WARPATH

THE SPINWARD FRINGE SERIES

Spinward Fringe Broadcast 0: Origins
Spinward Fringe Broadcast 1 and 2: Resurrection and Awakening
Spinward Fringe Broadcast 3: Triton
Spinward Fringe Broadcast 4: Frontline
Spinward Fringe Broadcast 5: Fracture
Spinward Fringe Broadcast 6: Fragments
The Expendable Few: A Spinward Fringe Novel
Spinward Fringe Broadcast 7: Framework
Spinward Fringe Broadcast 8: Renegades
Spinward Fringe Broadcast 9: Warpath
Spinward Fringe Broadcast 10: Coming Soon

OTHER BOOKS
By Randolph Lalonde
Brightwill
Dark Arts

For more information please visit:
www.RandolphLalonde.com

Spinward Fringe Broadcast 9

WARPATH

Randolph Lalonde

Foreground models created by Herminio Nieves – hns3d.com
Composition, lighting and rendering by Randolph Lalonde
Ebook formatting by Jesse Gordon

Print ISBN: 978-0-9937398-8-0
EBook ISBN: 978-0-9937398-7-3

PROLOGUE
FREEGROUND ALPHA

Some of the best strategies require sacrifice. Holographic images were not Admiral Jessica Rice's preferred method of watching anything, but there was something about watching news about Ayan Anderson as a full sized hologram that made her feel better overall. She admitted her desire to make amends and accept Ayan as her daughter to no one. When the burden of command lessened, and she had time alone, the young woman was always in the daydream future the Admiral tried to avoid indulging in.

"-through this conspiracy of ownership and the denial of rulership, Commander, or shall we call her 'Queen' Ayan Anderson has barely represented her settlements to the rest of the Rega Gain system," said the announcer over the holographic playback. "This news agency wasn't allowed access to their monitoring systems, so all our information is from testimony, our news gathering drones, and stories from the Stellarnet. This reporter is fairly confident in saying that, while it seems like the Queen of Haven Shore turns a cold shoulder towards the people outside her safe haven, those who have been fortunate enough to make it through her recruiting process are happy with their placements. They are given accommodations in trade for labour that are becoming increasingly rare as the fringes of human territories falls to the Order of Eden, corporate rule or lawless chaos. It's old socialism, or a new trade of freedom for safety, labour for a cot under a shield. Or, is it?"

Admiral Rice watched as holographic footage of Ayan arriving with a recruitment ship amidst a razed landscape. Small downed ships, pools of toxic materials and broken earth surrounded her and several heavily armed soldiers as they ushered people who looked no better than their surroundings into combat shuttles. Footage of what looked like a military complex followed, most likely taken from a great distance by one of the news drones the announcer mentioned. She immediately recognized it as a pre-fabricated Order of Eden base that Ayan's people had taken.

Several still images of Ayan and members of her council followed as the announcer continued. "With the history of selective humanitarianism Ayan has become somewhat well known for, I can't help but wonder why her Haven Shore council seems to have turned against her, along with Haven Shore's original populace. Information recently obtained by this reporter has revealed that fewer than forty one percent of her voting population supported her continuing activities on the Council, and she has not participated directly in proceedings for over a month. Even though she is the sole owner of nearly all of Haven Shore's assets, and has strong ties to the new Triton Fleet, I cannot help but wonder how much of the peace Haven Shore seems to enjoy is just an illusion created by her and the British Alliance." Admiral Rice couldn't help but scowl at the supposition. "How about you go get recruited and find out for yourself," she said in response to the story, dismissing the hologram with a flick of her wrist.

"I'm sorry, Admiral, it was the best recent news story I could find in the Sunspire's database," said the gentle voice of Gus, her personal artificial intelligence.

"Don't give it a second thought," she replied. It was time for her to walk the ship, and she wouldn't do it without looking like a crewmember. Admiral Rice took her sidearm, a stout, powerful plasma pistol, from her side table drawer and slipped it into the holster on her upper thigh. "Next time I'll have you review it for me though, then you can relay the facts."

"Along with the best images of your daughter," Gus said into her sub-dermal earpiece.

There was no arguing with him, after a year of using Gus, he'd learned everything there was to know about her, twice. The first time he'd become highly competent at predicting her moods and needs, he had to delete himself as a failsafe when political enemies managed to hack into his database. They got nothing, but she would make them pay for the setback as soon as she found out who was responsible, because Gus had to start learning all over again.

"How is Freeground Alpha doing?" Admiral Rice asked.

"The wormhole generator of Freeground's primary segment is almost finished charging, and all remaining residents have evacuated to the section of the station that will be transported through it," Gus replied as he provided an image of the thick inner ring of Freeground. The lights from thousands of transparent metal windows made it look alive, well inhabited compared to the rest of the station. Most of the rings surrounding Freeground Station were completely dark, abandoned as all but the most steadfast citizens left for other parts of the galaxy.

"Perhaps this is the wrong image," Gus said, changing the view so it focused on the lighted main ring.

"It's all right for me to grieve, Gus," Admiral Rice said. "This is the home I came to love, and it's near the end of its decline. That's some consolation."

"Ah, Freeground's population increased to two hundred ninety eight thousand and three last night, Admiral. Two children were born, both boys."

"Thank you for the silver lining." She made sure her uniform was in good order, a thick armoured red and black vacsuit, before leaving her sparsely decorated quarters. The Ironside was a fine ship, one of the last produced by Freeground Shipyards. It was a direct descendant of the improved Sunspire design, and had already seen nineteen engagements under the command of her captain, Harold Behr, a man only a few years her junior, but somehow he looked twenty years older. It was his twelfth ship, and he'd only lost one in combat.

She walked the well polished metal halls from her quarters to the port gunnery section, then to engineering. Only two crewmembers saluted out of the hundred or so she passed. They were new, unaware that she'd put out a standing order that crewmembers were to disregard the tradition of saluting the Admiral if they were working unless they were addressed.

"Admiral, we have an emergency," Gus announced in her subdermal communicator. The left side of Admiral Rice's vision was filled with an overlay of scrolling sensor data from the Ironside. She was receiving it at exactly the same time as the bridge, and recognized what was happening immediately.

"Channel open to the bridge," Gus informed her.

"Captain," was all she had to say.

"I know, this is the largest incursion yet," Captian Behr replied, "Battle Group One is already responding with energized flak bursts, we're moving into position."

It had become standard operating procedure over the last four months, since the Isek began their attacks. Opportunists to the core, a large faction of their society recognized that, with the Order of Eden on one side, and no major allies on the other, Freeground was truly alone again in a vast empty span of space. The Isek began jamming Freeground's communications, then they began bombarding missions. They realized after losing an outer ring and nearly a quarter million people in one of the first attacks, that energized flak and energy shielding was their only defence. The outer patrols were only so effective, the fleet they had was not large enough to maintain their borders.

Admiral Rice reviewed a segment of the sensor data and shook her head, walking into a lift at the same time. The readings indicated that the Isek were sending clusters of missiles in from almost all directions. "Battle Groups Two and three are to fall back to the departure point, reinforce the energy shielding surrounding Freeground Alpha. The less energy that main ring has to spend on shielding, the faster the main wormhole generator will charge. This attack may be our indication that the Isek has discovered our plan. In short, we are leaving as soon as conditions will allow, Captain, and not without the core of our station."

"Aye," Captain Behr replied.

Admiral Rice signalled the Sunspire, the lead ship for Battlegroup One to disband and begin their faster than light journey towards the Rega Gain system and Haven Shore immediately.

When Admiral Rice arrived on the bridge, he was finishing relaying the orders to his staff, who were calmly conducting themselves. She took the seat beside him and immediately began monitoring the countermeasures. The gleaming hull of the Ironside was as yet untouched by the long-range attacks as her many gun emplacements fired a stream of counterpunch rounds. They were made specifically to halt and obliterate incoming projectiles head-to-head, and the computer was managing their firing patterns so well that they were able to contribute to the defence of Freeground Alpha.

"Freeground Control reports that they only have enough power to create a wormhole to the near side of the Ironhead Nebula," Captain Behr said. "It's a no-go for the moment, Ma'am."

"We'll see," Admiral Rice said. "Open a channel."

Captain Behr nodded at his communication's chief, a young man who looked more like a security chief from his build. He opened a channel and put the communications on the bridge's secondary display, a hologram just to the left of the middle of the room. It stuttered occasionally, thanks to the jamming signals the Isek were generating. The laser communications systems weren't completely unaffected, but they were the only thing that still worked.

"Admiral Rice," said the responder. He was a thin-faced man who always looked a little too high strung for her liking. He wrung his hands, chewed his fingernails, or scowled when he thought no one was looking. Just a few years ago, the Admiralty would not have accepted him in their ranks, but needs forced them to advance people who barely made the grade.

"Admiral Pallon," she replied. "We knew this would come, the Isek want to wear us down before they send their cruisers in to take the last active segment of Freeground."

"We do not have enough power in the capacitors to open a wormhole through the Ironhead Nebula. We will arrive on the inside edge, possibly sustain damage thanks to the particles there, and we will definitely be in Order territory," Admiral Pallon replied, turning away from the holographic receiver.

"If we do not take this opportunity, while our ships are shielded and we have this much power in hand, we will not be able to leave at all. I am not looking forward to fighting to the death, or becoming the newest resident in the Isek slave camps," she told him. "I've already ordered Battle Group One out of the area, and the rest are falling back."

"Get them back in the field! Our defence will not be effective if-" red light flashed on Admiral Pallon's end, bathing the side of his face in its hue.

With a glance at her command and control console's screen on her wrist, Admiral Rice could see that Freeground Station had been struck by a group of missiles. Dormant sections had lost shielding, and were open to space in hundreds of places. They were already empty, powered down for the most part, but the decompressing hull of the massive structure warned at the fate that awaited the main ring of the station, Freeground Alpha, if something wasn't done.

"Pallon, deactivate the shielding surrounding the abandoned sections of Freeground and apply the energy to the wormhole generator. It's the only way."

"I'm sorry, Admiral Rice, I can't split my attention between convincing you that we are on the right course, and keeping things running smoothly," Admiral Pallon said.

Admiral Rice was out of her seat and on her way to the main communications console the moment Admiral Pallon's image disappeared.

"Give her command control, Lieutenant Feng," Captain Behr ordered as she arrived and pushed the heavily muscled communications officer out of the way.

"Aye," he replied, standing back and watching as he resumed his duties at another communications console.

"Captain, I regret to inform you that I am about to violate several military and civilian laws, and you'll probably have to take me into custody when I'm finished," Admiral Rice said.

"I have no idea what you're doing or what your intentions could be, so I see no reason to interfere," Captain Behr said, feigning ignorance.

"Captain, she's entering Freeground Alpha's remote command codes, probably so she can-" a junior communications officer started. He was silenced with a warning look from Lieutenant Feng. "Right, can't tell what she'll do Sir, probably nothing to worry about," he trailed off.

The main display at the front of the bridge focused on the primary ring of Freeground Station. Small areas of its hull flashed as hundreds of weapon emplacements fired at incoming missiles. Blue light began to shine from several rows of old emitters built into the broad surface of its upper sections. They formed a glowing ring, crowning the thickest, oldest section of the station for several seconds before a high-compression wormhole opened above it.

"Helm, get us into formation and inside that wormhole as soon as Freeground Alpha is under way," Captain Behr ordered.

"Aye, already on it, Captain."

"Admiral Rice!" shouted Admiral Pallon over the communications band. "You will be court martialled for this!"

"I don't care if both of us aren't admirals when this is over," Admiral Rice shouted back, "As long as we're both free and alive, I've done my duty." As if to punctuate her statement, emitters on the opposite side of the Freeground Alpha ring pulsed to life, pushing the massive ring into the wormhole above it.

The threshold of the wormhole was surprisingly rough, and Admiral Rice couldn't help but wonder for a moment if she'd done the right thing as she watched a few metres of old armour plating lift and detach from Freeground Alpha as it transitioned from normal space into the wormhole.

"Battlegroups Two and Three are in position, Group One is already out of the area," Captian Behr reported.

"Proceed through the wormhole, this end will only be here for another seventy seven seconds," Admiral Rice said as she checked the energy readings scrolling across her vision.

All that remained of Freeground Fleet, thirty-eight ships, made it through with three seconds to spare, and for those scant seconds Admiral Rice watched as the bulk of Freeground, the thirty-four massive, lightless rings they were leaving behind, were pulverized by Isek missiles. It was the longest minute of her life.

CHAPTER 1
A NEW JOURNEY

The comfort of the bed Jacob Valent laid in was unfamiliar, but magnificent, all enveloping. He didn't want to move, or open his eyes and let the world in. The last thing he remembered was Ayan's face looking down at him, filling his view, trying to smile, making all the right promises.

The rest came in a flash, that he had been rebuilt, but he couldn't remember the details of the surgery, or being saved from whatever attacked him. Without opening his eyes he flexed his fingers and toes, curling the soft, warm bedding in them. It felt like everything was where it should be, but at the same time, Jake was filled with the sensation that he was different.

There was a weight on his chest, only slight, but a weight nonetheless. He opened his eyes a crack. There was a little Nafalli mouth and above that, a tiny pink nose. She was laying above the sheets on his chest, flattened out on her stomach. "Zoe?" he whispered.

Her slumbering response was a puff of air from her twitching nose, then she yawned widely, revealing rows of sharp juvenile teeth. Her dark eyes barely opened as she smacked her lips and stared at him. Jake gently pulled a hand from under the sheets and the comforter and lightly stroked the top of the pup's head and neck. There was no doubt that he was using his own hand to pet the youngster, but it didn't feel like his own, it didn't look like it either. The fingers were thicker, they looked stronger, and that arm was bulkier, more muscular than the one he'd had before.

Zoe cooed and closed her eyes, fidgeting for a moment before flattening out once again. "Wonder who left you here to watch over me?" he asked in a croaking whisper. It was almost his voice, but the difference was unmistakeable. He looked around while stroking the young nafalli's back. He wasn't in Haven Shore, that was for certain. The light he initially mistook for morning rays were reflecting across the atmosphere of Tamber. None of the construction or finishing looked like the Triton, but the sounds of a mid-sized ship were absent, so he was most likely aboard a station.

The door opened soundlessly, letting in light his eyes weren't ready for. Doctor Messana with Alice close behind. Zoe and Jake both groaned at the sudden light, to the amusement of Alice, who sat down on the edge of the bed and took Jake's free hand. She was beaming, grinning from ear to ear.

Doctor Messana smiled as well, taking a seat in a bedside chair. "How do you feel, Jake?"

He was about to answer, but was interrupted by Zoe, who stood, stretched, then said; "Better now." She kissed him on the nose and ran from the room. He smiled at the toddler before responding. "Good, different, but good."

"There are going to be differences," Doctor Messana said, nodding. "Some big differences, just like we discussed before you agreed to go into the development tank, but physical therapy will be easier, and your physical strength will be closer to what you're used to. Not nearly as impressive as it was when you had the framework system, but your muscle mass is sixty percent higher than the average healthy human."

"I don't remember that discussion," Jake said, still not alarmed. "Can you refresh my memory?"

"It was the first day of physical therapy, and you noticed there were still a few scars left, and you were having a lot of difficulty with the basics. I offered to put you in a maturation tank for a few weeks so we could program your muscle memory, heal some deep scars that would take months to disappear otherwise, and build your muscle mass. The six weeks you were in there saved you nine months, most likely much more time."

"Okay, that seems familiar, but six weeks? I wouldn't agree to that long," Jake said. His whole body felt different, but he wasn't uncomfortable. What surprised him was how unburdened his mind felt. His head was clearer and less troubled than he could ever recall it being before. "Oh, and am I on something?"

"No, nothing at all," Doctor Messana said. "I'm afraid you're right, you didn't agree to six weeks, Jake, you agreed to two. After the two weeks passed, I didn't see the kind of progress you would expect, so I gave it more time. Now I know you'll be pleased with the level of development your body has accomplished."

"I didn't get a say, dad," Alice said quietly.

"Next time," Jake said, "You listen to her, but I'll let you off the hook this time. Seriously though, I feel like a weight has been lifted off my mind, it's hard to describe."

"The framework has been interacting with your brain throughout your entire life," Doctor Messana said, "It was one of the discoveries I made while researching your unique circumstances, so I knew there was a chance you'd feel different mentally as well. Part of that extended time in the maturation chamber was spent making sure that you could identify with your new body. It was essential that your mind did not reject your body, as it happens to clone transfers often enough."

Jake couldn't help but notice Alice, who watched his every reaction to what Doctor Messana was saying. "All right, did it work?" Jake asked.

Doctor Messana looked to Alice then back to Jake. "Your reaction to the reality of your situation will tell me that. Everything that made Jake Valent ended up in the bin. Nothing could be saved. Your brain, your everything was rebuilt or replaced while you were alive, so you're not going to feel like there was any interruption in your thoughts, and there wasn't, but every cell in your body is different. Genetically similar, but fresh, it's a miracle that medical science has gone so far that your brain could be destroyed and rebuilt at the same time, while we were able to make this body for you through a series of transplants and reconstructions. The end result is a completely new life with your mind intact, now without the restraints and directions of framework technology. That is how you should look at this, as a new life. If I were you, I'd keep my mind open to taking a whole new approach at how you live this one."

"Well, I'm not having a seizure, violent flashbacks, or even a case of mild surprise, so I think I'm good," he said, smiling at Alice. "So the framework is gone," Jake said.

"Yes, everything you were, except for all but your short term memories, are gone," Doctor Messana replied. "You're starting out with a clean slate, completely human. I've programmed your body with functional muscle memory, and I'm amazed at how well you're speaking, but I'm sure you're going to have to spend some time learning how to do a lot of things. Do you feel like trying to stand?"

"Yes," Jake said without hesitation.

Doctor Messana and Alice pulled the sheets aside to reveal a thicker, more muscled torso than Jake had before. His body felt heavier, but good, solid. He was wearing clean, white knee-length shorts. "So, I had trouble with recovery?"

"Yes, your muscle memory map didn't take, so you could barely speak, let alone walk."

"Okay, so what about this time? Was six weeks in the tank worth it?"

"So far you've been able to control your arms, you're speaking clearly, and we're about to find out if you can walk. I'd say it's much better this time, and you may be able to skip the first two or three months of physical therapy."

"It was bad, Dad," Alice said. "You couldn't stand being out of control, I'm glad you can't remember."

"So you might have opted for the six week treatment anyway?" Jake asked.

"If it meant avoiding that, yes," Alice replied. "But they wouldn't give me much information, so I didn't get to weigh in."

"That's all past," Doctor Messana said. "Let's see if you can take a few steps today."

"All right, time to get mobile," Jake said. He sat up, was immediately dizzy, and steadied himself. "Head just spun for a minute, I'm all right."

"Okay, take my hand," Doctor Messana said. "Alice, take the other one, just let him put his weight on you for balance."

"Don't worry, I could dead lift him," Alice said, immediately cringing as the words were heard. "Sorry, bad choice of words."

Jake laughed a little. "Time to get me on my feet," he said.

"Now, take it one motion at a time, relax and let your muscles tell you how it's done," Doctor Messana said, "that's what the muscle memory treatment is for."

Jake pulled himself up off the bed and onto his feet. His legs felt strong, but the deck seemed to sway a little. "Sure the dampers are working here?" he managed to say before he lost his balance and began to fall to his right. Alice caught him under his arm and propped him up.

"Relax, Jake," Doctor Messana said.

"Just put your feet under you," Alice whispered, helping him by gently pushing his foot back into place. She was a short pillar of strength and stability under his shoulder, unyielding and strong. "Now put your weight on it slowly."

Jake did so, and, slowly he found his stance. He leaned on Alice less and less, until he could feel himself starting to fall backwards. Alice supported him in time, her arm reaching as far across his broad back as it could. "I got you," she said. He leaned on her for stability and she practically held him up herself. He could move his legs, but his feet weren't listening nearly as well. He needed the support of his daughter and Doctor Messana to walk.

"That's a lot of progress for the first ten minutes," Doctor Messana said. "How about a first step?"

"No," Jake said, laughing nervously, then he instinctively stepped forward with one foot, and the other. He felt as though he were about to fall backwards, but leaned on Alice briefly to compensate.

"Well done," Doctor Messana said. "You'll be jogging in no time. There are a few people waiting for you in the next room, do you feel up to it?"

Jake nodded, slowly sitting back down on the bed with Alice's help.

"Good, the sooner we get you back to normal activities – moving, socializing – the sooner you'll be in shape. I'll go brief them."

Jake waited for her to leave. "Someone should tell her I wasn't the most social creature before all this."

Alice gave a short laugh. She pulled a regular vacsuit out from a box at the foot of the bed. It was already black with the markings of a captain, and WARLORD printed in white across the shoulders. "I don't feel like I've earned that back yet," he told her quietly.

She looked at it for a moment then used her command and control unit to change its colour to navy blue and remove the markings. "Better?"

"Looks right," he replied.

The suit did most of the work of dressing him, creeping across his skin as he put his feet in, but Alice helped him lean the right way so it could get access. It was a little demeaning, but Jake pushed his pride away. "I never thought about what it was like for you when you were first born as a human," he said to her.

"I'd almost forgotten that," Alice said, "I guess it's one of those things the framework is suppressing, it's all foggy. I sort of remember learning how to walk, talk. I was lucky, I had people there to help, mostly from pity I guess."

"I wish I was there for you," Jake said. "You didn't waste too much time waiting for me to hatch again."

"I visited," Alice said, looking a little guilty. "But, no, I didn't waste much time. Remmy convinced me to re-enter the Rangers when Anderson invited me back in. They've gotten better now that the standards are higher, I'm almost finished with the advanced tactical and encounter analysis training."

"So you're going back to the Rangers?" Jake asked.

"Yes, but Governor Anderson tells me that I'll be leading another team of rangers aboard the Warlord when it's back in full service, with your approval, of course. If that doesn't work out, I'll leave again and join your crew."

He was glad to see that she'd been busy while he was practically dead, and he would have to thank Remmy later for getting his daughter back into the Rangers. They would be a good option for her, since he didn't want her on the Warlord any longer.

"You okay, Dad?" Alice asked.

"Just wish I could have been there for you way back when you were taking your first steps," he lied.

"Ancient history, besides, you didn't even know," she said as he positioned his left arm so the vacsuit could close around him. "Ready to go?"

Jake took a deep breath and let it out. "Time for the great unveiling. I feel like I owe this to Doctor Messana. I'm her big success."

"Just concentrate on yourself," Alice said as she helped him up.

With her under his right arm, Jake took ponderous steps towards the door. When he finally made it across the room it opened to a hallway, where Ayan, Minh-Chu and Ashley all watched from a door on the other side.

Ayan was across the space and pressed into his arms in a moment. Minh-Chu put himself under his other arm. "Did they have to make the new model bigger than the last? I felt short before, but now I feel like a ten year old."

"Don't knock it, I hear it was the only model on the lot," Jake replied.

The room across the hall was filled with senior staff from the Warlord, the Triton and a pair of people who aided Doctor Messana while he was being rebuilt and his muscles were reprogrammed. He didn't remember them, but they spoke to him as though they'd known him all his life.

They brought him to a plush seat in the middle of a social room. There were several sofas and seats in a rough oval, and he could see imitation wood tables folded up and stacked in one corner. Everything looked relatively new, and he couldn't help but ask; "Where am I?" with a chuckle, amused that he couldn't piece it together himself.

"Oh, you're aboard the Solar Forge," Alice said.

Jake had never heard of the ship. His expression – a mix between bewilderment and mild irritation – must have indicated that to Ayan, who was sitting on the arm of his chair. "It's the ship construction and repair facility Lordander Corporation traded to Triton fleet."

"What did they trade for?" Jake asked.

A little of Ayan's joviality visibly drained, "we agreed to give refuge to a group of issyrian exiles who were escaping Clark Patterson and the Order of Eden."

"Did they know anything about them that we can use?" Jake asked.

"Part of the deal was that we wouldn't involve them in the fighting," Ayan explained quietly, "We've invited them to share what they want with us, but we haven't heard anything back about that yet. They're good people though, it seems like they really only want peace."

"Defectors from the other side's inner circle get to live in and near Haven Shore, but the people there won't have them. Those spoiled civilians protested, so you'll find most of them up here, learning how to run this place and going about their business while we figure out if they're really out of the war," Frost said as he entered the room with Stephanie and a few newer Warlord crewmembers in tow. He didn't let his irritation with the situation spoil the occasion. His grin could have lit up that side of the room as he took Jake's hand in both of his and shook it. "Still made of miracles, Captain," he said, and Jake could have sworn that there was a tear in the older man's eye.

"Not anymore, Frost. Looks like I'm just human now," Jake replied.

"Not to me," Frost replied, "Welcome back, lad. The Warlord's waiting, repaired and tested."

"Tested?"

"Acting Captain Vega has us on long range patrols, dropping sensor buoys. I'll admit, being able to come back to Tamber near every night has been good for the crew, restful, but the room fees are piling up. Makes me wish Stephanie, oops, sorry, Acting Captain Vega and I could have a little flat of our own down there."

"Frost," Ayan said, an edge to her voice that caught the attention of everyone on that side of the room. "I'm forgiving that entire tab for the Warlord's crew."

"But I just paid in full," Finn said, burying his forehead in his hand. He was just entering the room.

"I'll make sure you get a refund," Ayan said.

"Your little council won't like that," Frost said.

"Triton Fleet owns Haven Shore now, so I won't hear about it," Ayan replied, putting the order through on her arm unit, a thick transparent blue bracelet. It matched her dress, which was loosely fitted from hips to knee, and a tight scoop-neck design from the waist up. "And I was going to wait to announce this, but I just got word today. The Core World Authority has sent the final verdict down about ownership of the Rega Gain system. I technically own Tamber, while Triton Fleet has been acknowledged as the rightful victors over the Carthans, making this solar system our property. I'll give up Tamber to Triton Fleet again when I get the chance to do the paperwork. Owning a moon the size of Earth is a little too much for me to take on."

The room erupted in a wave of applause that made Ayan raise an eyebrow and smile. "So no more of this 'Queen' or 'Your Highness' business," she shouted over the din. "You call me 'Commodore' or 'Ma'am'."

"One last time then," Frost said, grinning as he stepped directly in front of her and bowed so low that his nose nearly touched the floor. "Greetings, your Majesty," he said with a flourish. Finn shook his head and Agameg cocked his. The majority of the room was tickled by the display, as was Jake.

Ashley broke through the semicircle of people that had gathered around Jake and nearly smothered him with an enthusiastic hug. "You look better than ever!" she said. "And you're smiling, a lot!"

"I swear she was picturing you in stitches and braces the whole time you were in recovery," Minh-Chu said. "I kept telling her; 'he's being remade, not stapled back together.'"

"How do you feel? I didn't hurt you, did I?" she asked, ignoring Minh-Chu.

"Better than before," Jake replied, conscious that his daughter, who was still a framework construct, was sitting to his right.

"Really? Wow, the Doc does great work," Ashley said. Zoe landed on her shoulder, jumping or falling from such a distance that Jake couldn't figure out where she'd come from. "This one spent the whole morning begging to visit you because I told her you were sick when she saw you wheeled by," Ashley said, holding one of Zoe's tiny hands.

"Better now," Zoe protested at full volume into Ashley's ear.

"Yes, we know," she replied, "Thank you Zoe."

"Thank you for your help," Jake said, capturing the Nafalli child's attention. "I don't know if I would have ever woken up if it weren't for you."

Zoe bounced onto Jake's chest, hugged his head, kissed him on the forehead then bounded off again. She used Ashley's shoulder as a post to look from then leap from when she spotted Panloo. "Off she goes, to tell everyone that she saved you," Ashley chuckled. "She'll be telling that story all week."

"She's growing faster now," Ayan said. "Last time I saw her she was five centimetres shorter. Are you sure it's all right for her to jump around like that though?"

"Panloo tells me Zoe is from a tree tribe," Ashley said. "You can't stop them from doing it at this age. She's broken her arm once though, so Panloo put a few rules in play, and Zoe's listening so far. I can't imagine what she'll be like when she's full grown."

"Beautiful, I'm sure," Ayan said with a smile that seemed a little too sure.

The rest of the night continued with a similar jovial feeling. Jacob never thought his survival would make so many people happy. He believed he had a core group of friends, and allies that would be relieved, but the room was full for hours, and when he was brought back to his bed, he couldn't recall how many people had stopped in front of where he sat all night to congratulate him on his recovery.

Alice was quiet for most of the evening, fetching non-inebriating drinks and listening to everyone who wanted a moment of Jacob's time. She left him with a kiss on the cheek as she said; "love you, Dad."

Ayan fixed him with an affectionate gaze, her big blue eyes unflinchingly staring into his as he looked up from his bed. "Thought I was about to lose you forever," she said.

"I'm here, more than ever," he replied, a question he refused to ask while he was so tired nagging at him. He aired another thought he'd been hiding all night instead. "It's as though I was experiencing everything from the opposite end of a long hallway, or through a thick filter before, and now that's gone. The framework was in the way before."

Ayan glanced to the doorway, where Jacob's daughter had passed a minute ago, then back at him. "You think she's having the same problem?"

"I don't know, but she's talked about suppressed memories, the framework won't allow her to age more than a few months, and I'm sure there are other things going on," Jake said, keeping a yawn from interrupting the last few words.

"Something we can talk more about tomorrow," Ayan said, sweeping Jacob's hair out of his face.

He caught her hand and squeezed it. "I'm still surprised you came back to me, if that's what this is," again, the denied question repeated itself in his head; *why did you leave in the first place? Was it for Liam?*

"That's what this is, if you want me back," Ayan said.

She had to know that he checked on her status, read her public reports and had pictures of her in his Crewcast profile. She was asking a question he was sure she knew the answer to already, but he didn't mind. "Yes," was all he said.

"On that note," Doctor Messana said as she seemed to appear in the doorway. "It's lights out. You start physical therapy tomorrow morning." She walked on, looking down at something she was reading on an old fashioned touch pad.

"I'll see you tomorrow, Alice will be here when you wake up," Ayan said, kissing him lightly. Her pillow-y soft lips lingered a moment before she hesitantly stood and left.

He laid there for a few moments longer, going over the events of the evening. He'd seen everyone who he considered important to him, with only one exception, Oz. He'd lost track of all the other people who cycled through the room.

It was easier to name the people who were conspicuously absent. Oz sent him a warm message, but could not leave the Triton, which was understandable. What Jake found slightly alarming was the absence of anyone from the British Alliance. He tried not to let it bother him, but he was sure there was something he was forgetting.

CHAPTER 2
PATROL

A pair of Uriel Fighters drifted along their patrol route around Kambis. The blue, green and brown ball of Tamber was well distant, a dot on the horizon of its more darkly surfaced parent. Minh-Chu Buu, or Ronin as he was known to his Fighter wing, Samurai Squadron, waved at it as it winked out of sight. They were crossing over to the dark side of Kambis, a looming giant that had once been the target of an incredible effort, complete environmental terraforming.

Hundreds of years before, people had begun digging deep canyons into the planet and removing the matter from it entirely in order to reduce its mass, stabilize the surface and reduce the worlds' gravity. They began another terraforming effort at the same time on Tamber, which was already a near match for Earth's gravity. Oxygenating the environment and transplanting life was easier there, it was estimated that results were seen in decades instead of centuries. That is why the contemporary belief was that the life on Tamber was to be used to seed the world it orbited, Kambis.

The people who originally started the process got as far as freeing the water trapped under Kambis' surface and oxygenating the atmosphere. They finished their work on Tamber, leaving a moon teeming with wild life by the time the Omnivirus killed most if not all of them. There were structures left behind on Kambis that people still marvelled at, but Minh-Chu had only seen the ones visible from orbit. He knew better than to risk a visit to the smaller planet bound wonders.

The cities of that giant world were all contained in domes with gravity control. Most of them perched on cliffs, or were wedged into the bottoms of canyons, and despite the attempts of Carthan and then British Alliance authorities to tame them, they remained wild and dangerous. None of those places were under the control of governments, but gangs and the others, who called themselves New Lords. The night side of Kambis came up, and the sparse lights of those cities decorated the landscape, along with patches of absolute blackness, canyons that were so deep that the scant light on the night side of the world was not at all evident. Even still, they were the most frequent trade partners with Tamber settlements, including Haven Shore. Within those havens for crime were traders, some of whom were honest, most of whom were somewhere between that and criminal. Many of them were necessary trading partners.

The shadow cast by Kambis submerged Ronin's barely lit cockpit in inky black. The distant lights of ships seemed distant and solitary.

"Hey, Ronin," Joyboy, Ronin's wingman for that patrol, called over their short range communications. "I've gotta admit something to you, man."

"What's that, Joyboy?" Ronin asked, bracing himself.

"When I saw you on the roster for this patrol, I traded to get the spot as your Wingman," he said.

"Oh," Ronin replied, relieved. "I thought you were going to tell me that Paula told you that her bouncing baby boy was actually mine."

"Uh, no, that's not funny."

"Well, you know she could have stolen some genetic material, bribed someone in Triton medical to-"

"Nope, Jim is completely mine and hers, man."

"Well, you know, he does look a bit-"

"Still not funny," Joyboy said.

Ronin laughed, he'd forgotten how easy it was to wind Joyboy up. "I'm just kidding. I'm really happy for both of you."

"The kid really has mellowed her out, she's pretty amazing now," Joyboy said. "You and Ashley thinking about having one?"

"No!" Ronin replied, surprising himself with how quickly the response came.

"Wow, had that one locked and loaded," Joyboy chuclked. "Something wrong?"

"We're just enjoying the early part of our thing together. Ash gets to exercise her maternal instincts on Zoe, and we babysit."

"Early part of your thing? You guys have been together almost a year, haven't you?" Joyboy said.

"Hey, your relationship with Paula went faster than light, doesn't mean Ashley and I don't get to have some fun before set-tling in," Ronin replied. "We have attended three weddings in the last six weeks though, so we might be headed there."

"You guys really are that serious? It's hard to tell, I mean peo-ple see you're crazy about each other, but there's no public dis-plays or anything. I know three guys in the Skyguard who have serious ambitions for her, if you know what I mean."

"Names, now," Ronin said in his best intimidating tone.

Joyboy laughed, "You won't get anything out of me. Seriously, though, you two have to make more appearances, like at the Oota Galoona, or something, and make a date out of it or some-thing."

"Look at you with the relationship advice," Ronin said.

"Hey, Paula really is planning our wedding, you're invited, by the way. I don't know if Ashley is, though. Paula still thinks she's an airhead who likes to take her clothes off."

"We'll think about it, but if Ashley isn't coming, neither am I," Ronin replied. "Maybe when Jake's on his feet the Warlord crew will hit Oota Galoona and the Pilot's Den. Call it another step in his physical therapy, dancing, imbibing, more dancing, maybe some falling."

"How is he doing? All I heard was that he survived whatever happened aboard that Order ship," Joyboy asked.

"There's an expression that Frost uses; 'That man's made of miracles,'" Ronin said, doing his best imitation of the grizzled Gunnery Chief.

"Hey, that was pretty good," Joyboy said.

"Thank you, I practice," Ronin replied. "Anyway, I'm starting to believe it too, but I think it had more to do with the Warlord's new doctor. A couple med techs I've met were pretty quick to mention that they didn't approve of her methods whenever they were near someone who would listen, but the results are good, so I'm not one to argue."

"Why? Did the new Doc think too far outside the box or something?"

"I'm no expert, so I don't know, but I've heard people call her a butcher more than once. Either way, that woman deserves credit. Jake was almost walking after waking up from recovery, and there's not a scar on him. He's a little taller, and looks like he took on a lot of muscle, but he's got functional hand-eye coordination, maybe even better, strength, and a full range of motion. Pretty good for a man with a body that was grown in pieces and put together in a day."

"Wow, that's amazing. There's almost a full blackout about the how and why of what happened to him through the fleet, so thanks for sharing. I was worried. I know I bitched about service on the Warlord sometimes while I was still there, but I'll follow him anywhere."

"You and me both," Ronin said. He knew that whatever he shared with Joyboy would be spread across the fleet by morning, and it would permeate Haven Shore by the end of the week. The opportunity was too good to pass up. "Between you, me and our flight recorders, I have to say it looks like this whole rebirth has made Jake better in the head too. He hurt his face from grinning at his Welcome Back To Life party, and Ayan says he's easier to be around, more present."

"Really? Man, maybe that framework tech was doing something," Joyboy concluded.

"Maybe, but no one knows for sure, so keep it quiet," Ronin said.

"Yeah, no problem."

He was sure Joyboy wouldn't. Tales of the Warlord Captain grinning from ear to ear would be everywhere before long.

"So, is Samurai Squadron going to be based on the Triton when we leave for the Ironhead Nebula?" Joyboy asked.

"I can't say," Ronin replied. "It depends on whether or not the Warlord is going to be part of the battle group."

"Oh, man, that would be cool. The Triton *and* the Warlord."

A warning appeared on Ronin's tactical system. The overlay in his helmet displayed an energy spike and indications of a decelerating ship headed for Kambis. It was already past the outer boundaries of the Rega Gain solar system. "Power up, we have incoming."

"I see it, Triton Flight Deck sees it too," Joyboy replied.

The Uriel Fighters' systems lit up, their thrusters pulsed as they got ready to manoeuvre. The projected displays in Ronin's cockpit showed a summary of communications between the Triton's Flight Deck, British Alliance Control, and Haven Shore on his right hand side. To the left the greater galaxy was represented, with listings for nearby objects, incoming ships and missions that could affect his situation. In front of him his fighter's solid state displays told him everything he needed to know about his and his wingman's ship, while the projected display over top of that provided all tactical data, and a shortened version of his current orders. His navigational assistant was also included in the overlay, showing nearby navnet routes for other ships, the course he and his wingman were supposed to follow on patrol, his actual position, mission timer, threats and gravity fields. A long red spike across his display showed the expected trajectory of the incoming craft. "Local Navnet has already assigned alternative routes to ships in our area," Ronin said. "That's coming in fast, it'll be here in fifty three seconds. We will be the closest ships."

"Is that a good thing?" Joyboy asked.

"It's decelerating fast enough so it won't make it to Kambis, but it's transmitted no header or warning signal," Ronin reported. He saw the British Alliance Control Centre hand all responsibility for the incoming craft to Triton Fleet, and shook his head. "Yup, some help they are."

"I'm overhearing the British Alliance ordering their patrol ships out of the area," Joyboy said.

"This is Triton Flight," said Ensign Dunbar, one of the communications officers aboard the Triton. "We have determined that the new ship in the region is a high speed Korin Industries Spaceliner. The wormhole trajectory suggests she departed Hosanna Station nine days ago. The helm is on autopilot, and has acknowledged our Navnet signal, so she will be entering high orbit around Kambis. You are to flank the spaceliner, scan it and await further orders."

An image of the one hundred and five metre long ship appeared on Ronin's main display as he and Joyboy began their approach, firing their engines at the rapidly decelerating ship. It had crossed the threshold from its wormhole into normal space, and continuing to slow down along the course sent to it by Triton's Navnet. "Acknowledged, beginning our approach."

Joyboy and Ronin stayed in formation as they accelerated towards the starliner. As he began decelerating and moving into position, Ronin couldn't help but admire the smooth, long lines of the ship's designs. Her quad rotary thrusters were cooling at the rear of the craft, while pot manoeuvring thrusters fired sporadically, making minor corrections to her course and position. "I can confirm, there is no human on the stick in that starliner," Ronin said.

"How do you figure?" Joyboy said.

Ronin began his sensor sweep of the ship while he explained. "Almost all pilots make major course corrections then smaller touches after, so you can see the manoeuvring thrusters firing for a couple seconds at a time. Automated pilots make minor adjustments sooner, and they're typically programmed to save fuel, so you see these quick pops and pulses from the thrusters instead."

"Unless you're watching Ronin," Joyboy said. "You only give your ship the thrust it needs, you don't waste anything if you can help it."

"Why thank you," Ronin said as he watched the detailed scan data come in. He read the raw feed instead of paying attention to the computer's interpretation.

"I'm saying you fly like a robot," Joyboy said.

"That is not nice," Ronin replied. "I fly artfully, like a stone skipping across water, or a fish in a pond."

"Like a drone on long patrol," Joyboy added.

Ronin knew his wingman was just trying to get a rise out of him, and shook his head. "The law of the good space farer: Only use the space, the energy, the food, water and air you need. Oh, and always be courteous first."

"Wow, never heard that one," Joyboy said.

"Something they taught us on Freeground, I don't remember a time when-" Ronin stopped as he saw that all the systems on the spaceliner were operating except for life support. There were six hundred and nine corpses aboard, and a pair of faint life readings. "You seeing this?"

"It's another ghost ship," Joyboy replied. "Fifth one this month."

"No, this one's strange. The others finished their deceleration cycle and went dead outside the solar system, this one was programmed to land right on our doorstep. It would have to be for the emergency deceleration system to be overridden, and the emergency beacon is dead, like it's not there at all." Ronin checked the fuel readings and the responses the spaceliner's computer was giving his fighter. "Communication is completely shut down, and this spaceliner should have enough fuel to go on to a few more systems before it needs to refuel, but there's nothing but fumes in the tanks."

"What do you think?"

"Triton Flight," Ronin addressed, "estimated time on a rescue team?"

"We should have one out there in nineteen to twenty two minutes," replied the communications officer.

"Not fast enough, there are two life signs on this spaceliner, and they're about to go out," Ronin replied. He took a closer look at the scans and could see that the only living things on the ship were crowded into a closet, connected to some kind of emergency support gear. "I'm going aboard, the landing bay is open and my fighter will fit."

"Wait for the rescue team," replied the communications officer.

"I don't detect any signs of a bomb, or anything else that could take me out. I'm going in with a support kit," Ronin said.

"I'm going with you," Joyboy said. "Triton can send a couple fighters to pilot us, and I have emergency training."

"Since when?"

"Finished the course three weeks ago."

"Oh," Ronin replied, turning his craft so it faced the small landing bay running alongside the lower half of the ship. "Time to get you some experience. Follow my lead going in."

"Aye, aye, Sir," Joyboy said.

As Ronin approached the landing deck he immediately recognized that the racks containing emergency escape craft were all empty. His Uriel fighter retracted all but two of his thruster pods, reducing the ship's profile so it could fit in one of the narrow slots for landing craft, and Ronin touched down. There was artificial gravity in the starliner, but he activated his landing clamps anyway. Nothing about the situation felt right.

He climbed out of his fighter, checking his sidearm before he reached behind the seat for the rescue kit. It was a metal case he could carry using its handle or easily affix to his back by touching it to his light armour. He opted to wear the kit and drew his sidearm as he watched Joyboy touch down with a thud. "Easy, this deck is so thin it may as well be decorative."

"Funny, ship looks really good from the outside," Joyboy replied. He was out of his cockpit and geared up in under a minute.

"Sure," Ronin replied, "But these starliner companies cut corners wherever they can. Why do you think we keep getting ghost ships arriving with depleted oxygen supplies or bad heating systems? They still use oxygen tanks and crappy scrubbers that only last about thirty trips, but the emergency deceleration systems are in great shape, because they couldn't dock anywhere worth flying to otherwise."

"Yeah, I get it, they're death traps if you don't maintain them constantly," Joyboy replied. "Paula goes on about it whenever a ghost ship drifts near the system."

"Ah, right, sorry," Ronin said. "Didn't mean to go on there." They saw the first corpse then, perfectly preserved in the vacuum of space in front of the airlock leading to the ship's interior.

"Okay, we have a high-powered plasma blast," he said as the forensic suite in his command and control unit analysed the body. "This one was killed using a close range weapon."

"Nearly cut in half with one shot," Joyboy muttered. "Looks like he was trying to stop whoever was leaving?"

"Yeah, or whoever launched all those pods," Ronin said. "All right, we're here to rescue two people. We scan and record everything else, we don't have time to analyse the scene."

"Aye, Sir," Joyboy replied. "Lead the way."

Ronin plugged an emergency power supply line from his backpack in to a jack at the bottom of the airlock door and triggered it open. He wordlessly led the way into the passenger area, where he and his wingman were confronted by a scene Ronin knew Joyboy would revisit in his dreams. The man was more trustworthy as a pilot and soldier by the day, but he hadn't truly seen anything like what was in front of them. Ronin had seen worse, but not by much.

The desperate expressions of the horror struck passengers were preserved by the airless cold. "Someone evacuated the air here," Joyboy said sadly. "Was it the computer? Holocaust Virus got in from an old inactive system somehow?"

"No time to analyse the scene, remember? Stick to the mission," Ronin said, sure that what he was seeing wasn't the result of a computer virus.

"Ronin, this is Oz. Triton Fleet Command is watching. Our rescue team leader is staying abreast of the situation and will be there in twelve minutes."

"This mission clock is ticking slower. The rescue team was supposed to be here in two minutes according to the first estimate your man gave me," Ronin said. "That puts response time at over thirty one minutes, Oz."

"That's why I'm giving you the official go-ahead. Rescue if you can, but if you can't, keep the situation stable if at all possible."

"What does that mean, 'keep the situation stable?'" Joyboy asked.

"It means that if we can't make the rescue ourselves, we shouldn't screw it up by making the attempt anyway," Ronin replied. "Welcome to a real rescue operation."

As the scant minutes it took to make it all the way to the front of the main passenger deck, past over a hundred corpses that were frozen in poses of dismay, anger and everything in between, it became plain to Ronin that quieting Joyboy was a mistake. He could see the man's stress readings climbing through the Crew-cast display in his helmet. "Looks like it happened quickly," Ronin said. "But you have to stop looking every passenger in the eye, Joyboy. Stay aware of the situation, there's nothing we can do for these people."

"Yeah," Joyboy replied, "Okay, yeah."

Ronin was relieved to finally come upon the closet where the faint life readings were emanating from. He examined the doors and took a detailed close range scan. "You seeing this, Triton?" Ronin said. "Two people, crammed together in a support bag made for one. The air recycler in there has almost had it."

"All right," Captain McPatrick replied. "We see the scan, that bag is still sealed, and one of them is conscious, but barely. If you get your emergency bag around them, it will take over for what's keeping them alive right now."

"Oh my God, that bag only kept their heads and torsos warm," Joyboy said. "And one of them has no legs, looks they were cut off before they were put in there. Who would do this?"

Ronin didn't comment, but got his emergency survival bag ready. It was a black self-forming bag that could wrap itself around up to four people and seal in seconds. It would provide heat, air, and medication to the people inside. It was one of the devices everyone adopted once they were found aboard the Triton in abundance, especially since they were so easy to fabricate. "You open the doors, I'll catch them."

"What?" Joyboy said.

"You open the doors, step out of the way, and I'll get them in here," Ronin said as he pointed to the bag spread out on the deck.

"Aye, aye," Joyboy said, all hesitation gone. He stepped in, spread the doors apart, and then stepped out of the way.

Ronin caught the intertwined passengers. The survival bag they were stuffed into was transparent, and he saw things he wished he didn't before he got them onto the deck and atop the Earth technology style bag. He watched as it enveloped them, sealed, inflated and shuffled as it infiltrated the rudimentary life support bag the passengers were found in. The readings on Ronin's helmet indicated that the pair were immediately put into deep stasis and would survive with serious medical attention. Their major organs were intact.

He squeezed his eyes shut and clamped his jaw, trying to shake the sunken feeling and nausea as he mentally reviewed what he saw before his emergency medical bag closed around the rescued couple. The woman had red hair, fair skin, and was being cradled by the male passenger, who had broad shoulders, was tall, and powerful looking. When the closet first opened he thought he was seeing Ayan and Jake, the likeness was just close enough.

"You okay, Ronin?" Joyboy asked.

"No," was all he could say.

CHAPTER 3
THE MESSAGE

Since he'd arrived in the Rega Gain system, Terry Ozark Mc-Patrick had seen many things. They ranged from the marvellous to the horrific, but he made sure he observed everything he could, regardless of how much he might want to turn away. The injustices visited upon the average Tamber citizen outside of Haven Shore's embrace were truly difficult to hear about. The number of times he wanted to lower the Triton over a city and wipe out the gangs so normal people could live in peace were beyond counting but he had to pick his war carefully.

There were Order and Regent Galactic forces slowly edging towards Rega Gain, testing their perimeter, and finding that they could come a little closer to the solar system each day. The Triton was ready, and in one week three mid-sized ships would be ready to accompany the carrier when Oz guided it towards Regent Galactic territory with the purpose of pushing back. That was the war he chose, and everyone in the Rega Gain solar system – gangster and citizen alike – would benefit if they managed to hold.

He was a military man, trained to be a problem solver, and he still enjoyed that kind of problem. The kind of problem where there were only one or two enemy flags to watch for, and the objective was to force the people carrying them to retreat or surrender. That was the kind of problem he enjoyed, not the kind of complicated situation that awaited him in the Triton's Medical Centre under heavy guard.

'They are deeply traumatized, I'm helping to keep them calm," remarked the Triton's overseer, a being created in the Sol System to serve as the ship's heart and advisor. Oz had come to depend on the telepathic link they shared. *Thank you, Geist, I'm going to have to take it from here. I want to hear the interview in their words before you play back any of their memories for me.* Oz thought in response.

'You don't want these mental images, I do not want to do that to you,' Geist replied.

The guards standing in front of the male victim's room parted and Oz stepped inside. He was thankful that the man was covered by the medical support bed, because the chart behind him marked that half of one arm, the better part of a leg, and his entire other arm had been removed. Oz assumed that they had frozen unevenly while he was stuck in the storage compartment aboard the spaceliner. The fellow was awake though, and noticed Oz right away.

"You look important," he said. "I'm Dom, short for Dominick."

Oz pulled a rolling stool to the man's bedside and smiled. "Hello, Dom, short for Dominick. I'm Admiral Terry Ozark Mc-Patrick, you can call me Oz. How are you doing here? They treating you well?"

"Well, just got a new nose, they fixed my chin and cheeks, and I barely felt a thing. Things are good. Well, except for a few other missing parts, but they tell me they're growing those for me, and I'll be getting them for free?" His question revealed uncertainty and doubt.

"You are, but if it makes you feel better, you do have something you can trade for our services. I need you to tell me what happened to you and your partner."

"The woman that Wheeler person put me with?" Dom asked. "I only know her name, Antonia Chandler. We never met before he put us together. Is she going to be all right? No one will tell me."

"She's going to be fine, but she got the worst of the injuries, even though, from the looks of how you were found, it seems like you were trying to keep her warm."

"When we woke up in that closet, she said that Wheeler cut off her legs so we would both fit in that emergency bag together. I still don't get that though, that closet had dozens of bags and suits for decompression. The seats even had decompression safety features built in."

"Okay, can you start at the beginning? From when the trouble started to happen." Oz would never forget the name, Wheeler. It belonged to a man who did not care who he betrayed, as long as he did what he wanted and got what he wanted.

"Okay, I was having a great flight to the Rega Gain system. I wanted to apply to join whatever fleet was forming behind the Warlord. I'm a structural engineer, but I thought I could make my experience work for them, and the British Alliance wouldn't have me because I got caught stealing a shuttle when I was fifteen. I didn't think the Warlord staff would care. The guy sitting beside me was coming here to work in the jungle, he said he already contacted Haven Shore and they had a place for him, he was a botanical technician named John. Kind of a nervous guy, but nice, really smart. We're talking about our families before the virus, I think everyone does these days unless it's too fresh, but my husband has been dead since day one, my dad didn't make it through the first week, so I just do it to keep their memory alive, but anyway," Dom turned his head to take a sip from a water tube near his cheek, and Oz helped move it into position. "Thank you," he said after a large gulp.

"No problem," Oz replied.

"All right, so we're talking up a storm, finally," Dom said. "and this guy walks to the front of the cabin and starts talking, saying that his name is Lucius Wheeler, and he won't be going all the way to Rega Gain with us. I could feel the ship slowing down, not like gravity, but the rumble of the retro thrusters. The safety restraints on our seats turn on, and we're all stuck there. He says he's sorry that only two people would be making it, and then singles me and Antonia out. Four guys, big, cyborgs from what I could tell, pluck us out of our seats, and drag us to the forward compartment where there were four dead attendants. Someone had shot them, as best as I could tell.

This guy, Wheeler, looks us over and says we'll do, then looks at the bag he's holding and says; 'some alterations are necessary.' One of his guys gets out this blade that's glowing white hot and starts coming towards me, then Wheeler grins and says, 'no, cut her legs off, if you cut his legs off, the two of them still won't fit.'"

I'm no hero, but I see the cyborg turn towards Antonia and I go for the side of him that isn't metal plated. No one caught me in time, so I try to tackle him, and he doesn't budge. He may as well be a support beam for all the difference I make, and that metal arm of his backhands me across the compartment. Wheeler leans down and tells me; 'give the people who find you a message for me. Tell them that they should have let me leave in peace, but they didn't, so now I'm going to take or destroy everything they have.' Then he knocks me out."

Dom turned for another sip of water, and Oz helped him once again. Oz was piecing the story together, what Wheeler was thinking when he chose Dom. From the report he'd already received, Antonia was roughly the same shape, and had the same hair colour as Ayan. Dom's complexion, height and hair matched Jake's. Wheeler probably thought he was being clever when he chose them to deliver his message.

"Thanks," Dom said as he finished sipping. "I woke up in the dark. The life support bag only had enough light for me to make out the top of Antonia's face. She told me they took her legs, and I could feel the cold coming. I didn't know what was going on, not really, but I wrapped myself around her as best I could. I couldn't check to see if she was bleeding, but I could feel something wet, all I could do was try to keep her warm. She was in so much pain, but she passed out a little while later. I did too when the air got thin."

"Whatever they used to cut her cauterized her wounds. They haven't woken her up yet. You kept her face and head warm enough so she didn't need the work you did though, her cheeks and nose are fine."

"That's something then," Dom said. "I wish I could tell you more, Oz. The next thing I remember is waking up here."

"That's plenty," Oz said. "I'm sorry this happened to you."

"Please, don't worry about it. It doesn't matter who this madman was after, or what his reasons were, he's the one who had it done. If I were the kind of man who could track down and punish people, I would make him pay, but I'll leave that to people like you. You look like that kind of man."

"He won't get away with this," Oz said, putting a hand on Dom's shoulder. "He'll get what's coming to him eventually. Until then, I'm wondering if you could use a job on a large carrier. We'll be under way by the time you're on your feet. I'm sure you'll find something worth doing aboard the Triton."

"On one condition," Dom said.

"What's that?"

"You visit me while I'm stuck here," he replied.

"You have a deal," Oz replied.

CHAPTER 4
PARALLELS

Jacob Valent could not walk. No thing in his memory was more frustrating, more difficult to cope with than that simple fact. For two days his daughter helped him in the morning for two hours, trying to get his feet, as useful as clubs, to support him while they dangled from inept ankles with little improvement.

He was thinking about his frustration and the sweat that he'd put into so little improvement when his hand slipped from one of the parallel bars and he fell to the mat like a marionette with its strings cut. It was the fifth time.

He kept his grumbling to himself, but could feel his face flushing red with frustration. Alice was patient and cool as she helped him back up. He didn't fight her at all, those bars seemed so far away from the padded deck, nearly impossible to reach from where he landed.

With her help he got them under his shoulders and pushed up. Another thing he didn't understand was why everything but walking seemed to come naturally. His hand-eye coordination was returning, he could sit up without assistance and his balance seemed a little unsteady, but improved. As soon as he tried to walk, his legs seemed to forget what they were supposed to be doing and go on strike.

Alice took a step back when he nodded, indicating that he felt steady again, even though he was only holding himself up on the parallel bars using his arms, there was no weight on his legs. The

recovery room aboard the Solar Forge was rectangular, two stories tall, and all the surfaces were a plasticized off white colour.
He had mats in one corner, a few balls of various sizes ranging
from small for throwing to large for sitting and balancing. Then
there were those damned parallel bars. "All right Jake, this is
easy," Doctor Messana said from the other end of what he'd
started calling 'the pill box.' "I programmed the muscle memory
in your legs, so they should already know what a walking motion
is, you only have to relax and urge yourself to do it, like you've
done thousands of times before."

Jake tried, but the response he got from his leg was a haphaz-
ard flop forward. He stared at the awkwardly placed foot. "Are
you sure you gave me the right legs? There isn't someone else
with mine having the same problem?"

Doctor Messana shook her head, her lips pursed. "You're still
trying to learn to walk when there's no need to. It's easier than
that. Your muscles know what to do, you just have to relax and
let them do it. You were standing on your own for a few seconds
a couple nights ago, remember how easy that was?"

Jake nodded and exhaled. Listening to the Doctor was becoming more frustrating by the minute. He looked at Alice, who had
a neutral expression. Jake took a step, or at least that's what he
commanded his left leg to do. He got more awkward lifting and
flopping instead.

"Okay, wait," Doctor Messana said, shaking her head again.

Alice looked almost as irritated as Jake felt, only she had her
back to the Doctor.

"You're concentrating on the small motions required to take
one step. Walking is a reflex combining balance and about two
hundred muscles working together, you can't control every single
one consciously. What I'd like you to do is forget about one step,
and just try to walk to the other end of the bars. Just take a deep

breath, relax and as soon as you finish exhaling, let go of the bars and walk to the other end. Alice, give him extra room."

Jake nodded to Alice, signalling that it was all right, and she took several steps back as he inhaled. He made several unwelcome realizations while he slowly exhaled: his hands were sweaty, his heart was pounding fast, and that the other end of the parallel bars seemed very far away.

He finished exhaling and let go of the bars, refusing to look down at his legs. The realization that he was standing, feeling steadier than he'd felt since waking up gave him a surge of confidence. He started to take his first step, then the whole training room went sideways, he smashed his ribs on the right parallel bar, the padding didn't seem to spare him any harm, then he finished falling between them, his impact on the mats knocking the wind out of him.

"This is easier than you're making it, Jake."

"Stop telling me how fucking easy this is!" Jake roared as soon as he caught a breath. "Does this look easy to you?"

"Fine! Do it the long way, learn to walk all over again!" Doctor Messana said before storming out of the room.

Alice was at his side, helping him back up. He was about to ask for a break, but glanced the other end of the parallel bars, less than three metres away. Even if he had to drag his feet, he'd make it. "I went too far," Jake muttered.

"She had it coming," Alice replied. "She couldn't have expected all that programming to work perfectly. I get my control freakiness from you, so I know what this is. You can't just trust a brand new pair of legs, and back, and bum to work together to keep you upright unless you've had something to do with it."

Jake smiled at her and nodded. "Yeah, I know. I just wish I was better at picking my battles. These bars are kicking my ass."

"We'll take it slower," Alice said. "One step at a time, first we just get those feet under you properly, then you move them forward without putting much weight on while you keep upright on the bars with your arms. Baby steps though."

Jake carefully concentrated on moving his thigh so his foot landed on the mat just in front of him, then put a little weight on it. The weight felt good, his leg was strong enough, but his footing was shaky. He shuffled forward a little with his right hand on the bars. "Where'd you learn about teaching someone to walk?" he asked as he started working on the other leg.

"Ayan, Oz, Minh-Chu and I all took a physical training course. Doctor Messana wasn't thrilled, but we did it anyway, it was Commander Anderson's idea. He said he went through the course before Ayan was reborn. He had to be prepared if all those memories he recreated in her head wouldn't attach to her physical body properly."

"Thank you," Jake said.

They didn't speak as Jake ponderously took baby steps all the way to the other end of the parallel bars. He was almost completely dependant on the bars, keeping most of his weight off his feet, but his legs were doing some of the motions, if clumsily, and it felt like progress.

"Now, we turn around," Alice said, moving to the opening in the bars behind him.

Jake decided to try the Doctor's advice one last time. He closed his eyes and simply desired to turn around one hundred and eighty degrees, willing his legs to do the work. He got one foot into position, and fell to the mats between the bars so suddenly that Alice couldn't catch him. The mats saved him from numerous bruises. He looked up from the floor at his daughter, who stared at him in utter shock. "time for a break?" she squeaked.

He couldn't help but laugh. "I guess we do this the hard way," he said as she sat down beside him.

CHAPTER 5
THE CODIS SYSTEM

The deep pore cleaning was always refreshing. A pretty, ultra slender attendant bot in a short red and green kimono handed Governor Tate a large towel as he exited the treatment booth.

"There is nothing like steam and a nano scrub to make you feel fresh and new," he said to her.

"Yes Sir, will there be anything else, Sir?" she asked.

"No, you just get in there and work your magic. The jets have to be cleaned as often as possible."

"Yes Sir, thank you sir," the bot replied. He would be almost convinced that she was human, except for her perfect obedience, that was something he'd had some difficulty inspiring with human servants in the past.

He towelled off as he walked into his living room, not thinking for a moment that he was being watched.

"Now that's something I'll never un-see," said a voice from the large recliner in the main area of his large, lavishly furnished home above the clouds. "You should look into the new fitness meds, I hear they have versions that won't trigger an allergic reaction or extreme flatulence for cases like yours, where you're a little over the ten percent body fat margin."

"Who let you in here?" Governor Tate asked, embarrassed, outraged and alarmed. He ran for the door of his study, where a rack of rare weapons awaited, only to have it close swiftly before he could grab one.

"I'm in your computer system, Governor," the stranger said. "No running, no hiding, and no sicking your poor, mistreated attendant bot on me. I'm amazed that you've had her for four months and still haven't named her. I think I'll call her Nancy, she looks a bit like a Nancy to me."

Governor Tate wrapped the towel around his waist, leaving his round belly hanging over. "I don't know who you are, but you're in more trouble than you could ever imagine. I'm the master of eleven inhabited worlds, and a fleet like you-"

"Nancy!" the stranger cried, snapping his fingers. "Get the Governor here something to wear, his uniform should do." He leaned forward and regarded Governor Tate with an impish grin. "You know who I am, just give your grey matter a minute to work through all those faces in all those reports. I'm somewhere near the top of the pile, I guarantee it."

The man's manner was infuriating. He was completely dismissive of the Governor's position and somehow in control of everything around him, so it seemed. There had to be a crack in the man's armour, or a piece of information that could help Tate out of his predicament, then this unwelcome guest would pay for his insolence. "I don't recall seeing you anywhere," he told the stranger. The man had hair down to his shoulders, a square visage, and eerily penetrating blue eyes. Details of his face shifted under the skin, then the lips expanded at the corners, and the nose flattened, shortened and Governor Tate recognized his visitor. "You are wanted for questioning in multiple sectors," he said, calming down. It was Wheeler, a man with a fleeting relationship to the Order of Eden at best. "Not to mention, you're still technically the property of Regent Galactic."

"So, your war torn toy is here," he replied, sitting back in the chair as he watched the helper bot deliver a dark green uniform to the Governor. "You Regent Galactic people get a real twist in your knickers when your technology grows a mind of its own. You know how to make us look good though, I'll admit."

"I'll never trust this one again," the Governor said as he pulled his trousers on. "It took five months for the fabrication centre to get her just right, but now that you've been in her head...."

"Then I'll take her. I'm sure you can have something else made," Wheeler replied. "Maybe something with a more human shape. The ultra slim models never really look human, do they?"

"What makes you think you'll walk out of here with anything? Even your freedom is a long shot at this point. I don't care that you're a murderer, or that you may have had something to do with the leadership changes at the top." Governor Tate told him. He only needed to know who his visitor was so he could read the situation and find his footing. Wheeler was a destructive force, even when he failed in his mission there was some kind of wreckage left in his wake. Even still, the only reason why Wheeler would beg an audience with the highest power in the Codis solar System was because he wanted something, and there were a number of things Tate could think of that Wheeler could deliver.

"I'm going to make you the leader of the Order of Eden," Wheeler said. "You're one of the only Governors who have passed on the framework program, and have been smart enough to stay away from the current leadership."

"Powerful people who get too close to Eve or that Beast tend to end up in their place with no hope of advancement or dead, with very little in their epitaph," Governor Tate said. His bot brought him a mug of nutmeg cocoa as he sat down in a firm armchair across from Wheeler. The drink was an all natural treat, the ingredients cost thousands of credits when they were available.

"Very good, Nancy, now could you record everything that is said here?" Wheeler asked. "I really do plan on taking you with me, and we'll make more than point zero zero seven percent use of that wonderful brain of yours."

A sip of his drink revealed a perfect texture, flavour and temperature, something he'd been trying to have his bot, Nancy, to master since she'd entered his home. "I don't know if I want control of the Order. They've fallen in line behind Eve, and the military feeds on the image of the Beast. They're zealots, near crazed."

"Then the Regent Galactic Forces, corporate control," Wheeler said, "That's even easier. You're right, the Order is so crazed now, it's like a bag of flaming cats. That is, except for the segments of the Order you already control. I hear recruitment is down thirty five percent thanks to Valent's game of Chinese Whispers."

"It'll come back up. People want the community and opportunity Order membership brings, and if I can do that without demanding the fervour that Eve does, then they'll see the rational choice."

"That's not going to be possible. Eve is coming here," Wheeler replied. "Just something I heard on the Order of Eden Command Network. She's going to gather your Order members into the fold."

"What? She travels with so large a group, getting her onto this side of the Ironhead Nebula would be a massive undertaking, I would have heard something," Governor Tate said.

"No, not if she had a double spreading her message elsewhere. She wants to surprise this sector, appear as though by some miracle," Wheeler said. "It'll work for some, and the rest of the Order followers here will see that, by taking her lead they can elevate themselves faster than they could if they just stayed here, fighting in your ranks. You're about to have a workforce shortfall on three of your planets, probably four. All the biggest ones, really."

"And you're going to tell me that you have the solution, that you can put me in a higher position than the Mother of the Order?"

"No, I'm going to put you up as her equal. I've seen across this digital landscape, the plains that remember our footsteps like they are pressed into stone. The Beast hates the zealotry and sacrifice that Eve demands as much or more than you do. He could use an ally in Regent Galactic too, especially on this side of the Iron Head Nebula, where the majority of their resources and fabrication assets are. If you drop all your suppositions about him, and forget his public persona, which is a farce, if you ask me, you'll find that he'll become an easy ally. I can get you in front of him through his own secure network, and I know you'll be able to take it from there if you respect him."

"That's all, just respect him," Governor Tate said, deeply interested. The Beast commanded forty two battle groups at last count, half a billion souls engaged in military service, and his forces grew every time they conquered a new outpost or world. Even his manufacturing capabilities were growing, especially over the previous two months. "There has to be more to it."

"There is, I knew the man, even before he changed. I'll walk you through it step by step, I'll even vouch for you. Once upon a time I had a hand in getting him into his position. But first, you need to agree to give me a carrier group. I'll fight your war my way, and I'll bloody all the enemies you have on this side of the Nebula. You think this is power? This solar system? It's a great money generator, and, yes, you could build something impressive here, but you haven't seen real power until the local systems start paying you tribute, until an entire sector feels they need to consult with your people before they do so much as take a deep breath. If you want to be remembered, to have the kind of power that generates a legend that can outlast Earthen Pharaohs, then let me help you, and give me what I need to draw blood from your enemies."

"A carrier group, that's-"

"A pittance," Wheeler said as he accepted an amber drink from Nancy. "Regent Galactic is waiting for a great leader, and you could be it. You just need the right backing."

"The Beast."

"Exactly," Wheeler replied. "And I need a carrier group. I need one of those carrier groups you have in orbit to get a few things done. All I want is Tamber, in the Rega Gain System. The rest is yours, along with the credit."

"One moon you intend to capture yourself?"

"Yes, get the carrier group ready this week, and I'll get you on the fast track to becoming the greatest leader this galaxy has ever seen. You have the mind for it, you have the fortitude, and now you'll have an in-road thanks to me."

"They'll need two weeks to prepare, in the meantime I expect to see significant process, I need to see this is working before you go on some warpath."

"Fair enough."

"Now, how do we get started?" Governor Tate asked, truly excited for the first time in years.

"Well, for a start, you'll never call the leader of the Order Military the Beast again. Call him Overlord Clark Patterson. He was human once, and he had a good soul."

CHAPTER 6
THE SOLAR FORGE'S ONLY PATIENT

Jake sat on a balancing seat that would sway left or right if he didn't actively hold himself in place. Jake had almost mastered it, and could stay up straight without much concentration. His room was unrecognizable thanks to the holographic display that surrounded him. He was in a rest period, true, but that didn't mean he had to rest his mind. He had been out of commission for weeks, and there was a lot to catch up on.

His recovery was going well, according to Alice and Oz, but it wasn't fast enough for Jake. Even with a parade of visitors throughout the day, life-like simulated experiences, and an endless stream of reports, he still felt like he had been placed in a corner away from the rest of the universe. He appreciated the fact that the Warlord was on patrol, training the new crew under Stephanie, Frost, Agameg, Finn and Minh-Chu. They were doing what he'd wish they would while he was off his feet, nothing serious and nothing overly dangerous. He still felt like he should be with them, like he was missing too much.

The Triton hadn't operated under his command for months, but he felt like there was too great a distance between it and him as well. Oz had that well in hand, Jake knew, but what he actually knew about the day to day operations of Triton Fleet could fit in a ten minute narrated report. An evolutionary kind of change was radiating from the Triton, and he felt like he was missing it. The captured Order of Eden Destroyer had become part of Triton Fleet after undergoing a refit inside the Solar Forge that lasted a little over two weeks. With the resdesign that Ayan's new engineering team along with Agameg, Frost and Finn put together, it would have taken six months in a normal shipyard. The Solar Forge was a wonder, and while Jake was recovering it was attending to ships that came from across the sector to join Triton Fleet and Haven Shore Defence. Lorander was truly allowing Triton Fleet do whatever they liked with their gift, to Jake's surprise. The Destroyer was even improved significantly during the refit. New exterior armour plates that could absorb incredible amounts of energy and emit nearly as much were added, along with advanced stealth systems. The lower cargo doors had been rebuilt so the main hold was a large hangar. The list went on with other minor improvements, some of which took two attempts to install properly, but one glaring oversight nagged at Jake: they hadn't found a captain worthy of the destroyer yet.

He returned his attention to the work the Solar Forge was doing. It had taken the repair systems only a day and a half to repair all the damage aboard the Warlord, inside and out. The skitters aboard learned from the much smaller reacher droids that the station used to do fine internal repairs as well. Reports of the Warlord's skitters efficiency rising were encouraging. The strides the Triton Fleet's technology was making was more than impressive, it indicated to Jake that there was a will in Lorander Corporation to see them become a major force against the Order of Eden.

Even if they used it as a tool to track the number of ships Triton Fleet had, the benefits still far outweighed that kind of drawback. Oz even had his people checking every ship for control or tracking devices that may have been planted by the mobile shipyard, but they found absolutely nothing. Watching what was going through the ship refurbishing and building facility was one of the more interesting things Jake had to do, and even though he could rarely feel the vibrations or hear the sound of machinery that was right under his feet, he felt like he was close to one of the main devices for change in the Rega Gain system.

The quiet of his small medical ward was stifling at times, and when he discovered that there were over three hundred trainees aboard the Solar Forge, he was relieved. Two days passed and he only saw them when he was on his way to the training room he'd come to call the pillbox. They were in Triton Fleet uniforms, and were specifically being trained to service the busy ship building vessel by the vessel itself and a few Lorander guides. Jake was convinced that this was another way for the Lorander Corporation to observe members of Triton Fleet, but, again, what they were trading for the opportunity was worth it. To Jake's surprise, all the issyrians who were once in the service of Clark Patterson were among the trainees. He had to wonder if Lorander foresaw that they would take an interest in the construction ship. It was a way for the group of issyrians to join Triton Fleet as non-combatants, a way around the agreement that won them safe Haven on Tamber.

The medical centre aboard was still empty, and it was where he spent much of his time. Even though he knew so much was going on aboard, he still felt separated from everything, a growing sensation that set Jacob Valent on edge.

It didn't take long before he broke down and called a map of recent patrols outside the Rega Gain system. The circular paths of British Alliance and Triton Fleet patrols hung in the air above him, traced by lines coloured blue, yellow, green and red. The red line was always furthest out, that was his ship and Minh-Chu's Samurai wing. Samurai Wing wasn't out there with the Warlord more than a third of the time, the mission didn't always require them.

"Engagement history for the period since Stephanie Vega has been Acting Captian," he told the computer. To his surprise there were five encounters. The first two occurred while Warlord was on high speed patrol, moving so fast that, when they returned to orbit around Tamber, an extra half hour had passed there. What amazed Jake was that one of the encounters were engaged and concluded at that speed.

The Warlord detected a weak signal that didn't match anything on the British Alliance's frontier. Within seconds the Warlord determined exactly where it came from, matched the shape of the ship with a Regent Galactic scout ship, and then the Warlord fired her main rail guns, destroying the scout ship completely. The whole engagement took less than two minutes to resolve.

During the second engagement the Warlord had time to slow down and follow the scout ship they found, and offered surrender terms. The ship self destructed, but transmitted an encrypted stream of data first. "Okay, there's something there," Jake said to himself. The data still hadn't been decrypted, but Triton Fleet was still working on it. He suspected they'd find sensor data from the scout ship along with a short log from whoever was aboard. What Jake found interesting was that it transmitted anything at all. That meant there was something else within range to receive the data. There was something launching these scouts, and it was within a light year of the Rega Gain system.

From then on at least part of the Samurai Squadron was present on the Warlord. Jake didn't have to check Stephanie's log to figure out why. She had come to the same conclusion he did.

"The next thing they came up on was three days later, the first Regent Galactic Cruiser we've seen," Minh-Chu said from the door. "You and Ayan review way too much of your data in hologram," he said. "Almost every time I visit she's looking at something in mid-air."

"Something like?" Jake asked.

"Reports, or she's building a database, or something for the skitters to put together," Minh-Chu replied, sitting on Jake's bed.

"What happened here?" Jake said, pointing at the third engagement on the map. A rogue planetary body had drifted past the Rega Gain system, and a tiny graphic of an explosion marked it as a combat encounter.

"Like I said, the Warlord was swinging by that rogue planet, and we found a Regent Galactic Cruiser hiding there. Me and two members of the Samurai squadron were already out of the hangar, following behind the Warlord to get our scans of the planet finished faster, and the cruiser came at us firing. To us, it came out of nowhere, but Stephanie's report includes a scan that broke through the cruiser's cloaking systems, and it bolted the moment it realized it was detected. We didn't even know they were using cloaking until then."

"What happened next?"

"I hid behind the Warlord," Minh-Chu said with a shrug. "I'm not proud to admit it, but I ordered my squadron to scatter, the cruiser threw everything at the fighters, I guess they thought they could get past the Warlord, but the fighters could be a problem."

"With the way your wing has been loading your ships, I don't blame them. You've managed to turn Uriels into full on gunships."

"Yeah, that's a necessary evil," Minh-Chu said. "With our patrols spread out so thin, even with a hundred eighty British Alliance ships out there at all times, we've got to fill the high risk spots, so we take half of what's on the deck before we go. That's what happens when a big government like the British Alliance plans on putting a grand frontier defence up and they fail right out of the gate."

Jake activated the recording of what happened to the cruiser in the last moments of the engagement. "I'm guessing the cruiser's decision to ignore the Warlord was a mistake."

"Oh yeah," Minh-Chu said. "Just play that section there." He gestured towards the graphic of the Warlord and the cruiser frozen in space. The Regent Galactic Cruiser was trying to leave the planet's orbit, its engines and beam weapons firing brightly. The ship was only two hundred eighty metres long, compared to a full sized destroyer, that was small. It was still larger than the Warlord in the space it took up, but it was half the Warlord's mass. "What did they do here?" Jake asked, pointing to the underbelly of the ship.

"They managed to fit turrets firing high speed rounds into your mine launching positions. They can be removed so you can launch mines too, but Captain Vega has been sticking with her configuration since the Warlord was fixed by the Solar Forge."

"Is it working?" Jake asked.

"For what we're doing out there? Absolutely. Watch, she ordered armour piercing screwhead rounds this time." Minh-Chu twitched his finger to the right and the playback began.

The Warlord fired her main weapons – the large railguns at the front of the ship and her new pulse cannons mounted across the top. The railguns fired once, partially bursting through the enemy ship's shields and showering the bridge with white-hot shrapnel. The pulse guns overloaded the enemies' shields, raking white beams of pure energy across their invisible barriers. By the time the cruiser was alongside the Warlord, the bottom half of Jake's ship was turned towards it, and those new turrets rained hard rounds down on the enemy ship's hull, breaking thrusters and compartments open.

"Surrender or die," Jake's voice said as the guns stopped, the power levels of the enemy ship dropped, and the Warlord took a position right above the cruiser, making it obvious that they were getting ready to make the kill.

"Yup, everything that comes out of that ship while it's in patrol sounds like you," Minh-Chu said. "Captain Vega's orders.

They even have a stand-in who is your height and build wearing armour that looks exactly the same. He boards and debarks from the ship whenever it's with the fleet."

"I'm alive and well everywhere except for in this room," Jake said.

"That's a dark way to look at it," Minh-Chu muttered.

The playback continued with the cruiser signalling its surrender. The report summary said that the Warlord latched onto it with the maxjack and hauled it all the way back home, to Tamber orbit. Teams from the Triton stripped it after the crew were placed in British Alliance custody, and the hull was processed for raw materials by the Solar Forge.

"That was the last cruiser that surrendered. The Warlord was forced to destroy the other two. There wasn't much to bring back."

"They fought to the last man," Jake said.

"That's exactly how Frost put it," Minh-Chu said, bringing the lights up to daylight level in the room.

"So the Warlord is doing fine without me," Jake said.

"I wouldn't put it that way," Minh-Chu said. "You are like the main gravitational force in the middle of that ship. When you're gone, things start floating away. Alice left for the Rangers, Agameg and Finn have been taking time to help with other parts of Triton Fleet, and other officers from your bridge are sharing what they've learned from close encounters with the Order and Regent Galactic. It's not the same ship, Jake. Sure, Steph is doing an incredible job. She tells people she learned from the best instead of taking credit for thinking past your style, but she can't keep the crew together like you can. She wants to see what you do with your ship next, not take your place."

"Maybe it's time for her to get her own command," Jake said. "There's this destroyer we have, Warlord still has the claim, technically."

"She won't take it unless you order her to," Minh-Chu said. "Her and Frost are your people, they don't want to leave your ship. Now, if you took command of the Barricade, they'd follow you in a second."

"I didn't even think about that," Jake said.

"Oz sure has," Minh-Chu said. "Just don't tell him I told you."

Jake was overwhelmed by a sinking feeling when he thought about the bridge of that ship. "No," he said.

"You like the agility of the Warlord, I get it," Minh-Chu said. "You should still think about it though."

Jake thought about commanding the ship and was filled with dread. "Chinese whispers," he muttered, not knowing where the words came from.

"Bad memories from that bridge," Minh-Chu said, nodding. "I think Oz will understand."

"What do you mean?" Jake asked. "I don't remember getting to the bridge, I've thought about it, trying to get there, but I just remember the hallway in the middle of the ship."

The colour drained from Minh-Chu's face, he looked as though he was seeing a foe he could not defeat or escape.

"What happened there? Did I die there for a while or-"

"You murdered someone there, Jake," Minh-Chu said quietly. "You menaced a junior member of the bridge staff in front of his mates when you couldn't find the captain and killed him to make a point."

Jake immediately gestured for the light in the room to be reduced and tried to call up the records of combat aboard the Barricade's bridge, but discovered he was locked out of that file. "What? I don't have access?" Jake exclaimed. "Bring it up, Minh, I need to see what happened."

Minh-Chu wordlessly accessed the file. "I'm coming to terms with this, Jake. Recruitment is down across the Order of Eden, especially on this side of the Iron Head Nebula. You did this to show that you'll give no quarter to your enemy, to scare people off."

"Play it," Jake said, "I need to know why I feel like the bridge of that ship is the worst place I've ever been, and that I've done something I'll regret for the rest of my life."

Minh-Chu stared at him a moment, then nodded. The playback began. Jake had a young officer in hand, and burned him with the heated end of his Violator Handgun as a form of torture, to get his attention. "We're going to play a game – it's called Chinese Whispers, only it'll be a short one." His recorded self said to his young captive. The boy was terrified, shaking, crying. The devil was at his back and there was no promise of mercy.

Jake could feel his heart racing, he didn't remember any of what he was seeing, but somehow knew it was true. "Don't do it," he whispered to the recorded image of himself. The recorded Jake threatened his captives, told them what would happen if the Captain or the codes for the ship wasn't revealed to him, then ordered the young officer to begin counting.

A tear rolled down Jake's cheek as the countdown continued, and he flinched so hard when the gun went off that he almost fell out of his seat. "No!" Jake shouted, "that's not me!"

He fell from his seat, trying to remember that moment and failing in the midst of a remorseful panic. "I can't remember, that can't be me!" he cried. Minh-Chu was on the floor with him, picking him up in his arms. Over his shoulder Jake caught a glimpse of his recorded self taking a young woman up by her pony tail and said; "stop playback." The computer froze the image there.

"You killed the one, the others survived and are in custody," Minh-Chu said.

"How did I do that?" Jake said, letting Minh-Chu hold him. "Why did I do that? I don't remember anything before that that could-" his meeting with an agent of the British Alliance returned to him. He was ordered to use fear, intimidation, but he was not ordered to murder. That was the way of the barbarian, the quick route that led your enemies to a feeling of being justi-fied in standing against you. That could not have been his way, but he knew that it was for a while.

"That's not me," Jake said. "You've got to know that's not me now."

"I know, old friend," Minh-Chu said. "I'm glad to have you back, you don't know how much."

CHAPTER 7
LONG RANGE COMMUNICATIONS

Governor Tate did not know how Wheeler found an Echo Corp communications device, or how he knew Clark Patterson, known as the Beast to most of his forces, had one. He did not know how Wheeler got his hands on the Beast's schedule, or how he could predict where the primary Order of Eden fleet would be next, but he had done that too.

If it weren't for Wheeler, the Governor would not be able to press a button and have the immediate attention of the Overlord of the Order of Eden Fleet in front of him holographically. "Governor Tate," Overlord Clark Patterson said. "I have been looking forward to meeting you, but I did not expect you to find me through the Echo network. We only captured the module two weeks ago."

"My sources informed me that you have one yesterday, it is a pleasure to finally address you outside of my weekly reports. I am impressed with how you have commanded the fleet since the coup, Overlord, but I didn't go to these lengths to contact you for praise alone, I'm afraid."

"Thank you for getting to the point, Governor," the Beast said.

The holographic image of his face was blurry, but that exoskeletal skull with its shifting, scraping plates made Governor Tate's skin crawl. "I am concerned about the impending arrival of our High Priestess, as her people have begun to call her, Eve. My branch of your military does not run on faith like her coterie does, they are military trained and believe that their service will improve their quality of life. This religious zeal that she inspires, it seems fickle, dangerous. It even seems difficult to direct."

"She inspires millions," Clark Patterson said in defence of Eve. That was unexpected.

"It all hinges on her, and her ability to deliver immortality and paradise. I have difficulty believing in her, and I can't help but suppose that a great number of her followers are sceptics who are going along for the ride because they see little alternative at the moment. They'll break away the moment they see an opportunity."

"You are one of the wealthiest people in four sectors," the Overlord said. "If I'm not mistaken. Paradise is within your grasp, even though you have responsibilities. How could you understand the struggle of people who were stranded, accosted by the Holocaust Virus? You cannot. At the same time I have to admit that you have a point, one that I've been thinking about for a while. My own fleet is performing exceptionally well without constant exposure to the religious side of the Order of Eden. Their gratitude for a place in this wounded galaxy and the camaraderie they feel towards each other keeps them in line. I concede one point to her, however. The ideas of immortality and paradise are intoxicating. I am in the process of founding my own paradise world right now, and have made many of my soldiers immortal by implanting them with framework technology and making them Knights of the Order. These things are enough to motivate my soldiers like nothing I've ever seen, even though a number of Order Knights have been destroyed. They are hailed as great heroes and few question that earning a place as a Knight is the best way to survive this war."

"But that's not religious zeal," the Governor pressed gently. "That's presenting your servicemen and women with rewards for improving themselves, for proving themselves. I award my top people in similar ways."

"Ah, but not in our ways," Overlord Patterson said, "Paradise and immortality do not have to be connected to religion any longer. Not when our control of high technology can make us seem like Gods. We don't have to call ourselves Gods, just leaders, but the result is the same. They will lay their lives at our feet. The difference is that we don't try to trick our people into thinking that we are somehow supernaturally superior, or some chosen prophet."

Wheeler had warned him about getting too deep into a debate. The Governor was to befriend the Beast, not argue with him, or try to change him. "You are absolutely right, Grand Admiral. I find myself wondering if I should follow your example in elevating some of my men to Order Knight status."

"You should. In fact, if you have a personal guard, I'd begin there," Grand Admiral Patterson said. "You should also create propaganda that promises your best and brightest an eventual place in paradise."

"Do I have to sacrifice a world for that purpose? Every place I govern has at least a little of its territory used for production," Governor Tate asked, hoping that he wouldn't have to ruin the balance he'd worked so hard to create across his Regent Galactic worlds.

"No, you are fortunate in that regard. Knowing that I will eventually lead my fleet around the Ironhead Nebula, I have studied your worlds. I am impressed at how money in Regent Galactic territory can change lives. So few people have a surplus of credit, and the few who do live like kings and queens. Offer them near limitless credit in your little Empire, then they can decide where paradise is for them, on one of your worlds."

Governor Tate was taken aback by the suggestion, it made so much sense and it was so simple. "I'm embarrassed that I didn't think of that myself, thank you, Grand Admiral."

"You're welcome, I'm sure you would have thought of it eventually. Make sure you offer these things and give a little before the Priestess of the Order arrives. I cannot stop her from visiting your worlds, nor do I suggest you do. In the meantime, I have new orders for you."

"Yes, Sir," Governor Tate said, straightening.

"You will also officially take Doha, Myrrin, and Chunu for your own. These worlds are too well civilized and politically powerful to exist so near your territory without being owned by Regent Galactic or you. I have reviewed your assets. I know you can do this within the week."

"Yes, Grand Admiral," Governor Tate replied.

"One more thing. Keep forces from Rega Gain contained. My intelligence tells me that their forces are growing, ships flock to the Triton Fleet."

"Let me be clear," Overlord Patterson said, raising a finger. "Contained. You are not to take the solar system. Maintain a reasonable perimeter and keep them within it. I know you have the resources to accomplish this."

"I will keep them contained, but leave the solar system itself alone. No bombardments or invasions," Governor Tate replied.

"It has been good speaking with you, Governor Tate. I look forward to your next update." The transmission ended.

Governor Tate was on his feet, pacing in the next instant.

Wheeler stepped into the room with a knowing grin on his face. "That went well, Governor."

"I thought so," Governor Tate said. "I can't believe it, he even gave me useful advice when I thought I had everything here taken care of. You'll earn that battle group yet, Lucious."

"It won't be long, you report to him again in three days, and you know what to do now."

"Absolutely. I have the Overlord's leave to purchase one of those planets, he as much told me to do it with my own funds. The other two can be squeezed through the supply line, I shut down all of Spacerwares operations for a week and people begin to starve. I blame their local governments and the people will look to me to solve the problem."

"Be careful, if one of those worlds turns on you, there will be ports filled with ships and people ready to join Triton Fleet, or start a revolt all their own."

The Governor dismissed his comment with a wave. "Don't worry, I've been planning this for years, I just needed approval from the board. Now I don't need to so much as send them a memo before the fact."

"Don't forget to appoint a few Order Knights and give them the right enhancements, the Overlord will be expecting that."

"Of course, I'll be happy to reward some lucky soul for great service," Governor Tate said. "Publicly, there will be a parade somewhere."

"Careful," Wheeler said. "Work on it, find the right person, someone who has made sacrifices, obeyed the rules of the Order and has climbed the organization's ladder, but still believes in you. Then propose your choice to the Overlord before you give them unlimited credit."

"Near unlimited," Governor Tate corrected, "The only person with unlimited credit in this sector is me. I see what you're saying though. All this has to have an air of collaboration, like I need just a little of his approval."

"Exactly," Wheeler replied.

CHAPTER 8
CONCERNED FRIENDS AND LOVERS

Minh-Chu was surprised when Ayan didn't answer the door to her new quarters aboard the Triton right away. She was finally in the ship's inner ring of quarters, surrounding the outside of the Botanical Gallery. There were a few larger Officer's quarters that went unused for the first year they had the ship, but with the refit complete, the well protected Officer's Quarters section was open. Despite a few whimpers about favouritism, Oz assigned them to his closest friends, who were all officers anyway, so there was no arguing with the decision. Minh-Chu and Ashley were supposed to occupy theirs two doors down, but after spending so much time in pilot berthing, neither of them were in a big hurry. Somehow all that space seemed strange, and living with Ashley was a little intimidating. There was no rush, however, the pair were busy trying to catch minutes together between their shifts and duties.

"Sure she's home?" Ashley asked from his side. They both carried bottles from the Oota Galoona, the non-human themed dance club inside the Triton. In his hand was a blue coloured bottle of Sideslider, a beverage known for its relaxing qualities, and in Ashley's hand was Paramour, one of her favourites. Minh-Chu liked it for the savoury smooth flavour, but had come to believe it was made for couples, not so much for parties, because of its tendency to make the drinkers much more affectionate than normal.

"Crewcast says she's here," Minh-Chu said, squeezing Ashley's hand.

"Sure she's not off doing shadowy stuff? Something no one's supposed to know about?" she asked in a whisper.

"What do you think she does?" Minh-Chu asked with a chuckle.

She smiled back at him sheepishly. "Well, her dad's some kind of former spy guy and the new Governor," Ashley shrugged. "She could be anywhere now that she's out of politics, she could do anything."

The door opened, revealing Lacey, dark haired, taller, and a little older looking than Ayan. It looked like she had just been arguing with someone. "Come on in, Ayan's just wrapping up."

One of the newer District Representatives from Haven Shore, Doug Hamlin, was standing in the middle of Ayan's living room, his arms crossed and his brow furrowed. "How can you expect me to sell that to my people? Two thirds of them are out there in the jungle harvesting on full shifts but my district's food alottment is restricted? It doesn't make sense."

"Everything goes to the military branches first," Ayan replied, "even if your people were responsible for all the food we ate, that product would still be gathered by the military at the collection site then transported to our depots where it's distributed fairly. That's just how it works now."

"No one is happy down here, people are threatening to leave my district all together."

"Tell them that it's the same everywhere, even up here, in the fleet. In fact, Fleet personnel are even more closely monitored."

"I'll believe that when I see it, and I'm sure no one down here will believe that either."

"That says more about your ineptitude than it does about how fair or unfair this situation is," Ayan replied. "The Fleet are providing more fairly for your people than the Council was, there are plenty of points about the system going into place tomorrow that you could focus on that your people can understand and appreciate. Supplies, infrastructure, and medical services are all going to improve for your district. In other districts they may see a drop in some things that they had in over abundance, but you'll find this is fair on balance, like those representatives have."

"So you admit that, while this policy is fair on balance, it may be unfair to some," replied Hamlin.

"No," Ayan replied flatly. "Let's talk about fair, shall we? Right now all of Haven Shore is allotted an extra seventeen dietary points. By the old British system, that's an extra twelve hundred calóries a day, and the majority of them don't come anywhere close to eating that. What you're asking me to do is to influence the military chain of command so that so-called limit is removed. Are you trying to get control over other districts by having more influence on the food your people provide? Is this a power play? If it is, I'll have you removed tonight. Reaching for power outside of your district is no longer legal, now you are in service to your district. The law prevents representatives from making a district serve them."

"Your accusation is baseless and hypocritical. If anyone is manipulating a system, it is you. The military is the ultimate system of control, and right now it's a helping hand, but at any time you can change the allotment and it will become a rod you can use to punish or flog my constituents. It doesn't matter that you're over-alotting Haven Shore's people now, I worry about-"

"You're talking about a situation that does not exist, and about a situation no one in this solar system has the power to change. I own Tamber in name, and I have placed it into the care of Triton Fleet to be overseen by the Governor. The laws that will govern resources are not up for debate. You go back to your people and tell them that the system is there to enforce fairness, so the people who service buildings, and build infrastructure are just as well fed as the people who grow and harvest our food. Tell them that they're doing such a good job right now that they're not only feeding the fleet that protects them well, but providing almost double the daily requirement of the population in Haven Shore while giving us enough to store away in case we have a short harvest later. Your people are to be congratulated, reassured, not represented by a reactionist idiot."

"You can't talk to me like that!"

"I'm not part of your council or who you should be lodging your complaint with, so I can tell you that you're a spoiled blowhard, and that you're on the verge of being exiled from the solar system because it sounds like you're trying to take control of an essential supply of food on Tamber, and there's no room for a power hungry beurocrat in the new government. Don't call my ident again," Ayan told him before slapping the bracelet style command and control unit on her wrist.

Lacey applauded lightly, chuckling a little. "That's the last one."

"Finally," Ayan said, a smile appearing as soon as she saw Minh-Chu and Ashley. The Ayan Minh-Chu knew and called friend was back in an instant, the strained diplomat was gone. She crossed the room and pushed herself between Minh-Chu and Ashley, pulling them into a three person hug. "This is a nice surprise."

"What was all that about?" Minh-Chu asked.

"I thought it would be a good idea to speak to each Council Member individually, an opportunity to thank them for their service and answer a few questions now that my father is officially the Governor."

"Best of intentions, most of them were receptive," Lacey said. "But a lot of them were like that, still fighting for rights they had no right to. It's as though they can't accept the Equal Priviledge laws that put them in the same conditions as the average citizen in their district."

"Oh, hon," Ashley cooed sympathetically as she gave Ayan an extra squeeze.

"I'm all right, it's the last time I have to speak to anyone on the Haven Shore Council, unless I want to," Ayan said as the trio split.

"We thought you'd like some company now that things are settling down and you're officially assigned to the Triton," Minh-Chu said, offering his bottle.

"And on your last night without Captain Valent," Ashley said with an impish grin. "Here's something for your first night with him, because I hear things are going well."

Ayan handed Minh-Chu's bottle to Lacey, who took it and said; "oh, we're opening this now. A nice big bottle of relaxer is just what this room needs."

"Thank you both, Lacey wanted to have a gathering tonight because my schedule is clear, but I convinced her to hold off at least a night, so Jake can be here," Ayan said as she received the smaller bottle from Ashley. "Speaking of Jake…" Ayan put the bottle on a side table set under an interior opening looking through to the kitchen. She activated a program on her transparent blue command and control unit and the blue material of her uniform turned green. The shape shifted into a dress with a plunging U-shaped neckline and a loose skirt that ended well above her bare knees. Ayan pulled the ring holding her curly red hair in a bun, letting it fall down just past her shoulders. "That's better."

Ashley whistled appreciatively, "You're definitely giving him something worth running to, nevermind walking."

"I couldn't have said it better," Lacey said, "He better know how lucky he is."

Minh-Chu couldn't help but recongize that Lacey compli-
mented Ayan's civillian side. For all the training and the soldierly
tendencies Ayan had, the second Ayan always knew how to relax
as a civilian when she had the chance, something Minh-Chu
never mastered. Lacey, in a skirt that was loosely stretched down
the length of her from shoulders to shins, was entirely civillian.
While she seemed to support the military, her point of view was
that of a civilian, something that was easily apparent from his
first conversation with her months before. She didn't have any
experience in the military, but she had plenty of opinions. He realized that Ashley wanted him to compliment Ayan when he felt
her nudge him with her elbow. "A lily is prettiest when her roots
are planted deeply, and her petals are open to the sun," he said,
realizing immediately that his witty declaration was more than a
little miscalculated when Ayan began blushing, Lacey chuckled
and Ashley's jaw dropped. "That didn't come out right," Minh-
Chu said in a rush. "I meant to say you work hard to look the
way you do, not that you have to work hard, the way you are,
and there's more to you than how you look, and that dress-"

"You should quit while you're ahead," Ashley whispered.

"Very pretty," Minh-Chu said, "Jake's very lucky. Are you visiting him soon?"

Lacey's sudden outburst of laughter came as a short shriek,
while Ayan blushed and laughed along. "Better," Ashley snickered.

Ayan cleared her throat and nodded. "I'm going to see him in
about an hour. Otherwise Lacey would be having a Thank
Goodness It's Over party for me tonight."

"Why before Jake can be here?" Ashley asked Lacey.

"If being friends with Ayan has taught me anything, it's that
you take full advantage of openings in her schedule when they
appear," Lacey said, uncapping the blue bottle of Sideslider. "I

have a feeling those openings will become even harder to reserve once Jake's free from captivity."

"Recovery," Ashley corrected.

"Oh, I call it captivity. When your information, the people you're allowed to see and your range of movement are controlled, I call it captivity."

"That's not happening, is it?" Ashley asked. "I mean, Doctor Messana told me and Minh that we should wait to visit until he's off the Solar Forge, and it made sense. She didn't want him too distracted. He still snuck in without any questions, too."

"You're on a list of hundreds of people who were told the same thing, dear," Lacey said as she touched the wall and used the simple interface that appeared to request a drawer from the kitchen just behind the wall. An opening appeared half a metre to her left and a drawer filled with fluted glasses slid open just above the sideboard table she put the bottle down on. "That Doctor's controlling what level of information he gets from the fleet, who can visit, pretty much everything. She even has the Solar Forge's artificial gravity systems pushing down on him all the time. Just him, it's completely localized, so he can come out being accustomed to one point four times standard gravity. It's no wonder he's covered in bruises. When he gets out tomorrow and realizes what's been going on without his knowledge, there may be a reckoning."

Minh-Chu had no idea that was happening, and immediately felt guilty for listening to Doctor Messana's request to only visit during group events. His only visit was an eventful, significant one two days before. A repeat visit probably would have been a real relief to his old friend. He was busy flying missions for Triton Fleet and for the British Alliance. He'd rarely been as busy, but he could have stopped in. Judging from Ayan's non-reaction, he could tell she knew exactly what Lacey was talking about. "He realizes he's not seeing the whole picture," Minh-Chu said. "I had to access some files for him the other day when he wanted some of the gaps in his memory filled in. He didn't take what he did on that bridge well."

"You showed him what happened on the Barricade?" Ayan asked.

"He wanted to know," Minh-Chu said. Ashley was quiet, she didn't like talking about it.

"We were told not to do that," Ayan said, "How did it go over."

"He had trouble," Min-Chu said. "We got through it." He made the decision not to tell Ayan, or anyone else, that he stayed for four hours after Jake broke down at the sight of the murder on that bridge. "It was hard, but I think he believes that he isn't that person anymore. There was something going on while he was a framework, I didn't see it as clearly as I do now, but there was something missing, something held back. Now he's all there, and this Jake wouldn't have done what he did on the bridge of the Barricade for anything."

Ayan still looked irritated, put off. "Doctor Marcelles told me there could be differences. Parts of his brain were rebuilt. How is he now?"

"He regrets what he did on the Barricade, more than I've regretted anything," Minh-Chu replied.

"Well that's something," Lacey said. "We can't have Captains running around murdering young officers, even if they are brainwashed."

"You have no idea what you're talking about," Ayan said. "I don't like what he did either, but it has made a real difference in the Order, one that might give us a chance."

"Yes, but the ends can't justify-" Lacey started.

"I don't have time to have this argument with you again," Ayan said. "I'm going to see him. Thank you both for coming, Minh, Ashley." Ayan said, leaving the room.

Minh-Chu was glad Ayan was going to see him, but he couldn't help but wonder if he should be asking for her forgiveness for breaking a rule he wasn't told about.

"Why would they hide that from him?" Ashley asked. "What he did, I mean. People are going to tell him as soon as he gets out, gets back to work."

"One recovery at a time, maybe?" Lacey said, putting the glasses away.

"Maybe," Minh-Chu said. He made a promise to himself then, to stay close to Jake and provide an extra set of eyes and ears. For the first time since he knew him, he had a feeling that his old friend might need protection.

CHAPTER 9
OPEN AND CLOSURE

Jake could not help but stare in awe as he watched the Lorander fabrication ship complete work on one of their new heavy gunships. It truly was a child of the Clever Dream.

To Jake's right there was a transparent bulkhead where he could watch new ships leave the Solar Forge, and in front of him was a larger transparent wall overlooking the testing area. Several Triton crewmembers rushed around the vessel with silver, round bodied skitter bots helping with the final inspection.

"Lewis will be proud," Jake muttered to himself as he admired the shape of the armoured hull. It was two short decks tall, twenty one metres long, and it bore a sleek, broad profile. "Proud, and more than a little envious." He chuckled as the seven pulse turrets rotated, part of the after construction check, he guessed. Each of those turrets had two barrels and a small missile launcher , that was on top of the ship's three torpedo launchers and single multi-purpose launcher, large enough for a medium sized mine or probe.

He almost forgot he was leaning against a railing as he watched the ship's thrusters light up the testing bay as they pulsed on for the first time. "What kind of automation do they have?" Jake asked.

"On board only," Alice replied. "No one outside the ship can take control of the automation systems, so it can only be hacked by someone on board, just like the original."

"What's happening to the Clever Dream now that we have these?"

"The Clever Dream and Lewis are being given back to Alice," Ayan said as she came down the ramp into the simple observation area. She was in a dress that left her legs mostly bare, and teased more with a short, loose skirt. The scooped neck drew his eyes up to her ample bosom, the top half of the dress was revealing too, and a tight fit. Her warm smile drew his gaze up further, and he returned the expression until she was in his arms. They kissed briefly and took a step back. "Wow," he said.

"Thank you," she replied.

"That's my cue," Alice said. "I have Tactical Trial Two in an hour, so I should start getting ready."

"How did One go?" Jake asked. He knew she wasn't stressed about the first tactical test, it was an urban warfare scenario, one he'd taken several times using a simulation interface.

"Good, I'm third in my class, but that was only because I didn't stay on top of my squad as much as I could have, something I'll work on," Alice said. "This one is going to be interesting though."

"Zero gravity tactical?" Ayan asked.

"Yup, I'll be lucky to pass," Alice said. "I gotta go get ready."

"I'll see you tomorrow morning," Jake said.

"If I pass today I'll have the third Tactical Trial tomorrow morning," Alice said. "So I'll see you tomorrow afternoon, or in the morning all defeated and mope-ey."

"Tomorrow afternoon," Jake said. "Good luck."

"Thanks, Dad," Alice said.

Jake stepped away from the railing, took three sure steps to her and gave her a hug before she left. Ayan was at his side as soon as his daughter started to leave. Instead of leaning on her, Jake moved back to the railing and lightly put his hand on it. His balance almost felt normal, and he barely needed help with his stability when he walked. "You know what I really like about this ship?"

"What's that?" Ayan asked as she moved to walk alongside him.

"Railings. There are railings everywhere, I have no idea why, but I'm thinking of having them installed in the Warlord," Jake replied.

"Zero gravity," Ayan said with a chuckle. "They're here for a crew to start the ship up from a dormant state."

"Ah, so everything shuts down if there's nothing to build or repair," Jake said. "I think I read that somewhere. I don't remember where, it feels like I've read half the database since I woke up, way too much time on my hands."

"Doctor Messana says you've been training most of the time, over ten hours a day yesterday, twelve the day before that," Ayan said. "The last few weeks since you've been awake read as though you are either sleeping or exercising."

"Walking, tossing a ball, more walking, weight training, swimming, more walking," Jake said. "I need to get ready, I can't spend more time than I have to here."

"We can keep the war warm while you're recovering," Ayan said, "your bruises tell me you're trying too hard. You have to slow down once you're off the station, too much training can do more harm than good."

Jake took a step away from the railing and picked Ayan up in his arms. His balance threatened to falter for a moment but he recovered. She was shocked, her eyes and mouth wide open. He took advantage and kissed her with vigour. Her arms wrapped around his neck, and she returned his kiss with the same passion.

He enjoyed the feeling of her against him. She was lighter than expected, but most importantly her reception was far more amorous than he could have ever guessed. That made the conversation he had to have with her more difficult to start. He didn't want to question what was growing between them, he wanted more long conversations with her, he wanted the casual pleasure of seeing her every day, and he wanted what he was feeling with her in his arms. It still felt temporary, as though she would be gone when he could walk on his own two feet without questioning the act of staying upright. It still felt as though she was there because she felt guilty about something.

He lowered her slowly, their lips parted gently and she remained encircled in his arms, catching her breath. "I wouldn't have been able to do that if I didn't work for it," Jake said.

"Happy surprise, that," she said, her big blue eyes looking up at him.

They remained standing together there quietly for a long moment, breathing together, swaying slightly as they looked at each other. Then Jake decided to ask the question that would break the moment. "Why did you leave last time? I need to know."

Ayan lowered her eyes and leaned her head against his chest. "I regret that," she said. "I got some very bad advice. Very bad, but convincing advice."

"From who?" Jake asked. If that was all it took, then what they had before couldn't have been worth much, he thought.

She looked up at him, searching his face for a moment before saying. "I like what's happening here, with us. No, I love this, I love us, right now, the way this feels and the time we've been spending talking about everything, just being together. I even want to take you home with me tonight, to get you out of here so we can have some time alone, unrecorded. I'm afraid the truth is going to break that."

Jake kept his mouth shut as his mind raced to the conclusion that she broke off their previous relationship to be with Liam Grady. That was what he expected her to say next, and he didn't know if it would break their relationship. He only knew that he lost respect for them both, Ayan and Liam, and that he was still irate about the whole thing.

"I'm going to tell you everything anyway, because you deserve the truth," Ayan said, carefully stepping out of their embrace and taking his hand. They walked down the corridor to a room designed for planning and examining star ships. It had several floating seats and was equipped with high quality holographic projectors hidden in the walls. "Privacy mode," Ayan told the computer sombrely. "Display Ayan Future Three around Jake and myself."

The room was filled with images running along a timeline stretching for twenty years. "This is what I have been able to piece together from my experience with the Victory Machine. I was able to use the Triton's neural scanner to rebuild most of the memory and I've run most of it down this timeline. The red marks are things I believe have not been fulfilled, or have failed to begin on time. The green marks along the timeline show things that have come true. So far, red and green are roughly equal. If there is a slash across a green marker, then it's something I had to bring into being myself, acting on the machine's advice."

"What are the black marks?" Jake asked, observing several circles along the timeline that correspond with the previous new year's eve.

"My breakup with you, Laura and Jason's deaths and the beginning of my relationship with Liam," Ayan said. "Things that were not predicted, the last of which was a terrible mistake. Nothing has gone right since then except for what I could build or gather together. I am a political failure, and I disappointed you when I left. I don't know if I can make that up to you, but, I can at least explain." Ayan enlarged the black dot marking the day that she left Jake and a full sized holographic image of Minh-Chu appeared. He was playing a guitar that looked exactly like the green, blocky instrument that had been given to him on New Year's Eve by Ashley. He looked much older than his current self, and wore a Stetson hat.

"The Victory Machine had something to say about us getting too close too soon, and it used this image of Minh to get that across. I asked the Victory Machine why he looked older in the future it presented, and it wouldn't tell me. Anyway, this is where the Victory Machine told me to step away from you," Ayan said, moving away from the image a little, but still standing off to the side. Jake sat down and watched as a much older Minh-Chu spoke to a hologram of Ayan.

"Make sure Jake doesn't get any bright ideas about direct revenge on the higher ups. There's no end to the anger he has for the Order of Eden and their leaders. From what the Machine can see, there's nothing wrong with him going after them indirectly. On the other hand, if he ever stands in front of Hampon, the Child Prophet, or Eve, Jake could literally become a different person. I can't tell you what will happen to him because the Victory Machine can't calculate it, and that's rare. This thing can calculate sky luge tournament standings eight years in advance and be ninety eight point six percent correct, so when it can't see the possible outcomes of something, it's a big deal. Worst case scenario: Jake kills Eve, or Hampon and humanity's chances of surviving the next century go down the crapper. Best case scenario: Jacob Valent is transformed by the experience, and his path changes drastically. Somewhere in between is just as likely, but do you really want to take the chance?"

"No, definitely not," Ayan replied.

"Neither would I. There's another thing. You have to send him on his way and put as much distance between you and him as you can for the next few days at least. It's the only way to make sure he's not in the wrong place at the wrong time. If you two get back together - and the chances are likely, trust me – he'll be burdened by guilt. He'll

focus on taking revenge on Wheeler, Thurge, and everyone else who was involved in that android that looked like him. You'll have trouble with him too, the memory of being assaulted by something that looked so much like him is still fresh, it's too soon."

"I know the difference, it was obvious," Ayan protested.

"The subconscious is like Supersticky, things stick to it until you break out the brand-name solvent, which is always sold separately, damn those corporate geniuses. You'll process your encounter with Android Jacob, but it'll take some time away from the real Jacob. What's more important to consider is how being with Jake will affect his thinking. He'll be focusing on you when he should be coordinating with a team. If he doesn't link up with a dependable crew and focus on being part of a competent group, if he's focused on you instead, his future gets real dark. You'll have to take care of him, and that'll darken your world too. You leave him, and he finds a good crowd. Well, good by his standards, anyway." Minh-Chu began playing the Hall Of The Mountain King as he continued.

"We're just about to find our way back to each other," Ayan said. "I can send him away for a few days, I don't have to leave him."

"If he sees you as his damsel if you're in trouble, it will distract him from a whole chain of events he has to forge. Sometimes the military policy of non-fraternization is the right one. Someone once said; if you truly love someone, you must set them free. If it's meant to be, they'll return. Trust. Just trust."

"How long?" Ayan asked. "How long do I have to stay away?"

"Oh, don't worry about that," Minh-Chu said. "Here's a real spoiler for you: you need time away too. You're changing so fast that you need to have a few new experiences. You'll be a different woman from week to week for a while, and when you come though, you're going to be just amazing. If you get tied down to Jake it'll be like turning the reverse thrusters up to full, and that won't do you any good. This breakup is a good thing, it feels like crap now, but you'll

see. Go it without him awhile, you'll thank me. Well, you won't be able to find me to thank me, but you get the point."

"I'll try," Ayan said. "I'll break it off with him and test your theory."

The image faded and Ayan walked back to the middle of the timeline before Jake could say anything. He didn't know what to say anyway. The Victory Machine wasn't right and it wasn't entirely wrong, as far as he was concerned. The breakup with Ayan did make it easier to stay away, to pursue intelligence that aided the Warlord in its mission, that was beneficial to both the British Alliance and Triton Fleet.

He pursued his missions without restraint, and finally arrived at a point where he was ruled by rage, where he became a murderer. Murder for a cause was still murder, even though the act caused a dip in Order of Eden recruitment that measured in tens of thousands in that sector alone. It wasn't enough to justify murder.

None of what he'd seen sat right. It still felt like the Victory Machine had a very easy time convincing Ayan to leave him, and, even though he knew it was an irrational reaction, that's still what he thought about most.

"Before you say anything, I need to show you something else," Ayan said. "The Victory Machine left me with a vision of children in a more distant, calculated future."

Ayan was about to touch a hollow dot to the far right of the timeline, but Jake blurted; "stop!" before she could, nearly falling out of his seat. "I don't want to see that part of the future."

Ayan turned and crossed the room to him, kneeling down, taking his hand in hers. "I have to share some of it, because it's what made leaving you possible. If the Victory Machine didn't show me a future with two children, one from you, and one from someone else, both of them beautiful, then I would have never been able to leave. It left me with the distinct impression that I still loved you, that we would be together in the future, but that I'd had a daughter somewhere in that time with someone else, but we came back together even after that. Leaving you was so hard, I was crushed, but knowing that we could still have a future made it possible. Now I want to begin that future, there's nothing in the way, and there's even evidence that the Victory Machine was wrong about some things, big things."

Jake looked to the timeline, then back to Ayan's sorrow struck face. She was impossible to say no to. It seemed that she had suffered more while they were apart than he had, even though he knew that she would have kept him calmer, he would have never murdered a bridge officer aboard the Order of Eden destroyer if she had stayed with him. She would have stood in his way. Then again, he already felt like the person he was before Doctor Messana saved him was entirely different, so he couldn't be sure. Looking down at her, into that heart shaped face that was more beautiful to him than any belonging to a digital model, or anyone he'd met, he realized that she was begging him.

This woman who had gone through so many trials with grace, accomplished things that he didn't even know how to start, could navigate government despite her own opinion of being a failure, was begging him to take her back. The woman who would feed the world orbited if it were a question of kindness instead of supply, and was more intelligent than he would ever be overall was waiting on his answer. Somehow the idea that she partially broke it off at the promise of children and a future where they were back together made it a little better, even though jealously at her past relationship with Liam still nagged him, but much less so than before.

There was only one other thing that argued against him taking her back unconditionally, and he voiced it. "I don't deserve you,"

Jake said as he reached down and tried to pull her up. He lost his balance and slipped out of his seat instead.

He'd had worse falls, and he'd managed to avoid falling on top of her, so he just remained flat on the deck. She joined him, rolling on top of him. "We can just stay down here awhile," she said. Her face was so close to his, with the merest motion he'd have his lips on hers. "What were you saying?"

."I don't deserve you," Jake repeated. "I'm a murderer, if there were still Galactic Courts, they'd have me in front of a local tribunal, and I'd deserve whatever sentence they passed down for murder."

"It's war, and if anything my experience in this life has taught me, it's that we can't take responsibility for what our past incarnations have done."

"Just because part of my mind was rebuilt and rewritten doesn't mean I'm not the same person. I have the same memories, I love the same people," Jake said, and was stopped by Ayan's smile.

"You're not the same," she whispered. "All the time I've spent with you in training, what you're saying here, I know you're a better man. I think it's your separation from that machine inside you. I didn't realize it before, but you seemed more distant then, now I feel like you're all here, and that comes with a man who can embrace guilt, who values life, and can love. Maybe we didn't belong together before, you as a framework and me, but we've both had a real rebirth now, and I think it's our time."

He allowed himself to look into her blue eyes and couldn't help but ask himself; *Maybe my atonement starts with making her happy, with putting her and everyone I love first? Maybe I can have this?* Before he realized it was about to happen, he was kissing her. His right hand crossed her back, his left caressed her lower back and he held her close for a long time while they indulged. He'd never felt anything so warm and intimate, nearly merging through body heat, soft lips and the soothing smell of her – earthy vanilla and something else he couldn't put a name to.

When she lifted her head up, her curly red hair drifted between them. She flipped it aside, breathing heavily. "That was not a goodbye kiss," she said with a new smile, one that was excited and amused and playful.

"We start over," Jake said. He couldn't believe what he was going to say next, and had to force it from his mind to his lips. By the time the words were in the air it was a groan. "Tomorrow morning."

"Oh, you don't mean that," Ayan replied with a chuckle. She lowered her forehead to his and briefly extended her lips to touch his. "But you're right," she sighed. "You're right. I came to tell you about a couple things anyway, didn't think we'd get like this." She shifted herself so her head laid on his chest. "You okay?"

"I'm fine. I've gotten to know this deck very well over the last few weeks, I might even come back every once and a while just to say hello with an awkward fall," Jake replied.

"I missed that," Ayan said. "Almost forgot you could be funny."

"I'm serious, deck and I are proper mates at this point," Jake persisted. "What did you come to tell me?"

Ayan took a deep breath and let it out slowly. "It's nothing to do with us."

"Okay, that's a relief," Jake said.

"Doctor Messana has been restricting information to the Solar Forge, especially you, filtering what she thinks may be distracting. So, a lot about how Regent Galactic are pressing in, how the British Alliance Frontier failed when they couldn't get critical stations in place, and how we've been finding spies in Haven Shore every week since you've been out. None of that's been made available to you."

"I'm getting out tomorrow morning," Jake reminded himself aloud. "Just help me get back up to speed and I'll try not to hold it against the Doctor, even though she had no right to do that to me."

"About that, you getting out tomorrow," Ayan said.

"What?" Jake asked, alarmed. "I *am* getting out tomorrow, right?"

"Yes, and I'll be here at oh-nine-hundred when you step off this station right on schedule."

"Okay, what about tomorrow?"

"The first thing you're going to notice tomorrow when you leave, maybe even when you wake up, is how much lighter you feel. How much easier it will probably be for you to stay on your feet."

"Why? Why would it be easier to walk off the station than inside?"

"Doctor Messana has been adjusting the gravity on you, just you. Whatever readings you saw about your environment were fake. Right now the localized field around you is at one point two eight standard units. When you picked me up earlier it was at one point four."

"So you weighed an extra forty percent more? You were still pretty light," Jake replied.

"Thank you, but no. The Lorander gravity systems on this ship are so precise that the gravity increase follows you as closely as a vacsuit. A really tight one, actually."

"Okay, so people around me wouldn't even know," Jake replied.

"Exactly. I found out because I was supervising construction of the new gunships. I don't think Doctor Messana ever meant for you to find out. But she does seem focused on having you recover as quickly and as thoroughly as possible, so I think her heart was in the right place. My father says he's only seen that kind of thing in strength training, not trauma recovery, he doubts that it speeds things up at all, because you'll spend time adjusting to lesser gravity later."

"So it's something I'll watch for," Jake said, reminding himself that if it weren't for Doctor Messana, he wouldn't be alive, laying on the deck with Ayan in his arms. "Anything else?"

"No," Ayan said, raising her head and looking at him. "You're really calm about all this," she said. "I thought you'd take the news differently."

"Why? It sounds like Doctor Messana was just trying to help. As long as I didn't miss anything critical while I was out, or here, then I can't say she did anything wrong. Time will tell if the increased gravity was a good idea."

"She changed your mind, too," Ayan said, "forced the rebuilt parts of your brain to be rewritten in a sequence that resembled an average human mind, ignoring the pattern you had as a framework."

"I know," Jake said. "I was too paranoid not to look at how I was put back together. I've even seen parts of the operation footage."

"No," Ayan gasped. "She restricts tactical data and news but lets you in on your whole medical file? I couldn't watch more than a few seconds of your operation."

"I guess she knew I'd notice that parts of my file were missing. Besides, I couldn't watch much of the operation either. I didn't think I had a squeamish bone in my body until I was a few minutes in, then I had to call it quits. I went back and looked at what I wanted to see later."

"What parts did you have to see?" Ayan asked.

"Mostly the later parts of reconstruction, when they were putting the new legs and parts of my lower torso together. I just had to see if the trouble I was having in recovery had anything to do with my new factory installed parts."

"And?"

"The comparisons to the kind of thing nature builds are almost perfect, and the differences are all minor improvements anyway."

"Improvements like?" Ayan asked with a teasing smile.

Jake laughed and shook his head. "Nothing to get excited about."

"Really? Maybe we should do a comparison scan."

"No scans on the first date," Jake said sternly.

Ayan rolled over and slowly stood up. "Something to look forward to," she said. "We should get off the deck though."

Jake wouldn't have admitted it while Ayan was still atop him, but his shoulders and head were getting sore from being on the hard surface. "I don't think the deck is as good a friend as I thought." He rolled over and carefully got to his feet, something that was impossible for him weeks before. Every time he stood on his own it was still a small victory. "Extra gravity," he muttered. "Can't wait to see what its like to try to walk in a normal environment."

Ayan put his arm around her shoulders. He looked down at her and smiled. "Where to now?" she asked.

His gaze wandered from her eyes, and eventually answered, "the guest lounge?"

"Good idea," Ayan said with a raised eyebrow. "Enjoying the view?"

Jake nodded, "Very distracting, you could be impeding my recovery."

"Oh, I can adjust the pattern," Ayan said, bringing an image of her dress up on her bulky command bracelet.

"That's all right, I think it's having the opposite effect, actually. I feel better already," Jake said in a rush.

"If you say so," Ayan replied. "But eyes front, soldier. I don't want you tripping on my watch."

"Aye," Jake replied.

"Besides, there's something I have to tell you about tomorrow morning."

"Oh?"

"There may be just a few people waiting for you when you arrive aboard the Triton. There are a few Captains who have been looking forward to meeting you."

"How many Captains?" Jake asked.

"Twenty eight, I think. The fleet is a little bigger than you remember," Ayan said. "Something else Doctor Messana thought might be distracting, news of new people in the fleet."

"Catch me up?" Jake asked.

"It'll be my pleasure," Ayan replied.

CHAPTER 10
THE PUSH

The gathering the night before hadn't kept Minh-Chu up for as long as he expected. Finn and Agameg brought a few new faces from the Warlord with them, unaware that the hostess wasn't going to be there. Ayan's absence made Lacey the hostess and centre of attention, and people were curious about the tall, dark British woman who had been at Ayan's side for months. She warmed to the attention, and was soon exchanging questions with Triton and Warlord crewmembers. She was curious about military life, and many of them were curious about Haven Shore, and her very political existence.

There were no arguments, even though politics, especially the recently rocky kind that were happening on Haven Shore could have been a minefield. Lacey was a born diplomat, and Minh-Chu was amazed at how she could turn conversation in a fairly harmless direction.

It wasn't a party where a lot of imbibing took place, though, more of a gathering where people exchanged scuttlebutt and shared what they brought. When it started getting late, the party broke up pleasantly, but calmly.

Minh-Chu missed Ayan's return to the apartment much later in the evening, but things must have gone well, since Jake indicated that he'd be at her place later that day through Crewcast. Minh-Chu looked forward to visiting, so did Ashley, he just had to get through his patrol in one piece.

He had great faith in his Wingman for the patrol operation, Dent, who had five solo kills against Order of Eden fighters, and several cooperative kills on corvette and other classes. He was competent, believed in staying in the present, and had a good mind for strategy.

They had one of the long patrols, taking them to the asteroid belt slowly drifting past the boundary of the Rega Gain solar system. "So, no British Alliance out here?" Dent asked through their private communications channel.

"Not so much as a satellite, which is one of the things we're looking for on scans," Minh-Chu replied.

"Oh, that wasn't in my briefing," Dent replied.

"Then I was supposed to brief you on it and forgot," Minh-Chu replied, feeling like an amateur.

"It's not a big deal, I would have noticed it on my scanner either way. Leave anything else out?"

Minh-Chu sent his list of objectives to Dent, "Nope, here's the whole thing."

"Let's see," Dent said, clearing his throat. "Watch for signs of enemy activity, report anomalous signals, forward transmission bursts, assist ships in distress, and scan for signs of damaged vessels in the Paulo Belt, especially the Ash Sen and the oh-seven-nine-dee-bee British Alliance communications satellite. Above all, observe and report, do not engage unless fired upon. Yup, you just left the search items off. My orders don't include those."

"Well, now you know," Minh-Chu said as he began his sensor sweep of the first section of the asteroid belt.

"The Ash Sen was a Carthan Battlecruiser, wasn't it?" Dent asked.

"Yup, was due in Kambis orbit five months ago but never reported. They figure there's a chance it crashed somewhere in this mess."

"On account of bad navigation," Dent said. "Love those Carthans, there's nothing like a two hundred billion Galactic Credit battlecruiser manned by a brainwashed convict crew."

"Did you hear that we'll be raising one of their battlecruisers from the surface of Kambis and repairing it in two weeks?" Minh-Chu said.

"There's actually a crashed Carthan ship worth salvaging whole?" Dent said.

"There is, I couldn't believe it either. It's almost spaceworthy right now, only the reactors need to be rebuilt, and a few thrusters, and the bridge was slagged, but overall, it's in fair shape for a losing ship."

"The fleet just keeps growing," Dent said. "Hey, I got a ping."

Minh-Chu saw a computerized response from a ship at the same time, a simple signal that told his Uriel Fighter that, somewhere in the asteroid field, there was a communications system on. "Cut power to everything but passive sensors," he said as he did so. "Make sure your navnet ident is off. We don't know what that is, so we don't want to broadcast what we are just yet."

"Might be too late," Dent said, "I didn't turn my ident off when we left Kambis navnet range."

Minh-Chu checked to see if Dent's fighter was still broadcasting it's operating identifier, and saw that it was off. "No worries, we'll know what kind of system just reached out to us from that asteroid group in a moment, I think."

They drifted in a parallel course to the asteroid field, moving a little faster. Minh-Chu watched his scan results, which were mostly reporting geological data from the nearest bodies of stone, ice, and iron. Through his display he could see the dark masses slowly tumbling through space, there wasn't enough light to make out most of the individual asteroids, but he knew they weren't as close together as they looked. There was plenty of room for ships to hide in there.

"Got something, Ronin!" Dent said.

Minh-Chu saw the data stream as his wingman reported it. "Data stream, what kind?"

"It has a Regent Galactic header," Dent reported, "Combat group identifier."

"All right, power everything up, sensors first. Let's do a deep scan for two seconds then hit our xetima boosters home."

As soon as Minh-Chu powered his systems on, his computer analysed the data stream from the asteroid field and concluded that it was from a Regent Galactic repair drone. "This is encrypted, my computer's working on it," he told Dent. "But small ships don't carry repair drones this big."

"Targeting the area with sensors, they're going to see us as plain as day if they don't already know we're here," Dent said.

"Or you *could* do that," Minh-Chu said.

The broad profile of a Regent Galactic Carrier appeared on Minh-Chu's screen and he hit his solid xetima thrusters. The inertial dampers whined as they strained to compensate for the sudden acceleration. He was relieved to see that Dent had followed his previous instructions, firing his thrusters at the same time. "Only have seven seconds of thrust left," Minh-Chu said.

"Same here, these things don't go long, but it's one hell of a ride when they go off," Dent replied.

Minh-Chu sent his sensor data to the British Alliance and Triton Fleet, knowing that it would take nine hours for the transmission to reach them. He opened a micro-wormhole to the safe deceleration area near Tamber and tried to retransmit, but his system reported a failure. He checked his communications system and immediately saw that the Regent Galactic forces in the asteroid field were jamming them.

"They're jamming us," Dent said over their secondary communications, a system that used direct laser linking instead of conventional ship to ship technology.

"I'm formulating a plan as we speak," Minh-Chu said as he let the micro-wormhole close. "But I'm sure Triton Fleet caught their jamming signal and they'll have the origin of my wormhole calculated in a couple minutes.

"So they'll know where we are and that something is stopping us from communicating," Dent said. "But it'll be a bit before we see friendly support."

"About an hour, I'm formulating a plan," Minh-Chu said.

The Asteroid field lit up with live ship signals, populating Minh-Chu's tactical display with readouts from fighters, gunships and several destroyers. The xetima pods burned out, their fuel exhausted, but they still had a good lead on the enemy. "Maintain full burn for the perimeter defence, " Minh-Chu said.

"Roger, Ronin, full burn to Harnen navnet space," Dent replied. "I just hope we don't have to land there, I hate that place."

"Well, that's where we're going," Minh-Chu said. "I'm calculating a wormhole trajectory that'll take us right into their emergency deceleration safe zone."

"Uh, Ronin, there's a bend in that trajectory," Dent said, referring to a curve in Minh-Chu's wormhole path that would take them up and around one of Harnen's moons.

"Not so large that my projector can't handle it," Minh-Chu said. "I'm using a few tricks I picked up from Ashley, they make this kind of course a lot easier to verify and correct."

"You're going to make corrections to the navigational computers' work?" Dent said.

Several flashes of weapons' fire lighted their cockpits. It wasn't high powered, but long range. Minh-Chu's shield reported three minor strikes, not enough to cause any concern, but if the ships behind them kept it up for the whole time it took them to get to safety, there wouldn't be anything left of their fighters, or them.

"Carry on, Wing Commander," Dent said, "But if you sink us into some kind of time compression space or something, you'll never hear the end of it."

"Bah, little chance of that," Minh-Chu said, looking over the navigation computer's work. "See? Nothing here but perfect transit calculations. Opening the wormhole, follow me in."

"Aye, Sir," Dent said.

The wormhole generator and power systems whined as the space in front of him distorted. He only had three seconds to scan it before deciding whether or not to evade, and was relieved when he saw the other end let out to Harnen Navnet space. "Here's hoping they take the signal noise those Rega Gain ships are making as our request for navnet coordinates on the other side." He said as his ship passed over the threshold and began the nine second transit through the wormhole.

"What?" Dent said as his fighter followed close behind. "Oh, God, I didn't think of that."

"I'm sure we'll be fine," Ronin said as he gripped the controls and glanced to his right, nodding at a small red holographic square that activated the emergency evasion systems in his ship. "Ready to evade standing bodies in the Navnet pattern." His ship crossed the far threshold, emerging from the wormhole, and he sent his ship into a port side turn, so Dent would be clear to emerge and pass on his starboard side.

There were only three large cargo ships in the area, and they were well out of the arrival space. The old Carthan station, where imported prison workers were programmed for service while they were still in the solar system, was nothing more than a tiny shining shard in the distance. They were headed in it's general direction, and would decelerate right past it in under a minute.

The wormhole closed behind Dent and the jamming signals that came through with he and Minh-Chu ended. "-Base, to

Uriel fighters. You are on approach to Anchor Station at high speeds, please state your intentions."

"This is Ronin, from Triton Fleet Samurai Squadron," Minh-Chu said as his thrusters fired at maximum in an effort to guide the ship into a smooth course past the station during his deceleration. He saw Dent slowly drift past, his ship looked like a white hot fireball with all of its thrusters firing. "There is at least one Regent Galactic Carrier and group on their way into the system, or getting ready to escape."

"Ronin, we recognize your ship ident. So this fleet is poising to attack or retreat? You couldn't tell which?" The British Alliance officer on the other end asked, sounding a little amused.

"I didn't stick around long enough to clarify, there was some weapons' fire involved. Transmit my sensor data and short automatic report to your command centre and Triton Fleet."

"I'll review the data and see if it rates high enough for priority transmission," replied the officer.

"You'll transmit this now. Do not take time to review them before you pass them on, this is not easy reading material, it is not bathroom data for your perusal, and it's not a field trip report."

"Sorry, that's not policy," the officer replied.

"Dent, do you still have enough juice in your cells to get a high compression wormhole transmission out?" Minh-Chu asked.

"Sure, I've been charging since we caught something on scanners," he replied. "I'll transmit that report from here."

"You are prohibited from opening any wormholes in the safe Navnet zone," another Officer from the station said sternly.

"Wait, are you just talking to me?" Minh-Chu said. "Because I was the one talking to your officer, and I'm the senior commander for Samurai Squadron, so-" Minh-Chu watched as Dent's micro wormhole opened, the transmission was sent, and it closed.

"We are talking to Dent! Your wingman! The one that just broke our harbour laws!" replied the second officer.

"Now, when you say 'We', is that the royal 'We' or are you representing a collective of some kind?" Minh-Chu asked.

"Oh, you were talking to me?" Dent asked, his voice loaded down with false regret. "I'm sorry, that won't happen again. I'm just used to reporting to my superiors as soon as I can when there's an invasion force in the area. Again, really sorry, won't happen again."

Minh-Chu reviewed the data himself. If the fleet decided to attack, they would be within range of the Anchor Station in just over an hour. He started a systems check.

CHAPTER 11
TRITON FLEET

Oz had learned to say 'no' early on in his training. It was one of the first things they broke into him when his real military training at the Junior Academy began. Freeground soldiers were all trained as problem solvers first. That meant looking at a problem from multiple angles, considering your options then being decisive. Normally, that meant denying a request was easy for Oz, but facing Alaka, who he had come to respect and like overall, was difficult.

"Why can't I join Triton Fleet?" Alaka pressed. His normally passive expression was drawn into a scowl. Oz swore he could see more grey around his pointed snout. Eleven new born nafali must have been taking their toll.

"You are one of the only truly trustworthy people on the ground who I can be sure will train new crewmembers on Tamber," Oz replied. "You're just too important there. I know Governor Anderson has been trying to get you into the Rangers, you'd see mixed action there. You'd train people, lead ground missions, boarding missions."

"Iloona and my daughters are taking care of the children, if that's what you're truly worried about, and I stay out of the Rangers so I can train people to live on Tamber, not just fight or survive there," Alaka said, his dark brown and blonde muzzle twitching. The time he'd spent in the outdoors on Tamber had done the Nafalli a lot of good, he had time to train people in the jungle there, most of it was spent with the children he had who weren't occupied with taking care of Illoona. As Oz understood it, that came to an end several weeks before, when Iloona gave birth to a brood of eleven tiny Nafalli children. Alaka was constantly at her side, despite what he was telling Oz. The logs were clear, Alaka spent less than four hours a day away from Iloona on average. "She would rather I go on a long hunt than spend any more time with her and our new borns. She is not accustomed to me being with her all the time. She tells me I'm 'under foot' or 'always over head,' whatever that's supposed to mean."

Oz recognized Lacey's terminology right away and couldn't help but smile a little. The woman didn't meddle, she was a great help to Iloona, but she did know how to help people find the right words. "The problem is not that you'll be separated from your family, not in this case," Oz said. "I really do want you on Tamber training people, watching them to make sure we're not taking our enemies in. You've already caught nine people who joined up for the wrong reasons."

"It's easy when you're paying attention," Alaka said, "The Rangers have rooted out ten times as many in a month. They are better at training people for security and law enforcement."

"Not for the Triton, not for the extended fleet we're building," Oz said, gesturing out the transparent bulkhead behind him to the Barricade, a ship that wouldn't be properly crewed for another two weeks at least. "If it makes you feel better, you're going to have to move trainees there while they train on the Barricade's systems, so you can get a couple weeks away that way. You can even bring your two eldest if you want them to get some technical training."

"I will argue this with you, Oz," Alaka growled. "I belong on the Triton. The fight you fly to is mine, the memory of my friends demand that I make myself part of it. Some of your people visited Pandem after it fell, but I lived there, my family lived there. I remember how alive it was, and all the friends who I couldn't save. Now I can join you in avenging them and stopping the people responsible from taking control of more territory, killing more people."

"What would your friends say about you leaving your family and an opportunity to train hundreds of people? I know you train fighters, and pickers, and people who study Tamber to live there without disturbing life there. The people in this fleet may not see it, but they're important to our survival, they help provide a home for us to go back to, and people like you make sure it's secure. You're a born hunter, I've seen you in action, and, yes, I'll miss you in a fight, but I'd rather have a thousand people you trained and have you guarding Haven Shore on the ground than have just one of you aboard. You can argue all you want, Alaka, but my answer won't change."

"I belong at the front," Alaka said. "I am a warrior in my prime. The squad of nafalia I brought for your inspection are all great hunters."

"Don't get me wrong, I would be proud to have your squad aboard, representing this ship on missions, but you are needed on Tamber, " Oz was interrupted by the alert alarm as it sounded once and the lighting tinted slightly red. "You and your squad are on a shuttle back home from the dorsal launch deck in two minutes, Alaka. You're my friend, but you still have to follow orders."

The Nafalli was obviously irritated, and looked around before sighing and nodding. "After the alert," he said. "My people will be disappointed."

"All right, let's see what this is," Oz said as he left the room for the bridge. Hausgeist didn't have to communicate how urgent the situation was with more than an emotion that Oz recognized immediately. He mentally put the entire fleet on alert and sent an advisory to Kambis Navnet.

The moment the doorway to the bridge slid open he had the lead communications officer, Lieutenant Commander Liara Erron at his side. Oz was always struck at how much she looked like his mother. Her long brown hair, soft features and a usually passive manner that made her easy to talk to. She looked much younger, in her early twenties if he had to guess, but the resemblance almost had him staring from time to time. She walked with him as he walked to the command seat at the centre of the bridge. "The patrol we sent to investigate the asteroids drifting through the system may have made an attempt to contact us, but their micro-wormhole burst was jammed. All we have is noise. We're analysing it now."

"Signal all orbital patrols, they are to coordinate with Tamber Defence to set up a defensive screen. Contact all our in-system assets, find out who is in range of that jamming signal, and if we can scramble stealthed scouts to that location in the next fifteen minutes. I want pilots and support crews in our new gunships, and our alert wing ready to launch in five minutes. This is not a drill."

"Sir, are you sure? This jammed signal doesn't conclusively indicate that we are dealing with anything serious, it could be smugglers, or illegal salvaging teams working on a wreck in that asteroid drift. Maybe one of our patrols tripped across someone trying to do something questionable, and they're being jammed so the perpetrators can buy time to get away," the Lieutenant Commander countered.

"That's very specific," Oz replied. "Do you know something I don't, Lieutenant Commander?"

"It used to happen all the time in Soroluna, smugglers and other interesting travellers meeting with people in shadow ports, trying to make contact with people on the edge of the core world cluster."

"Better safe than sorry, Liara," Oz said.

"Relaying orders to Flight, Sir," Liara said as she started back for the communications section of the bridge, a semi-circle of stations to the right of the command seating. "And I'll keep looking at that jamming signal, I'm pretty sure the transmitter used was Regent Galactic, but a lot of neutral ships use their comm systems."

Oz took a moment to allow Hausgiest, the Triton's first inhabitant, to elaborate on the feeling of alarm. His voice came through the audio system on the bridge. The crew knew Hausgiest as the ship's newly active artificial intelligence, and had no idea that it was a biological being. "Admiral, there is an unmistakable set of signatures in this jamming signal. One is Regent Galactic, just as the Lieutenant Commander has already determined, the other is Citadel, there is no doubting it."

"Citadel?" Oz asked.

"There is a Citadel ship in that asteroid field, and it is issuing commands. There is no doubt," the normally warm male voice of Hausgiest was strained, beyond concerned. "Somehow, the last functioning branch of Citadel has allied with Regent Galactic or the Order of Eden. There is no other explanation."

"But that's still a good guess," Lieutenant Commander Erron said. "Not certain."

"There is no other likely explanation for this combination of technologies and methods," replied Hausgiest.

"So we are facing Earth technology?" Victor Davis asked. He had taken the place of First Officer aboard the Triton.

"A true Sol System vessel would have been able to stop any transmission at the source, so there is a doubt that there is a Sol System ship here, but whoever jammed that transmission is certainly using Sol System software. I cannot determine how old it is, or any other details, however." Hausgiest replied. "The signal is mostly noise, there is little encoded within it."

"Are our updates all ready to go online?" Oz asked as he took a seat in the command chair. All eyes were on him, all the crew knew were the rumours of a Citadel assassin killing people aboard before he could be stopped. Most of them feared Citadel, and were in awe of Earth.

"Anti-Gravity shielding, the new point defence systems, particle beams, and everything else except for the experimental D-Transit Drive are ready," Agameg replied. "We are still weeks away from completing construction and testing."

"Well, we have what's important for now," Commander Davis said. "I'll work on putting our course together. Contact Governor Anderson, we might need him."

"I'll be on the Flight Deck," Oz said, standing and starting for the ramp leading down into the flight control and Mission Centre. He stopped and looked to Alaka, who seemed stranded between the bridge entrance and the command seats. "Why don't you make sure your team is geared up? Go see Chief Glassner in the armoury, your team's custom armour may be the challenge he's been looking for. Oh, and there are some large class weapons you might like there, just in case you need them while you're working on Tamber."

"A consolation for not getting my team's chosen assignment," Alaka said, nodding. "I accept."

"It's not like we'll have time to drop you off if Citadel is in the system," Oz said.

"Yes, Admiral," Alaka said, even more pleased than Oz expected.

Oz continued down to the Flight Control Deck where the crew were directing ship recovery and pre-launch operations. The crew of seventy people who directed traffic and watched the status of everything in scanning range through all the hours of the day had become a group of well trained experts. At any given time a little less than a third of them were on shift, but during combat operations, fifty crowded the large, protected area. Paula Mendle, one of three Flight Operations Chiefs, stepped down from the central command seat and moved to a display station seamlessly as Oz took his place there. "Who do we have on the umbilical right now?" he asked.

"We have the Fallen Star on the end, the Malcontent on link twelve, Eva Grey on link two, and five heavy gunships armed and ready for launch down the dorsal line," she replied. "We have the Warlord hard docked to dorsal mooring seven, and the Morrigan is on her way out of the primary landing bay. Captain Moira McFadden has offered the assistance of her ship and crew."

Oz had forgotten that Jake was already aboard the Triton, for some reason he thought the reception was going to be later, but he double checked the time and realized that almost all the new captains in the Triton Fleet were on their way to the Triton or were already aboard to meet Valent. His nervousness at having to tell Alaka and his entire team of nafali that they weren't going to be serving aboard the Triton had him thoroughly distracted through the entire morning. "Order all captains to their ships immediately. If they don't get off the Triton in ten minutes, they'll be stuck here for the duration of this alert."

"What's going on, Admiral?" asked a small holographic image of Governor Anderson.

"We have reason to believe that there is a Regent Galactic and Citadel presence in-system and I'm readying the Triton for a response," Oz said. "Can you direct the defence of Tamber from the Barricade? We still don't have a captain for her, the crew is still training, but the ship's ready."

"How long do I have?" Governor Anderson asked.

Being able to order a man he once called 'Doctor' aboard the First Light was still strange, but Oz pressed through it. "As fast as a combat shuttle will take you there. Most of the temporary crew are Rangers, you should feel right at home."

"Give me fifteen minutes and I'll be there," Governor Anderson said. The transmission ended.

"Who are we dropping from the umbilical?" Chief Paula Mendle asked. She had the hologram of the Triton's new tail floating between them. It was part of the ship's original design, but never added. It was a long, black multi-purpose appendage at the rear of the ship that could serve as an extended docking section, large antenna, or a focusing tube for energetic fields or beams. "Are the Fallen Star and Eva Grey ready to drop?"

"Yes, the crews have checked in," Chief Mendle replied.

"Good, decouple and send them into the standby area. Tell them they will receive further instructions from the Barricade," Oz replied.

"From Governor Anderson," she said. "He's going to take that ship for the Rangers, you know," she muttered disapprovingly.

"I know," Oz replied. "We have to leave something here when we go off to fight this war."

"With it's interdiction tech?" Chief Mendle said, shaking her head. "We haven't finished figuring out how to adapt that to the Triton."

"I know," Oz said. It was a discussion they'd had before, but they didn't have any other ships that could even hope to assist in the defence of Tamber if the British Alliance were to leave. That, and the Triton was ready, several other smaller ships were ready, if they remained behind to train the crew of the Barricade, they would spend weeks or months more out of the war. Oz had come to the conclusion that letting the Rangers take the Battlecruiser was best for everyone.

He looked upwards to the bridge and the communications system automatically routed his voice to the Captain's seat above. "Are we ready for departure?"

"We are," Commander Davis replied. "More data coming in, a report from Wing Commander Buu."

"Looking at it here," Oz said as he watched the data from Minh-Chu's report arrive and his crew of analysts and strategists dig into it like a ravenous pack. "Hold one minute."

"Admiral," said an image of Jacob Valent as it came up on screen. Alice was helping him into combat armour. "Warlord command, checking in. If you don't need him, I'd like Agameg back."

Oz couldn't help but smile at the sight of his friend in armour aboard his ship. "I'm afraid he's busy on my bridge, Jake. My system says you have Finn aboard, don't get greedy on me, Captain."

"We'll talk about this later. Should the Warlord decouple? We'll be ready in two minutes," he said.

"Piggyback through our wormhole in stealth mode. I'm linking you to our Flight Deck. Looks like the Samurai just found us a fight."

"I'll await further orders," Jake said. "Captain Valent out."

"Finally, some good news," Chief Mendle said. "About time he got back in the chair."

Oz shot her a warning look.

"What? He doesn't need to walk to take command of a ship. If I can work here with a belly out to here," she said, holding her hand almost a metre away from her middle, "then he can sit in his captain's chair and get us a few more ships."

The Chief may have lacked in sensitivity, but she was one of the best commanders Oz had ever seen. Her biggest problem overall was picking the worst time to start an argument. She rarely knew she was doing it, and Oz knew better than to be baited. "Hand all Navnet operations over to Haven Shore, please," he said.

"Yes, Sir," she replied without batting an eye.

"We've finished our analysis of Wing Commander Buu's scans," announced his lead Tactical Analyst, Lieutenant Gwen

Yore. She was a thin, bird-like woman who was ten years his senior, but she didn't look it. A refugee of New Australia, she seamlessly brought her expertise to his crew months before, along
with two hundred and three survivors from their capitol city,
Sydney. They came from another in a long list of great cities and
worlds that had been ravaged by the Holocaust Virus, then taken
by Regent Galactic.

"Go ahead," Oz said.

"Most of the scans are inconclusive, but he was right to respond quickly. There is at least a carrier in there, it's able to
shield its power core from scans, but close scrutiny of the asteroid field revealed the profile of a K-103 Class Combat carrier
and three destroyers, E-309's. Those are two generations older
than the Barricade, but they've been modified with low emission
shielding, not something we've seen in Regent Galactic technology before."

"What do you think about the possibility of Citadel's involvement?" Oz said.

"Too early to say conclusively, but there is external technologi-
cal influence in play. I believe that this hidden battlegroup is in
the solar system to launch stealth missions, to check on us and
the British Alliance. I expect that they will withdraw if they
think they were discovered."

"Unless there is more than one carrier group in there," Oz
said.

"I understand your need to plan for the worst," Lieutenant
Yore said, "But there's no indication that there is more than one
carrier group from these scans. While this is not a complete scan
of the asteroid field by any means, I don't believe we'd find
more."

"Your recommendation?" Oz asked.

"The British have confirmed that they are not ready to act yet.
This carrier group will be gone by the time they make a decision

and formulate a plan. We are ready, and the Triton alone has all her combat systems operational for the first time in her history. The Warlord is ready as well, and its combat level is that of a heavy destroyer in a stealth-capable package one eighth her size. With that in play, I recommend we make the decision for the British Alliance and force their hand. If we depart to block the escape of this carrier group, they will most likely order ships to support us. We should disable and capture everything we can if we find ourselves with the advantage, except for the carrier at the centre of their group."

"That gets destroyed," Oz said.

"Exactly, in the first seconds of the engagement if possible. My only other concern is that there is another carrier group in or near the system standing by, waiting for the forces protecting Kambis and Tamber to diminish so they can execute a direct attack. If that were to happen it would be from Kambis' daylight side, since most forces are in place to defend Tamber. I advise you to keep one ear turned its direction," Lieutenant Yore said.

"Thank you, Lieutenant," Oz said. She didn't stay at his side for further praise, but left to re-join her team and continue analysing data. "Five minute warning, we will be leaving orbit."

CHAPTER 12
THE CAPTAIN RETURNS

The temptation to explore the unfettered database of the War-lord for information that was kept from him while he was out of commission was almost too much to resist for Jake. He consoled himself with what mattered. The bridge of the relatively small warship was filled with some of the people he cared about most.

"I won't be here during the action, my job is to take care of what's going on aboard the ship and to be ready for incursions," Alice was telling Ayan to Jake's left as she showed her the security console.

Finn was getting Ayan's engineering console ready behind the command seat. To Jake's right Stephanie was giving Frost a brief kiss. "See you after," she told him. He responded by attempting to pinch her bottom, but was thwarted by her armoured hand.

Ashley was concentrating on going through the pre-flight checklist with her temporary co-pilot, Jim Nethidge. He was younger than she was, but one of the few trained navigators the Rangers had. He was on loan since her regular navigators were all off ship. The bleach blonde soldier seemed extremely calm, con-centrating on taking everything that Ashley was telling him in and helping with the checklist without any extra commentary.

Kadri Dutta, their communications and scan officer, was re-laxing at her station and noticed Jake looking across the bridge. She offered a warm smile. "Welcome back, Sir," she said quietly. "Sorry the reception was cancelled."

Jake leaned forward in his seat, whispering conspiratorially even though he knew everyone on the bridge would be able to hear him anyway. "I'd rather come back to this than that crowd waiting for me in the Triton's rear observation."

"Well, we know your weakness then," Kadri replied, "Large crowds."

The mission timer started counting down from five, and the list of events that would take place during the countdown appeared in front of him. "I feel for the people who planned it though, I'm sure they went to a lot of trouble," he said as he scanned through the mission timer details. The only ones that mattered to the Warlord were the orders to prepare while they remained docked, and the departure time.

"It's all right, don't worry," Ayan said. "I'm more excited about the welcome I'll be giving you when I get you back to quarters."

"Okay, yuck," Alice muttered under her breath.

Jake sobered himself by looking around the darkened bridge. The stations in front of him as well as those to his left and right were built more like cockpits, the seats sliding under the consoles and securing the people working in. There were extra stools that were stowed on arms underneath the consoles in between. Behind his command seat there was enough room for three consoles, two were related to engineering and one was multi-purposed.

Behind that, facing the rear wall of the small bridge were three more slide-in consoles, all spares that weren't currently in use. Kadri had a plan for expanding the communications and sciences staff aboard the ship if the mission required it, and Jake mentally promised himself that he'd take a closer look later.

He sat in the centre, upon a slightly raised dais. The Captain's seat was surprisingly comfortable despite its simplicity. Most of the displays he saw were holographically projected in front of him, the rest were at his crewman's stations or projected on the hull at the front of the bridge.

Ayan took her place behind him at an engineering station. "Thank you for bringing me on for this, Finn, I hope I'm not crowding you," she told her.

"Are you kidding?" Finn asked. "It's an honour. Besides, you can take care of things for me here if I have to run off and help with repairs in person."

The mission counter ticked down to three minutes and Jake nodded to himself. It didn't matter how nervous he was, there were some things all Captain's had to do before a major mission, a mission that could land them in the middle of a major conflict. "Kadri, open a channel ship-wide."

"Yes, Sir," she replied. "Your attention please for an announcement from our Captain," she announced gently. A green circle appeared in front of Jake's command seat, telling him that there was a channel open to the entire ship.

"We are at the fast end of the 'hurry up and wait' military paradigm, so this will be quick. I am proud of how this crew performed in my absence. You've made me proud, and now that I have returned to command, I vow to guide you through the coming war using all the resources at our disposal and whatever wisdom I can bring to this command. In two minutes we will be making a quick transit across the solar system, responding to a report that Regent Galactic have violated our borders. The Warlord's assignment is three fold: to assist the Triton in securing the area. To capture a military ship and transfer our command flag to its bridge. To return to Tamber orbital space with our prize. That is what the Warlord does, it takes from our enemies, and whatever it cannot take it destroys, so the Order and its allies are always thinking twice about continuing this conflict. I am proud to be with you again, there is no better crew."

Frost whistled loudly and brought about a brief round of applause on the bridge and down the pair of narrow hallways leading to it.

"Well done, Captain," Ayan said from behind him, only loudly enough for him to hear.

As the mission timer ticked to thirty seconds, the revelry was over, and all bulkhead doors were closing across the ship. A large wormhole formed in front of the Triton. As the large ship and the Warlord attached to it slipped inside, Jake caught a glimpse of a row of other medium sized vessels approximately the size of the Warlord forming up behind them. He knew who they were from the mission list, the reserves. If there was a real engagement on the other side, something that they could use help with, there were forty two more combat ready ships in the Triton Fleet, all ready to join the fray at a moment's notice.

The size of the Fleet had Jake in awe, but he blocked out distractions and got ready for what awaited them on the other side of the wormhole.

"Here we go," Finn sighed from his place at the Engineering station.

CHAPTER 13
BAFEK CITY

It hadn't become apparent to Governor Tate that he'd come to depend on the opinions and advice of his houseguest, the enigmatic Wheeler, until the man split off to go his own way for a day. He also trusted the man less and less as the distance between them grew. He knew Wheeler was keeping parts of his plan from him, and he suspected that time and distance would enable him, and if there was one thing he recognized in Wheeler, it was that he was a man that needed to be controlled.

The Governor had to put that out of his mind, however. He watched as the buildings of Bafek City drew nearer. The continent surrounding that tall skyline was a pit of brown marshes and blackened wastes. The planet was host to large deposits of heavy metals, and a unique soil mixture that released rare chemicals when it was burned. Lursur's land could be burned until the entire continent was black, then tilled and burned again hundreds of times before the expensive resource was fully harvested.

His armoured shuttle passed through the barrier that kept the tall city's air clean, and the grey-brown film that everyone outside of it had to live in. "May I ask you a question, Governor?" asked one of his new Order Knights. The soldier was a believer, a hero who saved two wealthy families from a rebel attack on Governor Tate's home world. He'd also fought in the previous expansion as a boarding officer who was involved in half a dozen successful combat operations. For the life of him, Governor Tate couldn't remember his name, but he was a perfect fit for one of the four Order Knight positions he decided to fill. The narrow faced helm muffled his voice, so it was almost indistinguishable from the sound of the other soldiers around him.

"Please do, it might distract me from the view," Governor Tate replied.

"Thank you," replied the Knight, one of a pair he took with him for this trip. "Isn't it strange for our Lady to choose this as her first meeting place in the solar system? Wouldn't one of the cleaner cities be a better choice?"

"She is here to recruit," Governor Tate said. "I suppose she believes that the people here are ready to follow her because the place is so drab, but most of the free people in Bafek live behind the barrier, in the city, so I don't know what she'll accomplish."

"I told you everyone outside the barrier was on indentured contract," said the other Order Knight, a woman who was a celebrated police sergeant. Governor Tate heard that there was an entire day and night of celebration when she was given her position and the gift of immortality through the new framework technology. "She can't recruit people who still owe money or are serving a punitive labour term."

"Exactly," Governor Tate said. "But there are still some free people outside of the clean air barrier, and on other continents that aren't so heavily worked. I suppose there are people who would rather live the adventure of being an Order Follower."

"If you pardon my forwardness, it doesn't sound like you believe, Governor," said the former police officer.

Governor Tate shook his head slightly. "I'm denied my place in paradise," he told her. "As Governor I follow the calling to serve the public, and that requires a practical mind," he said, trying to keep the practiced speech from sounding like a recitation. He crafted it at Wheeler's urging, a part of the man's advice on how to trick his people into thinking that he, their Governor, was one with the cause. The purpose? To keep from being put in an adversarial position across from Eve and her followers, something that Wheeler convinced him he could not afford. "I can't daydream of living on a lush world where the food is fresh and plentiful, presented on a platter morning noon and night. Those blue skies and perfect, sacred nights filled with beautiful people are something you and your fellow Knights can count on when you've earned your way to them, whereas I must maintain the supply chains, the defence and practical considerations that build such places," the flowery speech seemed so gaudy, overblown when he was practicing it with Wheeler, but aloud, in front of two Order Knights and twenty-six trained soldiers who were technically Regent Galactic military, it sounded like he really did believe, and he had their attention without even trying. He paused, sighed, and looked down at his hands as though they bore the callouses of endless work. They were perfect, manicured and clean, but he could almost convince himself of the fantasy. "Well, I will be here for decades longer, making sure paradise can be real for people just like you when your service elevates you to the worthy position. When my work is done, there will be a place for everyone who earns it, and maybe, just maybe there will be a place for me when it's time for me to put my burden down."

"Thank you, Governor," said the hero soldier Knight. A few soldiers quietly echoed his thanks.

The rest of the trip took place in silence, and Governor Tate did his best to look as though he was considering the burdens of caretaking for entire worlds as he watched the tall buildings slowly pass outside. He couldn't wait for the shuttle to touch down so he could move on with his day, and when they landed atop the central port spire, a tall, square structure with bays for over a hundred small and mid-sized ships, he couldn't help but breathe a sigh of relief.

The Order Knights led the way, with soldiers surrounding him, keeping pace as they walked down the broad ramp at the rear of the armoured shuttle. Five fighters, their escort, hovered near the edges of the landing platform. The unmistakeable scent of the Lursur continent, a slight burnt smell that seemed to stick to the nostrils for days afterwards, was in the fitful gusts of air around them.

A small Order of Eden combat shuttle swept down and landed expediently at the other end of the platform. As the ship eased onto the deck the ramp lowered, and before it had completely come down a group of three youthful people emerged, striding towards them. Something about their gait or disposition made the soldiers around Governor Tate tense.

He couldn't put his finger on it, but there was something about them that made the Governor uneasy. They wore some kind of slender equipment bag firmly strapped to their left legs, and an unusual sidearm on their right thighs. Their armour was unlike anything the Order had, smooth, with flexible padding instead of plates, and coloured dark brown with black. The colour shifted as they moved across the deck, making them difficult to focus on.

As they drew to within comfortable speaking distance, Governor Tate stepped forward to stand between his heavily armed Order Knights, and stopped as he looked into the eyes of the newcomers. Within their dark hoods he could see that their skin was extremely pale, two of them had jet black hair, while the one in the middle had perfectly white hair that was cut to a practical short length. Their eyes were washed of colour, their pupils and irises just grey enough to be distinguishable from their perfect whites. "We come in service of Eve, to speak to Governor Tate," said all three in unison.

"I understood that I'd be meeting with her personally," Governor Tate said, trying to act as though he wasn't completely taken aback by the performance.

"Lucius Wheeler avoids her, but he is a close confidant of yours. You will have to determine why he does not want to appear before her when he is so concerned with helping you inject yourself into the centre of the Order's politics," said the soldier in the middle.

"I don't know what she's been told, but I have no choice but to get involved, with her coming here."

"She has not been told," the trio said together. "We just learned it from the surface thoughts. Wheeler has become a part of your decision making process in very little time, and we know the man's history. He is as dangerous as he is useful. You will have to appear with him at your side if you wish to meet Eve in person. He must be read by a Trio Cell, just as you have been."

"I am the head of government here, no one ranks above me, especially not Wheeler," Governor Tate protested. "He isn't even a citizen."

"We understand why you may find our determination insulting," the trio said. The white haired woman in the centre stepped forward, speaking alone. "You have to put that aside. Citadel is allied with Eve now, and she trusts us to keep her safe so she can continue her work without worry."

"Citadel, I understand," Governor Tate said, doing his very best to disguise the fact that he had no idea what Citadel was. A slight smile broke the perfectly placid expressions of the trio in front of him, and he could only suppose they could hear the ignorance in his thoughts – if they could indeed read minds. It infuriated him, but he didn't care as long as his ignorance was hidden from his soldiers.

The trio turned to leave and Governor Tate let them go, even though he wanted to force them to produce Eve so she could answer his questions, so he could influence her to leave his indentured workforce alone. He would return with Wheeler, but not before he got some answers from the man about Citadel and so many other pressing matters.

CHAPTER 14
A SINGULAR ENCOUNTER

Admiral Terry Ozark McPatrick could feel the tension in Hausgiest's mind. It was in direct relation to the ship. Fourteen fighters were resting in the punters under the ship, all three hangars were ready to spring open and launch three gunships each, and the Warlord rested on a main mooring point, able to spring off at a moment's notice. The torpedo tubes were loaded, the new high energy particle weapons along the bottom of the ship were fully charged, missile turrets were loaded and ready behind their heavy hatches, and the gunnery deck along the top of the ship was prepared, patient, and silent.

They emerged from a very short trip through a wormhole, cloaked and manoeuvring away from their entrance point into the space near the drifting asteroid field. No one fired on their obvious position of arrival, and they were clear in good time, making it nearly impossible for most ships to find the Triton.

The Triton's main engines stopped flaring, manoeuvring thrusters and inertial shifting systems took over as they maintained a smooth but irregular course near the asteroid field. "There's something wrong here," said one of the analysts in the sensor and signal monitoring section of the bridge to Oz's right.

"What's that, Henrietta?" he asked her. She wasn't of military rank, but served on the bridge, paid for her keen eye and years of experience with two space exploration companies.

"The area around this asteroid cluster is too neat. There is no sign that this large group of high-mass bodies has drifted through something like a solar system, picking up garbage and other small bits as it goes through. That sort of thing isn't just common, it's inevitable, especially in a system like Rega Gain, where bits of trash and old tech are everywhere."

"What does that tell us?" Oz asked. "Do you think this is artificial?"

"Wait, Sir, I'm checking the trajectory against charts we have on hand and a few passive scans the Warlord did on recent patrols," she said. All the information came together in the middle of the bridge, where one of the main holographic projectors displayed an image of the solar system, the trajectory of the asteroid drift, and objects it would have passed near as it came into the system. "Sir," Henrietta said tentatively as several red circles highlighted small outer solar system meteor clusters and a large flotilla of old wreckage that was slowly drifting away from the Rega Gain system. "There's very little chance that this asteroid cluster made it through all that without hitting anything unless it was aimed, and that's not something I've seen."

"It's as though someone plotted its course well in advance, knowing where all that would be," said Ensign Pallot beside her. "But that's not the worst. Our passive scans have enough information to confirm the Wing Commander's readings. The composition of those asteroids doesn't match anything for a light year along its course."

Oz called up the navigational charts for the region and checked the history of the asteroid field. "It's been in the navigational charts for nine years," he muttered to himself. Hausgiest broke through all this thoughts with a realization. 'Citadel is here!'

"Wait," Oz said, holding a hand up to ward him off.

"Yes, Sir," Henrietta said.

He didn't bother correcting her assumption that he was telling her to wait. 'How do you know?' he asked Hausgiest.

"The Victory Machine predicted that Haven Shore would be significant in the war, that it would reveal the secret motivation behind the Order of Eden's formation and war. I can feel that something has been sent here to stop whatever they are afraid of in the Rega Gain system."

"We have a ship on scanners," Agameg said from the tactical station. "It is of Sol System design."

Hausgiest would not allow himself to be interrupted. "Ten years ago, Citadel put this assault into motion, sending this asteroid belt towards this position, at this time. They are here."

"How do you know?" Oz asked.

"I have contacted their on board Intelligence, and it tells me that they have allied with the Order of Eden to set the future to right. They demand that we surrender the Triton."

There was no wavering in Hausgiest's loyalty to Oz and his crew, a concern he'd had about what would happen if they ran into another Sol Defence ship, or another of his kind. He realized that he shouldn't have been concerned, in fact, it was sealing off seventy sections of the ship with heavy bulkhead doors and starting all their secondary power generation systems up. "Be calm, calculate the way ahead, don't panic," Oz said to the ship's steward, and he could feel Hausgiest ease a little.

"Sir, I don't see any data stream or ident contact between the Triton or the other ship," announced a communications officer.

"Don't worry about it, Ensign," Oz said, aware that Hausgiest's communication with the other ship was telepathic. He could feel a trace of the other ship's controller, it was much younger, perhaps only a few years old.

"They are directing weapons at us," Agameg said.

"With what kind of accuracy?" Oz asked.

"Ninety three point four percent," Agameg replied. "Our cloaking systems are ineffective."

"Deactivate all cloaking systems. Eject the Warlord with instructions to remain cloaked and to get some distance. Bring up our new shields, at least we have something they haven't seen yet," Oz said. At a glance he could see where the enemy ship was revealing itself.

It was called the Pontos. The narrow, flat face of the vessel was beginning to emerge from the far side of the asteroid field. Behind that four hundred metre tall face the hull split into two thick hull segments that extended three hundred metres behind. A forest of long antennae and long devices extended from the rear of the ship. A main hangar rested in the cleft between the two hulls, well protected by shields and thick hull plating. "Send the following to Pontos Command," Oz took a slow breath before continuing. For most of the crew, this was their first contact with anyone from Earth. "This is our opportunity to peacefully speak about major events in the galaxy and how we can resolve numerous issues that affect the lives of billions of people. The meeting of our two ships, and our leadership could bring about a new era, regardless of your recently formed alliance with the Order of Eden."

Lieutenant Commander Liara Erron stared at him for a moment with a surprised expression. Oz nodded, and the she sent the message without further delay.

"We wait," Oz said, standing and resisting the temptation to pace.

"All systems are ready for deployment," came the voice of Chief Mendle through his command seat.

Hausgiest sent one thought to him, then fell silent. 'You are wise to make this attempt. To avoid war is more valiant than winning one.'

"The Warlord is away," Agameg said. "There are no indications that the Pontos is tracking it."

Admiral McPatrick nodded and started to indulge in his urge to pace, slowly walking forwards and backwards in front of his command seat. "Good," he said. "Good, Jake will react to this in his own way. Good, good," he muttered to himself quietly. "How is your analysis of the Pontos coming?" he asked.

"Badly, but we can see an Order of Eden carrier hiding in the asteroid belt, they're not moving," replied Henrietta. "As for Pontos, the hull is reflecting most scanning signals just like the Triton's does."

"Older ship? Younger ship?" Oz said.

"Most likely much younger, but the weapons, from what we can see are inferior by a wide margin," Agameg reported. "The Order of Eden carrier is beginning to move."

"Incoming transmission," announced Lieutenant Commander Erron. She played it without waiting for the order. "We do this as a warning. Do not interfere with the Order of Eden. Do not ponder Citadel's purpose or act upon our people."

The Pontos opened a wormhole and passed into it. Three destroyers and two battlecruisers appeared on scanners, revealing themselves inside the asteroid field as they activated their main systems. The carrier began launching fighters. "This is a distraction," Oz said.

"Ready to launch fighters!" announced Chief Paula Mendle.

"Hold!" Oz shouted towards the Flight Deck underfoot. "Where does that wormhole go?"

"It led to Kambis Orbital Space," Agameg announced.; "Opposite Tamber, where we have the least defences."

"Warlord reports that they are moving in to block the incoming fighters and to fire main guns on that carrier," communications announced.

"Activate our cloaked torpedoes. Launch a full volley at that asteroid belt, ahead of the destroyers and that carrier when ready," Oz turned to the helm. "Navigation, send new orders to the Warlord: They are to do their best in delaying the carrier group, but to return to Kambis orbital space as soon as holding them is unreasonable."

"Yes, Sir," replied Liara. After scant seconds she reported; "They have acknowledged the new orders."

The torpedoes launched. Less than three seconds later anti-matter explosions filled the view in front of the Triton as hundreds of asteroids and smaller bodies were struck, some of the smaller ones spun into the interior of the field, stirring lower mass stone into a frenzy around the enemy battle group. "That should slow them down, we'll have to come back and clean that up later. All stations, prepare for short range wormhole travel into a combat zone. Let's show the galaxy what our Triton can do."

CHAPTER 15
DELAYING TACTICS

The tactical display in front of Jake's command seat did not lie. There was little he could do to further delay the remaining Order Ships while keeping the Warlord hidden. Even though they could fire cloaked, the amount of firepower they'd need would reveal their location. One enemy destroyer was caught by the colliding mass of asteroids at the rear; it was finished. Two more were leading the carrier in the small group out of the asteroid field, and the battlecruisers alongside that destroyer were working in concert with her to combine shield strength, staying close, displaying an impressive amount of fortitude for a smaller class of ship. Heavy fighters launched from the battlecruisers, staying close enough to add to the shield power of the trio of larger ships.

The carrier was not launching fighters. "Kadri, can you get a read on how well charged their wormhole generator is?" Jake asked.

"All the power in those ships is being directed to maintain their shields. Their wormhole emitter systems are cold," Kadri replied. "It looks like they expect someone to stir up the asteroid field even more."

"I can confirm," Ayan added. "Several of the shield emitters on the battlecruisers are overloaded, a few on the nose of that carrier are in the same shape. The fighters running alongside the battlecruisers are making up for the dead shield emitters."

Jake looked at the Warlord in relation to the emerging ships. No one would question his decision if he simply observed and then reported back to the fleet once the Order of Eden battle group was gone if their intention was to escape the system. If their intention was to follow the Pontos to Kambis and its moons, then he had an opportunity to do some damage to the battle group. Not enough to stop it, but he could get one shot that could make them less effective in the next phase of the engagement – a battle that could be coming to Kambis orbit.

"All batteries, all launchers," Jake started, "Load all of our antimatter rounds. We're only going to get one chance to make a first impression."

"We don't have much aboard, Sir," Frost said. "Maybe a minute's worth of constant firing for our guns, three shots on the railguns, and seven mines."

"We won't have long to fire," Jake told him. "Ashley, get us here," Jake said, gesturing at the tactical map he could read in his helmet. "Kadri, ship wide channel, please." Jake ordered.

"Please stand by for a message from our Captain," Kadri said into the open channel before nodding at Jake.

"The Pontos has just taken a wormhole in the direction of our home planet. The Triton has followed it, and our orders are to delay a small Order of Eden battle group that is about to leave the asteroid field here. The Warlord is small, but he's a scrapper, with more armour and weaponry than anything in his class. We're going to bloody their noses and bug out to Kambis Orbital space. For one minute I need your best as we bash these bastards with all our antimatter ammo, then I need everyone to do their best as we get to Kambis orbit, where we can get some backup. Let's take the fight to 'em. Seal all hatches and vacsuits."

Jake could see the enemy's aggressive scans on his tactical display, they knew there was something else out there with them, but they didn't seem to know what it was.

Ashley was moving the Warlord into position carefully, avoiding the strongest scanning signals. "Moving at stealth thrust," Ashley replied as they Warlord lowered itself into position right above the carrier. They were beside a large asteroid that was rolling through space alongside them that kept the sweeping scanners on an entire side of the carrier group from testing their stealth systems. The carrier itself was close enough to block most of the rest of the scans.

Jake could hear a distant clang under foot as the new rounds were loaded into the railguns. "Sir," Stephanie said over a private channel. "We are massively outmatched here, we could stand by and bug out when we know where they're going."

"Our orders are to delay these ships. We will have only seconds to do anything effective," Jake said.

"Why aren't we getting reinforcements from Kambis orbit?" she asked.

"Because, aside from the Triton, we are the heaviest class ship with a working cloaking system. Anyone else would be torn to shreds in minutes," Jake replied. They closed on the position he'd indicated, right beside a large asteroid, and only nine hundred metres above the carrier. Ashley pointed the Warlord's nose at the lead destroyer, less than three kilometres ahead. Those antimatter railgun rounds would land in exactly the right place.

"All stations, prepare to fire on my mark," Jake said. "Ashley, once all our mines are off, break off at full thrust and get us here, behind this cluster. Frost, fire all three railguns, then drop our mines. Gun emplacements will unload throughout this volley."

"Aye," Frost said. "All stations report ready."

Jake took a deep breath and let it out slowly, the Warlord had settled into the perfect position, the destroyers in the lead were almost completely clear of the asteroids, one was beginning to turn to the right. He watched one of the nearby asteroids approach from the carrier group's port side. One of the lead destroyers launched five rockets at it. They buried themselves in the surface of the asteroid and continued to thrust, slowing it down so it just grazed their shields. Even though it was only a light touch to the group's shields, it was enough to strain them. "Three, two, one, mark."

The deck plate under his feet rattled as all three of the Warlord's main railguns fired. Their shields reported a massive strike as soon as they impacted and detonated against the lead destroyer. The Warlord's shields were down to twenty three percent charge. Jake saw that extra power was being routed to the shield batteries. The Warlord's emitters had taken no damage, so they recharged their shields at a rate of three percent per second.

"Main sensors are overloaded," Kadri announced. "Switching."

The Warlord's gunners were so close to the carrier that they didn't need the sensor suite to score hits on the enemy ship. Their antimatter mines dropped, and Jake shifted to the edge of his seat. "Go, Ashley, get us out of here!" Their shields were only up to forty three percent, if they were too close to their antimatter mines when they went off, there would be nothing left of the Warlord.

All their thrusters fired at maximum burn, a glance at the exterior view on the bridge's main monitor revealed that the Warlord looked like a fireball from the middle back. He watched as they gained distance from their position above the carrier, skimming across the asteroid drift towards the upper edge of a cluster on the far side. They were only half way there when the carriers point defence guns fired at the mines, setting one off within a kilometre of the enemy's hull. The one set the other six off immediately and the blast struck the Warlord's hull hard enough for him to hear the thunderous blow through his helmet. They were far too close to the detonation. Jake hoped they'd have enough ship left to fly away from a fight he knew they'd lose.

The Warlord went dark, and emergency systems started coming online. They had inertial dampers, and most of their manoeuvring thrusters.

"Main communications systems are down," Kadri said. "Backups are taking over."

"All main thrusters are down, resetting," Finn said. "One through three are coming back on line, but four is disconnected."

"Secondary navigation array is coming back online," Ayan said. "The primary nav is reading dead."

"Targetting systems are offline," Frost said. "It is drawing no power."

The tactical display appeared on his helmet, signalling to Jake that they had a sensor and navigational system working. "Brace for impact!" he announced as he saw that they had been blasted off course just enough for the down-tilted nose of the Warlord to catch the edge of a large asteroid.

The inertial dampers saved them from most of the jostling, but Jake was still nearly pitched out of the command seat. "Shields?" he asked.

"Our aft shield emitters are slagged," Finn announced.

"We've lost all our port emitters from frame twenty three back, we can give you sixty percent coverage, about eleven percent power," Ayan added.

"Really?" Finn said. "Show me, quick."

"Give me whatever you can," Jake replied. "Weapons?"

"We have three guns left," Frost said. "Lost five crewmen in their turrets, one to an antimatter ammunition explosion, emplacement three is open to space."

"Seal that off, get our good side facing the enemy, and start plotting a wormhole course to Kambis orbit, safe arrival space," Jake said, seeing that the wormhole generator was intact and still charged. The Warlord had drifted past the asteroid field, and had luckily put itself under cover, the field was between them and the carrier group. "Launch fighters, we need them to stay close and to provide countermeasure fire in case those ships start sending guided missiles our way."

"Aye, fighter launch systems are up and running, launching," Frost said. "I'm surprised there's a straight line left on this ship after that. First pair are away."

"This is Carnie," announced one of the newest additions to the Samurai Squadron. "Me and Hottie are on station, ready to stop anything coming at the Warlord while you get things running. Initial scans of the carrier group show heavy damage, but I'm guessing they'll be able to recover enough to ruin our day."

Jake didn't know much about the new pair in the Samurai Squadron. He hadn't even met them, but Carnie was well known as an incredible shot, and Hottie was a man who did not enjoy his call sign in the least, but no one told Jake the story behind it. Both were phenomenal pilots that Minh-Chu had to fight with Triton Fleet for.

His tactical display told him two more fighters launched off the racks and another pair were being loaded. They may be able to provide the modest cover they needed.

"Main sensor array is up!" Kadri said, surprised. "Pin a medal on the tech that got that working again," she added. "I have a clear read on those destroyers. Full crews, the furthest one from us has no shields on its aft-port quarter, the other is turning to intercept us. The Carrier's shields are down on the fore-dorsal section, port launch bay is severely damaged, as well as the starboard launch bay, but their main hangar can only open a quarter of the way, and it is launching small ships. They don't look like fighters. Both the battlecruisers took light damage, they are moving into position above the carrier to cover with their shields."

Jake looked at the ships that the carrier was launching. "Those look like pods with a rocket on one end and some kind of cutter system on the front."

"Never seen anything like that before," Frost said. "There are four people in each."

"Carnie here," announced the pilot. "I'll have a firing solution on those in just a sec. We'll have all our birds out playing defence in a few seconds, Warlord, don't worry."

"Wormhole course plotted," Ashley said.

"Start opening it," Jake said. The carrier launched another wave of pods, it appeared on his tactical display as a line of twenty-four new contacts. "Hurry."

The first wave of six got clear of the asteroids between them and the warlord, and the fighters opened fire. The rockets on the back of the pods fired, sending them towards the Warlord at an alarming speed. Five were obliterated by their cover fire before they could finish the trip to the Warlord, the sixth was heavily damaged, but its momentum carried it past the fighters. It struck the hull of the Warlord and went spinning past it, directly through the point in space where they were generating their wormhole.

"Wormhole generation failed," Ashley's navigator announced. "The surface of that thing reflected enough energy to interrupt it."

"Do we have enough power to generate another right away?" Jake asked.

"Nope, it'll take eleven minutes," Ashley replied. "Could speed it up if we can get more power though."

"Warlord," Hottie said over his communicator from the cockpit of his fighter. "We have a problem, no way are we knocking all those pods out."

Jake saw what he was talking about. The pods were splitting up, getting enough distance from each other so the fighters and the Warlord would have trouble taking two or more out at a time. They fired their rocket engines, accelerating so quickly that the tactical display in Jake's helmet couldn't quite keep up.

"Our last turrets are helping with that," Frost said. "Something is going to get through."

"Counter incursion teams, get ready," Jake said.

Alice and Stephanie checked in as ready.

"One of those destroyers will have a firing solution on us in one minute and twelve seconds," Frost said.

"Get us under cover, Ash," Jake said. "Use the asteroids, we can't take direct hits from that ship."

"I'm trying," Ashley replied. "None of my thrusters are running at full power, and I'd be real happy if someone could jump-start my number four engine."

"On it," Finn said. "I have a damage control officer on his way out."

With a glance Jake could see that David Penton, a man he'd saved from slavery before they arrived on Tamber, was on his way through a maintenance hatch to the pylon holding thruster four. "He has the worst timing," he said under his breath. "Get that wormhole generator charging faster," Jake said.

The seven Samurai Squadron fighters fired at the incoming pods, sending streaks of automatic gunfire and missiles towards the approaching wall. Five heavy thuds sounded against the hull, followed by a rain of shrapnel. To Jake's amazement, David managed to avoid getting torn to shreds or crushed by hiding behind the thruster pylon in the nick of time. "Captain, I can see five pods attached to the hull. One is right above the power systems on our main rear thruster. All the pods are starting to cut."

"Just finish what you're doing and get back inside," Finn said.

"My team's going outside," Alice said over inter-ship communications.

"No," Stephanie replied over her communicator. "Stay in position, inside the ship. Your team will get killed out there. We don't all have David's luck."

"Aye," Alice replied.

"Sir, guided missiles from the lead destroyer!" Frost said.

"Turn our shields towards them, " Jake ordered. "Samurai, take them out before they get here."

"Roger," Carnie replied.

The small fighter group of seven couldn't be faulted for their performance. The lead destroyer and the carrier were each launching waves of five guided missiles, some of which wove between a few asteroids before entering the clear space around the Warlord. "They're jinky," Quack said from her cockpit. They were able to knock out the first fifteen guided missiles, before one got through.

To Jake's surprise, the missile turned into an arc at the last second, avoiding the heavy shields on their lower side, instead striking their weakly shielded dorsal side. The next two to get through did the same, doing no damage to the pods that were attached to the Warlord's hull, but destroying the shield emitters for the dorsal side of the ship. "They're after the bridge," Jake said.

"I hate this," Ashley said as she turned the Warlord, the number four thruster activated, giving her the power she needed to get them moving faster towards the closest cluster of asteroids. "We'll be under cover in a sec."

"I can't get back in," David said. "Going to thrust off and take my chances until search and rescue can pick me up. Wish me luck."

Even while the Warlord was under terrible assault, Jake couldn't help but wonder at David's coolness under pressure, and his bravery. His suit's emergency thrusters got him away from the Warlord, then he engaged his cloak. David would indeed be safe if he could get away from the shrapnel and other agents of destruction.

"Cover, squadron! Knock those missiles out!" Frost said as several hits registered on the hull.

"Breach, dorsal section," Finn announced. "Our main reactor is down. Our main engineering section is open to space. Two fires in adjacent compartments. Putting them out."

"Switching to secondary systems, but we can't keep the shields up, there's no way to route power to several generators, and we lost some people with that last volley," Ayan said.

"Most of our engineering staff," Finn added.

"The destroyer and carrier have stopped launching, their last volley is incoming," Frost said.

"Not going to get all of these," Carnie said. "We've taken hits, I'm down to one gun, sorry, Warlord."

Jake watched as the fighters, most of which took damage putting themselves between the missiles and the Warlord, sacrificing shields, and in some cases, parts of their ships to keep the missiles at bay, opened fire on the last volley. Fifteen heavy missiles cleared the asteroid field, and three were destroyed by Samurai squadron in the first second, seven in the two seconds that followed, and then six hit them, spiralling around the Warlord, seeking her bridge. Four struck in front of the bridge, the other two exploded through the hull, destroying crew quarters over their heads. Alarms went off, the doors at the rear of the compartment opened. The bridge was losing atmosphere. "How long until we can open a wormhole?" Jake asked, standing and transferring control of as many systems as he could to his command and control unit.

"Three minutes, nine seconds," Ashley said, surprised that her seat was retreating from her pilot station. "What's goin' on?"

"We're abandoning the bridge, falling back to a launch bay," Jake said. He was relieved to see that he was able to transfer pilot controls to Ashley's command and control unit, and that the wormhole generator was still charging. "We're going to have to keep the ship going while we get there."

"The first pod's cutters have broken through," Stephanie said. "If we blow these off with grenades, we lose all hull integrity in this section."

"I don't care, just kill those boarders," Jake replied. "And make sure you don't get sucked out with the atmosphere."

"Blowing one off," Stephanie said.

Frost opened a hatch at his feet and hurriedly handed rifles out to Ayan, Kadri, Finn and Jake. He also activated a small portable shield bot and took a case of ammunition.

Jake adjusted his rifle to the maximum setting, he would only be able to fire in bursts, and he only had a hundred and five shots, but they would be powerful enough to cut through most armour.

"Blew four grenades right at the base of the pod, didn't do a damn thing, those things are full-thickness welded to the hull, and they have shielding," Stephanie said. An explosion sounded over her comms and Jake only heard the sounds of gunfire and running.

"Steph! What is it?" Frost asked.

"Knights, four Order Knights in each pod," she replied.

Chapter 16
Kambis Orbit

"Okay, I don't like this," Dent said from his fighter where he held formation on Ronin's port side.

Ronin finished verifying what he was seeing on his tactical display. "Triton Fleet is on alert, but the Triton isn't here, neither is the Warlord or any of the new gunships." The recently organized group of forty two mid-sized ships were running a picket line near Tamber Orbit. Triton Fleet gunships and fighters were assisting, filling in soft sensor areas, where the time delay between scanning and receiving data was too long for larger ships. The Barricade and the British Alliance Fleet numbering three large carriers with three battlecruisers and nine destroyers each along with countless smaller ships watched over it all.

"I knew we were being misdirected when that British Lieutenant directed us back to the fleet," Dent said. "They've got Tamber locked down, this is not where the action is."

"It was a good order, he saw they were on alert, and sent us back," Ronin said, observing the situation and putting the pieces together. "I'm linking us up with Skyguard Squadron." He sent a hailing signal to Skyguard command.

"Slick to Ronin," addressed the leader of Skyguard.

"Ronin here. Did we miss the party?" Minh-Chu asked.

"Triton and the Warlord followed your lead up, the Barricade is our new operational carrier, so don't scratch that fighter. As big as it is, the Barricade is not a full carrier, it's got a fifth the capacity of the Triton and her crews are all green."

"Slow service, possibly bad service, gotcha. Any word on what they found out there?"

"I was hoping you could tell me," Slick replied.

"Wing Commander Ronin, this is Barricade Flight," said the familiar voice of Governor Anderson.

"Finally found a command seat, old man?" Ronin replied.

"Rushed into service at the last minute, glad I've been keeping an eye on this ship all along," he replied. "Otherwise I wouldn't know which end was up."

"Where do you want me?"

"The Morrigan could use some fighter support, they're patrolling the far side of Kambis."

"I see it, Slick and I will provide scout support. Any idea what we're watching for?"

"Admiral McPatrick was concerned that that carrier group you found was only part of an enemy strategy."

"Made to lure our best ships out of orbit so they could strike Tamber," Ronin said. "Command thinking. Tell me if there's anything else we can do."

"Aye, good hunting, Ronin," replied Governor Anderson.

Minh-Chu turned his fighter and thrust in the direction of the Morrigan, the armoured hauler Captain Moira McFadden, Frost's cousin, had just finished modifying. After she was finished with it, Ronin could only call it a pirate ship. She kept the six main rotary thrusters, but shortened the pylons they sat on so the ship wasn't such an easy target. She also kept the main thruster at the rear of the ship, but an extra layer of curved armour covered the entire ship.

Large disruption emitters dotted the bottom of the ship, made to damage shields at relatively short range. A long armoured box ran along one side of the ship where her version of a maxjack was hidden. Numerous arms, cutters and a pair of fortified docking hatches were ready to crack into a ship once it was disabled. The rest of the vessel was dotted with old fashioned energy pulse and railgun turrets.

"I'd love to see a simulated fight between the Morrigan and the Warlord," Dent said as they moved in closer. "Wouldn't like to see a real one though."

"That's a good idea for training the crews," Minh-Chu said. "I'll have to pass it by Jake and Moira when I get a chance."

"Captain McFadden here," the Captain of the Morrigan said through their communicators. "I understand you two are our new escort?"

"That's right, we're just getting into position," Minh-Chu replied.

"Split and cover our starboard and port sides," Captain McFadden said. "We're on our way to the dark side of Kambis."

"Expecting trouble?" Dent asked.

A wormhole opened between the Morrigan and the rest of the fleet, close enough to set off all of Ronin's energy and collision alarms. "Evasive action! Break to port! Break to port!" he ordered.

The pair of Uriel fighters thrust out of the way of the large newcomer. It was unlike any ship Minh-Chu had ever seen. "You're never allowed to ask that question again, Dent," he said as he and his wingman finished moving out of immediate danger.

"What is that? I've never seen that configuration," asked Captain McFadden.

Ronin's heart sank as the Sol Defence database finished looking up the ship's profile and transponder. "I have a record in my Target Identification Database. That is the Pontos, a ship made for Citadel, the covert oversight organization for Earth Defence. All information on that ship's systems is gone, deleted before the records could be updated."

"Citadel?" Captain McFadden asked. "What are they doing here?"

"Citadel ship," Governor Anderson addressed. "We are currently dealing with a crisis elsewhere in the solar system. I need you to declare friend or foe immediately."

Minh-Chu's tactical display lit up as the Citadel ship's shields flared, sending a wave of energy in all directions for over thirty five thousand kilometres. "My shields are down to nine percent," he said.

"Five," reported Dent, "five percent."

"Twenty eight percent," Captain McFadden said, "they are not friends."

"Dump your missile bays, head for that old observation station for cover," Minh-Chu ordered. He and dent opened their missile loading doors and ejected all their munitions in the direction of the Citadel ship. As they made the minimum safe distance from the munitions, they armed the lot of them. The guided munitions fired rockets, dragging their full launcher racks towards the enemy ship. "Hope that provides enough of a distraction."

"They're not targeting us at all," Dent said.

"Stop jinxing us!" Ronin replied as his canopy was lit up by several nearby flashes. "Morrigan, are you in need of our assistance?"

"No, you made the right call, running for cover, that ship is between us, you'd get ripped apart if you tried to cross the distance," Captain McFadden said. "We are staying clear of your munitions dump stunt though, we could have used some warning."

"They're not doing anything about it," Dent said. "No countermeasures."

Minh-Chu watched as the Morrigan opened fire with her turrets, and the flying bundles of missiles passed by, closing on the

Pontos. A barrage of energy bolts struck one of the bundles, detonating it and sending the rest of the missiles off course.

"Okay, that singed us around the edges," Captain McFadden said. "There was some antimatter in that load, yeah?"

"A little, that was one of Dent's loadouts, mine are a little heavier. There's an accumulation missile aboard," Minh-Chu said as he activated it. The guided missiles attached to the bundle were doing a fair job of turning the munitions back towards the enemy ship. His accumulator missile's reactor began charging up quickly. The Pontos fired several shots at it, but couldn't quite reach. "A blind spot, right behind that big bastard's main thrusters. I'm going to have to blow my racks, Captain McFadden, hurry up and get behind this observation post."

"Making best speed, Ronin," replied Captain McFadden. "How big is that accumulator going to build up? What kind of antimatter is it going to make?"

"Enough," Minh-Chu said, "I hope."

"This is the British Alliance ship William. Please cease and desist all combat activity and clear the area, we are launching defence fighters and drones."

Minh-Chu waited an extra three seconds as the Morrigan made it behind the abandoned observation station. It had already taken significant damage from the Pontos' pulse cannons. His gave his accumulator missile time to build a little more charge, then triggered the final stage of the small reactor's cycle, creating a small, unsafe amount of dense unshielded antimatter. The drifting rack of missiles flew apart, sending most of the munitions thrusting against the Pontos' shields. An instant after they finished impacting, the accumulator missile exploded, filling the area with white light.

"I'm sorry, say again, B.A. William?" Minh-Chu asked.

"-and drones are incoming, please fall back and refrain from detonating any other large munitions."

"Understood, B.A. William," replied Governor Anderson from the Barricade. "We will move to a holding position once we have a clear line of fire on the Pontos."

Minh-Chu's tactical display updated, indicating that he was to join the Barricade, the Morrigan and Dent had received the same orders. "B.A. William Command," he said, looking at the broad carrier on his tactical display as it launched thirty fighters at a time. "My biggest antimatter weapon only reduced that ship's exterior power readings by eleven percent, it still has a seriously high shield reading and its recharging fast."

"Thank you, Ronin," said someone from the command deck of that ship. There was no way Minh-Chu could know who they were or what rank they had. "We are aware, please follow your commander's orders."

"There's nothing we can do against that," Dent said. "Unless you've got another dozen accumulator missiles in your back pocket."

"Retreat," Minh-Chu said. "We'll merge our shields with the Morrigan, get a good field going." He guided his ship into position on the ship's port side as Dent did the same.

"Merging the field," Captain McFadden said. "Slave your controls to my helm please."

"Aye," Minh-Chu said as he watched the drones engage the Pontos. The ship hadn't done anything but reduce the shield power of everyone in the area. It wasn't firing at them like an enemy set to destroy its opponents. "The Pontos was more interested in distracting us," Minh-Chu said.

"I was just thinking the same thing," Captain McFadden said. "It's biding its time."

"The Barricade is performing a deep scan now, we just got a clear line of sight," Governor Anderson said. "Get into our group, now."

The trio of them broke cover, thrusting as quickly as they could into open space. Several bolts of energy struck their shields. One got through and Minh-Chu's eyes went wide as he saw what those blasts really were. "They are firing super-heated plasma contained in an energy field. Uriel fighters cannot take that kind of fire. Our cockpits are not strong enough."

Minh-Chu took control of his fighter. "Dent and I are going to move our ships to the front of the Morrigan, so you're between that ship and us. We'll still add to your shield's charge."

"My damage control team can confirm your readings, Ronin," Captain McFadden said. "Set your shields to charge as fast as they can, that single shot blasted a third of the way through our hull."

Once Dent and he were in a better position, Minh-Chu looked at the mess the Pontos was making of the British Alliance drones. Most of them were destroyed in two shots – one to break their shields down, and another to superheat large portions of their instruments – and Minh-Chu couldn't help but feel lucky that he wasn't a member of the fighter squadron moving in behind the drones. They were British pilots, incredibly talented, well trained, well disciplined. Their fighters weren't half as well armed or as manoeuvrable as their Uriels, but they did have more armour and better shields.

"They're going to get killed," Dent said. "The Brits have to move their destroyers in faster."

Minh-Chu could see there were fourteen British Alliance destroyers and nine corvettes coming around the planet, but they would not be able to find a firing solution for another minute, up to two in some cases. Most of the drones were reduced to rubble by the time the manned fighters were launching missiles, and Minh-Chu had to force himself not to look away as the Pontos began firing on the British pilots.

The Pontos began to move towards Kambis rapidly, opening large doors along the front of the ship. "The energy readings on whatever is in there are off the charts."

"We see it, that's what we've been trying to get a good scan of," Governor Anderson said. "As far as we can scan so far, there are antimatter solids, and they are charging a separate shield system."

Minh-Chu had an idea as to what it was, but shook his head instead of saying it aloud.

"Governor, send an evacuation order to Kambis, right now!" Captain McFadden said.

Minh-Chu's tactical screen updated with an evacuation order for Kambis. "Ronin, do you know what that is?" asked his old wingman, Slick, on a private channel.

"A large armoured casing, independent propulsion, shielding and solid antimatter in the centre." Minh-Chu said. "That's enough power in one weapon to wipe out a fleet in tight formation, but they're headed for Kambis' atmosphere."

"So, that's a planet killer," Slick said, "That's what you're thinking."

"Look at the scan data," Minh-Chu replied. "I can't see what else it could be. There are half a billion people down there." Minh-Chu grasped at his controls, only to discover they were under the control of the Morrigan. He turned the slave circuit off and thrust away from the combat hauler.

"Ronin! Get back here right now!" Captian McFadden ordered. "What do you think you can do?"

"I'll think of something on my way there," Minh-Chu said. He looked at the doors at the front of the Pontos, still opening. They still had powerful energy shields protecting what was inside.

"There's nothing you can do!" Captain McFadden said. "Ronin, listen, if that's a planet burner, then we're going to need you more than ever."

"Too many people look to you to lead them," added Governor Anderson. "If you close in and try something heroic, you're going to get slagged before you reach your target. Those destroyers are about to clear the planet, and they're not going to hold their shells for you to try whatever you have in mind. Fall back, that's an order, Wing Commander."

Minh-Chu gritted his teeth, staring at the Pontos thrusting away, then flipped his fighter and thrust away from the dark planet of Kambis. A field of debris was forming around the Citadel ship made of the broken hulls of British Alliance drones and the wreckage of manned fighters. Those small ships couldn't make any difference. "There are half a billion people on that planet right now." He set his navigational computer to automatically move back into formation with the Morrigan and punched between the buttons on his console. "You better tear that ship up!"

The first of the British destroyers began firing their shells, striking the side of the Pontos to no immediate effect. The Barricade fired all its guns, even the railguns of the Morrigan were firing in a continuous stream, the tips of their barrels turning red.

The rest of the Triton Fleet left behind to defend Tamber were finally out from behind the moon, and began firing. The Pontos began to slow as it closed in on the outer atmosphere of the planet.

"This is the Triton, we need an update on the situation," came Oz's voice over Minh-Chu's communicator as the Triton appeared on his tactical display.

"The Pontos is about to launch a weapon towards Kambis, we are unsure, but it is most likely a planet wide weapon of mass destruction," replied Governor Anderson from the Barricade.

"Triton, fall back so we can increase our level of response," ordered British Alliance command.

"Firing a volley of torpedoes and everything we have as we clear the area," Oz replied. The Triton had come in ninety eight thousand kilometres behind the Pontos, it was well out of range of any splash damage the British Alliance could hit the ship with. It was also in a position to block the Pontos' escape.

Regardless, Captain McPatrick, Minh-Chu's old friend Oz, obeyed orders, firing a volley of torpedoes and fired all its non-energy weapons across the nearly one hundred thousand kilometre distance separating it and the Pontos on their way out.

The Triton's efforts, the constant volleys from the British Alliance Destroyers, the Barricades roaring guns, and the solid projectile fire from hundreds of smaller ships brought the Pontos' shields down to low levels, and scarred the side of the vessel, but the enemy ship somehow managed to maintain a functional energy barrier. It was just enough to keep the vessel moving towards Kambis, on whatever mission it was sent to complete

Minh-Chu could barely stand to watch as his tactical sensors illustrated an oblong object firing sideways from the front of the Pontos. The ship's cargo doors closed behind it and the Pontos turned at a speed that seemed impossible for a ship its size.

The object it launched into the atmosphere of Kambis accelerated through the atmosphere, its shields creating a fireball many times its size. As soon as it was in the open atmosphere it burst into more pieces than Minh-Chu's tactical systems could track, and the shards triggered an antimatter alarm.

"Tell me this isn't happening, Minh," Dent said. "I knew people down there."

"We cannot let this drive us to destruction," Minh-Chu said on an open channel, "or murder, or waste. Take the Pontos, and as many crewmembers as you can alive. We need to know why this is happening, people will never stop asking."

As soon as the silver shelled projectile finished entering the atmosphere, the two hundred ten metre long case split open and fell away. Thousands of shards of solid antimatter, each with their own containment shield, split in all directions, moving at speeds that Minh-Chu's sensors could not track in real time. Once they were dispersed around the planet, the energy field expanded, and each solid antimatter shard became a gas covering thousands of metres.

Chatter on all fleet communications bands stopped for a moment, as the antimatter gas was suspended in Kambis's atmosphere by the isolation fields separating it from normal matter. Then the fields ran out of power, and the gaseous antimatter made contact with normal matter, and, for a moment that no one would forget, Kambis turned white and blue as it was enveloped by an explosion unlike any ever recorded.

CHAPTER 17
IN FLAMES

The bridge of the Triton was silent until Henrietta gently announced; "The entire planet has been struck by an antimatter explosion. There are no signs of city ruins, and most of the atmosphere has been burned away. Kambis's surface is on fire."

"Thank you, Henrietta," Oz said. "Agameg, how is the Pontos doing?"

"Energy readings indicate that their shield is holding at three percent. I believe they are drawing on power reserves, and doubt that they will survive long enough to leave the gravity of the planet and an escape into a wormhole."

"Signal the British Alliance, they are to cease heavy weapons fire immediately. Ronin is right, we are capturing that ship. People will need answers."

"Transmission sent," answered Lieutenant Commander Erron. "We have a reply."

"This is Admiral Charon, we will eliminate this threat. The weapons aboard that ship are enough to significantly damage the fleet," said a firm female voice.

"Cease fire, you are here by invitation of Triton Fleet," Oz said just as sternly.

"A moment, Admiral," replied Admiral Charon.

He turned to Agameg, "Launch all our gunships, hold on launching anything smaller. Load high yield torpedoes and prepare for single firing, we'll launch them sequentially if we have to at all. Tell the gunnery bay to load EMP rounds only and begin firing on their shields."

"Admiral McPatrick," replied Admiral Charon. "We are recalling our combat support ships and ceasing fire. Good hunting, Triton, we will be here if you need us."

"Signal the Barricade," Oz said. "They are to close and begin emitting interdiction fields so the Pontos can't get away. He looked to Panloo at the helm. "Close in, present our front and sides, do not give them a large target to fire on."

"Aye," she replied.

"Sir," Agameg said, alarm in his voice. "The Warlord and Samurai squadron are coming through a wormhole seventy thousand kilometres behind us. The Warlord is firing their thrusters in an emergency deceleration pattern. They are badly damaged, the rest of Samurai squadron is damaged, but they are reporting that they are still combat ready. Three are reporting low ammunition."

"Oz," Jake said over the emergency communications band. A hologram of him in his vacsuit armour appeared with just enough of a background to suggest that he was in his quarters. "We have a carrier, two battlecruisers, and two destroyers coming in behind us. I did my best to slow them down in the asteroid field. We've lost people, and have taken serious damage, our bridge is open to space. A few missiles brought a small group of Order Knights aboard. We have jettisoned all our escape craft with the injured aboard and they are awaiting rescue."

"Ordering British Alliance forces to support you, get clear, Warlord, and take care of your incursion," Oz replied. "We'll request that they begin a recovery operation."

"Thanks, working on it," Jake said, cocking a wide bore short rifle with four barrels.

"Open a channel to British Alliance defence," Oz said.

"This is Admiral Charon, I've been eavesdropping. We will intercept the incoming carriers, and I'm sending three corvettes to recover the Warlord's wounded. That is, if you want the help."

"Be my guest, Admiral," Oz replied. The light of an intense explosion drowned out the illumination shed by the fires on Kambis' surface for a moment. "Tactical, what was that?"

"Someone detonated a cloaked electromagnetic pulse bomb directly aft of the Pontos. It flashed no more than ten metres away from its hull. The Pontos' hull is undamaged, systems are unchanged, but its shields are gone."

"Request for communication from the Clever Dream," Lieutenant Commander Erron announced.

"Lieutenant Garrison here. Lewis wouldn't let me keep him out of this one," said the communication. "Where do you want us?"

"Remain cloaked and stand ready to assist. You're not even on the Triton's scanners, so I doubt anyone else has found your location."

"I'd rather be fighting," Lewis said.

"You will be," Oz said. "Do you happen to have any of those super EMP's left?"

"I may have six left, Admiral," Lewis replied. "Do you have a target?"

"I might, just stay out of sight for now," Oz replied.

"Fine," Lewis replied peevishly.

"All Triton Group ships, focus your fire on the Pontos' weapons and main thrusters." Oz ordered.

Victor Davis took a seat in the second command seat beside Oz. "You heard the admiral, tactical. Focus on weapons first so our fighters can get close."

"It's time, Paula," Oz said. "Launch all fighters."

"Three large wormholes opening thirty one thousand kilometres aft," Agameg announced. "The Warlord is manoeuvring to cross in front of them."

"Jake, what are you doing? I have the British closing in so they can engage."

CHAPTER 18
THE WARLORD

"We're dropping our primary EMP weapon in front of the carriers and abandoning ship," Jake replied from where he stood behind Frost, who had both hands on the manual lever for the latest version of the Big Surprise. Originally, the Big Surprise was a large electromagnetic pulse bomb that the crew built on to as various initiations and rituals were observed. The original was used during the Battle of Port Rush.

The new Big Surprise was the same size, but constructed of top-end components with heavy shielding, propulsion and guidance systems. "Drop our payload now, Frost." Jake said after making sure everyone's vacsuits were sealed.

"Aye, we barely knew ye, farewell," Frost said as he pulled the creaking lever. The bay doors swung open and the black, oblong missile was pushed into space. Its rocket engine fired immediately, thrusting towards the newly arrived Order of Eden carrier group.

"Ash, start the thruster firing sequence," Jake ordered over his communicator. He got all the confirmation he needed when he felt the deck rumble through the soles of his boots. She was in another group of survivors, surrounded by Warlord soldiers on the other side of the ship.

He'd never been so tired in his life. They had been running through the ship, shooting, fighting since the boarders' missile tubes rammed through the hull. Half the engineering crew in the

centre of the ship were injured or killed in the first three minutes.

They disabled their cloaking systems first, then the bridge
took intensive fire, and Jake barely got everyone out before it was
breached. The Order Knights were efficient, terrifying, and knew
where to hit them. They didn't care who they killed, as long as
they took the Warlord out of the fight. Jake didn't want to be
around to see the second part of their plan.

"Falling back to the aft cargo bay," Stephanie said. "They're
breaking through here."

"Here too!" Ayan said, coming down the hallway leading to
the launch room with three soldiers in tow. She slung her rifle
and closed the hatch behind her. "There are four doors between
us and them, but this is the biggest compartment."

Jake looked to the open launch doors then to Frost. "Alice is
falling back to this compartment with the rest of the survivors.
It's about do get crowded."

"What're you thinking, Jake?" Frost asked, a twinkle in his
eye.

"The whole crew will be isolated in three main compartments,
we could take the last thirteen Knights out, but there would be
heavy losses."

"But what else can we do? We have to stand and fight," Alice
said over their encrypted communications channel.

"We can still carry this fight forward," Jake said. "With help,
but not on this ship." Jake nearly fell over as he hurriedly turned
towards a control panel. His vacsuit armour helped him restore
his balance. "Can you control the maxjack from here?"

"Aye, I can use this and my control unit," Frost said.

"What? What are we doing?" Ayan asked, looking from Jake
to Frost.

"We're going to take one of those pretty battlecruisers coming
after us," Frost said.

"Exactly, and we have to stay in control of the Warlord remotely while we do this, or it could all go wrong," Jake added. "Can you coordinate with Oz and get us a few hundred soldiers? We're going to need their help."

"A few hundred?" Ayan asked, wide-eyed.

"Aye, taking the Barricade was easy," Frost said.

"It was a ship full of amateurs, greenbacks," Stephanie added over the communications channel. "We're in the rear cargo hold. Killed two Knights on the way, sealed off all entrances. We should have about ten minutes before they break through, maybe more."

"Weld armour plates over the doors, there are spares secured under the Uriel launch rails."

"I see them, on it," Stephanie said.

"Okay, so I'm ordering a couple hundred soldiers," Ayan said.

"Wait three seconds," Finn said as he stared at his command and control unit. "Two, one," he counted.

Jake's heart skipped a beat as all of his electronics flickered for a moment, but they returned to normal before there was reason to panic. "There goes the Big Surprise, I guess they didn't manage to destroy it before it went off after all."

"Open a channel now?" Ayan asked.

"Yup, hope you can get one," Frost said.

"Triton, this is Ayan aboard the Warlord," she said.

"Good to hear from you, Commodore, this is Commander Victor Davis, the Admiral is a little busy," Victor replied. "Great work on that EMP bomb, the carrier groups' shields are almost completely down. Our readings indicate that you fried a lot of electronics in the noses of those ships."

"How about the battecruisers specifically? Did any of them get hit harder than the others?" she asked.

"Three ate that blast pretty heavily, at a range of about five hundred metres. Why?"

"We want one," Ayan said. "I'm not sure what's about to happen exactly, but we are still fighting Order Knights here, and are going to change location to one of the destroyers heavily affected by our surprise. We need boarding teams to follow us in."

"Also, we need someone to blast those hangar doors open," Jake said as he finished syncing his command and control unit with the flight controls for the Warlord. He sent a signal to Ashley relieving her of pilot duties, and telling her to stand by.

"Right, so an order of boarding teams with a side of crazy pilots, if you please?" Ayan asked. "About two or three hundred of the former and as many of the latter as you can spare."

"We have a Clever Dream itching to get involved," Victor answered.

"Ronin here," Minh-Chu interjected. "Glad to see most of you made it through. Samurai squadron, support the Clever Dream's run, fire on active weaponry. We only have to clear a path to the fore hangar."

"This is Triton Flight, I'm sending three gunships and Terror Squad to assist," Chief Mendle said.

"We have our cover," Jake said under his breath. He began turning the Warlord, and one of the main thruster pods stopped firing. "We have a Knight cutting power to systems."

"Well at least he's not trying to cut through the doors like the rest of them," Stephanie retorted.

"I can still fly this thing with three main thrusters," Jake said, nodding to Frost.

"Maxjack is working fine, I don't think they know we're planning anything interesting," Frost replied.

"This is Alaka," announced a warm, low voice over their communicators. "Triton has given me command of twenty squads. I will lead them with my own. We are loading into gunships and shuttles now. Thank you."

"No, thank you!" Ayan said, excitedly.

"We begin launching in two minutes," Alaka said.

"Have you chosen a ship yet, Jake?" Ronin asked. "We kind of need to know which one we need to blow open."

"What looks good to you?" Jake said as he focused most of his attention on guiding the Warlord back into the direction of the enemy Order of Eden fleet. He only had access to basic information. The shapes of each ship with their major systems and positions relative to his ship were visible. The Warlord's sensors weren't capable of determining more.

"Well," Ronin mused nonchalantly. "I think it's between two. One is called the Blessed Mission, and it's sort of off-white, and the other is called Eternity, and it's more of a light-grey-ish." Minh-Chu waited a moment then burst; "I don't know! They're about the same, with about the same level of damage from the electromagnetic pulse, their forward sensors are equally dead. Pick left or right?"

"I'll take the Blessed Mission," Jake said, "and I already have a new name picked out."

"That's bad luck, you know," Dent said. "Renaming a ship."

"Luck is for games and fools," Jake said. "We're not playing and if we're fools, we'll be the last to know." He had the Warlord thrusting towards the Blessed Mission's main hangar and was busy making fine adjustments. "We'll be on that deck in one minute and twenty four seconds or we'll collide with that door in one minute and twenty two seconds."

"On it," Ronin replied. "We'll get that open."

"What do you want me to do? Grip the deck once we're down?" Frost asked.

"Yes, we'll have to use the maxjack like articulated landing gear," Jake said. "We'll only have three minutes to leave the War-lord once we touch down. I'm setting the autopilot so it takes off after that time then heads for the least damaged destroyer, that one there," Jake said as he marked the furthest destroyer from them on his comm unit's small holographic tactical display. "I need you to set the maxjack to grip the hull of that ship as soon as it makes contact. I'm linking the maxjack with the containment systems for our antimatter reserves."

"But, the Warlord!" Finn said.

"It's always been more a weapon than a ship," Jake said. "Today it'll be a bomb, and it's going to save lives."

"Aye," Frost said. "Easy to set up. There it is, done."

"I'll finish the antimatter link," Ayan said.

Jake saw a large explosion on the starboard side of the Blessed Mission and realized that the British Alliance was still firing on it with their largest munitions. "Oz, can you tell the British to stop shelling my new ship?" he asked over scrambled communications between the Warlord and Triton Fleet.

"This is the Triton Flight Deck, we're signalling them now and marking your target," replied Chief Mendle. "I think they were just trying to keep them off balance until the last moment."

"Tell them that they're on the hook for any holes I find once we're aboard," Jake shot back.

The last preparations were completed in silence. Jake could see enough through his sensors to know that the Clever Dream fired a vicious volley of missiles at the pair of destroyers defending the carrier central to the Order of Eden battle group, further delaying their fighter operations. The ship hadn't been able to get a single vessel off its deck since entering the area.

The fighters accompanying the Clever Dream was split between supporting the large gunship, which seemed to gleefully skip through the battlefield as it disappeared and reappeared, cloaking itself between volleys and targeting the weapons on the battlecruiser the Warlord wasn't flying towards and its two accompanying destroyers.

The enemy carrier was beginning to recharge shields and restore systems to its forward section, however, and the Order of

Eden war machine seemed to invite the British Alliance carrier groups into closer combat, as many of their long range munitions were countered before reaching their targets. Jake could see that they were headed for a close fight, the battlecruiser they planned to take could not be allowed to join the fighting, or it would have to be destroyed, regardless of whether he and his people were aboard.

"Finally," Jake sighed as a third surgical missile strike opened a large hole in the hangar doors of the Blessed Mission. The Warlord's upper port thruster scraped a jagged edge as the ship passed through. Everyone cringed as the vessel touched down hard and scraped for several metres.

Finn, Frost, Alice, Ayan and most of the people gathered in the starboard cargo area looked to Jake. "I'm rusty!" he announced with a shrug. "Disembark, quick, cover our exit. We can't let any of the Knights leave the Warlord." He picked up a shield droid with narrow treads and a one metre tall emitter rod, activated it and handed it to Alice as she passed. "Drop this ahead of you, before you go through that hatch," he told her, pointing at the doors the Big Surprise passed through only minutes before.

"Okay, hurry up and get off the ship," Alice said.

"Don't worry," Jake told her. "Just provide cover for the first group with your team."

Jake helped most of the people with him jump down through the launch doors, Ayan and Frost were the last through before he dropped through himself.

"Check in," Jake said. "My group is out."

"Alice here, my group and the Rangers are out."

"Stephanie here, my group and about three hundred two skitters are out."

Jake checked their lists against the confirmed casualty list Crewcast was keeping and nodded. One hundred sixty seven people made it off the Warlord, the dead they left behind would be cremated with the ship. The British Alliance reported that they'd located all seven of the Warlord's escape vessels and rescue operations were under way.

The hangar was illuminated by the firing thrusters of gunships taking turns dropping their soldiers off, not taking time to land, they literally walked off the debarkation ramps and fell to the deck in groups of fourteen, except for Alaka's squad of nafali soldiers, who leapt clear of their gunship. They looked even larger in their specially made vacsuit armour. The metal plates were painted with snarling faces and jagged symbols in the Nafalli language.

The deployment was so quick and practiced that the enemy defending the landing bay, hiding behind shuttles and taking cover in hatchways, were driven back by the shock of it. Three automated shield droids dropped from one of the slim Triton combat shuttles. They rolled towards the Warlord crewmembers, expanding their protective barriers to join the energy shields that were already being projected by the bots Jake and his crew had already activated. All in all, over four hundred crewmembers and armoured troops filled the main launch bay, crowding the enemy defenders, blasting them into corners and incinerating them within minutes. Jake didn't have the opportunity to fire a shot, stuck in the middle of the deployment pattern.

A hatch from the Warlord burst open and an Order Knight emerged, his shield bending the light around him. The force of every soldier and crewman left from the Warlord was on him before he could fire a shot. Within three seconds, the landed boarding crews joined in.

Jake only had a chance to fire two of his explosive shells before there was nothing left of the Knight but a narrow crater on the deck. The timer for the Warlord's departure continued to count down, and Jake couldn't stop glancing at it. "Clear the hangar doors," he ordered as it counted down to nine. The boarding crew craft did their best to move to the side, leave, or hover near the deck.

The Warlord's thrusters pulsed, then fired gently, lifting up with a precarious wobble before backing out through the hole in the launch doors. Jake took a deep breath as it disappeared from sight. "Give 'em hell, one last time," he said. "Thanks for keeping us alive."

Alaka dropped down with one other member of his boarding crew. He'd replaced the fighter class weapon he once carried with a new two barrel weapon that was only a little shorter, still nearly as tall as Ayan, who stood beside Jake. From what he could see, the top portion was some kind of beam weapon, while the bottom barrel was a rapid fire shrapnel gun, made to rip through infantry but not through thick hull plates. "Where do you want us, Captain?" Alaka asked.

"Now that's a sight," Frost muttered wide eyed at the towering pair of Nafali.

"Alice's squad and the maintenance crew will clear the ships in this bay. Stephanie's people will go with you. How does the main causeway look?"

"Our scans show troops regrouping there," Alaka replied. "They are blocking the only way to the bridge."

"We're going to take it in one rush, cloaked. Remmy's Rangers are going to start heading for engineering, just in case the crew decides to try to activate a self-destruct. I'd like him to take half the boarding teams with him."

"Aye," Alaka replied. "There may not be enough room for them to move through the choke points."

"Use lesser routes, clear rooms as best as you can along the way," Jake said. "Remmy will be able to direct them in more detail, he's one of the best Rangers I've seen."

"Aye, they will follow his orders," Alaka said.

"All units, engage cloaking systems," Jake ordered. In the space of seven seconds it appeared as though every crewmember from the Warlord, and every boarder from the Triton disappeared. Jake knew that the odds that Regent Galactic technology had caught up to their cloaking systems were very low. The ship would be theirs if they could avoid any serious missteps.

CHAPTER 19
VICTORY'S END

Oz could feel the slightest impression of what was going on between Hausgiest and the being at the core of the other ship. After all the time he'd spent mentally connected to Hausgiest, learning about him, asking him questions about his existence, he'd never considered that the heart of a Sol Defence ship could hate another of its kind. There it was, at the edge of Oz's perception, the awareness that Hausgiest was trying to calm the Pontos' living intelligence down, to ease its hatred of him and the crew Hausgiest's extended body, the Triton, was host to.

"Admiral," Agameg addressed from his station at tactical. "That last torpedo took out the Pontos' main thrusters, they are adrift with minimal thrust power."

"Hold fire," Oz ordered. "All stations; hold fire. Get me a deep scan of that ship, I want to know everything now that her shields are down, right down to the DNA of the captain," he said. "What is wrong with this thing?" he said under his breath. "Why are we so significant to Citadel that they've trained their intelligence to hate us?"

Victor only gave him a momentary glance. He was aware that there was something more going on in Oz's head, a discussion that would come up later, Oz was sure.

'The being in control of the Pontos was tortured,' Hausgiest replied telepathically. 'Another controller, older than me, was in its mind. It is a believer in Citadel, perhaps a component of its leadership. It tortured him, it brainwashed the heart of the Pontos into believing in the Order of Eden, in a destiny that required the success of this mission, but it took months of torture.'

'That's possible?' Oz asked mentally.

'Only in the young,' Hausgeist replied. 'He wants to show me the conviction of his belief! He is pushing his reactors past their limit to charge his shields so he can buy time to prepare another planetary attack weapon. This time he's going to detonate it while it's still inside the ship! He wants to destroy all the ships in range.'

"Could we break through its shields?" Oz asked aloud, forgetting that the people around him could not hear Hausgiest's last statement.

"They are drawing power from their last planetary weapon," Hausgiest replied through the bridge sound system. "Their shields will be fully charged in nine seconds."

"Fire all weapons, reverse away from the Pontos," Oz ordered. "Maintain fire while we retreat behind Kambis' horizon." He sat in the command seat and looked at the tactical display for a moment. The Barricade and the British Alliance were moving to close on the Order of Eden carrier group, which was too close to the Pontos. The only segment of combattants that weren't already too close to the Pontos, and drawing closer, were the mid-sized ships in Triton Fleet, who were returning to Tamber orbit just in case there was a third prong to the Order's offensive. "Open a channel to all ships," Oz said. "This is Admiral Mc-Patrick. The Pontos is about to self destruct, get as much distance as you can. Fire on that ship if you can, maybe we can knock out some of its powered systems."

"Sir, one of the Pontos' gunships is hailing us on an open channel," announced communications.

"Let's hear it," Oz said.

"Triton Command, most of the crew aboard that ship are dead, the intelligence and the first officer have taken control. They have activated another antimatter cluster weapon. We surrender and request asylum. Our weapons are powering down."

"Is there any way to shut it down?" Oz asked.

"No, you must get as much distance as you can or get your fleet on the other side of the planet."

"Can you get there yourself?" Oz asked.

"We have about ten minutes before it activates, so, yes, but not with every ship in the system firing on us," replied the pilot.

Oz silenced his side of the communication using his command and control unit. "You scanned their ship?" he asked the analysts to his left.

"We did, his missile bay is empty, and their weapons are powered down. Approximately nine percent shield power left. There are no signs of antimatter, and the gunship is powered using a pair of fusion reactors that cannot be set to explode."

"Do your scans confirm what he's saying?"

"Yes," Henrietta said without a hint of doubt in her tone. "I have been able to confirm everything the Triton AI and this defector are saying with our scan data."

"All right," Oz said. He turned to communications. "We've got our prisoner then. Notify all forces that they are not to be fired upon unless they open fire. They are our prisoners. We'll take physical control of their shuttle when we've gotten distance from the Pontos." He turned the channel to the gunship back on. "Pilot, you are clear to pass through our space and join us on the other side of Kambis. Stay close to the Triton, do not arm weapons. We will perform boarding operations as soon as we're clear of this situation."

"Thank you, Admiral," replied the pilot. The channel closed.

The main tactical display on the bridge made it clear that the entire Triton Fleet, including the Barricade, was in retreat along with the British Alliance. Most of the Order of Eden carrier group were too damaged to make good speed out of the system, but one destroyer was able to make it into a wormhole as soon as the Barricade's interdiction systems were turned away from it.

"Any word on how the Warlord crew's boarding operation is going? What am I seeing here?" Oz asked as he focused in on an image of the Warlord lightly colliding with the side of an Order of Eden Battlecruiser.

"Captain Valent converted his ship into an antimatter bomb," Agameg said. "So once it struck the side of that vessel, the Eternity, it would clamp on with the maxjack and explode like a focused charge. The Eternity, the Blessed Mission and the Redeemer Three, the main combat carrier all opened fire on the Warlord with directed electromagnetic pulse beams before it could complete its task, so it will not explode. The antimatter containment fail safes are in place, and the Warlord is now empty and relatively harmless."

"That's something I never thought I'd hear. The Warlord: empty and relatively harmless," Victor said. "I sent Captain Valent a message about our new problem. He tells me they will be able to take control of the Blessed Mission and get her out of the way in time."

"That's insane. Recall all fighters and order the gunships to move to the other side of the planet," Oz said. "What can our shields do to protect us against the blast?"

"We're working on that math right now," Henrietta said hurriedly. "Let me guess, you want to know if you can move the Triton in right here," she highlighted a spot on the map in front of the Blessed Mission, seemingly far from the Pontos on the tactical map. "Then charge up our shields to protect it."

"Exactly."

"Nope, not going to work," Henrietta said, shaking her head. "That blast is going to be way too hot. If this second planet burner has as much antimatter as the first, then there's no way."

"Jake," Oz said, opening a direct channel. "You have to get that ship into a wormhole, you have about eight minutes, maybe less."

Chapter 20
Rushing The Blessed Mission

Jake fired all four barrels of his short rifle at the blast doors in front of him. The gel loads covered a two metre wide section and filled the hallway with white light as it began burning through the metal. "Working on getting to the bridge now. Any advice you could offer would be appreciated."

"Do you think you'll make it?" Oz asked.

Jake looked to Ayan, who was scanning the door as the gel burned through. "That'll take ninety three seconds to get through," she said. "There will be soldiers on the other side."

"Any way around?" Jake asked as he looked at his tactical display. Their scans of the ship were complete, but that offered little comfort as he realized that there was no way around that bulkhead.

"No," Minh-Chu said from behind him. "Dent and I already did some stealthed recon. This whole front section of the ship is closed off, and this door is the thinnest point."

Ayan gave him a brief hug. "What are you doing here?"

"Someone left the front door wide open and we were out of ammo, so I thought we'd visit," Minh-Chu said. "The whole Samurai Squadron is stealthing around looking for a place for a hull buster Sticky had. Bad time?"

The hallway shook as heavy weapons fire announced the progress of Alaka's team. Jake looked to the white light of the thermalitic gel burning through the blast doors then back to

Minh-Chu. "Good timing, I think Alaka's team just cornered the Order squad he was tracking."

"Cargo bay three, Captain," Alaka announced through his communicator. "We could use some help. The enemy may retreat in your direction."

"Is there a good place to break through with a hull buster over there?" Jake asked as he dropped two mines in front of the door he was burning through.

"As good as any, a nice wide loading door leading aft," Alaka replied.

"That's hilarious," Dent said to Minh-Chu. "They'll come through the door thinking there's a whole bunch of us waiting for them once it burns through and…"

"We all get the picture," Minh-Chu said. "After those go off, this whole hallway will be impossible to get through. You have a really dark idea of funny."

The group started running, following the three heavily armoured guards in front of Jake and Ayan, who were equally armoured. Jake was thankful for the mild stims that were keeping him going, and the vacsuit that was helping him keep his balance. He tried to reload his quad barrel rifle while running, but decided to wait when he nearly fumbled his shells. "How is the access to the rest of the ship?"

"I'm headed to Alaka's position too," Remmy said. "All the systems in the forward section of the ship are dead. Some thanks to electromagnetic pulse damage, others have been cut off from engineering, I assume to keep us from taking control."

"This is a smart crew," Jake said. "I hate that." He stowed his quad barrel rifle and did his best to let his vacsuit teach him to run, keep him balanced and moving forward. He'd never been so tired in his life, sweat dripped down his face. He was thankful that his suit had a system that gently dried him and sequestered the sweat for processing along with other waste.

The dark run down the hallways was a quick one, they had no time to waste. According to his timer, the Triton expected the Pontos to explode in five minutes and fifty-seven seconds. "Alaka, get your people behind cover and stop firing on the enemy immediately. I've got to try something before we all get slagged." He stopped in front of a pair of large doors that led into cargo bay three.

"Aye, finding cover and ceasing fire," Alaka said.

"Oh, and use your stealth systems to get into position if you can, this might not work," Jake said. He took a few seconds to catch his breath then opened communications on all channels. "This is Captain Valent, looking to contact the Captain of the Blessed Mission. I would like to offer a ceasefire so we can take a wormhole away from Kambis. The Pontos is about to explode, taking this ship and its crew with it."

The response was so immediate that it surprised Jake. "Never," said a young male voice. "I would have destroyed this ship already if I wasn't sure we would repel your attack and take you captive. Your ship is adrift outside, our sister ship survived your ill-conceived attack. Now I will have the honour of watching you die with us. My immortal frame will preserve me, and I-"

Jake closed the channel, cutting him off. "All units, this is now a seek and destroy mission. Take no prisoners, give no quarter unless our enemy approaches without weapons and hands raised. We are not going to the bridge, our new goal is to get to the nearest working control node and to get this ship to safety. Anyone standing in the way of our mission is to be killed quickly, efficiently. Execute my orders immediately."

Jake could feel an explosion from the cargo bay on the other side of the door, and the rumble of gunfire. His tactical display updated with information from Remmy's team. They were about to join the fighting through the cargo bay door on the opposite side.

"You all right?" Ayan asked.

He hadn't realized it, but he was still breathing heavily. He ordered a round of fortifying medications and stims through his command and control unit and drew his quad rifle. His thoughts seemed to focus, the urgent need for air abated, allowing him to get his breathing under control, and he even felt firmer on his feet. "Better than ever," Jake said.

"About time we got about the business of taking this ship," Frost said.

"Aye," Jake agreed. He nodded towards Stephanie and her boarding team, and they pulled the manual lever for the door. The tall pair of cargo bay doors opened, revealing an unfair firefight. Alaka's team, sixty three Triton troops and Remmy's Rangers had the last of the Order of Eden soldiers cornered. There was another group sneaking through the corridors around the cargo bay just in case reinforcements were needed.

Jake could see there was still a little hesitation in how his orders were being executed. The Order of Eden group, reduced to only four, had been driven back behind a stack of heavily armoured metal crates. They were peeking out from behind to burst fire at their enemies whenever their shields were charged just enough. There was no time to press a surrender.

Jake set the firing power on his quad barrel rifle low, and angled it up. He fired the first grenade in a smooth arc so it landed right beside the crates. It was a miss, but close enough for him to find his range. One of the hold-outs was frightened out of cover and was immediately torn apart by the boarding team's weapons. Jake fired two more grenades and hit the mark, incinerating the rest. "Let's get that hull buster up here, now!" Jake ordered. To his surprise, three hull busters were brought forward by the boarding parties in addition to the one carried by a rather short and slender pilot from behind him. "Um, do you really still need mine?" she asked.

172 · RANDOLPH LALONDE

"Damn right we do," Stephanie said, "Thanks Sticky, we're going to make sure there are extra ration credits loaded for our new galley once we get through this." She took the hull buster and led her boarding party back down the hallway they came.

The rest of the boarding parties affixed the circular shaped plasma charges to the three interior cargo bay doors that led into the main section of the ship. In the meantime, Jake opened another comm channel on all frequencies. "Your Captain has sealed your fate. I have ordered my teams to execute anyone who does not surrender the instant we make contact. Those who surrender will be treated fairly, and most importantly, you will survive this because we will get this ship out of the radius of the Pontos' self destruct action. You can broadcast your surrender signal to me on any channel, I will receive it." Jake was surprised to hear an ear-stinging guffaw of a laugh over the secure boarding party channel.

"Oh, c'mon Remmy, what's so funny?" Alice chastised. "We're about to get slagged because of a bunch of religious fanatic idiots."

"I don't know, it shouldn't be funny, I'm sorry, maybe it's the tension," Remmy said through suppressed laughter. "Still working the mission, Captain, don't worry."

"Weirdo-butthead," Alice shot back.

"All right," Ayan said, "let's get ready to breach those doors." The skitters who abandoned the Warlord with them, along with the shield droid that survived the initial fighting in the landing bay rushed between them.

Jake followed as the hull busters fired. Super-hot plasma melted through the doors. The armoured cup that focused the plasma heated to red by the time they were finished. The shield droid moved ahead while the skitters leapt onto the interior doors and pried the circular hull busters off before the boarding teams had time to get to it.

A gust of atmosphere from the other side of the door rushed out, pulling a crewman in a flimsy vacsuit through the middle door. Jake, Ayan, Minh-Chu and several of their comrades couldn't help but flinch sympathetically as the crewman bounced off a heavy crate, pinwheeled through the air, rebounded off the ceiling then crashed against the far wall of the cargo bay. "Think he survived that?" Frost asked. "Poor lad."

"Nope, definitely not," replied one Warlord soldier from behind.

"Hold your fire!" shouted someone from the inside. "We surrender!" shouted another. The atmosphere on the other side was held in by an isolation field of a type Jake had never seen before, keeping the rest of an engineering team safe on the other side. "We work for Regent Galactic, the contract with the Order isn't worth this!" exclaimed a third. The dashes across the chest of his thin navy blue vacuum suit marked him as a Quality Assurance Manager, equivalent in rank to a Junior Chief.

There were forty-two of them, all gathered in a main concourse intersection. "We've got a terminal open for you right there," their leader said shakily, pointing just behind him as he slowly lowered himself to the deck, putting his hands behind his head. "My password and clearance chip are already in."

Ayan rushed forward, the skitters around her heels. By the time she got to the panel, the skitters had pulled a line from the console free. They held it out so she could connect it to her command and control unit. "Installing our flag software, here's hoping the operating system here is close enough to the Barricade's for this to work."

Jake checked what was happening through his command and control unit. The flag software uploaded seamlessly and overwrote the permissions files for the ship in seconds, replacing them with new files that made the ship property of Triton Fleet, locking out all but two security codes. If it weren't for the surrender of one of their enemies with an access code, it would have taken much longer to work. How much longer, Jake could only guess, but with two minutes and one second left on the clock before the Pontos exploded, he guessed it would have been too much. "I need someone to do the calculations here," Ayan said.

Minh-Chu and Ashley both rushed forward under the protection of several boarding team members. "Can you just get us out of the solar system please?" asked Frost. "No fancy calculations necessary, just get us far enough."

"Shush, that's the plan," Ashley said. "Here, Minh, check my math," she said, stepping away from the console.

"She's done?" asked one of their new prisoners. "That's too fast, that can't be right."

Jake nudged him in the side with his boot as he passed. "Silence is survival," he growled. He didn't want to kill anyone else, but he didn't have to let his captives know.

"It's good, generating wormhole, tipping the ship into it, and catching the Warlord against the port wing," he said.

Jake flinched and sucked air in through his teeth as he heard a distant collision and scraping sound.

"Don't worry, Captain," Frost said with a chuckle, "It'll buff right out."

* * *

"All fighters recovered," Chief Mendle announced from the flight deck beneath Oz's feet. "All but one of our gunships are out of the danger area, rescue operations on Ripsaw's gunship were successful, he and his Senoir Operations Officer are stable in stasis."

"Bring them aboard as soon as the Triton is clear," Oz said. He looked back to the tactical hologram in the centre of the bridge. He was on his feet, staring at the Blessed Mission as it slowly collided with the Warlord, heading for a wormhole it had just generated. "I wouldn't have thought of that," he muttered.

"C'mon, Jake," Victor said from beside him, startling Oz.

He looked back to the tactical display in time to see the Blessed Mission slip into the wormhole. The Warlord was precariously balanced against a port side section of hull that jutted out three times as wide as the smaller ship. "Minh, if that works, you'll be the talk of the Pilot's Den for weeks."

"He'll be the talk of the pilot's den for months if it doesn't," Victor remarked.

The battlecruiser and the Warlord disappeared from sight as they finished transitioning into the wormhole, leaving two Order of Eden destroyers and their carrier behind. The destroyers manoeuvred in front of the carrier, shuttles moved from them to the larger ship at a frenzied pace. The thick landing bay doors closed, leaving several shuttles stranded.

The timer estimating when the Pontos would explode counted down from one minute and ten seconds. "How accurate is that?" Victor asked.

Oz looked to his analysis team. Henrietta and the analyst beside her both shrugged. "Could be off by as much as thirty seconds," she said.

"Fifty, maybe even more," added the officer beside her.

She shot him a withering look.

"Well, true, right?" he whispered back.

She only had time to nod once before the sensors aboard the Triton were overloaded with an antimatter explosion larger than anyone in that solar system had ever seen.

"I'm sorry," Oz said before the light diminished.

'It's all right,' Hausgiest replied in his thoughts. 'The Pontos was so consumed with hate, and so corrupted by the cause of Citadel, that there was no saving him.'

"Hausgiest, could you determine the enemy ship's cause? Why are Citadel getting involved with the Order of Eden?" he asked as the bridge crew watched their systems reset. Oz wanted the crew to hear the answer, it had already made its mark on his mind.

"The Citadel crew had the Pontos' intelligence fully convinced that once the Order's enemies were defeated, they would turn towards the Sol System. The Order of Eden has promised Citadel their assistance in taking control of the home world. The Pontos believed that we were allied with Sol Defence because of our involvement with the Lorander Corporation."

"Why would our connection with Lorander make anyone think we were with Sol Defence?" Victor asked.

"I plan on asking them that as soon as we've finished securing orbital space. Have our allies checked in?" Oz asked.

"The British Alliance and the Barricade have checked in," Agameg replied. "The rest are coming in slowly as they recover from the blast."

"The carrier group?" Oz asked as he watched the tactical display slowly repopulate and update.

"The enemy carrier is severely damaged. Main thrusters are destroyed, their transponder is broadcasting an automated emergency signal. The battlecruiser and the destroyer that were holding position in front of the carrier are dead in space, sensors are still resetting, but I doubt we will find survivors."

"Any report from Tamber?" Oz asked.

"They were on the other side of Kambis," Henrietta said quietly. "Haven Shore is fine, they had a minor flash, only two of our military installations are down as far as I can tell."

"I think its safe to assume they lost power in the flash," added Lieutenant Commander Erron. "Their emergency drills put reset time at roughly nine minutes for the eastern-most base, and six minutes and thirty two seconds for our base at Un-Tam. I'll tell you as soon as they report in. Cursory scans forwarded from British Alliance Command confirm that our bases are still there, life signs are consistent with their expected compliment."

"That's something," Oz said. "Did our British Alliance or Lorander friends lose anything in the blast?"

"The British lost a minor orbital platform, but everyone got out in time. Lorander is fine," replied Lieutenant Commander Erron.

"Flight," Oz said, looking through the floor. It did not become transparent, and his seat did not rebroadcast his voice to the level below. He walked to the ramp instead. "How long until we can get ships to the Blessed Mission?"

"I don't know," Chief Mendle said. "Everything's still rebooting, the Triton may have weathered that pulse fine, but our fighters will take a minute. I'm not going to launch anything without a diagnostic. Our new gunships are all fine though, Clever Dream already checked in and wants to go after them."

"Tell Leiutenant Garrison to go ahead. He can have any gunship that's still in fighting shape to go with him," Oz replied.

"British Alliance Navnet just went down," one of the Flight Crew announced. "Critical transmitter failure."

"What about Haven Shore?" Oz asked.

"They're good, but three of the communications satellites they use to forward commands are down," Chief Mendle said. "Looks like we'll have to move into position and become a relay until we can get satellites in position around what's left of Kambis."

"Let me guess, everything on that side of Kambis is-"

"Obliterated!" Chief Mendle said, throwing up her hands. "Ka-frikkin-boom!"

"All right, looks like the Triton is stuck here for a while, coordinate with the Barricade, see if we can get some help," Oz said.

"What? From those untrained monkeys? The only place I wouldn't take directions from a Ranger is space, especially when they've barely had time to learn to point their *own ship* in the right direction. No thanks, we're fine, Admiral. We'll keep ships from colliding into each other and get temporary relay sattellites back in orbit by the end of our shift. But hey, while we're talking about help, why don't you open communications with the Lorander ship over there? Maybe they'll give us a hand with clean up after staying out of a fight that cost us a resource-rich planet and nearly burned Tamber back into the stone age."

"Tell me if there's anything we can do," Oz said, returning to the bridge.

"I love how she takes an attack on the ship personally," Victor said. "Not that I don't."

"I know, I'm just glad her language has improved since she became a mom," Oz replied.

'You would not be so impressed if you could hear her thoughts,' Hausgiest told him telepathically. 'I have never sensed such irritation. It goes beyond what language could share.'

"Let's see if we can get a few more people down there to help her direct traffic," Oz told Victor.

"Good idea," he replied, standing up and starting for the Flight Deck.

Chapter 21
Lead From The Middle

With the first group of captives taken and bound behind them, the crew moved on, leaving a single stealthed squad to watch over their prisoners. Jake, Minh-Chu, Alice and Ayan were exploring corridors well behind one of the forward groups. In his current condition, Jake couldn't bring himself to inconvenience one of the forward boarding teams by joining their number. Stephanie, Alaka and Remmy had it well in hand. Besides, he wanted to stay near Ayan, Minh-Chu, and the least armoured members of his crew behind them.

Three heavily armoured soldiers took the lead as they carefully traversed the central section of the ship. Most of them hadn't been on a simulated boarding operation, let alone the real thing. Jake knew they were the safest group with Alaka's squads ahead, Stephanie's to the right, and Remmy's Rangers to the left. Alice's squad moved behind them as a rear guard.

The first minutes after exiting the wormhole were the worst. The ship was silent except for the diminishing hums of systems powering down. It took only minutes to get everyone organized into their squads and moving. They all scanned rooms as they moved. Alaka's boarding teams across the front of their formation took the most captives as they went, killing only five soldiers, stunning and binding thirty-seven crewmembers.

Jake listened in on the action, which was quick in every case, wishing he was at the front. Everyone in command knew that would be a mistake, including him. He was being kept on his feet by stims, his balance was assisted by his suit. He could still give competent commands from the centre of their troops formation. That was his best role.

The first escape pod to launch was the most startling. It happened just ahead and two decks above them, a loud ping and the blast of a booster firing against the interior door. It was followed by several more, Jake lost count after seventeen. "How many people per pod?" Jake asked.

"Twenty eight," Ayan replied. "Every fifth one has a micro wormhole generator. It'll take them about an hour to charge."

"That explains why we're finding so few crew," Alaka said. "There is no fight here, our scans show nineteen life signs aft."

Jake looked at the tactical readouts of the rear of the ship in time to see the nine life signs move rapidly away from the ship, obviously in a pod. "There they go," Jake said. A movement in the corner of his eye caught his attention, and he looked up just in time to see a trio of grenades bounce across the hallway in front of them. "Everyone down!" Jake said as he raised his rifle and tried to fire at the grenades with a gel suspension round, meant to expand around a target and affix it to a surface. He didn't know if the gel round would help in the least, but it was all he had time to do.

The explosion struck him and the three soldiers in front of him before he could tell if he got the round off. Smoke and fire filled the broad causeway after the initial explosion, and Jake was immediately on his feet. His heads up display informed him that painkillers had been administered locally, nanobots and recovery injections were administered before he was fully on his feet. One of the soldiers in front of him was already being put into emergency stasis, the other two were unconscious, and their automated medical systems were treating them. Ayan's life signs were solid, but her armour was ruptured on the left hand side. Her arm was broken and burned, something the nanobots and recovery meds were already taking care of. Everyone else got off lucky.

A shadow moved towards them through the black smoke at great speed. Jake was almost fully on his feet, and lowered his shoulder into the oncoming shape. "Get back!" Jake said as he felt the heavy form collide with him hard enough to knock him onto his back. The enemy soldier's shields were up, the sensation of a shield clashing with metal was unmistakeable. He could feel the stock of a rifle trapped under his left leg, and he scrambled for it as he saw the shape of an Order Knight in full armour.

The hallway was filled with bright flashing light from his right, Ayan was down on one knee, firing a rifle loaded with anti-framework rounds on full automatic. He could hear her screaming through her clenched teeth as the nearby explosions of dozens of rounds on her enemy and the wall behind him immediately raised the temperature of that section of the hallway past what normal skin could tolerate. Her bare arm and a small section of her shoulder were scorched by the time her suit created a thin emergency seal.

The Order Knight was across the corridor before Jake could stop him, knocking Ayan's rifle out of her hands and sending her several metres down the hallway. By the time he turned towards Jake, he had the rifle that was trapped under his leg in hand, and he opened fire.

With the Order Knight less than two metres away, he was able to fire eleven rounds before the Knight grabbed the rifle out of his hands as though Jake was a toddler and the weapon was a toy. A monofilament blade emerged from the Knight's wrist armour.

A flash of silver passed between Jake and the Knight before he could bring his weapon down on Jake, and his enemy seemed to hesitate. Jake looked up and saw Minh-Chu standing off to the side with a nanoblade raised high, it had the hilt of a traditional samurai sword. "Fall down," he said as he kicked the Order Knight's shoulder. The Knight's head rolled free.

Jake was up and at Ayan's side in the next instant. The crisis was over, but there could be more Knights nearby.

"Come in, Jake, we read weapon's fire in your section and are responding," Remmy said urgently.

Ayan nodded as Jake helped her up. "Emergency treatment's taking care of me, I'm okay."

"This is Ronin," Minh-Chu said in response to Remmy's communication. "We're all right, but we're going to have to increase the intensity of our scans and re-clear the ship. We had to put down an Order Knight here. Getting ready to dispose of it now," he said as he helped one of the soldiers who were in the front up.

"All right, we'll start a volumetric scan of the ship interior," Remmy said. "We're near a primary terminal, looks like flight operations. Requesting cover while we get ready to fly this bird home. Pretty sure we have tow systems so we can bring the Warlord with us."

"I'll send two squads your way, Remmy. Another two squads are already on their way to the Captain's group," Alaka replied. "Volumetric scanning shows movement in sector twenty one. There is at least one more Knight aboard. We are moving to close around him. Don't worry about any more Knights or spooks, Captain, we know they're here, and we will finish this hunt for you. Get your group together and move to the Ranger's position. That is the most secure position aboard."

"Acknowledged, we'll head over as soon as we finish cleaning up here," he replied. Jake couldn't help but look at Ayan for an extra moment. Her heavy armour was split open on the left side, but the temporary vacsuit had closed the gap, and his medical readings on her said she was completely healed. He was left with the thought that he could have lost her just moments before, and he could have been killed if it wasn't for her. "You saved my ass there," he said. "Kicked some too."

"I don't train with the Rangers for nothing," Ayan said. "You did pretty well yourself, but I think we both owe Minh a drink."

They joined Minh-Chu as he picked up the remains of the Order Knight. Jake's command and control unit warned him that the Knight was already beginning to regenerate a new head. The warning on his heads up display was enough to spur everyone into motion. "Do we blow him up here?" asked Ashley, who looked frazzled and worried.

Jake looked around for a moment then noticed something on the map display inside his visor. "Nearest airlock, this way!" he said as he put himself under one arm of the heavy Order Knight. "I'm calling dibs on his rifle," Jake said as he and Minh-Chu dragged him through a hatchway to the right, down a ramp then into a debarkation room made for droids and crewmembers tasked with making repairs on the outer hull. They dropped him on top of the airlock hatch at their feet.

"Wait!" Ayan said, running to catch up, holding the Knight's de-helmed head at arms length with both hands. "His head!"

"Yup," Jake said as he folded a grenade and the last three explosive rounds he had for his ruined quad rifle into the Knight's chest armour.

Minh-Chu accepted the head and put it down on the hatch. "This is for you," he said to it as he pushed a grenade into its mouth and set the timer to three minutes to match the timer Jake had set.

Jake punched the inner door button. The hatch opened and the Order Knight's corpse fell into the outer hatch. "Did it look like his eyes are moving?" Jake asked.

"No, it's all in your head," Minh-Chu said, prompting an "Oh, God!" response from where Dent watched with everyone else at the end of the hallway. "Cheesy!"

"Silence! Jinxy pilot!" Minh-Chu shouted over his shoulder as they watched the inner door close behind the Order Knight.

"All right, adding a little extra pressure to the outer cabin," Jake said as he turned one of the environmental dials.

"Everyone say buh-bye to the Knight who tried to murder us," Minh-Chu said as he floppily waved his hand at the Knight's corpse through the airlock window.

Jake looked over his shoulder at the small crowd that had gathered at the end of the service hallway in time to see most of them emulating Minh-Chu's wave and saying 'buh-bye." He tapped the button to open the exterior door then pressed YES when the control screen asked him if he was sure.

The Order Knight and his head were sent out into space along with the rush of pressurized air in the airlock. Several people, Ashley and Dent included, squeezed into the service hallway so they could watch through the airlock window. "How long did you guys set the timer?" asked Dent.

"Three minutes," Jake replied.

"That seems long now," Minh-Chu said.

"I know, right?" Ayan remarked. "I can't even see him any-more."

"Better safe than sorry," Dent replied.

"There he is," Minh-Chu said, pointing through the window. "My scanner says he's got a new head and he's just about to wake up."

"That could be trouble," Jake muttered. "If he-" He was inter-rupted by a flash of light in the distance. "Nevermind," Jake said with a smile.

"You sure that got him?" Dent asked.

"Disintegration grenade," Jake replied. "One of my last ones."

"Those are illegal pretty much everywhere, aren't they?" Dent asked.

"Let's see about joining Remmy in that control room," Jake said. "I have a crew here that would like to get warmed up to their new ship while it gets cleared."

CHAPTER 22
THE IMPORTANCE OF BEING FLEXIBLE

Industrial buildings always seemed depressing to Governor Tate. Blockish factories, fabrication buildings that stretched out for kilometres, and refineries that grew up like forests of tubes and towers. The business of industrial support for a modern solar system was a dirty one. To be told that the Mother of the Order of Eden would be landing in the middle of one such industrial forest, atop the Xane Company building, was a shock. The change in her plans was inconvenient. He had security set up for the space she was supposed to use. Now it would be used to play a giant holographic version of whatever happened on top of the boring, dirty space she'd chosen at the last minute.

There was nothing special about that building, it was only a cap for an industrial lake. From the outside it looked like a flat roofed structure that was two storeys tall with a landing field atop it, and landing fields around. It was where they stored refined materials that were ready for transport off world. If she said something he would regret, he would have to smooth things over with the people at Xane, one of his top one hundred taxpayers.

He was there at the appointed time, with his four Order Knights and no one else, as he was told. Standing on the top of the Xane Company building, he had time to admire the optical illusion of the place's flat top. It was so large that the reflection of the morning sun against the metal tricked the eye into seeing a silvery lake in the distance. Governor Tate knew there was no water on the roof, it hadn't rained over Xane Company territory for months. He remembered hearing that what he was seeing was once called a mirage effect.

"People who were wandering the desert used to be tricked by mirages like these," he said aloud, pointing across the rooftop. "Like that, the shimmer in the distance there." His Order Knights, who were most likely as bored as he was, stepped a little closer so they could hear him. They hung on his every word. "The sand is really quartz on most worlds, and the sun would create reflections on it. At a distance you'd see what looked like water. Some would run towards it, others would keep trudging on, and all of the dead would be found on their bellies. Skeletons frozen in the act of reaching for something that was almost never there."

"That's rather dark for such a nice morning, Governor," said a voice behind him.

The Order Knights whirled, raising their rifles at Wheeler, who only smiled and half raised his hands. "I come in peace."

"It's all right," Governor Tate said. "If this one wanted to kill me, I would have been found in pieces weeks ago."

"Would you be found at all?" Wheeler asked, cocking his head and smiling a little.

The Order Knights lowered their rifles and allowed Wheeler into the protective box formation they maintained around the Governor. "How was your time away?"

"I didn't go far, just had to reassure my small crew," Wheeler said. "Had a strategic talk with a few of them, sent another pair off on an errand. With Citadel here, it's amazing what kind of information I can tap into."

"Like?" Governor Tate asked.

"Logs from the Triton, ending about a year ago," Wheeler said. "They had someone aboard who transmitted everything. As far as Citadel can tell, no one on the Triton knows the leak happened."

"Do you think I could get a copy?" Governor Tate asked, waving his hand low, indicating to his guards that he was all right. He started walking away from them, and Wheeler followed.

"That depends if you're still the real power in this solar system by the time Eve is finished here," Wheeler replied.

"I get the feeling there's a lot you're not telling me." Governor Tate said. Everything he saw so far about this visit was unnerving. He could learn almost nothing about Citadel from the networks, and everything he found advised travellers to stay away from their ships, their bases if one was found, or to leave anyone who claimed to be from Citadel alone. Everything online told him to run in the other direction if he saw one, but the problem was that they were there, in his solar system, and he had a distinct feeling that they wanted something from him, something he didn't want to part with. "Something about this, here, today, and I think it's time you started letting me in on all the intelligence you've been gathering. Intelligence that someone like you, someone who can escape notice in Regent Galactic territory, can get to."

"You know, there's something I like about you Governor," Wheeler replied. "So I think I will start sharing. I think it's time, but you have to start moving faster on delivering on your promise. I need ships."

"I will," Governor Tate said with more enthusiasm than was honest.

"I've learned about Citadel, it cost me a G-Terminal, but I was able to hack into their basic information systems," Wheeler replied. "And what they keep in their lowest security data storage would put you down on your knees in supplication, so whatever happens today, keep piety in mind."

"In my own solar system?" Governor Tate said, irritated at Wheeler's statements as much as he barely knew what the man was talking about. "What is a G-Terminal, anyway?"

"It's a low-latency communications unit that hides the user by piggybacking on the identification of other people accessing a network. I was connected long enough to get what I wanted, and probably a few things you want, but it's going to cost you."

"What? What do you have and what will it cost me?" Governor Tate asked.

"Let's just get through this," Wheeler said, gesturing at the crowd gathering on the landing field below the edge of the roof. There were hundreds there, but there was room for a hundred thousand or more on the large concrete landing field. A few workers were already setting up a barricade on the rooftop sixty metres from where they stood. "You'll have a better idea of what you need afterwards, and I'll know how soon I'll need those ships."

For the first time since Wheeler appeared in his apartment, Governor Tate took a good look at the man. He had scraggly long hair down to his shoulders, his face didn't conform to the kind of attractiveness that fashion dictated in his sector, the narrow, almost pretty man-boy that was idolized on most of his worlds was entirely absent. Wheeler's face was broad, with strong, expressive features, and he didn't look young, he looked almost wind-worn, at least that was what his face seemed like that day. Was that Wheeler's true face? It was the one the Governor had seen on wanted notices from the British Alliance.

Wheeler didn't sport a sidearm, but he still had that waist length jacket. There were espionage devices in there, his scans told him weeks ago, electronic parts, and strange drugs no one on his staff could put a purpose to. The boots Wheeler wore were military, and they looked old, scuffed. If anything, Governor Tate would say that Wheeler looked like a constant traveller. "What really brought you here?" he asked him. "Honestly, without giving me an answer that leads to more questions."

Wheeler seemed intrigued by the question. He watched the masses gather below, dozens at a time as he answered. A few transit shuttles were arriving, the first of many. "You are a powerful man who seems to have decided he doesn't need to increase his scope quickly. You manage what you have well, but you could be greater, you could be better. This war is only a season in a long year, and you could come out of it with more power than you ever imagined."

"All right, that's me, that's the door you promised to open," Governor Tate said. "What about you?"

"No fixer can live up to his full potential if they don't have territory. Territory they can learn all the details of, become well known in, respected. I am homeless, and worse, I only have a few crewmembers, no ship I'd put my name on, and one half of the galaxy wants me in prison or dead. I have information though, and ways to get more, so where would you go? What would you do, especially if you saw a Governor getting a little thick in the middle, an administrator who is waiting to be a real leader again? I saw that, and I said to myself; 'Lucious, why don't you go over there and introduce yourself? Show him a few tricks, like entering without breaking, and teach him a few things you've come to know, like how to talk to the most frightening commander in five sectors?' So I did, and so I started getting to know this space you've taken control of, and I think it's a good place for a fixer like me. I'm simply a man who helps people get what they want in trade for a few things I like. I want my piece of revenge on some people who got the three largest governments in the Core Worlds looking for me, and that's already in the works, but what else do I want? That's what you're asking. What does this Wheeler weirdo want in my back yard? What am I going to have to trade when he offers me something I can't afford to refuse?" Wheeler sat up on the ledge, the gathering masses behind him.

"I don't know," Governor Tate said. Whatever, whoever Wheeler was, it was always amusing to watch him talk. "That's exactly what I need to know."

"I want to be connected again," Wheeler said, pushing his hands together as though overcoming some resistance between them. "Not brain-bud, neutrally wireless connected like other idiots who got themselves addicted to the virtual fields of useless information and burned out, or let their enemies get the upper hand while they were reading a million different menus from a million different restaurants without realizing that they were doing it because they were starving.

"I connect, but I look at the networked wasteland of gossip and data, find what I need and get out. I want to get connected to a network with reach, like that big, fat Regent Galactic, Order of Eden network that's chock full of humans who don't know they're in the middle of two of the biggest social experiments in history. On one hand you have religious crazies and the people who play along for a hot meal. Some of them actually believe, and are trying to elevate themselves, bravo. On the other you have commercialism, and billions of people who don't realize they're slaves to the debt they're always trying to work off. Not these people," Wheeler said, waving so broadly that it looked like he was about to fall off his perch on the building's edge. "No, they know they're slaves, they can feel it in the chemical film on their skin, smell it when they wake up in the morning and taste it in that same air whenever one of your refineries opens the exhaust up for a few minutes. I'm talking about the people who live well in your solar system, beyond your solar system. They think they're working for a living, paying into a dream, staying upwardly mobile, and making a home for their kids, so they can do better than they did when they grow up. Those people are living in an experiment run by you, by Regent Galactic and the thousands of corporations that own hundreds of worlds, and you, my Governor, balance the scales in your solar system so well that most of those people will never know. I'll recruit the special ones from those folks and you'll never miss them. They are the malcontents, the people who know how to play your game and win, some of them are even like me, fixers who can get you anything you want." Several beaten shuttles started landing in the massive lot behind Wheeler, dropping off people by the hundred. "They're the people who don't fit in your culture, and they don't fit in with the Order of Eden types either, so you won't miss them."

"Then? When you have your people together?" Governor Tate asked.

"That's it, Governor," Wheeler said. "After I get my revenge they'll keep me interested. I'll be the one who delivered them from debt and monotony. We'll find something to do, and I bet we'll live pretty well while we're at it, too. Today I'm here because you asked me to be, and because I'm looking for a few good men and women I can entice onto my crew."

"You still need a ship," Governor Tate said, pleased that he mentioned something that Wheeler neglected to mention in his list of needs.

"For what I want to do, I'll need a carrier group," Wheeler said. "Something I'm not afraid to work for, but I'm not going to wait forever."

"You're a few trillion short," Governor Tate said. "It's going to take you some time and impressive work to earn your way there."

"I'm sure I'll find an opportunity," Wheeler said.

They watched the crowd below them grow. It was joined by food shuttles that sold cheap beverages and cheaper sustenance, but the lines were long. By mid-morning Wheeler and Governor Tate were both bored with watching, and they were relieved when the first Order of Eden fighters streaked overhead. The new four thruster design was impressive. At the end of four pylons attached to an elongated fighter fuselage was a long thruster that could fire forward or backwards. The ships would be unable to glide if they lost power in an atmosphere, but from what Governor Tate understood, they carried enough fuel to last days.

His facilities had manufactured thousands of them, but he was only allowed to keep a few hundred for his personal fleet. There were what seemed to be hundreds of the fighters in the air after a few moments. They flew in a slow circle high over the rooftop. Three broad nosed combat shuttles descended through the middle slowly.

The crowd that gathered on the roof had come just close enough so Governor Tate could see the awed expression on their faces. With a glance below he could see that they were silently watching the decent as well, the only difference being that many of the adults held half-eaten wraps, and a few children had toy ships or dolls in hand, purchased from the same vendors who brought food.

The shuttles finally touched down, and a large hologram of the lead shuttle hatch appeared above them, large enough for all to see, as it dropped open. Eve emerged in a long green and white dress, her hair pushed back and aloft by a wind Governor Tate could not feel from where he stood only fifteen metres away. Her arms were outstretched, her smile was wide and beaming. "I have finally come to you!" she announced.

The hologram above was twenty metres high, and through some trick of optics, it looked like you were looking up at Eve as though you were in a kneeling position in front of her, regardless of where you were. She was actually taller than the Governor expected, a littler taller than he was. She crossed the distance between them and took both his hands in hers. Her open smile and a brief kiss she gave him on his cheek were more disarming than he expected.

Her smile barely wavered for a second when she saw Wheeler, but she did not offer him the same respect or warmth. "Do I speak to your people with your blessing, Governor?" she asked.

"Yes," he replied.

She turned her back on him and strode to the middle of the front of the rooftop. Eve waved at the larger of the two crowds below with her right hand, and the smaller to her left, on the rooftop behind the shuttles with the other. "Many of you have been waiting a long time for me to come to you," she said, her voice carried over the crowd through hidden amplification. "I have been on the other side of the Iron Head Nebula, a place filled with danger, lawlessness, and the violence of this war. The people who would keep you poor, directionless and suppressed live in that vast space, and I crossed it for you." She extended her arms and clapped, as though applauding the growing crowd. With a fleet of transports arriving, Governor Tate was sure there would be over a hundred thousand there in minutes. The cheering was already deafening. "She speaks as though she crossed it on her own wings," he said under his breath.

"Respect and gratitude," Wheeler said, joining the audience in their applause. "We are her grateful servants."

Despite her simple, but regal attire in her simple silk textured dress, Eve seemed to be full of energy and youthful. She seemed almost approachable. Governor Tate did his best to smile as he clapped his hands for the last few seconds of applause.

"I will be here, on this side of the nebula for months, years, and even when it's time for me to move on, I will leave the promise to return behind me. Like all the people who work to escalate themselves every day in this Order, I recite my vow; 'I serve this Order. My service will make me immortal. My service will elevate me to paradise.' That's what this is all about, that's why I'm here. I am breaking the doors down for you just by being here. So many of you have not been educated on what the

Order of Eden is, so the first thing I will do, with the permission of your generous Governor, is educate you," she turned towards Governor Tate, half bowed, then applauded him.

To his surprise, the crowd joined in on her applause. He returned her gesture, half bowing. By the time he was standing straight again, only two seconds later, certainly not three, the applause was stopping. It was difficult not to be disappointed that she'd moved on, facing the crowd again. She was conducting the entire affair expertly, and Governor Tate's worry only grew as it went on. They already liked her more than their Governor, who had provided opportunities for billions.

"The Order of Eden is a simple organization that does a remarkable number of things," Eve said. "All are welcome, joining is as simple as approaching a member and asking them to take you to the Gate. That is the cost. You must ask. No credit must be given, no coins will be taken from you, and no property will be offered in trade of a membership, those days are over. We are interested in seeing how high you can rise in our organization, and we will help you elevate yourselves, because you will serve yourself and us better as you live up to your potential."

"After you ask to be taken to the Gate, you will be brought to one of our Entrances where we will ask you about everything you are leaving behind. You no longer have to worry about the bad things, debt, poverty, adversity, or strife. You are under the Order's protection, and even early on your brothers and sisters in the Order will protect you. We want to know if you're leaving good things behind. Family, treasured possessions, even pets are things we don't want you to be parted from. We'll do our best to find lost family members so they can join you, and, if the life of an initiate will permit you to have your most treasured possessions with you, we'll make that happen for you as well. Oh, and pets? I have a pride of Kawaii Cats that I breed in the little spare time I have, so you should be able to keep a pet of your own. We will keep any pet you enter the Order with in stasis for you through your Orientation Phase, your time as an Initiate, and they'll be waiting for you when you elevate yourself to a state of mental fortitude where that kind of companionship is welcome. Some of our Initiates progress so fast, that they're reunited with their pets within two weeks." Eve took a breath, looked across the crowd. "Some of you don't believe any of this, but you'll have an opportunity to ask someone in the Order, and they'll tell you that I'm not lying. Word would spread very quickly if I were. Aside from the good things I mentioned, we provide food, lodgings, appropriate work for your talents. Are you an artist? Do you enjoy building? Gardening? We have a place for you, and if you have no interesting skills, I can tell you that we'll find one in you. So many Initiates who told me that they were uninteresting, and just wanted a safe place to sleep and a good meal were actually full of potential. They were so busy pursuing survival in their old lives that they would have never found it without the support of the Order."

Governor Tate could see she was already winning the crowd, why she was stopping, looking at them without saying a word, he didn't know. Eve peered at the masses as though seeing them for the first time, her smile waning. Concern slowly overwhelmed her expression, and finally she turned around and beckoned someone forward. It was a man and woman in a filthy work suit. They looked like processing plant workers, and Governor Tate knew that they were containment workers just by seeing their reddened eyes and thin hair. They probably only had three fingernails left between them, and at least one of them was fighting a special condition called suit rot. It was an issue with skin infections caused by ill-fitting and unclean protective wear, something workers had been asking their employers and the Justice Offices to remedy for years wherever people had to wear heavy protective clothing in the solar system.

196 · RANDOLPH LALONDE

Two white and green robed followers, as clean as fresh clones, led the filthy suited couple to Eve. She seemed to take them in with her gaze, examining them from head to toe. "What are your names?" Eve asked them.

"I'm Yonda," said the woman without hesitation. "This is my husband, Merig." He looked like he was trying to shy away from whatever digital recorder was capturing his image then projecting it above.

Eve took Yonda's hand and unfastened her gloves, revealing puffy reddened skin and scarred fingers with no nails. She continued on to the other glove, then unfastened her husbands gloves. His hands were blackened in several places, suggesting that the seals on his wrists were most likely faulty. It was everything Governor Tate could do to keep himself from stopping the scene from taking place. He caught himself taking a step forward and stopped.

When Eve was finished taking the couple's heavy gloves off she took one of each of the hands. "You are both hard workers," she said.

"Yes," Yonda said quietly.

"You don't ask for more than you've earned," Eve continued.

"No, we never," said Merig.

"It has been hard for you, and you have children, don't you?" Eve asked.

Yonda nodded, a tear shaking from her eye. "Three, three girls," Merig said, suddenly the proud one, the one with something to say. Governor Tate could strangle him.

"I am not promising a paradise you won't have to earn yourself," Eve said. "You will still have to work, but we will take care of you, we will take care of your family. You may have to defend the Order if you join, one of you may become a soldier for a while,""

The couple in front of Eve didn't say anything, they just stared at her, frozen, with their suit rotten hands in hers. Merig nodded after a long moment, then his wife nodded.

"Have all of you ever sat around a table without having to worry about how you will feed your family? Without worrying about what kind of food you're giving them?" Eve asked. She paused for a long moment, then allowed herself a little smile. "Have your daughters ever seen a garden?"

Yonda shook her head and wiped tears away with her free hand. Her husband mouthed the word 'no,' but no sound emerged. The vast audience was silent, except for one voice who shouted; "Take them to the Gate!"

"You only have to ask," Eve said quietly, but the amplification ensured that she was heard. "For yourselves and your daughters."

"Take us to the Gate," Yonda said, looking to her husband, who nodded his agreement, then looked to Eve. "Take us to the Gate."

Eve embraced both of them, throwing her weight against them. They caught her and they shared a tearful moment before Eve withdrew, revealing stains and smears on her white and green dress. The crowd didn't know how to react, there were gasps, gaping mouths and covered eyes, but when she laughed, looking down at the garment and her dirty hands, they joined in. "Seems we could all use a good wash," she told the couple.

Without another glance at herself, Eve turned back to the larger crowd on the landing lot. "Yonda and Merig are so much further along than they realize, I'm so excited because I know they'll do well. Their children will be raised in an environment with education, good food, other children and they'll watch their parents elevate themselves, thriving as adults, as good role models. That is the first story I'm here to tell you. It's your story, most of it hasn't happened yet, your lives have barely begun, and once you are shown to the Gate, you'll see that path ahead. Yonda and

Merig are going to find their children in whatever care centre they left them in this morning, then they're going to be shown to quarters where they can rest together as a family. The next day they'll spend time at our Welcome Centre with their children and we'll find out how far along they really are. They'll have a chance to look over all their opportunities, and after three days they'll tell us," Eve emphasized the last then paused. "*They will tell us,*" she repeated. "Do you hear that? *They will tell us* how quickly they want to rise in the Order by choosing what they will do, and on the seventh day, they will be doing it. They will be on the path to immortality, to paradise."

Governor Tate noticed that Order Knights in heavy black and green armour started slowly moving to the left and right of Eve. They were far enough away from her to avoid being captured on the holographic image projected above, but they were definitely getting between him and Eve. Overhead he saw a cloud of long shuttles approaching, and it only confirmed what he suspected. Xane Company and several other operations in the area were about to lose the majority of their employees. Most of them weren't legally bound to their employers by a contract, just desperate for a payday and out of opportunities. They came cheap, they were trapped in their employee housing, and he knew that most of them didn't think that was enough. "I knew that's why she changed the location," Governor Tate said. "I was afraid of this."

"Do you want to join them?" Eve asked the audience. The air was filled with the deafening roar of workers on top of the building and in front of it. "Order shuttles are landing now, be patient, be courteous to all the people around you, and your journey can begin today. You can be aboard one of our ships taking your first steps up." She spread her arms wide, fully revealing her ruined dress and the black smears on her neck and cheeks from embracing her example couple, looked up and said; "I serve this Order. My service will make me immortal. My service will elevate me to paradise. I embrace my fate, the fate of all humanity to be the superior beings in the universe."

By the time she was striding back to her shuttle, there were twenty Order Knights between her and the Governor. He didn't warrant so much as a glance from her. "Knock her off her perch and I'll give you whatever you want," Governor Tate whispered to Wheeler.

CHAPTER 23
CLEAN UP

The reserve control centre of the Blessed Mission was a small room with control stations all around. Jake leaned on the control console in the middle, depending more on the display inside his helmet to tell him what was going on than the display in front of him.

He could see several craft approaching the Warlord, British rescue teams who offered to board the ship and attempt to clear the Order Knights. If he weren't so tired, and if they didn't already have their hands full taking a larger ship, he would have told them to stop entirely and he'd lead a team himself. Oz had his own solution. He sent three combat shuttles from the Triton with what had to be the last of their soldiers, and two shuttles with Rangers aboard were on their way from the Barricade. The British Alliance shuttles were called back, seeing that the situation was under control.

He wished he were there, in the lead shuttle. It was his ship. He'd known its hull and bones for what felt like a lifetime. He redesigned it, saw it built, made numerous deals for everything from her deck plating to landing gear. He should be in the lead shuttle, rifle in hand, ready to take it back.

"The bridge is fried, so are the main antenna arrays, and secondary sensor suite," reported Frost. "Everything electrical between frames nine and one are burned out. We did a little too good a job with that EMP. There's other damage too, mostly hull breaches from taking hits in the asteroid field. Two of our main thrusters aren't worth powering up either, we're limping."

"I was only asking if we could scan the Warlord, Frost," Jake replied. "Now I feel like taking a trip through the airlock without a vacsuit."

"No need to meet the deep cold in your birthday suit, Captain. I've got a scanning array working, looks like this ship has three," Kadri said. "Scanning the Warlord now, Sir."

"While that's going on," Ayan said, putting herself under one of his arms. "I've confirmed that the reactors, launch bay, cargo sections, berths, and most of the rest of the ship behind frame eleven is in great shape. Lorander will be able to fix this up in a couple days, if you aren't making any modifications."

"What if I want to make modifications?" Jake asked.

"Well, depends on which modifications you want, but if they're like the Barricade, then a week. Maybe four days if it's a rush and you get bots in on it."

Jake brought up the main schematic of the ship. It was a new model and class to him – Seamark Industries Heavy Battlecruiser Version 4.221, built for Regent Galactic. There was one launch and recovery deck that looked like a squashed tube running along the bottom of the ship. It could open in several locations along the sides, but the largest openings were at the rear and the front. It already had several Sol Defence system upgrades, from Citadel, no doubt, including the shields and the thrusters. There were several upgrades on the bridge, all of which were most likely fried.

Jake couldn't help but admit that he was impressed by the ship's missile systems, and the directed electromagnetic pulse beams installed along the side, rear and front of the ship too. He looked at the maximum output the beams were capable of and shook his head. "No wonder the Warlord was stopped."

There were only twenty eight paired gun turrets spread across the hull, but they were all sixty three millimetre shell guns that could fire several different kinds of loads. They were wasted on the Order of Eden. They were using solid slugs. There were countermeasure turrets that were completely computerized, and a few antimissile micro-drone launchers, but other than that, the ship depended on her heavy fighters to round out their power in a fire fight. Much of their firepower was rendered useless during their last engagement in the asteroid field, either by the proximity of the asteroids, or the carrier they were helping to shield. That wouldn't happen again if Jake kept the ship.

"We're getting an antimatter containment alarm from the Warlord," Kadri said. "It started right before I finished my scan. Someone aboard is tampering with the antimatter systems."

"Those damned Order Knights," Frost said under his breath. "Bloody zealots won't let themselves be taken."

"Order those shuttles away from the Warlord," Jake said, feeling whatever consolation he'd taken in capturing another Order of Eden ship slipping away.

"They're already halting their advance," Frost said. "They should all be at a safe range in-"

The Warlord was replaced with a white-blue fireball for two seconds. There was no sign of the Warlord after the light faded. Ashley flinched, stepping back from her terminal and backing into Jake's. "Oh my God!" she shrieked, her hands covering her face.

Minh-Chu locked the pilot's controls and turned, taking her into his arms gently. Jake moved to take their place at the pilot's console, leaving Ayan at the command station. She caught his arm at the last moment. He looked at her and nodded slowly, indicating that he was all right.

He wasn't. A lump in his throat refused to be pressed down, and all they'd lost that day was brought into sharp focus. The pilot controls were almost exactly the same as the Triton's, easy to use, with all the information you needed right in front of him. He was thankful, the last thing he needed was to fail at holding the ship on a safe course.

"All the shuttles survived, one's engines are dead, rescue operations are already taking place," Kadri said quietly.

"It was only a ship," Minh-Chu said to Ashley. "We'll make better memories on another one."

"Oh!" Kadri said from the communications station. "You're not going to believe this! David Penton, they just brought him in."

"This is Tamber Ranger Rescue Shuttle Nine," said a female voice over the intercom. "I think this is yours, Captain Valent. He's asking if you have a Nerine aboard the Blessed Mission, and if he can come aboard for a reunion?"

"David?" asked a young female voice. Jake remembered her well, she was another of the slaves he freed before Tamber, a young woman who served the captain of the Palamo.

"I'm here, they're bringing me aboard," David replied.

"David!" Nerine shrieked, "Oh my God, don't ever do that again!" everyone could hear that, despite her excitement, she was crying.

"I'll just put those two on their own private channel," Kadri said. "And tell the shuttle to proceed."

"Signal Alaka-" Jake started, looking over his shoulder.

"To make sure the way is clear between them," Ayan finished for him from the command terminal. "I don't want to see an Order Knight make that a horror at the last minute."

"We have to get looked at by something with a better scanning suite," Jake said. "Kadri, send a request to that Lorander Cruiser for a full scan of the ship. We need to know for sure if there are any Order Knights aboard. Volumetric scans aren't perfect."

"All right, you know what they'll say," Kadri said. "Lorander Cruiser Intrepid. This is Blessed Mission, now running under Triton Fleet flag. We request a full scan of our vessel to verify that we don't have any stowaways or other surprises aboard."

"Blessed Mission, we are on our way. Please hold your course," came the reply the instant she finished speaking.

"Here's to silver linings and little miracles," Frost said.

"Captain!" exclaimed Remmy over their secure communications band. "One of our captives just detonated a biological bomb in the hold. We got a little rattled, but our personal shields saved us. No one else survived."

"Never mind," Frost sighed. "I'll start looking for silver linings and granted wishes tomorrow," he muttered under his breath.

"So, forty two captives, all dead?" Jake asked. "No one can be saved?"

"Confirmed. The bio-bomber just said; 'for the Order!' then set himself off," Remmy said. "There's nothing for a medic to do here, whatever bio-bomb was mixing in that fanatic's belly was enough to wipe everyone around him out, and we had them corralled in a corner of this cargo hold pretty close. I mean, we're talking red and grey goo here, I've never seen anything like it. I'm sorry, Captain."

"Nothing you could do, I'm sure," Jake replied. "As long as all your people are all right."

"They are. I'm surprised the explosion didn't set off any alarms."

"The sensors are dead in that section," Finn replied. "Goo? Really? Have some respect."

"Sorry, Sir," Remmy replied. "I'll call up a thesaurus on my comm here and see if I can find something just as descriptive but more refined for your tender ears. Oh, here's one, 'muck', or would you prefer 'sliced and diced mishmash of humanity?' I just made that up myself."

"That's enough, Remmy," Jake said gently, catching a glimpse of Finn shaking his head, and Frost doing his best not to laugh.

"Permission to seal off this cargo hold and join the scanning crew?" Remmy asked.

"Granted, leave a remote scanner on in that room though," Jake said. "Just in case."

"Today can't get any worse," Dent muttered as he joined Jake at the pilot's station.

"Jinx!" Minh-Chu said, jabbing his finger. That brought a little chuckle from Ashley, so he pressed on. "As Wing Commander of Samurai Squadron, I hereby strip you of your call sign, Dent."

"You wouldn't," Dent said. "Who would fly with me if…"

"Your new call sign is Jinx!" Minh-Chu said. "I'm putting it on record."

"Oh, no!" Ashley said, laughing.

Jake had to admit that it was amusing, several of the crew in the room agreed with their snickers and slowly shaking heads. "You can fly shuttles for me, Jinx," Jake said. "I'll keep you busy."

"Well, I'm a pariah," Jinx said as he watched the call sign on the front of his uniform change from Dent to Jinx. "I'll have to take you up on that, Captain."

"Adversity helps one develop good character," Minh-Chu said. "You're going to be a very reliable, interesting man thanks to that new name."

"I'm going to be a bored shuttle pilot," Jinx said as he checked in to the navigational console.

"I'll fly with you," Ashley said as she gave Minh-Chu a peck on the cheek and started back to her station.

Jake stepped back and let her take over. Ashley was one of the most emotional people he knew, but she had a wonderful habit of springing back, especially when there was someone else nearby who needed cheering up. Jake always admired that about her.

Chapter 24
Ellis City

The airspace above Ellis was under the control of the Order of Eden. Patrolled, locked down, cordoned off and scanned ninety times per second. The shining city of Ellis was no longer a piece of his territory.

It didn't irritate him. It infuriated him. Even still, no one seemed to notice or care if they did recognize a change. The traffic between the gleaming buildings standing like blades of steel grass in a field of green and blue was bustling. All sky traffic was limited to a one thousand metre ceiling, which would be plenty of space for anywhere else, but this was Ellis. Everyone wanted to be there, there was something for everyone to covet, and no one could have it all in one trip. The land of the beautiful and the powerful, Governor Tate didn't have the stomach for the place.

Fashion seemed to change nightly in the clubs, the sports were either destructive or brutally over-hyped with more logos and shouting announcers than actual action. The gambling, shows and barely understandable trends of the ultra-rich ruled the centre of the city. The Circle Grand was lit up as though they were signalling God, and as far as they were concerned, they were.

He wondered how quickly Eve would try to recruit people if she realized that over seventy percent of the residents in Ellis were miserable hourly wage slaves. Most of them were trying to live lifestyles they couldn't afford and were deeply in debt. It was a fantastic source of indentured workers for other, more demanding work in worse climates.

"This is fantastic," Wheeler said, his eyes wide and his grin wide. "I love Regent Galactic territory, it's as if the Holocaust Virus never happened." He watched through the window of the armed shuttle as they made their way through dense sky traffic.

"It didn't happen here," Governor Tate said irritably. "That was the point of Regent Galactic providing the technology to take payment from people who could afford to get on the safety list. The rest were either killed by bots or put into camps for their own protection."

"Work camps," Wheeler said. "Still haven't closed those down yet, have you? Brilliant work, I know exactly how it was carried out. You are one of the greediest people I've ever heard of, and you're good at it."

The pair were silent for several minutes then, staring out at the seemingly endless forest of buildings. Light in thousands of windows kept the night at bay. The route was pre-programmed, but people were stupid, and Governor Tate didn't want to be the loser in a collision with some idiot who thought he could do a better job of flying his shuttle than the autopilot. The armed shuttle could survive most head-on collisions with normal vehicles. The Governor wondered how Wheeler would fare if he tossed him through the sliding door. He was exactly the kind of person who would fit in somewhere of the middle of Ellis, with his unique style and difficult to determine age. The fall might be nothing more than an inconvenience for someone like him, a framework. He almost chuckled at the mental picture of Wheeler regenerating, dusting himself off, and stumbling down the street to join the nightlife.

"You get bored of this kind of place fast," Governor Tate said, allowing himself a moment to look through the window at the holographic billboard lights flashing by. "I haven't enjoyed this place for fifteen years, probably more."

"You should lighten up," Wheeler said. "What's the purpose of power if you can't party for free every once in a while? I'm sure there are crowds of people here who would pay to have drinks with the Governor."

"More who would pay to have me killed," Tate said. He immediately regretted revealing that fact. The silence that followed made him wonder how interesting it really was to Wheeler, who was quietly looking through the window.

The shuttle set down gently on a platform ringed with Order Knights bearing rifles, standing perfectly still. A woman in white and green robes greeted them as the door slid open. "Lucius Wheeler, Governor Tate. You are welcome," she said with a bow. "None others are allowed inside."

The top of the building Eve had taken as her own while she spent time in the solar system was one of the worst designed the Governor had ever seen. Then again, that was counter to popular opinion. The main portion of the building below was an octagonal stalk that stretched for sixty-three stories, and the top was shaped like a giant onion. Round, white, and with windows that were typically long and tall, the thing was ridiculous. There were perhaps a hundred people in the solar system that could afford a night in the penthouse, and Governor Tate got the sinking feeling that Eve may have kicked out someone who could make life difficult for him later.

Wheeler practically marched for the doorway, his hair flicking in the wind as he traversed the platform. The guards parted, and the doors opened. "I did not expect to see you," Eve said, taking his hand for a moment then letting it go.

"I'm surprised you weren't told I'd be around by your new Citadel friends. They're interesting people, right?" Wheeler said with a smile.

"They are a driven people," Eve said, turning to the Governor. "Thank you for indulging me, Governor. I am humbled by your system's hospitality."

The room was circular, with plush furniture and stylized, elongated white sculptures of dogs and birds in alcoves along the walls between doorways leading deeper into the penthouse suite. The lights were low, and the white walls were shaded in red thanks to a hologram that dominated the centre of the room. A planet turned slowly, burning in hues of red and yellow.

Eve motioned for them to sit down in the circular sofas in the middle of the room, and the trio equal distances from each other. "I can't spend too much time with you, I'm afraid. There is a party scheduled for me later this evening where I'm going to meet some of the main social figures. Sometimes greeting the few at the gates can bring greater masses, I must attend."

Wheeler was staring at the hologram, his brow furrowed. Governor Tate decided to ignore him and the monstrosity above. "I'm sure duty calls," he said, doing his best to be pleasant. "I have been putting out fires all day with companies who are low on workers. Your shuttles are picking people up at their homes every night. Your representatives are going to housing complexes and inviting people away from their jobs, from their lives."

"I'm here to improve life, and to build the Order's numbers in this sector. The defence is only getting harder. Building a new society takes more labour and management than droids can be trusted with," Eve said. "I have a number in mind, and when we've shown that many to the gates, I'll move on."

"That Gate business, that's new," Governor Tate said, looking for a rational edge to the conversation.

"I've made some refinements over the last few months. The Order of Eden didn't have enough ceremony, enough pageantry to be satisfying to people. We've grown past the cash cult that Hampon started. We still take ownership of most of our initiate's property eventually, but they trade it willingly for help in elevating themselves, so there is value, there is a trade, and ceremonies mark real progress."

Governor Tate looked to Wheeler, who actually looked a little angry as he gazed up at the hologram, and settled on the notion that the strange man would be no help. "I'm still facing worker shortfalls, and hearing nothing but bad news from some very powerful people. People who deliver on threats, make entire industrial sectors tremble."

"I'm sorry, perhaps you could repurpose non-essential robotics to fill the gaps?" Eve said, her pleasant manner fading. "This suite comes with eleven servant bots, I'm sure whoever stays here next could get along fine with two or three?"

"I thought the Order and Regent Galactic were partners."

"You and the corporation you own a small piece of are contractors," Eve said. "And I'm afraid there's no clause that can make your employees feel unsafe in joining the Order. We know we'll protect them, that there's nothing you or your partners can do. You make them miserable, so I'll make them whole. Don't worry, once I've recruited twenty eight million, we'll move on. Of course it could go higher, training could take time, and we may have to put some facilities on the ground just in case some of our new initiates are slower than others."

"That is it," Wheeler said, a note of realization in his voice, not outrage. "That's Kambis, I can see her moons."

"Yes. Citadel and I decided we had to make examples of the terrorists in the Rega Gain system. I wanted them to burn Tamber, but they resisted, something about the size of the spectacle being more effective and Tamber being too well defended. I think it sets the appropriate example. It's quite pretty too, an improvement on the half terraformed world that it once was."

Wheeler stood up and paced a few steps. "How is it that you're just as messed up as the last person who last used that body?" he asked, running his hands through his hair, snapping strands as he encountered knots. Then he spoke with increasing ferocity and volume. "Oh yeah, you probably don't know much about her, Gloria Parker, my old First Mate. They scooped her brains out to get yours in there, but they must have left a dollop of crazy behind, because that's a planet you just scorched!" He turned on Governor Tate then, whipping a pointed finger in his direction. "I told you I would deliver Rega Gain, all I wanted was Tamber, you and the Order could have the rest."

"You didn't tell me," Eve said coolly. "He didn't tell me either."

"You didn't give anyone a chance!" Wheeler said in a burst. "You came across the nebula and sent ships to set fire to worlds! Citadel is a monster, and you're slipping into bed with them! Does Clark know you're making deals with the worst gang in the galaxy?" He turned to the Governor who was enjoying the show. It was good to see Wheeler put in his place. "Tate, you have no idea what she's brought here. These people could take control of the Order, just yank the reigns away from her in a week, maybe they've already started. I got into their database, just the one they let their kids and special visitors see, but I saw enough. It took Sol Defence sixty-three years to kick them out, and they're still paranoid that some Citadel spies are still around! This," Wheeler said, pointing at the rotating hologram of Kambis on fire. "This is them! This is what they do for shits and giggles when they think someone is stepping too far out of line, the only difference is that they can reveal themselves now that they have Eve under control."

Eight Order Knights entered the room, and Wheeler laughed. He looked at the Governor then. "Good luck, really," he told him. "Do everything she says, give her everything she wants, then I might see you someday." He disappeared completely, and Governor Tate was left alone with Eve and her eight armoured Knights.

"That man is nothing but bad luck," Eve said.

"So I've noticed," Governor Tate said. "I'll take my leave, if you don't mind. I think I have some security concerns to address."

"I understand," Eve said. "Do we have an understanding regarding my recruitment needs?"

Governor Tate stopped, half risen from the sofa and tried to answer as naturally as possible. "I only ask that you give me some warning, so I can try to placate my partners with indentured workers, or robots, as you recommended."

"I think that is only fair," Eve said.

Governor Tate made his way to the shuttle as quickly as he could without running. Once he was inside he let his frustrations out by bashing the seat in front of him hard enough to feel the solid frame beneath the padding. He was alone again, he didn't care so much before, but somehow having Wheeler around made him feel like he was going to somehow roll back the clock, become a more vital man again. An interesting man who wasn't sneered at by most, and envied by the rest. He saw the same possibility for his entire solar system with Wheeler around, and the people in it. He silently vowed to improve life for the people he owned once the Order was gone and the economy was in balance. He would not be forever known as the Governor who used an entire solar system for his own gain. There had to be a better legacy for him, with or without Wheeler.

CHAPTER 25
A VISITOR IN THE NIGHT

Governor Tate woke from a deep sleep. He could swear he was dreaming of his childhood, his time with his family at the lakeside in Dol-Ne, when he was still innocent and the order of the day was play.

He had his arms around a new companion robot he'd ordered that evening. It was a mild consolation, made sweeter because it looked so much like Eve. There was something about using that image that made it easier for him to quiet his mind before falling asleep.

The artificial companion's warmth felt real, the sounds and motions of her breathing were perfect. Normally high quality a companion provided such comfort that he slept through the night. He started looking around the room and was startled by the weight of someone sitting on the bed. "Don't panic, Ansel, or should I call you Governor? No one has called you by your first name in a long time, have they?" a soothing voice asked him. He couldn't quite figure out if it was male or female. "That restoration system they replaced your appendix with is really good, it's going to take a minute or so for you to fade."

Governor Tate tried to fumble his way out of bed but found that he couldn't move. "What's going on? What have you done?"

"I've killed you," said the figure sitting at the foot of his bed. "You can't feel it, but your organs are shutting down. I'm just keeping you company so you don't have to die alone beside that thing. The rest of my trio thought it was fitting, but I guess I have a little more sympathy for you. You're a living being, even if not for much longer."

"Why?" was all Governor Tate could think to say. His vision was getting blurry. "Help me!" he tried to shout, not at his assassin, but to anyone, even the useless bot who feigned sleep at his side. It came out as a whisper. He was having trouble breathing.

"We're replacing you with someone who is going to look just like you, but they're going to work for Citadel. Wheeler gave you up the instant we cornered him, provided all the information we needed to infiltrate your home and a great record of your private life to save his own. We'll have no problem inserting an imposter. In fact, I guarantee that, after you die of that poison in about nine seconds, he'll enjoy your life more than you ever did. We'll even get that approval rating up, maybe put some low cost life improvement measures in place so your legacy is a good one. Don't worry, we'll do a better job of running things, you'll look pretty good in the end."

Governor Tate tried to breathe, but his body remained still. The world was fading, and all he could think of was how much he wanted Eve and especially Wheeler dead.

CHAPTER 26
A CHOICE BETWEEN FRIENDS

Finn was in full armour. He still wasn't used to the bulkier, heavier suit. The practice of putting technicians and engineers in full armour was proven many times over though, so he wouldn't argue with it. He interrupted Remmy mid-yawn with his thought. "Did you see what David did yesterday?" he asked.

"Yeah, saw it in the mission report. Took me three hours to go through the mandatory sections, but I couldn't stop watching," he said. "I'm sorry you lost your engineering team."

Finn said; "thank you," then tried to change the topic as quickly as possible. "I knocked myself out using the recommended sleeping dose last night, but I still feel like I didn't sleep a wink."

"Stress," Remmy said, suppressing another yawn. "Followed by waiting." He gestured at the busy launch bay aboard the Blessed Mission. They were waiting in the rear section, where ships were moving on and off with regularity as interior repairs were getting underway. Every uniform they could think of was on display as they carried kits and supplies aboard. Crews from the Triton, British Alliance, Haven Shore and the Rangers were boarding, all dedicated to getting the Blessed Mission into shape as quickly as possible.

A shuttle from Haven Shore dropped its hatch open and a wave of skitters, too many for Finn to count, surged forth. A tall, older man in a loose Haven Shore construction uniform followed them out. "Remember, you're just pulling unsalvageable systems, no building, no improving, and absolutely no improvising!" he shouted after them.

"Lee!" Remmy called out to him. "How'd they get you off the ground?"

"Wait at the lift!" he barked at the skitters before turning towards Remmy and approaching with a surprised smile. "I haven't seen you in two months, how's it going?" he said, extending a long hand.

"Ups and downs, lost the Warlord, lost Kambis," Remmy replied casually. "But I found a collection of ancient animated shows last week, so I'm pretending it all balances out. This is Lieutenant Billy Finn. Engineering branch of," Remmy hesitated, looking at the Warlord marking on his armour.

The tall Foreman didn't wait for the rest of the introduction, but extended his hand. "I'm Lee Romita, one of the Senior Foremen on Haven Shore. Well, guess I'm a general builder now, just got an enlistment invitation from the Triton and the first place the commander sends me is here. Nice that it was an invitation and not a draft, but if they knew my wife, they'd know she would force me to go, if I didn't want to go already."

Finn shook his hand and nodded. "That's Triton Fleet. Not enough highly skilled people to go around. How is Haven Shore?"

"Well, people are talking about what happened to Kambis. A lot of people are thinking of leaving, but no one's sure they would be much safer in any other solar system. Besides, most of the well armed ships have joined Triton Fleet, so chartering a lift out of this solar system is expensive. Doesn't much matter to me anymore though, the family and I are going to be aboard the Triton, I think. One of the Fleet ships, anyway. When I enlisted this morning, everyone else signed up. I'll never forget the fireworks when Kambis went up in flames, anyone who does that is worth fighting. Felt like the world was ending last night, but they say

Tamber's atmosphere's so thick that there's not going to be any noticeable difference with Kambis burning. Your military bases down there are all back online, in case word hasn't reached you."

"I heard," Finn said. "Do think we're going to have more supply problems with the trade from Kambis gone?" he asked.

"I think so, but you wouldn't be able to tell from the supply barge that's docked along the starboard side. I'd say the British Alliance are putting their backs into getting this bird back together," Lee said.

"Yeah, you hear anything about what they expect in trade?" Remmy asked.

"Sure, it was in this morning's briefing when I went up to the Triton. New Admiral in charge and Governor Anderson has given them a little chunk of land for them to build a military base on Tamber. I'm sure we're getting more than supplies and people to fix that ship in trade for the land, but I'd say this is a good start to an alliance we can all see working. Big trading going on last night, I hear your Captain Valent and Ayan have been making deals too. I'm guessing we'll see more cooperation, now that the Order has made an impression that we won't soon forget. They say fires will burn on Kambis for a hundred years. Makes me wonder what chemicals they had in storage on that planet."

"Guess we'll never know," Remmy said.

"Unless we test the air, I'd imagine the atmosphere's pretty thin there now though," Finn added.

"That's just the thing," Lee said. "It's going to build up and thicken again with the ash and smoke. That planet will probably look black from orbit in a week."

"I should have thought of that," Finn said. "Must be tired."

"Don't talk about tired," Remmy said, fighting a yawn. "You'll keep me tired, and we'll yawn all morning."

"So, what are you two doing here, waiting for a ride?" Lee asked with a chuckle.

"A shuttle from the Triton's picking us up," Remmy replied. "Has a comms expert and a commander who is going to take us to the Fallen Star. It took a heavy hit during the fighting, most everyone was killed, including Doctor Messana and all but one of her technicians. There's an old vault they need us to get into. Last night something inside activated and killed the entire crew with some kind of radiation blast."

"What? I didn't hear about that," Lee said. "That's terrible."

"I know," Remmy said. "I'm going because I've been through that ship before. They say there's no harmful radiation left, but we'll be sealed up, so it doesn't matter."

"I volunteered," Finn said, fighting a yawn. "But now I don't know why. I could have stayed here and been just as useful."

"You're off shift, Lieutenant's orders," Remmy said. "If the engineer we're meeting on the shuttle is any good, we won't need you. You could go get some rack time."

"As soon as my head touches the pillow I'll be wide awake, I'll bet any amount of leisure cred I wouldn't get any sleep and I'd be bored out of my mind," Finn replied.

"I know that feeling," Lee said. "Well, good catching up, but I have to be going, otherwise my new team here is going to get started without me." He pointed his thumb over his shoulder, where the crowd of skitters were waiting in a stacked box formation. Some of the little round domed, multi-legged droids were flashing red and quietly whooping at not being given permission to go through the ship's interior door. Lee started walking towards them, some of the whoops got louder at the sight of him approaching. "Oh, hold on."

"Are you really okay to do this?" Remmy asked Finn quietly.

He slept like the dead the night before, but woke up thinking that he'd be seeing half the people on his engineering team. In the short time he slumbered on that Regent Galactic manufactured bunk, on a mattress that had been softened by who knew how many enemy soldiers, he'd managed to forget that his team were almost all dead. The last thing he wanted to do was see that bunk again. "I'd rather do something than sit around and look at pictures of an engineering team that took months to get together on the Warlord. I wasn't friends with most of them, a lot of them thought I was too young to be their boss, but I still can't believe they're gone. I can't believe the Warlord's gone." Finn's command and control unit sent a tiny buzz through his vacsuit and he glanced at it without thinking. "Why did I look? I knew it could only be bad news," he said, holding his arm unit up so Remmy could see that he just got a notification from Crewcast that the Warlord crew were officially unassigned from that ship. "It's going to be like this for weeks, I'll be reminded that I was just lucky the bridge wasn't hit instead."

Remmy put a hand on his shoulder and looked him in the eye as though visors didn't separate them. "Hey, I know exactly what you're going through. The guy I followed into space, I guess you'd call him my first Captain Valent, is leading half the Order of Eden military. The woman he loved and, well, I never told her, but she was a sister to me, got smeared right in front of us. Shitloads of other people I cared about got killed, and I don't forget them. I don't keep them in my public Crewcast file, it's an encrypted thing I don't look at every day, but I remember them, I crack that file more often than I like people to see."

"Yeah, one-up me," Finn said. "My loss isn't as big as your loss."

"That's not what I'm saying," Remmy said. "I'm telling you that there isn't a person anywhere that hasn't lost someone, whether it's to some seriously screwed up adventures like me, or because of the Holocaust, so many people are finding a way to keep going. I think that's half of what keeps us on our feet, that there are other people who refuse to fall down. What's on the other half of that equation? Well, I'm just too annoying to die. You'll have to find your own reason to make that balance. Maybe it's because so many people do respect you. Hell, you have the Admiral and the most feared Captain in at least two sectors fighting over you and Agameg."

"Yeah, about that," Finn said, catching a glimpse of the Clever Dream drifting into the launch bay. A crew list came up with Agameg in second command behind Lieutenant Garrison.

Remmy turned in time to see the ship gracefully set down on the deck. "My comm is telling me that's our mission transport," he said. "I didn't think we were expecting trouble."

"Neither did I," Finn said. "Maybe a stubborn door, but nothing more serious than that."

"Well, it is a vault," Remmy said, attaching his rifle to a short line on his chest and starting towards the Clever Dream's port side ramp. "Are you going to be okay for this, whatever it is?"

"Yeah, like I said, I'd rather be busy," Finn replied.

Agameg greeted them with a smile that was a little wide to be human, something Finn was used to. The bounds of the human shape weren't always keenly adhered to by his best friend, but he was getting better at imitating the general shape. The cilia that Agameg once let dangle loose from his cheekbones were replaced with solid cheeks. The colour of his skin overall was still a little off, on the pink side so he looked like he was about to blush, and his eyes were still true issyrian size, green ovals that took up nearly half of his face, but they always seemed friendly. His nose was a little more than a bump on his face, with slightly larger, rounder holes than before, and his mouth was much more detailed, starting to look like slim human lips. Too much time had passed since he last served with Agameg, the better part of two months, and he could see his friend was very happy to see him. "I have found a pheromone match for you," he whispered. "I have only once noticed such a perfect fit, and that was after Captain Valent was rebuilt last time. She is sitting in the cargo hold with the rest of the people who want to transfer here."

"Wow, awkward!" Remmy said far too loudly for Finn's taste. "Hey, don't tell him who it is, I want to see if your nose science is on the money."

"On the money?" Agameg asked.

"Accurate," Finn said, "he means accurate. I think he's kidding, but it can be hard to tell."

"This is no laughing matter, and it goes well past my nose. In fact, if I were out of my vacsuit my entire body would be sensing whatever passes through the air, you cannot imagine how much I can learn from simply standing in an atmosphere," Agameg protested.

"I know, I'm sorry, Lieutenant Commander," Remmy said.

"I think he has the right idea though," Finn said. "Don't point her out, because then I'll have all kinds of expectations, and pressure."

"Humans let this stuff happen naturally," Remmy said. "Sometimes it seems random, but we find our way through."

"You don't realize how hard it was to find a match for Finn at all," Agameg said. "I've been secretly keeping my senses keen to finding one since he and Ashley failed to connect."

"You and Ashley? Pretty pilot, favourite instructor Ashley?" Remmy asked Finn.

"For a minute," Finn replied. "We're just friends now."

"Breeding is important for humanity now," Agameg pressed.

"Whoa there!" Remmy said, laughing. "We don't breed well under pressure, or when we know we're being smelled."

"This is funny?" Agameg said as he started leading them down the main corridor to the hold at the rear of the ship.

"Not really," Finn said.

"Oh, it's all funny," Remmy countered.

222 · RANDOLPH LALONDE

"But, seriously," Finn said to Agameg. "Thank you for looking for me, it's good to know there's someone out there, at least chemically. Wait. She doesn't know, does she?"

"No, that would be a strange thing to do. Everyone is in here," Agameg reminded quietly, a glimmer of excitement in his eyes.

"Okay," Finn said, more nervous than he could remember ever being. "But really don't tell me who it is. I just want to be myself, that way if anything happens, it'll come naturally."

"I'm going to step in if it looks like things are about to fail," Agameg said.

"Oh my God," Remmy said, "everyone should have a wing-man like you!"

"I'm a terrible pilot," Agameg said. "I don't know what this one's talking about half the time," he said to Finn.

"I'll explain later," Finn replied. "Just, no matchmaking today, okay?"

"If you say so. It is good to be on a mission with you," Agameg said. "That's enough for today."

The double doors slid open to reveal a modestly sized hangar with a temporary rack of seats and a heavy set of airlock doors at the rear. They were all temporary modifications.

The forty-nine seats were crammed into the space, and there were only a few left closest to the temporary airlock. Finn tried not to pay attention to how many women were in the crowd – it was about half, so at least twenty-two by his estimation – or if he'd met them before – most of them were wearing new Triton vacsuits of every colour from every department, and he could only recognize three – and he failed at ignoring them completely.

Lieutenant Commander Stephanie Vega came through the airlock, barely giving it enough time to finish opening, and looked around. "Okay, this is more than we need." She pointed to a random Ensign from the Triton crew wearing a blue Engineering Department vacsuit. "You, why are you here?"

"I'm here for the mission," she replied, not looking up from her slender command and control unit.

"What mission?" Stephanie asked, all business.

"I heard that if we went on this mission we would be able to transfer to the new crew," she replied.

"You know, like the end of a ladder match in sims?" added another crewmember in a white vacsuit, marking him as a general maintenance crewman. "Finish a mission, get an opportunity for a better one?"

Stephanie's mouth twitched into a lopsided smile, it wasn't a happy one. "So, there was a rumour out there that said that if you signed up for this mission, you got to do what, exactly?"

"Join the new crew under Captain Valent," said a woman in a black and gold vacsuit with the rank insignia of Lieutenant Commander on her wrists. She toyed with a hair-tie, sitting back in her seat without showing a hint of nervousness. "I'm here because this ship needs me more than the Triton, there are plenty of people in communications there, a few waiting for my job. I'm the only analyst who signed up, but I think most of the other people here came because someone put a list of available engineering positions up. Oh, and there are four more commuter shuttles coming. All from Haven Shore."

Stephanie glanced at her command and control unit then looked over the crew. "Okay, looks like there was a mix up. The list of the engineering positions and this mission got combined in the system and everyone except for the people on *my* list are getting off this ship and going to work on the Blessed Mission starting today. That means training, hauling skid loads of parts that were burned out in the fighting to shuttles headed to a recycling barge, and it means a solid twelve hour day," Stephanie said so her voice could be heard clearly across the compartment. She raised it even more when a few crewmembers started groaning. "Hey, it's all good news. You get to sign up for the Captain's new crew, and you'll have a small part in repairing his ship for him. I have three people on my list, their names are Lieutenant Commander Billy Finn, Sargent Remmy Sands from the Rangers, and Lieutenant Commander Liara Erron. Everyone else, get off my mission craft!" She stepped aside and directed everyone towards the airlock with a sweep of her arm.

"I'm not on the list?" Agameg asked, alarmed. He squeezed between the seats and the crewmembers to speak to Lieutenant Commander Stephanie Vega, who greeted him with a smile. "I'm not on the mission list?" he asked her, touching her command and control unit.

"You're not on any list, Commander," Stephanie said. "You've been bumped up in rank past me, couldn't have happened to a better crewman. Only thing is, you're not assigned to a ship or any missions right now."

Agameg looked at his command and control unit, then at Finn, who was moving towards the pair at a slower pace through the departing crewmembers. "I'm a Commander in Triton Fleet but not on Triton? Not on this ship? Not on any ship?" Agameg asked no one in particular. "Why? Why has this happened? I transferred to Captain Valent staff last night."

"It's okay, Aggie," Stephanie said, comforting him with a hand on his arm.

"Why?" Agameg whispered to himself, then he flinched at something he saw on his command unit screen. "Ayan is Engineering Chief? Rank of Captain now? She was Commodore, how can she be a Captain now? And Engineering Chief?"

"Hey," Stephanie said. "Tell me what's going on," she said.

"Is he all right? It looks like his head is about to explode," Remmy asked Finn in a whisper.

"I've seen him like this once before, the night after Ramirez died," Finn said, stepping in beside Agameg. "What's going on, just start at the beginning, okay?"

Agameg squeezed his eyes shut for a moment then slowly opened them, the green tint was slowly being replaced with red. "I saw there was an open slot for an Engineering Chief on Captain's crew last night. You would be one Chief, and I would be the other Chief. Different shifts, different Chiefs. Split responsibility, very efficient."

"Okay, so you signed up for that," Stephanie said.

"Yes, I contacted Hausgiest, and he said that was all right, there was someone to replace me on Triton permanently because five people were almost finished training with me. He would finish training them. He made sure my name went to the top and this," he tapped his command and control unit, "said I was the new Chief, the second Chief. I would have a security watch too, day after tomorrow. It told me to come here. Now it says Captain Ayan is the new Chief. Finn and I are now missing from all lists." He held his command unit up to show Finn and Stephanie. "We are not assigned." He took a breath, his large, oval eyes reddening. "We have no jobs."

"Okay, we're going to get moving on this mission," Stephanie said. "You're coming with us if you can calm down, and I'll sort this out."

"You'll sort it out," Agameg said anxiously.

"Yes, I'm sure it's a simple error," she reassured. Finn could already see she was calling up Captain Valent's ident on her command and control unit.

"We're ready to go," Lieutenant Commander Erron said into the ship intercom at the rear of the cargo bay as the airlock closed. She held her hair tie between her teeth as she started bundling her hair into a ponytail.

"Just confirming destination, because things got confusing for a bit there," Lieutenant Garrison replied over the intercom. "We're going to be docking with the Fallen Star?"

"Exactement," she replied.

"That's Old French for 'exactly,'" Lewis said over the intercom. "In case you were wondering, Lieutenant."

"I know," Lieutenant Garrison said with a sigh. "Thank you, Lewis. We'll be taking off as soon as we get the all-clear from the Solar Forge. Should be about a minute."

"Thank you, Lieutenant," Liara said.

"The Blessed Mission is docking with the Solar Forge already?" Finn asked her, aware that Agameg was practically attached to his side. Issyrians didn't do well without stability, and Agameg's stability was his job. It was a central part of his identity.

"I guess," Liara replied. "I don't know what's going on, to be honest, only that my request for the communications position went through late last night, and I'm already assigned to this mission. The brief hasn't been sent yet. Oh, and I'm getting a bunk and a welcome packet later today. All us new crew are getting crammed into a little aft berthing while the rest of the ship gets some work done. I think I signed up prematurely, but there were only three communications positions, and I qualified for just one."

Finn could see Agameg's eyes turning green again, and he knew, beyond a shadow of a doubt, why his mood was turning so quickly. He could feel the butterflies gathering in his stomach, so he stepped forward and offered his hand before he lost his nerve. "I'm Billy," he said. "Finn, everyone calls me Finn, it's a thing with last names from the Samson, which you probably know as the Warlord. Whew, lots of names changed in the last year, I guess. Well, but not my name, they pretty much always called me Finn."

Remmy, grinning from ear to ear behind Liara mouthed the words; 'Are you okay?' then rolled his eyes and turned away.

"I'm Liara," she said with an amused smile. She tapped her wrist to bare her hand then tapped his to retract his suit from fingers to wrist. "We shake hands like this where I come from."

She grasped his hand, and he couldn't help but notice how warm and soft hers was. "Shaking hands with gloves on is like lying, you're only pretending to touch someone."

"I'm Remmy Sands," he said, approaching from behind her with a big smile. His right hand was bare and extended. "Just call me Remmy. I'll be the security for this trip," he said to her as she tentatively shook his hand.

"No, you're our guide for this trip," Stephanie said as she finished looking at her command and control unit. "Agameg and I are security, Finn is our tech, Liara is our communications and legal specialist. She's also a trained therapist with a medical degree."

"Pardon me, Lieutenant Commander, but that last part isn't quite right," Liara said. "I'm a trained crisis worker, it was about three months of training and a year experience. As for that medical degree, I can read a detailed med scan, and do some emergency work, but I'm not a physician. Oh, and I can deliver a baby in an emergency if nothing goes wrong. I think the Triton's Artificial Intelligence processed my records wrong."

"Your training still fills more gaps than most, and you have a knack for data retrieval," Stephanie replied. "So seal up your suit and start reading the mission brief so we can all figure out what we'll be doing aboard the Fallen Star this morning."

"Yes, Ma'am," Liara said without a moment's hesitation.

"We'll be meeting a medical technician when we get there. He was one of Messana's team and wasn't aboard during the incident. The Captain may have questions about him later, we're screening medics more thoroughly these days."

The sound of the landing struts retracting told Finn that they were taking off. He opened the mission file on his command and control unit and tried to concentrate.

"Did you find out what's going on?" Agameg asked as he looked at the file on his comm unit.

"Jake is in a meeting with the fleet commanders from this solar system, but he said it really was a mix up and he'll have news when he has a minute," Stephanie replied. "I think that's the least of the news we can expect when this meeting is over."

CHAPTER 27
PRIORITIES

Every muscle he knew he had, some he suspected must exist, and many he didn't know he had were sore. Ayan's first glance at him as she picked him up from his small quarters sent her into a fit of laughter. "Oh, the look on your face," she said. "It's as if you're asking the universe what you did to deserve this."

"The auto-medic said this is normal for someone in my condition after the kind of activity I had yesterday. I told it that I was in great condition, then it agreed and told me not to take so many stims."

That only brought on feigned sympathy, a hug, and an extended, "aw, poor thing," from Ayan. "Did you get any sleep?"

"The mattress in there is more like a torture device, but yeah, I was out like a light," Jake replied. "We have a meeting. Did you sleep?"

"Better than I have in months," Ayan replied, pulling at the collar of her form-fitted engineering blue uniform. "I busted myself down to the rank of Captain and put myself in the position of Fleet Engineer, with my father's blessing. He's taking over everything I was slated to do as Commodore with his staff tomorrow."

"That's giving up a lot," Jake said. "I know you really enjoyed working on the ship redesign with me last night, but are you sure you want to get clear of everything associated with Tamber?"

"I've never been so sure," Ayan said. "I'll have to spend time on different ships though, I can't just remain aboard one all the time, but I know this is something I want to do. Overseeing the condition of Triton Fleet and helping all the Chiefs keep their ships in shape is really exciting. I honestly think this is where I can do the most good. You don't seem very happy for me."

"Oh, no, I am, I'm really happy, it sounds perfect, and I know everyone wants you in that position. It just hurts to walk," he replied.

"Good thing the War Room is only three frames back from here," Ayan said with a chuckle.

Jake noticed that Ayan's command and control unit flashed and nodded at it, "What's that all about?" his flashed red then, and he looked at it. PRIORITY LEVEL RED was written over the meeting he was already trudging towards on his morning schedule. "Okay, something's up."

"That's an alert from the British," Ayan said. "There's no other information."

The pair hurried down the busy corridor, work on the ship was beginning under Frost's command already. There wasn't much damage where they were, in the upper decks of the aft section, so that was the area they were finishing first.

Several skitters carrying sealed replacement circuits and extra tools that didn't fit under their little silver domes rushed by along the wall. Triton technicians, trained on Sol Defence technology lagged behind with a cart carrying several EMP hardened oval computer nodes, a welcome reminder that every computer aboard the Blessed Mission was being replaced. The Triton sacrificed its entire store of spare parts so the Blessed Mission could get a head start, but the computer nodes would be replenished soon thanks to the secondary fabrication line on the Solar Forge.

They entered the War Room, which had a simple, thick round hatch with a Triton Fleet guard standing to each side. "The locking systems in this section of the ship are not functioning, Sir," said one of them.

"All right, if anyone else wants in, signal me first and I'll tell you if they're cleared. Other than that, no one gets through that door," Jake said.

"Yes, Sir," replied the guard in heavy black armour.

The war room was far more well furnished than Jake expected. The ten swivel seats at the long table were heavily padded, and two short sofas at the rear were deep and plush. He dared not sit down on either of those, at least not while important things were happening. Holograms of Governor Anderson and Oz were already standing at one end of the table. Ayan took a seat at the other, while Jake sat down beside her with a sigh of relief.

"He's a little sore today," Ayan explained.

"The price we pay," Oz said. "Welcome to the human race."

"A sign of old age, Jake," Admiral Anderson said. "Maybe it's time for you to lock your clock, stop aging while you're in your prime."

"Not a bad idea," Jake said. "But this has nothing to do with age, just muscles doing what they're not used to yet. So, why are we at red level?"

"Admiral Charon elevated the urgency of the mission," Governor Anderson said. "I'm putting her through our encrypted channel now."

"Good morning, ladies, gentleman," Admiral Charon said from where her hologram appeared to the left of the table. All the holograms looked perfectly real, and the sound was projected from each person's perceived location. It looked like all the attendees sat down with Jake and Ayan. "I understand you have some business to get through before we share our intelligence, thank you for letting me sit in," she said.

"I'm surprised you're interested," Jake replied as he projected his notes from his command and control unit to the table top.

"Unlike the previous Officer in charge of maintaining ties with your people, I have a real interest. I believe Triton Fleet is a legitimate entity here, and can have a significant impact on the sector, given the right support. Now, please, go ahead."

"Oz?" Jake said, motioning for his friend to begin.

"There are three major missions running from the Triton's flight deck right now. First, we are sending repair crews to the Norridge, Gambit's Pledge and the Fallen Star. Second, we are assisting the Rangers with rescue operations near Kambis. Several ships were caught in the flash when the planet was attacked. We estimate that there are over three hundred small ships and escape pods in or near Kambis orbit. Thirdly and lastly, our squadrons are coordinating with the British Alliance in maintaining a patrol. Minh-Chu would be here, but he is leading the first patrol with Samurai Squadron. Other than some light repairs on the Triton which will wrap up this afternoon, and our continual scanning of the area for more survivors, there's nothing worth reporting."

Governor Anderson stood and began his report. "The Rangers are doing everything they can on the surface of Tamber to rescue people in remote areas that still have no power, but we could use some assistance from the British Alliance. With the removal of Kambis from our supply trade network, we will have to look further for our supplies and step up our own production. Three manufacturing grade fabricators are in need of parts, we might be able to keep them going for another two days, but after that we'll be down to one materializing fabricator. I have people in Haven Shore who are native to this sector trying to contact potential suppliers from nearby solar systems so we can get trade going quickly, but we don't have the ships we need to transport the amount of supplies we'll need."

"I may have some contacts for you," Jake said. "And I know of three shipping companies that are against the Order of Eden. They're small, but they take trade as payment, and they can be trusted."

"Thank you, I'll take you up on that," Governor Anderson said. "Food is not going to be a problem for Haven Shore and our military bases, our third growing tower just finished delivering its first crop, but the rest of Tamber is going to start running out in a week or less. Warlords and gang bosses, the people who have taken control of most of the cities on Tamber, don't keep a large stockpile, and most of them were trading with or stealing from Kambis. We're in for a rough time unless trade is made top priority after defence," Governor Anderson took a moment to look at another document and continued. "If we manage to grow and import enough supplies, we may be able to take people in as high crime areas run out of food. If not, those areas will only get much worse."

"Haven Shore, our military bases, and the equipment we have are running well, but I'm putting a hold on recruiting for now. It comes back to maintaining our stockpile of food. We have a month's worth in storage already thanks to a bumper crop in the jungle, but we can't sacrifice our security to save people. As our stores grow, we'll start bringing more people in."

"The Council was eager to hear my plans this morning, that's my next meeting. They seemed more open to my leadership than before, so I expect relations will be good, considering I'm putting their people first. With regards to leadership, my daughter, Ayan has stepped down from her rank as Commodore, and fully dedicated herself to the maintenance and progress of Triton Fleet, as the new Fleet Engineer. There are other details to operations on Tamber, but those are the highlights. I'm submitting a report compiled by my staff detailing everything else this week. Your turn, Jake, I hear the Blessed Mission is a busy ship today."

Jake was not looking forward to his part in the meeting. He decided to get the grim news out of the way first. "At oh-three-hundred hours last night, we received an emergency signal from the Fallen Star, a Freeground research ship delivered to us from

234 · Randolph Lalonde

former allies to Clark Patterson, one of the Order of Eden leaders. We were the closest ship in the area, so we dispatched the Clever Dream for a closer look. Emergency boarding teams discovered that the ship had been damaged in Kambis' flash. None of the crew noticed the damage because it took place in a sealed, experimental system, which was inside the main lab's vault. All we know at this point is that this faster than light system may have been overloaded, and it released something inside the ship that killed all organic life instantly before powering down. All but one of the issyrians who brought this ship to us were killed. We haven't been able to determine why so many issyrians were aboard. Two of Doctor Messana's medical team survived because they were sleeping aboard the Triton, but the rest, and the Doctor herself are all dead. A lab in which she was doing research we only found out about this morning is still sealed, and there is a faint life sign inside. It is a vault, so we can't even tell you want kind of life it is other than it has a pulse, and a human body temperature."

"What kind of research was she doing, if I'm permitted to know?" asked Admiral Charon.

"Doctor Messana was conducting research on framework technology using the first lab in which it was developed. She was trying to find a way to safely extract framework technology from any person. Her plan was to use a different regeneration technology to replace the voids left behind by the correct living tissue during the extraction."

"I'm sorry, Captain Valent. Your daughter has framework technology, as I understand it, this must have been important to you."

"I didn't know she was pursuing that line of research," Jake said, keeping a stiff upper lip. "But I think it will be important to us all, so I'm sending a team of my best, most experienced officers with someone who has had a great deal of experience aboard the Fallen Star to investigate this morning. They will enter as soon as the Triton's cutting crew is finished getting through the airlock and determining that all systems are down."

"Please keep me in the loop," Admiral Charon said. "The British Alliance, and British Security Forces will be very grateful for any information regarding framework systems."

"I will," Jake said, taking the full meaning of her words. There was a trade to be had there. "Moving on, there isn't much else going on with the Blessed Mission. A full examination of her systems is under way. We expect to be finished today, thanks to the Solar Forge. The refit begins tomorrow, and continues for one more day before she gets re-christened."

"My turn, then," Admiral Charon said. "Recovery operations continue on the Order of Eden ships that were wrecked during the battle. We are willing to give you any ships that can be restored. We expect that you will have one destroyer and the Blessed Mission's sister ship in your possession by the end of he week . We have captured nine enemy combatants, twenty-four enemy service men and women, and killed three Order Knights with no losses."

"Thank you," Oz said. "With those ships we may really become a significant force in the area."

"You're welcome, Admiral McPatrick, and the British Alliance only wants your continued cooperation in return. On to the next item, two more carrier fleets are now en-route to the Rega Gain system. They will be here soon, exactly when, and where they are coming from are details I cannot reveal. Now, on to the matter of cooperation, the British Defence Force is officially grateful to Captain Jacob Valent and his valiant crew for his sacrifice in battle, and for turning the entire contents of the computer systems of the Blessed Mission over to us for analysis. We finished decrypting all of the files twenty-eight minutes ago, and will share everything with you if you agree that the possession of this data remains secret, accessible only to trusted officers. We invite you to check the contents of the file system against the raw file tables to make sure everything is there."

"We will, thank you," Ayan said.

"Before I disclose the nature of the information we recovered, I have to relay a message from the British Alliance Central Command. They approve of our alliance, but I've been asked to confirm that Captain Valent's new ship is following the same laws as the Triton."

Considering that his crew was about to swell past two thousand, he was a little embarrassed that it wasn't something he'd considered. "Yes, we're using the same ranking system, regulations and laws. We're all one fleet," he replied. "I thought that was obvious."

"I'm sorry, I just needed it on record. Central Command is having me report back on your conduct, it's always like this with new allies. Now, on to the most important discovery of this morning. The Order of Eden have determined the location of Freeground Alpha, the central hub of Freeground Station," Admiral Charon pressed on, delivering the information she had as quickly and as clearly as possible despite the dropped jaws and gaping eyes at the table. "We determined, without a doubt that Freeground Alpha was forced to abandon the rest of the station because they were increasingly under attack by a force who had been given an incentive to destroy Freeground by the Order of Eden. Freeground Alpha and a fleet of ships escaped through a wormhole that led them as close to the Rega Gain system as they could manage. From the data we recovered we were able to determine their approximate location, which is somewhere half way through the coreward side of the Iron Head Nebula."

"What can we spare to help them?" Governor Anderson asked.

"You can spare everything but time and the Governor," Admiral Charon said. "As I said, two more carrier groups are on their way, they will be here soon, so orbital defence will not be an issue. I need someone competent to coordinate with on the ground, however, and I submit that it should be you, Governor, even though it's not my place to do so."

"She's right," Oz said. "I wouldn't expect anyone to defend Haven Shore better."

"I was outcast by Freeground," Governor Anderson said. "Not officially, but it's true. As much as I want to help, I think the better choice is to send the Triton and the Barricade."

"No, the Barricade is a perfect heavy defence and patrol ship," Jake said. "It's going to take a couple days, but when we're finished with the Blessed Mission, it's going to be a good ship for fighting in a large nebula. It's more manoeuvrable, and I can add hangar space under the extra armour she already has on her sides. Keep the Barricade here, those interdiction systems are useful, and worth studying. Keep training her crew, their response time was too slow yesterday for anything more intense."

"You have more than one good point," Governor Anderson said. "We'll keep it here, and by the time you get back, her crew will be ready for anything."

"I am sorry to bring you this news," Admiral Charon said. "But the cooperation we've had in just the last two days has led us to important intelligence, open communication, and a renewed sense of purpose for everyone here. Aside from the approximate location of Freeground Alpha and the fleet, we also have recent deployment reports and ship movements from the Order of Eden. We also have confirmation that Citadel has formed an alliance with them, and that their queen bee is nearby. Our plan is to help you shore up the defence here so you can help Freeground Alpha, then to join you in fighting the Order of Eden. As a show of good faith, I'm sending two destroyers and a drone ship with you. They are under your command, Admiral McPatrick. Their only agenda is to assist you in your mission to

238 · RANDOLPH LALONDE

aid Freeground Alpha. Take care of them, these ships are under the command of my best Captains."

"Thank you, Admiral," Oz said, surprised.

"Other affairs are calling me away, and I think it's a good time for me to let you start working out the details of your next mission, so good hunting," Admiral Charon said, ending the transmission with a salute.

Jake's command and control unit chirped at him with a message from Stephanie:

DID YOU JUST FIRE FINN AND AGAMEG THEN REPLACE THEM WITH AYAN?

He couldn't help but snicker, drawing the attention of everyone virtually and physically at the table. "Sorry, I think there was a mix up in the new crew," Jake said. "A couple people are out of jobs until I fix it." He hurriedly tapped a reply.

MAJOR MEETING. WILL FIX IT AS SOON AS I'M OUT.

"Carl," Oz said, addressing Governor Anderson. "How big was the population of Freeground when you were there last?"

"Anyone who could get a pass off the station to another world that wasn't hit hard by the Holocaust was doing it, unless they were part of the political movement in charge. Last I heard, the military was about to take charge. I'd guess that about half of the people left could fit into the Alpha ring. If people kept leaving afterwards, maybe they fit them all. I can't be sure."

"The decrypted data is coming through now, starting with the Freeground Alpha package," Ayan said as she motioned to spread the information across the table. "There's a lot here, I think."

"Freeground Alpha is in hiding," Jake said as he sifted through the Order of Eden patrol logs inside the nebula. "It's not all here, this ship wasn't privy to all the details, but it did run with two patrols. There have been skirmishes, but they've only seen Freeground Alpha inside the nebula once. The ship that saw it, the Sacred Redeemer, was destroyed shortly after sighting it by Freeground ships."

"The Alpha ring moved since," Oz said, summarizing another set of log entries. "This log is only four days old, and it says they're starting their search from scratch. Ayan, could Freeground Alpha open wormholes inside the nebula?"

"Not far reaching ones," Ayan said. "I'm sure they open them whenever they find large pockets of clear space inside the nebula, but from what I'm seeing, the Order is guarding as many of those pockets as they can. Without someone to clear the way, it's going to take them years to get through."

"More like decades," Jake said. "The Iron Head nebula is huge, and every effort I've heard of to create a lane through it has been abandoned because of the war."

"So, are you sure you don't want to take the Barricade?" Oz asked Jake.

"Yes, there are Sol Defence systems in the Blessed Mission, so it'll take a quarter the time it would to train people, and I'll have more room for gunships after we add two hangars."

"That's going to deplete the Solar Forge's raw materials, we'll have almost nothing left," Governor Anderson said.

"Drag what's left of that Order carrier over to the Solar Forge, you'll be good for a while," Jake replied flatly.

'You're right," Governor Anderson replied. "I'm going to review this data while I keep things going down here. We'll coordinate through the secure network." He disappeared before anyone could say farewell.

"Blunt," Ayan said.

"Sorry, we need to keep our priorities straight," Jake replied.

"I meant him," she replied. "I agree with you. This ship and her crew has to be ready by the end of the week, and if we're going into the Iron Head Nebula, we'll need to make more modifications using more materials."

"If we cut back on some of the modifications you're planning, we could be out there in three days," Oz replied.

"Let's compromise," Jake said, bringing up the redesign for the Blessed Mission he'd worked on the night before with Ayan. "We'll build these two hangars, make sure they're spaceworthy, but all the systems inside will be set up so we can build the interiors while we're under way. We'll save tons of materials if we skip making fresh mattresses," he cringed visibly. "Computers get a complete refit, something we can't avoid because none of the Regent Galactic components can be trusted, and the essential defence and offense modifications get finished, but no cloaking systems get installed. That'll save us an entire day."

"Are you sure?" Oz asked.

"Cloaking systems are defeated easily in a nebula anyway, so we'll have filters and hull maintenance droids added to every ship going instead. Those will keep any particles that get through our shields from wearing us down too much. We can do that ourselves while other things are going on. There, just with those cuts, I've got this ship ready in three days, nine hours."

"If you gave up on moving the bridge, you'd save twenty three hours."

"No, I'm not riding up front like an idiot, that's the worst part of this ship, the bridge is right on the nose, the sooner I get that turned into a leisure area, the better." Jake said.

Oz laughed and nodded. "I get it, don't worry. All right, that's a compromise to the good for me. I'll break down and give you four days to customize your ship, and I want to be listening in when you tell your crew that they'll have to build those hangar interiors the old fashioned way."

"If you let us borrow a dozen heavy suits, you have a deal," Jake said.

"You got it," Oz said. "I'm going to keep studying this, but I have to get to work on the Triton."

"All right, talk to you later, Oz," Ayan said.

"Good luck," Jake added. "Damn, I should have asked for forty suits."

Oz's hologram faded out, and Ayan turned to Jake and asked; "Why 'good luck?'"

"Oh, because I'm hiring Agameg and Finn as co-Chiefs on my staff right now," Jake replied, making the crew changes on his command and control unit. "They were mine in the beginning, and he can't keep 'em now."

"Greedy," Ayan teased.

"Needy," Jake replied. "I'll need them both working together to streamline things on the ship."

He finished making his adjustments, then helped Ayan look through patrol reports and encounter logs from the Iron Head nebula. The Blessed Mission was with one of the carrier groups that escorted Eve's Command Carrier through the clearest part of the nebula. It broke off to assist with patrols, and Jake was just starting to take a closer look at the navigational data when he noticed that Ayan was just staring off into space.

He lightly brushed her cheek. She responded with a smile, but she looked worried.

"Hey, are you all right?" Jake asked.

"Yeah, I just can't stop thinking like Freeground is still home," she said. "But that's an illusion, they're transplanted memories. I'm still technically from there, I was made with their equipment, Carl is my father, but I didn't have a childhood there. I replaced someone they lost."

"You're more than a replacement," Jake told her quietly.

"I know," Ayan said. "And I can't deny that seeing Freeground stranded pulls at me, but can we really, should we really rush off to save them when we've barely begun to build something here? What if it's all gone by the time we get back? Or if one of our ships doesn't make it back."

"What if we find a way to bring Freeground Alpha here?" Jake said. "What if we already had access to the technology?"

"The Fallen Star," Ayan said. "They barely know how their faster than light system works, we can't trust it even though it's faster than anything we've ever seen. It probably killed everyone aboard that ship."

"Probably," Jake countered. "We don't know for sure, there are other experiments in storage aboard that ship that no one has been able to investigate yet. One of them could have activated because of the flash's radiation. Besides, there's someone else who can understand technology like their FTL prototype," Jake said.

"I thought of Lorander, more than once, weeks ago while you were still out. They'll never help us with the war against the Order. At best, they may permanently deactivate something like that, so us kids don't hurt ourselves trying to figure it out."

"What about a war with Citadel?" Jake asked. "I think a planet on fire is enough of a reason for another meeting with Lorander."

"Okay, but you talk to them this time," Ayan said. "I've already heard their speech about keeping advanced technology away from less advanced people four times."

"Sounds good," Jake said, his eyes widening as his back twitched. "I think it's time for a muscle relaxer."

CHAPTER 28
THE FALLEN STAR

The Fallen Star's secure airlock door was cracked open by the Triton's technical team in large powered suits that were more like wearable tanks. The thick, featureless plate door had slid in place the moment the ship lost power, welding itself into place. It gave Finn the impression that they were breaking into a forbidden space, like a tomb.

The team removed the outer plate, revealing the normal outer airlock door. "All yours," the technical team leader announced.

He watched as a medical technician, marked by his red uniform, pulled himself along the outer hull and connected a power unit to the airlock. He punched in a code and was inside in seconds. "Hold up, Ensign Rinett," Stephanie said.

"Sorry, I thought I'd get inside and out of the way so you could dock with the Clever Dream," he said.

"All right, go through the inner airlock, and hold there,' she said.

The outer airlock doors closed behind him, and Finn couldn't help but notice that the Medical Technician didn't wait once he was inside. He disappeared into the ship.

The Clever Dream docked perfectly only a minute later, and the airlock matched its air pressure to the ship quickly. The doors opened, revealing the dark interior of the Fallen Star.

There was no power, no light, and no gravity. Stephanie led the way, firing a thin illuminated line at the opposite end of the hull then affixing it to the inside of the airlock door jamb.

"Okay, kids, just head on through the airlock, grab the line and use it to slowly move towards the main corridor. From there we'll follow Remmy."

"Can't believe I'm back in this ship again," Remmy said as he followed Stephanie. As they crossed the threshold between the Clever Dream's round airlock doors and the Fallen Star, they became nearly weightless in the microgravity, drifting off the deck. "The first time I was here, there were dead issyrians, people, frameworks getting fed on by some kind of edxi bugs," he sighed. "Now at least there are just some dead scientists and a few crew. Speaking of scientists, where's our Med Tech?"

"Ensign Rinett, why have you gone ahead to the vault door?" Stephanie asked over their communications channel.

There was no answer.

"He's checked into our channel," Liara said. "He can hear you."

"Ensign Rinett, reply. I will freeze your suit and you will not be able to move if you do not reply."

"Don't worry, Lieutenant Commander," Ensign Rinett replied. "I'm just seeing if I can get some power to the Vault door here, getting a head start."

"Stop what you're doing," Stephanie ordered.

"All right, I'll be here waiting for you," he replied.

"Okay, everyone in, quick," Stephanie said over her proximity channel so only Alaka, Remmy, Liara and Finn could hear. "He's up to something."

Finn was next to go through the airlock. He'd had a lot of experience in weightlessness during repairs, and a little during college, so the transition was easy. He drifted through the middle of the airlock without a problem.

"Oh boy," he heard Liara say as she caught up to him very quickly. He caught her by the arm and they split their momentum, drifting forward through the airlock and towards the ceiling. He stretched his free arm towards the line and caught it firmly, stopping them both from tumbling out of control and pulling her close in the process. They lightly collided, her face-plate bumping into his. "Nice catch," she said with a nervous smile. "I've never done this before."

"What? Investigate a ghost ship?" Remmy asked. "Or get to see an engineering nerd up close. That glow you're seeing isn't his charming personality, it's side effects from the reactor room."

"Weightlessness," she said as she grabbed the line above Finn's head. "Thank you," she said to him before pulling herself ahead.

"You're welcome," Finn replied suppressing the urge to correct Remmy on his assumptions about radiation, and reactors.

"I think Remmy is trying to compete with you," Agameg said on a private channel between him and Finn. "He will fail, I will make sure of it."

Finn switched to their private channel. "Don't worry about it, this isn't a mating dance."

"Finn, take a scan," Stephanie said as the group reached the centre point of the ship. There were smaller corridors leading to the sides with airlocks at each end, and a larger corridor leading fore and aft. The only light came from the safety line. Much of the details in the hall were in shadow, but Finn could see the out-line of a floating corpse down the aft end of the hall. He pulled his high-powered scanner out of his pocket. It was an oval shaped device with a simple screen, a short ranged holographic projector, and dense plating on the outside. Small doors opened up along the sides of the centimetre thick device so it could take air samples and other ambient readings. He linked up with the Clever Dream's sensor suite for a broader sweep. "I'm seeing nor-mal radiation readings, no sign that there are any systems build-ing up a charge, and the Ensign, he's still trying to get through the vault door."

"Do you think we're clear to run power from the Clever Dream, get some lights and gravity on?" Stephanie asked.

"I don't recommend it," Finn replied. "Not until I can see that the D-Drive isn't still trying to draw power. If we turn the lights on when that thing's trying to activate, it could wipe out anyone without serious protection, or worse."

"Good thinking," Stephanie said. "Let's catch up."

Finn and the rest of the group followed her down the line as fast as they could, controlling their considerable speed by keeping both hands on the strand running down the middle of the hallway. Three corpses drifted past. None of them had their vacsuits sealed, and one looked like he was dressed for bed. It struck him then that they were probably all on their night cycle when the device that killed them released its charge. A glance at his scanner proved his theory. Most of the corpses were in their bunks. He looked up just in time to slow down at the main vault door and land beside Stephanie.

"I've got something on my security scanner," Agameg said, forwarding it to the group. A silhouette of three vacsuit protected corpses appeared on Finn's heads' up display. Their bodies and heads were drifting separately. "That did not happen because of an overload," he replied. "Or an other-dimensional event."

"What happened there?" Liara asked.

"There's someone dangerous aboard," Stephanie said. "Intensify scanning."

They arrived at the vault door and Stephanie immediately yanked the Medical Technican around by the shoulder so he faced her. "Okay, explain why it is so important for you to get in ahead of us."

Finn stopped himself against the vault door and shifted to the control panel. "He's been trying to pry this open," he said, looking at the edge of the control pad. "Can't get in that way."

"Those marks aren't from me," Ensign Rinett said. "Well, a couple are."

"Everyone shield up," Stephanie said.

Finn activated his own shield and checked to make sure everyone else's were working. Liara was last to get her shield up. "I don't like this," she whispered as she joined Finn against the Vault door. Agameg, Stephanie and Remmy drew their rifles and formed a half-circle around them, leaving Ensign Rinett the Medical Technician outside. "Get in there, I'm signalling for backup," Stephanie said.

Finn hurriedly pulled a portable power cell from his left thigh pocket. "I'm going to have to pull a Valent," he said.

"What's 'a Valent?'" asked Liara.

"Oh, I remember," Alaka said. "He is going to use a pair of circuit infiltrators, like long needles, to connect to the door system. They are very thin, and fit between the keys and the bezel."

"Oh, I think I saw that in an old sim once," Liara said.

Finn was keenly aware that he was being watched as he slipped two thin, needle like infiltrators into the keypad so they touched a powered circuit. "It's a good hack, as long as you get the power and location right. If you get the location wrong, you're just not connecting. If you get the power wrong, you can burn out the door mechanism." He scanned the circuit and adjusted his battery cell to match the power requirements.

"You could also trigger the vault security mechanism," Remmy added. "So the door panel gets disabled forever. Don't mess up."

"Thanks for your vote of confidence," Finn said as he activated his power cell. The door panel's number keys lit up. "Now we just need the codes."

"The first sequence is-" the Medical Technician started.

"No, just tap them in," Finn said.

"Oh, and hey," Stephanie said over her shoulder to Ensign Rinett. "If you enter in a remote deletion code instead, we'll know. I have one of the top communications officers in the fleet here. Then we'll see what Captain Valent will do with you. Remember the last time someone really pissed him off?"

"I do," Agameg said. "He strapped them to the front of a shuttle and used them to test their vacsuits on re-entry. I think one of them survived."

"Don't worry," said Ensign Rinett. "Here you go." He punched in a sequence of twenty-four numbers and stepped away as the vault door opened. Finn caught him touch a button on the power unit he'd brought with him, a small palm sized square, and saw the overload warning appear on the side. He grabbed the Ensign's arm and knocked the power unit out of his hand. It went spiralling into the lab inside the vault, bouncing against the front of a workstation. He didn't wait to tell anyone what was going on, just grabbed his own power unit, yanking the wires free from the door panel and pushed off.

"That battery is on a power build-up!" Agameg said.

Finn caught the small power unit against his chest, clutched it with his hand. He did his best to ignore colliding with the workstation and tied the lead wires of his power unit to the posts on Ensign Rinett's. "Make a hole!" he said, trying to twist in the air so he could see the vault door. The power unit the Ensign brought was more powerful than the one he had, he knew there was a possibility that it would still overload.

Stephanie and Remmy pushed on each other to get out of the way, and Finn tossed the two connected power cells down the hallway. It made it past the drifting corpses and out of sight before his suit registered a power transfer from one power cell to the other along with a low-powered electronic pulse. His pack was fried, which was no matter, he could get another, and Ensign Rinett's was fully discharged.

"Wait," Stephanie said. "Everyone replay your scanner logs. I think I saw something."

Finn set his scanner to replay the previous five seconds at a tenth the speed and half way through he glimpsed what she saw. It was the shape of a woman in a stealth suit that didn't look like the type of vacsuit anyone he knew used. He was about to report it when Stephanie's shields registered a hit from a nano-blade.

She opened fire in a burst in front of her only to have her rifle knocked aside. The tether keeping her rifle attached to her chest kept it from spinning away from her, but her assailant was grappling with her, the stealth functions interrupted by Stephanie's shields.

Remmy took aim.

"Shoot the bitch!" Stephanie shouted as she tried to hold her assailant's arm away and find leverage while they twisted together in the microgravity. "I have shields, she doesn't!"

Remmy and Agameg opened fire in bursts, mostly hitting Stephanie's assailant. The suit she was wearing managed to resist several bursts before it was breached, and the rounds of their rifles tore through the woman's lower torso before they could stop. The rifles were made to break through heavy armour, to kill framework soldiers. Finn never wanted to see what they would do to an unprotected human, but he did then. After only one burst from Agameg and a half-burst from Remmy, Stephanie's assailant's torso and legs were only held together by a thin strand of flesh. Blood began to fill the doorway of the vault.

Liara finally managed to get out of the doorway, and Finn caught her as she drifted into the lab. "You okay?" he asked.

"It's going to take me a while to forget that," she replied.

"Where's our backup?" Stephanie asked on the security channel, her side of the conversation was carried over proximity radio. "There is Citadel aboard, you get here and start scanning now." She moved through the vault door, directing Agameg and Remmy to do the same. "Grab him," she told Remmy.

The emitters in Remmy's armoured suit, hidden under rows of horizontal armour slats and usually used for shielding, brightened as he used them as micro-thrusters to move to Ensign Rinett. "You're coming with us," he said as he grabbed him by the arm then put restraints on his wrists with a practiced hand. "C'mon," he said as he pulled him through the vault door.

"Circle up, softies in the middle," Stephanie said. "That means you, Finn, Liara and Rinett." Once they were in the middle of a small circle formed with them in the centre, Alaka, Remmy and Stephanie on the outside, they waited.

Finn took a look at the interior of the vault section of the ship over Alaka's shoulder. To him, it looked like a large research lab. If someone wasn't told, they may not realize it was a vault at all. It only had three antennae reaching outside that could be cut off when the vault was sealed, and one door. That, along with a consistent layer of armour around the entire lab, made it the largest vault he'd ever seen outside of one that was made for a cargo hauler. He took a scan of the D-Drive inside the rear of the vault and saw no power readings. "The D-Drive is completely discharged. I can see its settings from here too. If I were to guess, that Citadel spy we caught set it to overload, then deactivated it when the crew were killed."

"So are you guessing that it's deactivated, or is it completely turned off?" Stephanie asked.

"It's off. She turned it off."

"Triton security here," they heard over their communicators. "We heard that, Chief Finn. Can we activate systems?"

"Yes, go ahead," Finn replied.

"All right. Lights and gravity are coming back on, get those feet pointed at the deck." The lights came on in a flash, and Finn concentrated on not looking at the gore at the door. The gravity followed gradually, and Liara grabbed his hand.

"Okay, never done this part," she said. They slowly descended the half metre that separated their feet from the floor. "Oh, that's better."

The first squad of fourteen Triton Fleet security officers entered, rifles at the ready, in black armoured uniforms. They moved directly down the main hall to the vault door. "Here as ordered, three more squads behind us," Commander Victor Davis reported.

"Start your volumetric scans," Stephanie said. "Vault first."

"Aye," he said. "Split to port and starboard sides, scan slow." He ordered. He turned back to Stephanie, stepping over the corpse carefully. "The Triton did a close range scan of the rest of the ship. We discovered a cloaked equipment case in compartment EG-11, but that's it. Looks like Citadel only managed to get one aboard yesterday. The British are spreading their ships out, scanning for the agent's ship, but that'll take a while."

"So you can confirm this is a Citadel agent?" Stephanie asked.

"Yes, Ma'am," Victor Davis replied. The armour she's wearing matches what we have on record exactly. Do you know what she was after?"

"I have an analyst and a pair of engineers here who might be able to find out." Stephanie said. She pulled a flexible, hard strip from the collar of the dead Citadel agent after a moment of struggling and handed it to Liara. "Hook this up and start trying to find out whatever you can."

"It's probably got some pretty serious security, but I'll get something for you," she said.

"Finn, Agameg, you two check the D-Drive, get as many details as you can on its operation, and disable the controls that can activate it from outside the vault."

"We already have a full analysis from the Triton Engineering team that studied it before they started building one," Agameg said.

252 · RANDOLPH LALONDE

"I want to know if this Citadel Agent changed anything, so do what you have to." She turned to Commander Davis. "Do you mind if your people stick around while I finish my mission?"

"Not at all, we'll even help you catalogue this place."

"Remmy," Stephanie said. "Get into the computer system and see if you can find out what the Ensign was trying to hide. Don't let him out of your sight. Oh, and see if you can find evidence that the D-Drive was used as a weapon on purpose."

"It was," Remmy said from one of the workstations. The Medical Technician was standing beside him, watching the holographic records pass above the desk. "This guy led me right to it. The automated logs record the aft airlock opening then closing right before the flash. The D-Drive's emitter array was then connected right before Kambis went up. It looks like whoever did it knew what was going to happen to the planet and when. It was disconnected right after the flash, so the power build up would end in some sort of..." Remmy trailed off.

"Trans-dimensional contamination event," finished Ensign Rinett.

"Yeah, I'll believe that when Captain Valent starts recruiting Kawaii Kittens for his next boarding team," Remmy scoffed. "Some sort of high energy event that renders biological matter inert."

"It's exotic particles from an open dimensional rift passing through organic matter, at best, you don't know what they'll do, at worst, they prove to be too high energy and biological matter can't survive. As far as I understand it, that's what happens when you open an uncontrolled rift. No one on this crew had their suit sealed, so they were killed instantly."

"Except for the Citadel Agent, who knew it was coming," Stephanie said.

Finn started looking through a ring of interface ports for something to match the computer taken from the Citadel Agent as he listened in.

"I didn't know she was aboard, I wasn't even aboard the Fallen Star when all this happened, I was on the Triton, applying for assignment to Triton Fleet when the whole attack took place. I never got back to the Fallen Star. I don't know anything about Citadel, well, no more than Remmy."

"That's Officer Sands, to you," Remmy said.

"Sorry, Officer," Ensign Rinett said.

"Lieutenant Commander Vega!" shouted an alarmed Triton soldier. "We found something."

"Oh, no!" Ensign Rinett said. "Don't touch that!"

"What?" Remmy asked. "You can't even see where they are, or what they're doing, don't touch what?"

Finn saw Stephanie rush to the other side of the lab. "I need my team here, now. Everyone."

Remmy handed Ensign Rinett off to a pair of Triton Security Officers then joined Finn and Liara as they walked quickly to the next aisle of workstations. There were two rows of research grade stasis pods facing each other, with a dozen on each side and workstation pedestals in the middle.

Finn joined Agameg, where he was standing in front of one with a young woman inside. "This scans very strangely," he said.

"Stop scanning," shouted Ensign Rinett desperately, from across the lab. "No one was supposed to see!"

"This girl's DNA," Agameg said as he gently touched the transparent steel surface of the pod. "I cannot believe what I'm seeing."

"They're all dead," Liara said as she finished her own scans.

Commander Davis joined them, and was raising his own command and control unit to do a focused scan when Stephanie waved him off. "Okay, stop. Wipe your data, now," she told him.

"I'm just doing my jo-"

"I don't give a shit!" Stephanie burst. "You and your men will wipe everything from your scan records on this area of the lab immediately, and you won't report this, you will not talk about this to anyone."

"I outrank you, Lieutenant Commander," Commander Davis said. He looked at the scan results then entered a command. His expression had completely changed by the time he looked back to Stephanie. "I apologize. This is not Fleet business. I've locked the scan results under a Top Secret categorization. That's the best I can do."

"I'll take it," Stephanie said. "Keep your men quiet on this."

Agameg looked to Finn with an expression of bewilderment and sadness. "The dead girl here is Captain Valent and Captain Anderson's daughter," he whispered over their private channel. "The other six girls are also the same, but they are all damaged frameworks. This one is human."

"I didn't see that, did I?" Liara asked, not privy to what Alaka was saying.

"Why would someone do this?" Alaka asked over open proximity radio.

"I don't know, but we're going to find out for the Valent and Anderson families," Stephanie said. "Liara, can you start digging into the logs and see what they were doing here? I'm going to make sure that Ensign Rinett gets sedated then carried to the brig."

"We can take care of that for you," Commander Davis said. "My teams have cleared the ship for the second time. There are definitely no hidden agents aboard."

"Thank you," Stephanie said. "Can you leave a squad to keep people off the ship while we work?"

"No problem," Commander Davis said.

"Finn," Stephanie said, turning to him and Agameg. "You two go take a look at this D-Drive and learn everything you can about it. I don't have the education or brains you two do, but if I'm right, and the logs showing that the crew actually used this to get here a couple months ago are true, then the whole fleet could start fighting over it. Hell, the whole sector."

"All right, we'll start working on it," Finn replied. "You do realize that there's another prototype being built aboard Captain Valent's new ship?" he asked.

"I wasn't informed," Stephanie replied. "So I'm the last to know about this, okay."

Finn started walking away, towards the aft workstations, but Liara caught his arm. "Do you think you two could do it from these work stations?" she asked, motioning towards the pedestal workstations in the aisle between the stasis tubes. "I feel like I'm being watched," she said, eying the stasis tubes to her left, where corpses in different conditions were suspended in thick fluid.

"Yes," Agameg said. "All the stations are connected."

CHAPTER 29
THE TRITON FLEET SHUFFLE

Minh-Chu had to admit that the feeling of piloting one of the new gunships was an improvement over the Uriel Fighter he had gotten used to. The controls were more robust, the thrust was higher, and the shields and armour were far more resistant to damage. He could feel the mass as he decelerated towards the Triton's port side hangar. "Ronin, this is Triton Flight, wave off, wave off. You are being redirected."

The new course appeared on Minh-Chu's Navnet display and he veered away from the Triton towards the Solar Forge. "Acknowledged, following course three eight nine two five on Triton Fleet Navnet. Thank you for telling me at the last possible second."

"It was ordered from a Lieutenant assigned to your ship, Ronin," Chief Paula Mendle said. "Good luck."

"A Lieutenant," Minh-Chu said to himself. There was a great deal of personnel shuffling, with Captain Valent's crew growing to take control of the Blessed Mission, or whatever the ship would be called once work was finished on it.

He allowed the computer system to send images directly to his visual cortex. He could sense the ship's shape, its location and which direction it was travelling in. The wireless signals being sent to his cortex also gave him a perfectly clear view of every direction around the ship. Minh-Chu was still getting used to it, and it took a great amount of focus, because he could see with his eyes at the same time. What his hands and feet were doing in the cockpit was perfectly visible to him, and there was a screen that the system blocked out while he was 'sensing' with his brain directly. It was the most recent generation of Sol Defence technology, combined with systems from the Clever Dream, but the visual cortex link was something that Lorander left in the Solar Forge.

The more ships they built, the more they modified and refitted, the more people recognized that Lorander hadn't just given them a facility to build ships with, they gave them many new systems and improvements that were easy to adapt, and even easier to learn. The ship already knew him, and he'd only flown it for one patrol. His reaction speeds were already much higher, and he could feel the thrusters turning, firing, propelling him towards the Solar Forge along his desired course. He could see everything around him. Tamber was still peeking out from the shadow of Kambis, where red and yellow flames could still be seen through black clouds.

The Blessed Mission was half way into the Solar Forge's main manufacturing bay. Millions of tons of metal and other materials from old ships, parts of an old orbital observation station were being fed into the top of the factory. It would take three quarters of the Blessed Mission's current mass in materials to make all the modifications that Jake wanted for his new ship, and the miraculous part was that it would take only days.

Minh-Chu couldn't help but extend his course using Navnet so he could circle around the entire extended Solar Forge. The broken hull of one of the Order Destroyers was already almost in place for recycling, it hung in the space above the forge, gutted and dark while small but powerful tug bots worked to cut it down into smaller pieces. The lights Minh-Chu could see on the Blessed Missions aft quarter were starting to go out. The narrow rear of the ship was about to change. The schematics for the ships' rebuild illustrated that there would be four large thruster pods added along with broad armour plating across the top and bottom with two more hangars between.

There would be new turrets, an extension to the existing beam weapon system, and an array of main cannons added as well, bringing the ship's firepower to a level that would make most destroyers run from a one-on-one fight. He'd also heard of a new system that was top secret, even above his rank of Wing Commander. No one in his department was to know it's nature, at least not yet.

The indicator on his heads' up display telling him that the Solar Forge was ready to take control of his controls for docking lit up, and he transferred them to the computer. In under a minute, his fighter was slowed to a stop, lowered to one of the starboard docking ports, then connected to an airlock. He was still getting out of his seat when the airlock door opened.

The Lieutenant he was supposed to meet was on the other side of the door, according to the indicators inside his helmet. He carefully walked across the small interior of his shuttle, which was docked to the Solar Forge sideways, then pulled himself up through the docking hatch. Gravity switched on him as he passed through, the hatch was on the side of the Solar Forge, so he grabbed a rail along the wall on the other side, and tucked, so he rolled onto his feet. It took him a moment to recover his balance, it seemed like the world just tilted ninety degrees.

"I can't kiss you with your helmet on," Ashley said.

He pulled his helmet off. She was wearing a black and silver tube dress that was both almost too short, and almost too low cut. The shimmering, stretched cloth dress was one of his favourites on her, and she knew it, though she normally wore it in red or blue. The new colours marked her as a combat pilot, a new development since that morning, but she was definitely out of uniform.

She was positively beaming, her dark eyes were alive with excitement. There was good news, and she couldn't wait to tell him. Ashley wrapped her arms around his neck and kissed him as though there weren't crewmen and women at both ends of the hallway. He closed his eyes and enjoyed her warmth for a moment before prompting a surprised squeal from her by abruptly pulling her closer. "Hey, stop mooshing faces, public place here," Alice said from behind Ashley.

Minh-Chu and Ashley parted laughing. "Hi," Ashley said to him. "Missed you this morning."

"Early patrol, first time getting my hands on one of these," Minh-Chu said.

"Good test?" Ashley asked.

"It's a great fighter. What's this about you being a Lieutenant now?" he asked.

"It's all shaking up," Alice answered for her.

The couple started walking towards the main hall leading towards the centre of the Solar Forge, where a large Mess Hall that looked more like a ballroom had been built. He could hear the rumbling ramble of voices at the far end of the corridor as the doors opened and closed to admit an Ensign in blue, marking him as a member of the engineering team.

"She got promoted to Lieutenant, no more lead helmswoman title," Alice told Minh-Chu. "Nothing changed for you except for where you're stationed."

"That's not exactly true." Minh-Chu said. "I have to put together three squadrons in the next three days. I used to be in control of one, with a crew of ten. Sure, they're transferring everyone who can fly a combat mission or operate a welding torch from Haven Shore to the fleet, but I have to figure out how these people fit together to make a real Space Superiority Wing."

"You're already a Wing Commander, you know what that's like. I've been ordered to remain with the Rangers, I'm not even a part of Triton Fleet! Even Remmy's been given the opportunity to join up, but I've got *orders* to get grounded."

"Did you talk to your Dad?" Minh-Chu asked.

Ashley's nod told him the answer only a second in advance of Alice's mildly shrill answer. "No, he doesn't have time. First he was in an important meeting, and I couldn't even get through because I don't have a rank in the Fleet, then he was busy, now he's on his way in to Captain's Mast, so who knows how long that's going to take. I don't think he even knows I'm trying to get through to him."

"He's going to be leaving the Blessed Mission and moving in here with the rest of the crew this afternoon. He should be on the Solar Forge for a few days, I'll send him a notice telling him to contact you," Minh-Chu said.

"Ashley just did," Alice replied.

Minh-Chu opened his mouth to speak, but was interrupted as Alice went on. "I don't know what the best thing for me is half the time, how does he know? What am I supposed to do with the Rangers here anyway?"

"Help tame Tamber? Defend our favourite moon?" Minh-Chu offered. "Become a better soldier than anyone I know by the time you're twenty?"

"You're no help," Alice said. "I'm going to go see if I can find Governor Anderson. Maybe I can get this changed if I go from the top down." She stomped off towards a side corridor that would take her to a shuttle bay.

"They don't make smaller boots for people her size?" Minh-Chu asked, noticing, not for the first time, how comically large the soles of her combat boots seemed on her.

"I love it," Ashley said quietly. "Sometimes she looks like she's a kid playing in her dad's shoes."

"I heard that!" Alice screeched over her shoulder.

"She's been rolling back for a couple days, resetting so she's physically sixteen again," Ashley said quietly after waiting a few moments for Alice to go around the corner and out of sight. "She's rigged her medical tracker so she can see it now."

"I didn't know," Minh-Chu replied. "Haven Shore is the best place for her though. The Rangers will take care of her, and I think they respect her there."

"They do," Ashley said. "She's officially an Officer now, not just a returning trainee."

"Did she say Captain's Mast?" Minh-Chu said, checking his command and control unit for details. The accused was an officer he'd never heard of.

"Reason number two of three that I know I'm in the military, officially, like a real military," Ashley said. "The Governor, Ayan, Oz, and Captain Valent are all going."

"You say that like it's a social gathering," Minh-Chu said with a smirk.

"We didn't exactly have that on the Samson," Ashley said. "Captain kept things pretty informal but watched the whole crew. No one got much past him."

"Now, with a bigger crew, and war you know things will be different."

"I know, it really clicked this morning when reason number one I knew I was in the military came along. I got officer registration forms."

Ashley looked as serious as she ever did at the helm, and they stopped in front of the entrance to the Mess Hall. "What do you think?" He knew the forms she was talking about, he got a version of them before his patrol began and opted in for career registration.

"Three year term with no babies, my age gets locked, my health gets monitored and my skill level has to fit in a margin this wide," she said, holding her hands a few centimetres apart. "Unless they go up, then the margin moves up."

"There's more latitude than that, and there are exceptions to that rule," Minh-Chu said, leading her through the doors and to a table beside it. "I can walk you through the details, but you can think about this, you don't have to serve in the military."

"You are," Ashley said, sitting close to him. "I know there's no question, you're signing up."

"Freeground is where I come from. My family is safe, they're not there anymore, but-"

"I understand," Ashley said.

"You don't have to sign up because I did," Minh-Chu said. "It's hard, military families live with a lot of difficulties, but I'll serve to defend you, and Haven Shore."

They watched as the Blessed Mission locked into place part way in to the main manufacturing bay. The first thing a large manipulator arm did to the hull was scrub the name of the ship, OOE BLESSED MISSION, off. The hall was filled with the sounds of over two hundred people cheering.

Minh-Chu learned a long time ago that women didn't always need their problems fixed, sometimes they needed to be listened to while they worked their problems out themselves. It was that lesson from his sisters that he heeded then, and took Ashley's hand.

"You said military families," Ashley said to him. "Is that me?" she looked at him, expectant and as beautiful as he'd ever seen her. "That's me, for you?"

"I love you, Ashley," he told her. "Someday I'd like you to meet my family, we'll go there, they'll embarrass me, adore and adopt you. They'll do that because my grandfather used to tell us that we should all be fortunate enough to have two families, the one we're born to, and the one we choose when we meet some- one we can't live without. I know you don't have the family you were born to, but I want to be the family you choose." He wished, more than anything, that he had a ring in his pocket. That would be the moment to propose, the moment to demonstrate to her that he wanted to be with her forever, but there was no ring. There would be, he promised himself, and soon.

"Minh," Ashley said, hugging him as a tear rolled down her cheek. "Yes," she said against his ear. "A family of two."

"A start," Minh-Chu said. "A legendary start."

"But no babies for three years," she said. "I want to sign up because I love Haven Shore, I love Zoe, and Panloo, and so many things I've seen here. I never even got to see Kambis, and it's gone, someone did that." She looked back towards the ship in the manufacturing bay. The windows ran the length of the Mess Hall wall. "I can't believe it, people who hate us, people who want to take control of everything did that to us. They burned a whole planet. That can't happen."

"You have two days to back out, so there's time to think about it," Minh-Chu offered quietly.

"No, I'm going. Panloo is staying though," she said. "For Zoe, and so there's at least one good civilian pilot on Tamber. Most of the people I trained are signed up already."

"Welcome to Triton Fleet," Minh-Chu said.

Ashley smiled and said; "Thanks. Going to be a while before I get to wear anything other than a standard uniform. Or heels, no heels in the military."

"Thank God," Minh-Chu said. "I could break an ankle trying to get to my fighter in heels."

She laughed. "I'd love to see you try to walk in heels."

"Watch what you wish for," Minh-Chu replied.

"No aging, either. We get our clocks stopped. Maybe you could get a rollback? You know, just far enough to get rid of the grey hair?"

"I do not have grey hair!" Minh-Chu replied, feigning outrage. He knew he had a few creeping in. He'd coloured three only days before with gel. "And I have the constitution of a twenty year old."

"Well, I can confirm the second part," Ashley said. "Do you think we have time to check out our temporary officer's quarters? Are you off duty?"

"I have to check on Samurai Squadron in about an hour," he said.

"Let's go!" she said, practically pulling him out of his seat as she stood and leaned towards the door with his hands in hers. He did not offer resistance, and was impressed at how quickly she could walk in heels.

CHAPTER 30
THE LEGACY OF DOCTOR MESSANA

If there was one thing that Finn was grateful for, it was that he wouldn't have to share his report with Jake and Ayan while they were standing in front of the stasis tubes they discovered. He was still uneasy about where they were presenting their information, however.

Stephanie showed Liara, Agameg and Finn to the Captain's Mast Room aboard the Blessed Mission. It was a small room with a table that ran the length of the middle. There was a door on either side of the table with five seats on one side and two on the other. Finn, Agameg and Liara stood on the side with two chairs in front of Stephanie.

The other side of the table with five seats was empty.

"Are we in trouble?" Agameg asked. Finn was thankful he asked first, it was the question on his mind.

"No," Stephanie answered. "But you're going to witness the first sentence passed on anyone in the new Triton Fleet. That is, after you give your report and answer questions."

"This is the room for examining people's actions then assigning punishment," Agameg said.

"Yes, under the laws we have to follow now that our crew size is going up to about three thousand, yes it is," Stephanie answered.

"But not all bad things happen in this room," Liara said. "The Uniform Code of Justice they're using from Freeground designates this room for a lot of official functions that require multiple Officers. Don't worry, Agameg."

"This is one of the only rooms that will not be changing at all when the Blessed Mission's modifications are complete. I'm glad to hear it will have a broader purpose," Agameg said. "Friends call me Aggie,"

"Okay," Liara replied. "Thank you. My friends call me when they need a lawyer."

"I do not like this room," Agameg said, visibly looking around at the plain white table, the white walls, and the white ceiling.

"I thought that was funny," Liara whispered to herself.

"It was," Stephanie told her.

The door on the other side of the table opened to admit Captain Ayan Anderson, Captain Jacob Valent, Governor Carl Anderson, and Admiral Terry Ozark McPatrick. They took their seats quietly, there was just enough room for them. "I call this session to order, everything from this point will be recorded and sealed. Bring the accused in."

The door behind Finn opened and Ensign Rinett was escorted in. He was still in his red vacsuit uniform. Stephanie guided him to stand beside her at the rear of the room. "You will be silent until all reports are made, and all testimony is given. Do you understand."

"Yes, I do," he said, visibly worried. "I don't recognize this court, or this process, for the record."

"This isn't a trial, it is a review and sentencing under new Triton Fleet Law," Oz said. "You will be silent unless called upon to speak or you will be restrained for these proceedings."

"I don't recognize this court," he repeated. "But I'll listen."

"As required by our allies, the British Alliance," Governor Anderson announced. "We are to have a Uniform Code of Justice in order to operate as a fleet in an area where they are posting defensive forces. In response, we have declared that we are operating under the Freeground Military Uniform Code of Justice with limited revisions, so it has been renamed the Triton Fleet Military Uniform Code of Justice, a copy can be provided upon request. After reviewing your actions, this command has examined evidence that calls your conduct into question. The Admiral will now lead the proceedings for Triton Fleet."

"In six hours," Rinett scoffed. "You were able to review my actions and all the evidence in six hours? This is just a show you're putting on so you don't look like tyrants. It won't work, everyone will know anyway."

"You'll speak when addressed," Governor Anderson said firmly.

Oz looked to Finn and said; "Please render the report you prepared."

It took Finn a moment to gather his thoughts, he was just getting over the fact that he had been drawn into some kind of justice proceeding focused on Rinette. "Chief Agameg and I examined the use logs, testing information and technology of the D-Drive, or Dimension Drive that was found installed on the Fallen Star. It took us five hours today."

"What did you find?" Ayan asked.

"I've only confirmed what the engineering teams that analysed it before found. It is what it seems to be, a drive that is made to open a rift in space to a place between dimensions where limits of normal space-time are not the same. It does not transit a ship into another dimension entirely. The drive then creates an elongated energy field, similar to a wormhole, to a plotted destination where another rift opens. It draws energy from the space it is in so it cannot run out of power before it transits back to normal space. If it builds up a charge and cannot release it by creating a second rift so the ship can transit back to normal space-time, it will open a rift at the end of it's emitter's range so it can expend energy, but some energy from the other side can be let through

in this case. The drive didn't have a connection to external emitters last night, because someone enabled the vault's seal between
the D-Drive and the emitter, so it released the energy inside the
ship."

"Did you find any evidence that Ensign Rinett tampered with
any systems that would cause this?" Jake asked.

"No, he was not aboard when the tampering took place," Finn
replied. He wanted to go into more detail, to tell them it was a
Citadel Agent, but he remembered what his instructors in college
told him about justice on a ship. Only answer the questions you
are asked, and give the details that are requested of you.

"Chief Agameg Price," Jake addressed. "Are your findings different from Chief Billy Finn's in any way?"

"My report came to the same conclusions, and did not find
the Ensign at fault," Agameg replied. "I did create an accurate
holographic model of how the drive works, however, but the Ensign didn't have anything to do with that either."

"We see this Ensign cleared of any involvement with sabotag-
ing the D-Drive," Oz said. "Now, on to the report we read half
an hour ago from Lieutenant Commander Liara Erron. Please,
relay your report to this panel."

"Sir," she started officially, sharply, only regarding Admiral
McPatrick. "I reviewed the logs left by Ensign Rinett, Doctor
Messana and the rest of her team aboard the Fallen Star. Ensign
Rinett was a member of the team assigned to catalogue the experiments and research materials in storage aboard the Fallen
Star's vault lab. He notified Doctor Messana that he had discovered one of the original labs where framework technology was
developed, and proposed that there could be a way to remove
framework technology from a subject. A week later Doctor Messana moved aboard the Fallen Star and began research. Over the
next four weeks her team worked on a software solution to trick
a framework into regenerating the entire body, then removing it-

self as part of the process, materializing human flesh and bone as voids appeared in the body. Doctor Messana called Officer Alice Valent in for a routine physical and used the opportunity to make a copy of the hardware device containing the patterns for her current form, and the next form she'd evolve into when she was forced to materialize most of her body due to illness or injury. Ensign Rinett stole framework skeletons from a Un-Tam, a Haven Shore military base using a security pass issued by Doctor Messana. They began using them as test subjects, since the software they were developing worked in simulation. Six failed, as evidenced by the inert frameworks we discovered in the vault, but the last one was a success."

"Can you detail the successful experiment for us, Ensign Rinett?" asked Ayan. Her expression may as well have been cast from iron, there was no emotion to be found there.

Ensign Rinett stepped forward, dragging his feet. "What do you mean?"

"How did this process you develop work?" Governor Anderson asked.

"Oh," the Ensign said. "We transplanted Alice's data into a perfect copy of the hardware that we scanned in her, installed it into the framework platform, or skeleton, as most people call it. Then we put it in the stasis tube and activate it, making sure that the subject is perfectly sedated. Then we start the software patch-"

"You are missing something!" Jacob Valent shouted, pounding the table. Ensign Rinett jerked backwards. Liana and Finn flinched as well. Ayan put her hand on his shoulder and he settled back in his seat.

"The Lieutenant Commander's report gives us one more detail before your software was installed," Oz said. "Tell us what that is please."

"We installed a scan of Alice Valent's memories," he said quietly. "But we made sure the subjects never woke up, we needed that for proper testing, to make sure that the entire personality was transferred and that the subject didn't suffer any loss through the process," he added in a rush.

"Go on," Governor Anderson said.

"We made sure the memories were intact, that she was a match for Alice in every way," Ensign Rinett said. "Then we applied Doctor Messana's software and sent a false injury message to the framework itself so it would begin regeneration. She's right, the first six were failures, and we euthanized all of them, they never woke up. They never knew they existed. The last one was a success. She was perfectly human, and we were surprised to see that even the change in DNA went through without any problems. As the original Alice we made, she had the parentage of an unknown female donor and Jacob Valent. She evolved, her DNA was exactly as if she were the daughter of Jacob Valent and Ayan Anderson. Doctor Messana said that it was built into the imprint, like a part of the subconscious' wishful thinking."

"And three days ago, Messana woke her up," Ayan said. "Were those the records you were trying to erase?"

"I never tried to erase records," Ensign Rinett said, shaking his head slowly.

"Lieutenant Commander Vega?" Jake addressed, stone faced again.

"I witnessed the Ensign trying to enter the vault ahead of us, and later trying to overload a battery so it would emit an electromagnetic pulse. I can only guess that he was trying to damage data inside the vault, even though I'm told that the damage that could do would have been minimal since most systems in the Fallen Star are hardened against electromagnetic interference."

"You cannot definitively state that this Ensign tried to destroy evidence?" Governor Anderson asked.

"I cannot. I can testify to him attempting to enter a secured space, and that he attempted to improvise an explosive device, that is all," Stephanie replied.

"The explosive charge is serious enough," Oz said. "Lieutenant Commander Erron, were you able to determine if the Ensign had anything to do with the death of Alice Valent's copy?"

"From surveillance footage and research reports that were Doctor Messana's research team's files, I determined that he did not have anything to do with her death," Liara answered. She spoke even more stiffly during the rest of her statement. "Their research subject was awake for thirty three minutes before she objected to being confined to the lab and they had to sedate her. She believed that she was Alice Valent. She wanted to see Captain Valent, and Captain Anderson. They held her down, sedated her, and then put her back into stasis after a thorough examination. She was killed when the D-Drive overloaded. My findings were confirmed by Chief Agameg Price."

"There are crimes there," Oz said quietly. "But they would take longer to pursue and we do not want any of the experiments with Alice's physiology in the public record. I hereby find you guilty of endangering your fellow crewmembers by creating, arming and attempting to detonate an explosive device in the form of a power source set to overload. I also find you guilty of attempting to damage property with that same device. These charges give me all the justification I need to eject you from service with Triton Fleet. I require an Officer to oversee your removal."

"I volunteer," Stephanie said.

"Accepted."

Governor Anderson cleared his throat before speaking. "As Governor of Tamber, I recognize the crime you have been convicted of by Triton Fleet and see cause to revoke your citizenship.

You will be conducted safely out of the system aboard the next available transport."

"Lieutenant Commander Liara Erron," Oz said to her. "You are the new Communications and Legal Officer in Captain Valent's staff. Are you satisfied with how today's proceedings were conducted?"

"Yes I am," she said with no hesitation.

"Lieutenant Commander Vega," Jake said to her. "You are the head of my Security Staff. Are you satisfied that Mister Rinette has come to no harm, and has not been abused during these proceedings?"

"Yes I am," Stephanie replied.

"If there is any person in this room who feels they have not been honest with their testimony, please say so now," Governor Anderson said. They waited for what seemed like ten minutes, but Finn's command and control unit said it had only been ten seconds by the time he looked at it. "Then these proceedings have concluded. Good luck out there, Mister Rinette."

"I can't survive out there, I don't have any money," Rinette said as Stephanie led him to the door by his arm. "We made important medical discoveries, the framework system can be controlled now, it opens a whole new field of cybernetics!"

"You'll get whatever pay we owe you after we finish estimating the cost of whatever repairs we'll have to make because of your bomb," she said to him. "I'm sure someone else will continue your work ethically."

"I'm sorry," Ayan said. "That wasn't pleasant, I know. But we couldn't arbitrarily throw him out of the system. If it were three days ago, when we're not forming closer ties to the British Alliance then we could have done anything to him, but now, with this being so personal, we had to demonstrate some kind of process."

"He is being discharged and deported on an explosives charge you can prove, Ma'am," Liara said with a smile. "As a trained lawyer, I can say that these military proceedings can seem a little rushed and lopsided, but in this case the charge, the proceedings and the sentence were perfect. I couldn't invalidate this case if I had a whole legal team."

"Thank you for reporting, you're all dismissed. You understand that these proceedings, aside from the explosive charges and the sentence, are top secret?" Oz asked.

"Yes," Finn said.

"I do," Liara added.

"Yes," Agameg said. "Alice, the real Alice is well?"

"Yes, she's fine," Jake said. "And we have someone investigating whether or not this cure is real, but no one can know anything about that vault, or the D-Drive, or that you'll be overseeing it's installation aboard this ship. Lieutenant Commander Erron will make sure there is no chatter or record describing the drive, Chiefs Agameg and Finn will direct the installation, and Lieutenant Commander Vega will oversee security as soon as she delivers Mister Rinett to the Caraway Company Starliner that's set to arrive in about an hour. It's time for us to get off this ship, before we hold up the Solar Forge's work. Take a rest for lunch, then start getting ready, you have your work cut out for you."

Finn couldn't help but feel satisfied with the long morning he had as they left the room.

"Isn't he supposed to get a defence?" Agameg asked Liana.

"You're thinking of human civilian courts," Liana said with a smile. She seemed happy with the outcome. "In military courts like that, you have the evidence against you for everything the court wants to prove presented, then there's a sentencing depending on what the Officers decide, and then you get an appeal. The system is made to trust the Officers overseeing the process because they get into much bigger trouble if they're reviewed and it's found that their rulings were unfair. That, and it's made to be fast, so a ship can keep running."

"That's the way I was told it was aboard ship," Finn said. "When I was in college."

"Oh," Agameg said. "Rinett will have difficulty appealing from wherever he's going, I think."

CHAPTER 31
PORT CHALMERS, KAMBIS, MINUTES BEFORE
THE ATTACK

Bismark Industries. It was a name Burke would never forget. He had been studying their ships for weeks, and was finally almost ready to steal one from Port Chalmers, when a planet wide alarm was activated. He was sitting in one of the many ports on Kambis when he heard a thunder crack in the sky, and people started panicking.

He didn't know what was going on, only that his luck had most likely run out, whatever karmic payback he had coming was probably a few seconds from dropping on his shoulders. Burke's version of Karma was more an enhanced theory of cosmic give-and-take, but that didn't matter. There was something dark and red in the sky, and it wouldn't get him.

He picked a terminal, his sidearm in hand, setting off port alarms in the tallest section of Port Chalmers. Security personnel, most of them hired goons by the Termi Cartel, spotted him at the last possible second. He knew where he was going, and the security doors that started closing in front of him as he headed down the gangway to the small interplanetary transport he was watching wouldn't stop him.

He moved faster than he could remember, rushing down the gangway towards the heavy airlock door that was slowly closing. "Wait! Boarding pass! I have a boarding pass!" he shouted. It was a lie. The Steward, in one of those terrible white and blue uniforms they all wore with silly hats that looked like some arts and crafts project that turned out boring saw his sidearm and tried to push the door closed faster. "It's only a precaution!" he shouted, lying as he fired several shots at the door, his wild, running aim only managed to scorch the door's light armour.

He collided with the door, pushed through the narrow space and almost got all the way through. His right boot was a little bit too wide by the time his body pressed into the cabin. He deactivated the armour seal at the top of his boot and yanked his foot free before the door finished closing, crushing his boot to less than millimetre thickness.

"Boarding pass?" the steward asked, his voice cracking.

Burke pretended to search through the pockets of his long brown coat as he looked around at the inside of the small passenger carrier. It was already taking off in a hurry, alarms were going off, and the back four rows of passengers were all staring at him. "Must have left it back in the terminal. We making an emergency takeoff?"

"Yes, Sir," the steward said. "Can I have your name? I'm sure I can find you on our manifest if-"

An antimatter alarm went off on the personal scanner built into his coat. He used his ocular implant's display to bring up a view from a Bismark Industries satellite and involuntarily yelped as he saw that the antimatter alert was closing in around them. "Time to go!" he shouted, holstering his weapon, so he wouldn't set off the interior intruder nullification systems. He had never moved so fast in his life. "Get into one of these lifeboats, or you're dead!" he shouted as he stopped at the front of the small craft and opened a panel in the floor. The roar of the rocket thrusters firing as hard as they could filled the cabin. The display overlaid onto his sight showed the antimatter cloud spreading across the globe. "Too fast! Not gonna make it!" he said as he dropped into one of the escape craft. It activated and he looked for the controls. PUSH ONLY IN CASE OF EMERGENCY said some white writing above a big red button. He slapped it and crossed his arms atop his chest.

The escape pod closed and he was launched from the small, fifty person transit ship's fore, straight towards space. He watched the status display as the rocket at the rear of the escape craft indicated that gravity was slowing him down. "Oh, please, oh please, oh please, I'll save an orphanage if you just get me out of this. Like, one just chock full of the ugliest kids or something."

Whether it was because of his prayer, or luck, or physics and a willingness to run, the escape pod left the atmosphere or Kambis behind. The antimatter warning spread to the entire planet. "Oh, that's still going to kill me at this range," he said. "Emergency coordinates!"

A low quality screen slipped out in front of him with a navigational display. He tapped the coordinates he knew would take him somewhere safe onto the screen. "Voice command: use standard navigational routes to execute this transit," he told the computer. "Execute!"

The computer screen displayed a rosebud slowly growing then flowering. "What's that? Your progress screen?" he asked, shouting loud enough to make his own ears ring. "C'mon!"

The rose blossomed on the screen and the hyperspace escape pod accelerated away from Kambis orbit at hyper-speed.

"Thank you for choosing Bismark Industries for your escape. Please remain completely still for the initiation of cold stasis, provided by our partners at GoChill. Remember, when you need to preserve living or dead matter for an undetermined amount of time, use GoChill."

"No freezing! It's a short trip! I won't even have time to get-"

The cold stasis systems activated, and Burke was stopped mid sentence.

CHAPTER 32
CURRENT TIME, AN ASTEROID IN DEAD SPACE

"Hungry!" was the first word out of Burke's mouth. He was freezing, shivering, and the knock-off vacsuit under his clothing was just starting to warm him up. It would happen slowly.

A big, mechanical hand reached into the pod and hauled him up onto his unsteady feet beside the pod. "I'm sure we can get you something, mate," said Otto, a towering cyborg who had very little human left. Even his human skin had a sheen to it, indicating that it had been replaced with synthetic armoured flesh. "What happened to your other boot?"

"Short story, long explanation, not really worth going into," Burke said, shivering, feeling the moisture in his sinuses start to drain, and his gut rumble. Cold stasis didn't exactly freeze people, but it came very close, and there was nothing he hated more, even though it had saved his life twice. He looked at his surroundings. He was in some kind of small hangar. There were a few newer model Order of Eden fighters nearby, and through the window he could see there was a larger bay with a stone ceiling. They were in an asteroid.

"I tell you to bring me a ship, and that's what you come in?" Wheeler shouted. "Burke, man," he laughed. "You've gotta aim higher!"

"Kambis," Burke said through chattering teeth. "Probably gone."

"Yeah, I know, it's not gone though. Good as gone, on fire for a century or two thanks to all the crap they left sequestered for terraforming on that rock," Wheeler replied.

"We lost everyone there?" asked Otto.

"I think I only got out because I was waiting for a planet hopper to leave. I've been checking out Bismark's patrol ships for you, figured I'd have one for you in a few," Burke took a deep, steadying breath. The air was nice and warm. "A few days. I got all the scheduling info from Port Chalmers, for all the good it'll do, and a bunch of scans."

"You're the worst backup plan I've ever had," Wheeler said.

"He's unlucky," Otto said. "Don't think there was anything he could do about the planet blowing up."

"It caught fire," Wheeler corrected exasperatedly. "It did not blow up."

Otto picked up a chair, brought it to Burke and sat him down in it. "Better?" he asked.

"Yeah, thanks Otto, now make me a sandwich," Burke said.

"All we got is forma, and the E-Meals from the Order," Otto said apologetically.

"Just kidding, man," Burke said.

"Okay," Wheeler said. "All I've got is a connection to the Order of Eden network. We'll have to take something they're bringing in. Something my little crew can manage to take."

"If you're connected, then you've got the command codes?" Burke asked.

"Yeah, but things didn't go well, that's why I'm here to greet you personally, not just Otto and the others," Wheeler replied.

"What do you mean, didn't go well? They're not after you now, are they?"

"No, they're not after me, but they don't want me in their club either, I'm not exactly a devotee they can trust."

"So you didn't get a ship," Burke said. It was a damning situation. He knew getting stuck with Otto and Wheeler's small mercenary crew in the middle of no where could lead to the break up of the crew, and he'd be alone again, penniless. The only thing he could lay claim to were his ripper gun, his clothing, and the pod he came in. "I got the entry code system figured out for Bismark ships, I made a hack."

"I got a ship," Wheeler said. "It's just a small customs corvette from the Codis System, and it's out of date. Slow hyperdrive, small disabling weapons, you know, nothing worth keeping if we can get something better."

"I've been improving the thrusters," Otto said. "Got an extra eleven point nine percent."

"Yes, Otto," Wheeler said. "We're all proud."

"So, let's put a plan together," Burke said, his shivering finally starting to subside. "Like I said, I got the travel routes, not just from Kambis, but for Bismark Industries, they've got hundreds of haulers and transports. They've got some ports we can go to, I'm sure I can find us something bigger. Something newer, we just need a few more crew, some guns, maybe a few supplies."

"Guns and supplies, we've got," Otto said. "No sandwiches though."

"You didn't say all of Bismark's routes before," Wheeler replied, smiling.

"Sorry," Burke said, then he leaned towards Wheeler and shouted. "I have the courses and timetable for the entire fleet for the next month!" He leaned back in his chair, coughed once and quietly asked; "Was that clear enough?"

"And you can crack their security?" Wheeler asked.

"Yes, I figured out their security software," Burke replied, consciously not offering any details.

"Congratulations, you're important again," Wheeler said.

Chapter 33
In Memoriam

Visiting the Everin building was always surreal for Finn. The mountainous structure looked like the pictures of an Issyrian clutch he'd seen once, with oval sections closely affixed to each other, making one large, shining structure. This one reached for the sky, whereas the traditional underwater homes of the issyrians often rested in piles, wedged into crevasses on ocean floors.

He was supposed to be helping to oversee the third day of the rebuild on Captain Valent's new ship, but he was invited to the main floor of the Everin building that morning. There would be a memorial, and the engineering staff he lost would be featured. There were hundreds of people gathered inside the main floor, and thousands outside.

Agameg stood at his side amongst the officers from the Triton and Captain Valent's crew. Most of the leadership from Haven Shore was in attendance on the other side of the circle surrounding the covered monument. All he could tell was that it stood approximately three metres tall, and was semi-circular.

Governor Anderson stood in front of it looking across the crowd. "This monument wasn't supposed to be finished for another month, but I was approached by the team of artists who were sculpting this in their spare time. They wanted to devote their full attention to it since so many of our people are leaving tomorrow. I believe they have accomplished a miracle in the short time they had, and that their work will serve to remind us of the heavy cost paid for the peace we have in Haven Shore.

Please, let your first round of applause be for them and their hard work." He pointed to a group of sculptors, most of whom seemed sheepish, except for three, who had their heads bowed.

The grey sheet covering the monument was lifted by cables drawn overhead, to reveal a crowd of stone people standing in an incomplete circle on a flat pedestal. In the middle of the pedestal was an etching of Haven Shore's main island with a circle of words Finn couldn't make out from where he was standing.

Jason and Laura Everin stood prominently between all the other stone people, facing each other, holding hands and gazing into each other's eyes. The rest of the semicircle of stone people were frozen in natural poses, as though they had gathered for a celebration with each other. They were all people who died during their arrival on Tamber and the year that followed. Several of them, near the outer edge on one side, were from his engineering team.

Angela and Yolanda, who were as driven as he was to earn their way to Chief. Rain, Oscilla, and Frank, who were inseparable for their last few weeks of service. There was a plaque at their feet that the five of them were tilting upward together. The sight of them struck so deep, he almost forgot to applaud. He knew he'd have to speak at the end of the presentation, and clamped his jaws together, refusing to let a tear roll. He could not think about them until the moment was over, he had something important to say.

The applause abated, and a representative of the crafters stepped forward. She was in a red Triton Fleet Uniform, marked as an Ensign. "It reads," she said aloud as she arrived at the open centre of the monument. "For the sacrifices made in our founding year. In recognition of those who lost their lives while building a safe place for wanderers. May this serve as a monument to all who have protected and will protect Tamber," she looked to the crowd facing the open section of the monument, momentarily taken aback by their number. "It was our pleasure, our honour to make this in their honour."

She quietly returned to the group of sculptors, only two of them were in Triton uniform, the others wore various workers suits that marked them as pickers, maintenance people, and builders from the island. Finn was surprised at how many people he didn't recognize in the monument, including three children that couldn't have been over five years old. Two stood with a woman who smiled down at them, holding their hands.

There was a smaller one on the other side smiling towards the centre. She was a little girl with curly hair who looked like she was about to pull a prank on someone. Her minder was a tall man with broad shoulders, who looked down with pride. "So many people I never noticed," Finn whispered.

"We worked whenever we were not fighting," Agameg replied as quietly.

"Normally, at a ceremony like this," Governor Anderson said, "we would read all the names of those honoured aloud, but the list is still being built. When you take a closer look at this monument on your own, you will be able to see profiles of everyone this monument represents, and of everyone who sacrifices their lives in defence of Haven Shore and the war we wage against those who would harm us. Now, I would like to call two esteemed members of our government forward. Councillor Mischa Konev and Director Lacey Rosedale."

Governor Anderson stepped aside and Councillor Mischa Konev took his place. She wore loose skirts, had sun browned skin and dark curls that cascaded down past her shoulders. She waited for Lacey Rosedale to join her, wearing a similar loose black dress. She was much taller, and paler. "There is a special plaque on this statue dedicated to a person who is important to Haven Shore and Tamber," Lacey said. "I believe she will be remembered with pride, and with reverence. She is the only living person celebrated on this monument." She looked to Mischa.

Mischa Konev continued. "Captain Ayan Anderson negotiated with a difficult military occupier to find a group of refugees a place to safely build a home. In one year she directed the construction of this building. During that year more people came, and she found ways to keep them housed along with her father, our Governor. We are here because she had the vision and the tenacity to lead us through our first year, and when our first real home was built, she began to organize a government so we had representation. Thanks to her, we have a home, and Triton Fleet has something to protect." She looked over to Lacey who patted the corner of her eye dry and shook her head. "Director Rosedale was supposed to finish this speech, but she'd like me to continue for her."

There was a modest ripple of laughter across the crowd. Councillor Konev smiled, waited a moment then pressed on. "I think she's teary-eyed because our Founder is preparing to leave us. She is joining Triton Fleet so she can defend what she built. She will be overseeing the fitness of the Fleet as it leads the war against the Order of Eden. We wish all of them God speed and Good hunting. We'll keep the home fires burning."

Finn looked to his left, where he knew Captain Anderson was standing beside Captain Valent. He was not surprised to see her trying not to cry, dabbing her eyes with a tissue. Captain Valent had his arm around her shoulders.

The Counsellor and Director returned to the circle of people standing around the monument, and Governor Anderson took his place again. "I am only the Master of Ceremonies today, but I have to say this about the man who is about to speak. He is the bravest fighter I have ever met, a Captain who is so well respected that the Admiral of Triton Fleet told me that he should speak for the Fleet instead of the Admiral himself. I have never met a soldier who can seize an opportunity like this man. I present Captain Jacob Valent."

Captain Valent quietly checked with Ayan and then motioned to Finn, who had actually forgotten that he was supposed to speak before his Captain. Alice and Ayan stood together, arm in arm, as Captain Valent began walking towards the monument.

Finn followed him. "Say what you came to say," Captain Valent told him in a whisper. "If you have trouble with crowds, just look up, forget they're there."

Finn turned and faced the crowd. Instead of looking up, he looked at Agameg for a moment. "The Holocaust," he paused, the sound of his own voice over the public address system surprised him. "It has given us all something in common. We have all lost someone." Liara stepped into the spot he was in before, beside Agameg, her big brown eyes stared at him from across the grand lobby floor. His heart skipped a beat, he forgot what he was about to say next so he glanced at his command and control unit, which sent a private scrolling message into his line of sight. He started by reading the first few words. "I left my family because I wanted a better life for myself, I didn't want to work on the docks, or at the refinery. They are gone now. Most of them survived the Holocaust Virus at first, but I later discovered that the Order of Eden seized their world, and they were killed. I carry my grief with my crewmates, because our stories are similar. We don't have to ask, we do not ask." He paused and glanced at the images of his lost engineering team to his left and closed his eyes for a moment.

"Do you want me to finish for you?" Jake asked, resting a hand on his shoulder.

Finn shook his head and took one step forward. "I did not know my Engineering Team well, but I will never forget one night in the Mess Hall of the Warlord, when rank was not an issue, and we shared. We asked, 'where is your family?' I don't remember how it started, but the stories were told." He saw Frost, Stephanie, Kadri and several other former Warlord crewmembers all nodding, remembering that night. "Everyone's story was told that night. There were moments of sadness, anger, celebration, and even laughter. After that I did feel like I knew them, and they knew me. While we served we became a family, and I will never forget them. I will never forget the Warlord, and I will not stop fighting until I am sure the people who would murder our families are gone."

Finn thought he would be deafened by the crush of applause that followed his statement. His head was throbbing, and he knew his face had turned red, but he walked back to his place beside Agameg with a stiffened-straight back and his eyes looking straight ahead. Agameg and Liara were the first to embrace him, and several of the Warlord crew followed.

Captain Valent remained at the foot of the monument and waited. By the time Finn turned back towards him, the crowd was silent. Finn was amongst the crew of the Warlord, Liara closest on his left, and Agameg on his right, he noticed Frost was tear stricken, wiping his reddened face.

Their Captain was stoic. "The Warlord is gone," he said. "Admiral McPatrick and I have decided that no ship bearing that name will ever serve in Triton Fleet, in honour of those who died aboard. During the final moments of that ship's service it delivered us to another, one that required the efforts of hundreds of soldiers and my crew to secure. I'm not going to regale you with a story, or tell you why this monument was erected. I'm not going to render a speech about war or why we fight. I will only tell you that tomorrow I take command of a new ship, and, after days of trying to decide what that ship will be called, I have finally chosen a name. This name will be familiar to you all for many different reasons. My ship will not be the first to bear it, not by far, but I cannot imagine a more appropriate one. In honour of the warriors who have lost their lives defending the Triton during our journey here, who died before all this was built, and everyone who has defended Tamber, I am calling the newest Triton Fleet fighting ship the *Revenge*."

Frost was the first to whistle and applause, as though startled by the sound of the name. The rest of the crowd joined in, especially people who were about to begin their service with Triton Fleet. Frost's voice still managed to raise above the din. "Yes, lad! Yes, lad! Show me the paint and the brush and hang me over the side!" he thundered. "To the ores, to the crows' nest, to the rigging, to the tiller and the guns! A crew and ship and Captain on the high seas, our work is not done!" he recited from his favourite ancient movie, Pirates Are We. "Until our prize is taken, until the day is won!" he finished. Finn had heard him speak about it from time to time, but Finn had never been able to find a copy. He decided he'd start trying.

Whether it was his enthusiasm that drove the audience to it, or the thought of finally fighting the Order of Eden in a meaningful way, the applause was deafening. While it rolled on, Ayan stepped forward along with Alice, the five Haven Shore Counsellors who decided to attend and the Governor. They stopped to stand in front of the open end of the semicircle of stone people and bowed towards the monument. A hologram of Kambis before it was set on fire appeared in the middle of the stone men, women and children.

Liara kissed Finn on the cheek and said; "Yours was the best speech. I'm sorry you lost so many people. Thank you for being brave enough to say what all of us are feeling."

He didn't know what to say, so he lightly squeezed her hand and muttered; "Thank you," which he thought was the weakest response he could imagine.

"Thank you, Finn," Agameg said. "I am glad to be serving aboard the Revenge with you. There is no other place I'd rather be."

"Aye," Frost agreed, still frenzied enough for Finn to want to shrink back a little. "We're finally going to take it to 'em. We're going to make one hell of a mess."

Stephanie led him towards the centre, where many people were gathering as synthetic champagne was being handed out. "He has been sober for weeks," Agameg said. "The only difference I can see is that he is easier to understand, and fights with Stephanie less. Not much less, but less."

"He used to drink a lot?" Liara asked.

"Only off duty," Agameg replied. "But, yes. He was one of the only humans who seemed to enjoy alcohol. Most of you prefer non-poisonous inebriants."

"Speaking of which, I have the night off," Liara said.

Finn wanted to join her more than anything, and he looked at her smiling face. He could count the number of times he'd noticed when he was being flirted with on one hand, and left no uncertainty that he could add one to the total.

"Finn and I have duty aboard the Solar Forge," Agameg said before he could stop himself. "I can tell he wants to stay, but it's going to take both of us and much of the technical staff to ensure that the final modifications are complete. He really wants to stay though, even in a crowd this dense, my senses leave no doubt."

"Thank you, Agameg," Liara said. "I'll see you aboard tomorrow," she said. "Unless you finish early, then call me, okay?"

"Absolutely," Finn replied.

"I'll make sure he does not forget," Agameg added.

CHAPTER 34
FATHER AND DAUGHTER

The celebration was not something most of the members of the new Triton Fleet had time for. That included Captain Jacob Valent more than anyone. Even still, Ayan broke off from their group to have a few minutes of family time with her father before departing for the Triton, and Jake made sure he was joined by Alice as he walked from the Everin building down the long street leading to the main port building. He took one of the side exits to avoid the crowd, wishing that the Council wasn't blocked on whether to start work on the exterior transit system, or the main port building. All major construction in Haven Shore was at a stand still, something Ayan wouldn't talk about.

After shaking several hands, and ignoring all but Lacey and Misca from the Council and other arms of Haven Shore politics, he was able to sneak away with his daughter. They weren't outside of the Everin building before she asked; "Why are you dumping me on the Rangers?"

She wanted a confrontation. "You know that's changed over the last few days. You're staying in Haven Shore, but I'm giving you choices," Jake said. "They do want you to continue with them, though." Jake replied.

"You mean the Governor and you decided I should stay on Tamber, and you're keeping me busy. I get an illusion of choice, but they're all just activities, like I'm some little girl you sit in a corner. What did I do? Was it the people I lost? I'm sorry, I play it over and over in my head, and I can tell you about a million things I should have done instead. What can I do? I screwed up, but I don't deserve to be abandoned."

"You didn't do anything wrong," Jake said. "And no one wants to abandon you. I'm just going into dangerous territory you're not ready for. If I had a choice, you'd never be in danger again, not for the rest of your life. Especially now that you're having trouble," Jake said. "You have nightmares, trouble with crowds, and a lot of people in command have those problems sometimes. You need time to heal, to be away from the kind of stress that's hurting you."

"I just helped take an enemy ship," Alice said. "I've proven myself."

"No, you've proven yourself on a crew like the Warlord used to have. Over the last few days I've realized that if I keep pushing people like I did on the Warlord, I will get them killed. The Warlord was a grinder, and with the way that was running, you were one of the next people that ship would use up." Jake told her firmly.

"But you can change that whenever you want, put me in a place where I'm useful on your ship. Not command, maybe. I can learn so much from you, or even Stephanie."

Jake drew her into an empty office beside the Everin Building main doors. "You're having nightmares, your anxiety level is too high, and your tracker has alerted medical that you lost track of where you were twice while I was out of commission. None of that is your fault, and it's not permanent either."

"So I get therapy, while everyone else gets to take pills and do exercises for three days while they're on light duty. Weeks of therapy, maybe months," Alice replied sullenly. "While all I can do is train."

"They are teaching you coping mechanisms that you didn't have," Jake said. "If you're set on serving in the military, you're going to need them."

"I know, but can't there be a counsellor on your ship?" Alice said. "You know that's where I want to be, what if something happens to you? What good am I here?"

Jake could tell she was trying to turn the conversation back into a confrontation and took her shoulders in his hands. "I love you," he told her. "I need take responsibility for you as your Dad. If I let you serve and burn out on my own ship, or let you get involved with something you can't handle, I will not be able to live with myself." He pressed on through her tears, tipping her chin up so he was looking into her eyes. "I am making sure you are in the safest place, with the best people, doing the best thing I can imagine for you. For all the time I spent in rehabilitation, and all the time after, even when I was so busy I could barely breathe, I thought about what is best for you. I can not stop thinking about that while you're in pain, especially when that pain is from a situation I put you in. You are such a clever, kind and incredible young woman, and you don't deserve the nightmares, or panic attacks. You don't deserve a father who would put you in a position that dangerous either, and that's who I was."

"No, you were a hero who ignored limits, and-" Alice said through a veil of tears.

"I was selfish and angry," Jake said. "I let it drive my decisions. I did not consider what I was doing to you when I left you in charge of security on the Warlord. You were not ready, and you could have been killed. Since I woke up on the Solar Forge I have realized that I'm not that man now. I understand the responsibilities I have more, and I love you more than that man ever could. You are so incredible; you could do anything, inside or outside of the military. So, I'm going to give you a choice. You can either enter the Rangers Officer Training Program, the Triton Fleet Officer's Program, or take a few weeks in Haven Shore and find a job that you love outside of the military. Keep in mind, your therapy will continue, that's non-negotiable."

He could tell those were not the options she was hoping for, but he'd said something that calmed her down. "Triton Fleet Officer's Program. What's that? I've never heard of that," she sniffed.

Jake took her hand and started for the door. This was a conversation he was ready to have. She dried her tears and they headed for the side exit. There was a paved path leading to the landing fields that was being crowded by jungle growth. The trees offered shade from the sun, their leaves rustling in the breeze. On the clearer side of the path on their left they could see the silver domes ahead. Small ships took off and landed on the paved temporary port slips two kilometres ahead. "Once you sign up, there won't be any quitting until I'm back. They get custody of you," Jake told her.

"Seriously?" she asked, surprised. "I'm too old for that, aren't I?"

"Are we talking chronologically, or judging physically?" He asked. "Because physically, you're about sixteen, maybe eighteen, and age of majority is twenty on Tamber. If we're talking chronologically..." Jake finished with a shrug.

"Yeah, yeah, what's the Triton Fleet thing?" she asked.

"The Officer's Program is a new nine month school where you are specifically trained to perform as a self sufficient soldier, behave as an officer, and train your mind to command regardless of the conditions you and your unit are in."

"Another thing designed by Governor Anderson using Freeground ideas," Alice said.

"Actually, it's a hybrid program. Triton staff along with the artificial intelligence there, some of it is from Freeground Fleet, and the rest is based on the Rangers physical program."

"Which I would ace even without framework tech," Alice said proudly. "Every time this thing rolls me back to a soft girl, I've been able to get all muscly and fit. I bet it's no different when you're just human."

"I'll tell you in a few months," Jake said.

"Oh, right, sorry," she replied.

"It's okay. I started off right, let's see if I can keep fit, or fall to flab in that Captain's chair."

"You'd better not. So, what's the point of this training?" Alice asked.

"Some of our best officers are staying behind to train a new crop. Most of them are young, some as young as sixteen, but mature enough to attend. The next voyage the Triton and the Revenge take is going to be hard, because we have to train our people to work together. Many of our officers were trained by completely different military organizations, and even though we've adopted one uniform set of rules, most people won't know them by the time we set out. Everyone is going to be learning at the same time, as fast as they can, and the commanders are going to have to prevent disaster on a daily basis because of all those differences. What we want going forward are graduating classes of Officers who know the rules, know how they are to be enforced, who can fight, and take command responsibly. You already know so much from Ranger training, and have been tested so many times that you've already qualified. The six months you spend in fast track training will count towards a three year term of service with Freeground Fleet."

"So I'll be in the fleet, training for command?" Alice said.

"Yes, and your performance in all respects determines your placement when you graduate. That's something your framework technology can't help with, not really. Sure, physical fitness won't be much of an issue, but most of the factors in your placement are mental, so you're going to have to work your brain."

"There will be sims, right?" Alice asked hopefully.

"So many sims," Jake replied. "But everything will be geared towards you and your class learning essential command skills. We want you to graduate and be better officers than most of the people on our ships. There's going to be secondary training too, like a real Academy, but what you do after you graduate the primary Officer Program will be your choice," Jake said, hesitating a moment before continuing. "Under the new uniform code, you'll be considered an adult at that point. You'll get the Clever Dream and Lewis back if he's not committed to an important mission, and I won't be able to tell you what to do unless you're under my command."

"Seriously?" Alice asked, all the moroseness replaced with excitement.

"Yes, but it won't be easy. The fast track does in six months what nine months of training is designed to do, so there won't be a lot of breaks. You'll have to eat, sleep, and breathe Fleet, go to every therapy session. If any problems come up, you have to report them right away and do exactly what your instructors, commanders and therapists tell you to do."

"I guess I'm selling my soul to the Fleet for a while at least. Wait, did you say something about three years?" she asked.

"Yes. By entering, you agree to a three year term of service," Jake replied.

She thought for a moment, and he wasn't surprised when she said. "Sign me up, but, there won't be room for all of us when we graduate, it sounds like a big program."

He stopped, turned towards her and shook his head. "No," he said. "Only the best will be attending. The first class is capped at ninety, and the testing will require they prove that they are suited for a command position as an officer already. The test is in one week. You'll have to learn the uniform code, look over your materials from the Rangers, and refresh on your pilot procedure. I've already sent a message to Lacey, she's willing to help."

"Lacey?" Alice asked.

"She's agreed to help you with learning the law component of the test," Jake said. "You have to pass it, or you skip the fast track class, who will graduate in six months instead of nine, and start with the normal entrants who get recommended for the next session in two months. They'll be in the course for nine months, no fast tracking again for at least a year."

"So, I could be an officer on a ship in six months?" Alice asked.

He couldn't help but smile at the excitement. "Yes, or you could continue with the Rangers, take their Officer Program, or take a civilian position. I mean, it's nice here," Jake said, gesturing to the tropical jungle threatening to take the path back.

"Triton Fleet, I'll study, take the tests, and you'll see me on your bridge in six months," she said.

"Oh, you think you'll place that high?" Jake teased. "Ambitious, you're going to have to work hard."

"Not a problem," Alice said. Resuming the walk to the port buildings, dragging Jake's hand behind her.

CHAPTER 35
LORANDER

Jake set the new Triton Fleet gunship down at the mouth of a large cave unevenly, cringing as the ship wobbled on its landing gear before adjusting and settling. "Any landing you can walk away from…" he said to himself as he climbed out of the cockpit seat and popped the top hatch open. He was still thinking of the tearful parting he'd had with his daughter.

Everything was fine from the path to the landing pad that had been cordoned off for Triton Fleet combat vessels. As soon as she saw the gunship he'd borrowed to get to his next destination, she began tearing up. She had no arguments for him, only questions. When did he expect to return? How hard did the mission look? Would his crew be ready? It all concluded in a tearful; "I'm going to miss you so much, Dad."

He'd never felt a pang like that, even though he was sure he loved his daughter when he was still a framework. Leaving her behind never drove him near tears. "I'll miss you too," he told her. "Just be good to yourself. I'll contact you when I can."

He made an effort to focus on the moment. He was about to meet a Lorander representative. They didn't tell him to come unarmed, or give him a list of precautions or protocols. They only told him to arrive alone and tell no one of the location of their meeting.

He slid down the front of the fighter and dropped onto his feet, something he wouldn't have tried only three days before. Jogging with Ayan in the mornings was a great way to spend time with her, but more importantly it was the second-to-last phase of his rehabilitation.

He couldn't help but think of Doctor Messana. He was furious with her, but she didn't deserve to die the way she did. Someone in Citadel knew what was being done on that ship, possibly with the dimension drive, possibly with another experiment like the one Messana was running, and they wanted it to stop. Citadel was not an organization that planned its operations poorly. Whatever they intended to do aboard the Fallen Star was already done. Attacking Stephanie was the Citadel Operative's method of committing suicide. Jake was fairly sure they could have found a way to escape if they wanted to, and killing one of his officers was not the most effective way to damage Triton Fleet.

With the operative from Citadel gone, they would have no more answers. All they were left with was that ship, and the experiments that led Messana to break the trust of her Captain and one of her patients. There were people investigating whether or not the cure for framework technology was really as safe as the logs showed. If Messana developed most of that solution, he owed her thanks, but he'd never forgive her for breaking ethical boundaries.

He'd seen the footage of the copy of his daughter awake, thinking that she was the real Alice, and questioning the medical technicians for a long time before trying to leave. She had been transformed into a late teens human girl who really did look like a split between himself and Ayan. Watching her scream for him, try to get to any communicator, then get overpowered was hard. Seeing her suspended in a stasis tube, dead, haunted him. His daughter got her wish, she could grow out of her teen years into a woman, mature, remember and feel like any human, only it was a duplicate, and she died when everyone else on the Fallen Star did. He was happy the ship was being dismantled, most of the experiments carefully catalogued and stored.

Ayan took the sight of a girl who looked like her and Jake in the log footage just as hard. The revelation that Alice cared for her so much that she wanted to be linked to her through DNA was a beautiful thing, but the ruthless experimentation and testing with a duplicate was horrific. Ayan could not look at the failed versions of Alice in the tubes, or the corpse that represented a complete success. That young woman would have been a daughter to her if she survived and was rescued, Jake knew. That may have caused serious drama with Alice, but there was also a chance that the pair would see each other as twins eventually. The timing of the monument ceremony was perfect. Ayan and Jake had an opportunity to mourn that loss in secret, right in front of everyone.

Jake's attention was called back to the present, as he took in the view from the mouth of the cave. He was still on Tamber, but on the opposite side from Haven Shore. Sometimes he forgot that Tamber was so large, less than two percent smaller than Earth, he was told. Not that it was a good comparison. He'd never been to Earth, and knew little about it. The light brown dust at his feet matched the flat lands that stretched out from the cave entrance for as far as the eye could see. Failed terraforming had coated the surface with a crust, and the sun baked it solid. The cave behind him was an anomaly at the base of a mountain. His scans revealed that there was a spring inside with clean water.

"Captain Jacob Valent," said a calm, pleasant voice. "I am honoured to meet the commander, and intrigued by the man. I am Oru."

Jake dusted off his lightly armoured vacsuit and tugged his black long coat straight. Ayan had another one made, since the old design didn't fit. He walked into the cave, minding his step, and got a good look at the man he had come to meet. He was only a little shorter, and wore a white uniform with gold trim.

"You look military," Jake said as he shook the man's hand. His grip was firm.

"I am, but not the same way you are. You go to fight a war, I will be retreating from it," Oru said. "I sense that you're a man who appreciates truth and brevity, so I won't delay in telling you that Lorander is leaving the galaxy."

"So you see us losing?" Jake asked, unable to be anything but calm in the placid space, under the influence of Oru's mood. There was a still blue pool inside the cave, illuminated by unseen lights under the water.

"No, I can't predict that. Even though there are people in my society that believe they can, I know the future is usually uncertain. We all see the coming of an all-consuming war. We can't afford it. There aren't enough of us in this galaxy to make enough of a difference, so we are retreating to a place we have a firm grasp on, where our existence will not be contested."

"Where?"

Oru smiled at Jake. "You might find out someday. Survive this first, then we'll see," he took a deep breath and let it out in a rush before continuing. "But you come for help."

"Yes," Jake said. "We need to finish the research on something we found."

"The dimension drive," Oru said. "Something we've been trying to master for centuries. The one you are installing in your ship will work, but it's still dangerous because you do not understand it. We barely understood the scans we took when the Fallen Star arrived in orbit. Then we realized, the Order of Eden stole that technology from the Edxians. That is their preferred mode of travel between stars. Once we discovered the origin of the technology, we were able to adapt it, and we have five working dimension drives, all of which have been tested."

"They work?" Jake asked. "You were able to build them from scratch, and they work?"

"They do, all of them. We even tried weapon enabling one because we wanted to know why there was no record of an Edxi ship doing that very thing. We discovered what your scientists will soon find out from the records on the Fallen Star. Opening a single rift in dimensional space allows for random exotic radiation, most of which is difficult to measure or detect, to pass into our space. Much of it is not harmful, but there are types that kill organic life instantly, some will melt your hardest metals. The effect is unpredictable, and the dimension drives are not made to control rifts that way. They are made to open a rift, create a tunnel through the space between dimensions like a wormhole, and open another rift at the other end when your ship arrives. A balancing reflex in nature forces both rifts to close within seconds of a ship passing through, so no single rift is open for long. Your vessel is protected by the wormhole tunnel, which has a powerful directionality since natural laws demand the rifts close, and that your ship does not exist outside of its dimension. The forces that would act on a ship without that tunnel are destructive beyond anything we know."

"So weaponizing the dimension drive is suicide," Jake said, not at all disappointed. "But is it faster?"

"It is an invisible means of travel," Oru said. "And it is so much faster that Lorander owes you its thanks. But, you know the dimension drive aboard the Triton will never work."

"I didn't until now," Jake replied.

Oru laughed and sat down on the edge of the pool. "I think we would enjoy each other's company, Captain Valent. We've been watching the dimension drive's construction, and the copy aboard the Triton is missing a few things. It's also being made in such a way that no one will ever be able to configure it properly. We'll give you all the information you need to make dimension drives, and to fix the Triton's system. There is one condition."

"Name it," Jake replied. The advantage they were being given was colossal. He was almost afraid to tell Ayan that he'd gotten as much help from Lorander as she did.

"Protect the technology, even from allies. The dimension drive has the potential to change the shape of the galaxy, and humanity on the whole is not ready. Besides, you should maintain this tactical advantage for Haven Shore for as long as you can. The destruction of Kambis was a blow not even we expected. Without this technology, Tamber will be unable to get supplies to and from trading partners fast enough to survive."

"I can't argue with that," Jake said. "So, you knew I was coming here to ask for your help with this, and you just offer it freely," Jake said.

"We want Haven Shore and Triton Fleet to have the best chance possible in the coming century. I would love to return some day and see this arid landscape lush with life. Tamber has so much potential, and Haven Shore has had a surprisingly good start, even though Ayan does not see it that way. I'm told she hides many regrets, and feels disappointed in her work so far. That is something you can help her with."

"I didn't know our relationship was a large concern for Lorander," Jake said.

"It is for a few of our leaders, the ones who are more interested in watching than doing. I'm just passing some advice along. I'm more interested in the overall picture here in the Rega Gain system. The odds are against your people, but it is possible that this planet could become a golden civilization. Until I met you, I didn't believe it, but now I know. You are not the war machine you once were, you are human, and better for it."

Jake didn't normally like being analysed, but Oru was only confirming what he already felt. "What else can you give us that will help?"

"We've already augmented several changes you were making to your new ship, working through the Solar Forge. Our specialists are certain that Agameg and Finn suspect that there are Lorander modifications to the ship, so we're not worried about them understanding the systems. If they return from the mission you're going on, they will have learned enough about the technology to apply it to designs the Solar Forge works from in the future. There is a lot to learn from the Solar Forge, protect it well."

"I have a daughter," Jake started, watching Oru's reaction carefully.

"Have your medical staff review the experiments," Oru said. "Don't let that work go to waste, Doctor Messana was willing to sacrifice her career to find a cure."

"You really were watching everything here," Jake said.

"That is how we learn these days," Oru replied. "But it wasn't always that way."

"Lorander is more than a Corporation," Jake said, sure that their meeting would end on that question.

"Why are the most important questions so seldom asked?" Oru asked no one in partucular, looking out to the water. "We are a different evolutionary branch of humanity. Hundreds of years ago, Lorander Corporation, a human exploration company, discovered the home world of my people, and discovered humanoid life that almost completely matched their own. The difference was an extra ten or so thousand years of evolution, and my ancestors were intrigued by your culture.

There were terrible cultural conflicts when Lorander Corporation ships began showing up in number. So many of my people wanted to embrace the vigorous lifestyle of humanity, but there were others who didn't believe in the culture. They saw a tendency towards conflict stemming from ideas of religion and territory that we had left behind many generations before. The melding of cultures took a century, but eventually my people began exploring our small corner of the universe, because a culture of curiosity was the result of that turbulent time. People think we are powerful because we have advanced weaponry, but the few warriors in my culture prize protection and precision over brute force. They sent me because I have the dubious honour of being a warrior in a society of scientists and explorers. My entire career has been one of finding ways to protect my people while doing as little harm as possible to the people who would steal from us, or try to destroy us. I'm going off track, answering questions that are drifting through your mind instead of addressing your central curiosity."

Jake nodded, that was exactly what was happening.

"I'm not used to being able to read a mind," Oru told him. "I'm getting a great deal of assistance. Back to your central question. Lorander Corporation is a label our ships and our people wear when we're near the races of this galaxy. We bring back wonders from the universe and trade for what we need, and we offer your people opportunities to join us so our cultural evolution can continue at a human pace. The best thing about this is that we look just like you, so gaining your trust is relatively easy. The exchange between cultures is easy now that we've been at it for so long too."

"But it's one way," Jake said. "You take people in and learn from them, but your people don't join us the same way."

"Is that what you think?" Oru said with an amused smile. "The thought never occurred to you that some of my people find living in sectors of the galaxy dominated by humans irresistible. You would be surprised at how many Lorander people you've met."

"That gets me thinking," Jake replied.

"I'm sorry, I could answer questions about my people for days, but I am short on time. Before I go, I need to tell you that there are worlds in the Iron Head nebula, civilized worlds that haven't been taken by the Order of Eden. You can find allies there, some of whom may be critical to your success in this war. Save Freeground, but don't ignore a good opportunity if you find one."

Jake was irritated at not being able to ask more questions, he wished the meeting would continue for the whole afternoon, and he knew the sense of calm he felt in that cave would be gone as soon as the meeting was over. "Can you tell me anything else that will help us defeat the Edxi. The Order I can fight, but I know they're hiding the Edxi from the galaxy."

"Humanity only believes what it can see, what it can experience," Oru said, standing up. "You can tell everyone that the Edxi are using worlds in this galaxy for their broods, sacrificing millions of humans and other species while they're at it, but they will not know how dire the situation is until they feel sympathy for the victims, until they see the savagery of the brood. You only have to tell your people exactly where it is happening and show them the right recordings. Look for a story that makes you personally outraged and saddened at the same time, then share it."

"I understand," Jake replied.

"I knew you would," Oru said. He looked from the placid pool to the cave entrance. "You know, this spring leads to the water table. It wouldn't take much effort to pump water from here to there," he gestured towards the hard baked dirt. "Add some minerals to the water and a forest will grow out of that inert terraforming crust."

Jake glanced at the pool, then to where Oru was standing only to discover that he'd disappeared. His command and control unit was immediately busy downloading hundreds of gigabytes of data. "Well, good luck Oru, and thank you."

CHAPTER 36
STOP SHOTS

The medical bay of the Revenge seemed cramped. There were nine treatments beds and two surgical bays from what Finn could see. He knew from the specifications that it was next door to a large briefing room on one side, the brig on the other, and a small officer's wardroom at the end. All those walls were made so they could collapse, and grow the medical bay into a much bigger trauma centre. He silently hoped that he wouldn't see the need for that.

Remmy and Ashley came through the main doors, the chattering of crewmen and women in line in the hallway outside came through the door with her while it remained opened. "I mean, I get this whole, clock-stopping thing, and I think it's time, I'm old enough to be this age forever, but the birth control?" Remmy was saying. "If all the women are getting their eggs scrambled, I don't know why the guys need a vasectomy."

"We're not getting our eggs scrambled, they're just going to stop dropping for a while," Ashley said, sitting on the treatment bed beside Finn. "Heya," she said, bumping his shoulder with hers. "Getting your stop shot?"

"Okay, so you're not losing anything, but you still can't have kids, so why us guys too?" Remmy replied.

"Because guests and people off this ship may not have proper birth control," Ashley said. "Crewmen on leave inseminating small populations aren't going to help win the war. It'll just make visits back that way more awkward."

"Do you really think we run around the galaxy, using our willies as a loose lady detector?" Remmy asked.

"I remember those old science fiction shows you showed us on the Warlord. That captain you idolize would stick it in a power socket if you put lipstick and a dress on it," Ashley replied.

Finn couldn't help but laugh at the mental image. He felt much less nervous about the stop shot. He knew there were adverse reactions in a small number of patients, otherwise their command and control units would synthesize the dose they needed, and there would be no reason for the visit to the med bay.

"Okay, that's a bad example," Remmy said, holding his hands up. "Humans hadn't even been to the moon yet."

The door opened and a tall medical technician with a dark beard and darker hair strode into the room. "I'm Ensign Levine," he announced to them. "Sleeves up, everyone. You are the last officers not to have your stop shots, and there are about three hundred enlisted crewmen waiting. He picked up an injector the size of his forearm. "My bots are stuck in a loading bay, and they're having trouble finding my med techs, so it's just me right now, unless you can train one of those skitters to pop people in the arm with this thing?" he asked Finn.

"That's not really what they're made for, but-" Finn said, looking at the injector a little closer. The business end was the same as the painless devices he'd seen before, it just had an extra large reservoir for medication.

"Oh, don't worry about its size," Ensign Levine said, gesticulating with it as he spoke. "Won't even feel like a bug bite."

Remmy was staring at it, horrified. "Why is it so…"

"Convenient?" he asked as he nonchalantly touched it to Finn's shoulder. He felt a cold sensation on the small spot for a few seconds, but there was no pain. "There's enough medication in here to treat two hundred women and three hundred men with stop shots. It's a miracle, really," he said, suddenly spinning on his heel and touching it to Remmy's arm. "Gotcha!"

He held it up in front of Ashley, who bared her shoulder for him. "Here you go," he said as he touched it to her arm. "You may be in for a little swelling for a couple hours, but that'll be it. You are not going to have a bad reaction, I can tell already."

"What about us?" Remmy asked, alarmed.

"Oh, men can have a bad reaction within the first three minutes after the injection, after that, you're clear. You will stop aging, and the nanobots are already on their way to cut and tie your vasa differentia. You won't even notice."

"But, side effects?" Remmy asked.

"Well, there's always the possibility that your testicals will panic and jump up right into your abdomen. You'll sound like a nine year old, but you'll have the singing voice of an angel."

Remmy looked terrified and confused, and Finn couldn't help but let the silence extend for as long as the medical technician allowed, which was almost too long. Ensign Levine slapped Remmy on the thigh and said. "Nah, that's never happened. The worst you'll get is some irritation because some nervous men develop the unconscious need to scratch or grope themselves. Other than that, the only thing you'll notice is the absence of any little ankle biters after a few years with the same partner." He checked his command and control unit, stared at it for a few seconds then said; "and you're all good! No adverse reactions, see ya in three years if you want to breed when your service is done."

"You are an evil man," Remmy said as he left.

"Leave the door open on your way out, I have to do that to a few hundred more today," he called after him. He looked to Finn then. "Seriously, if you could do something about the medical bots in the loading bay?"

"I'll send a message down, get them to deliver them sooner," Finn said.

"All yours, the officers are all taken care of," Remmy announced to the crewmen and women at the door. The long line shuffled forward as people started entering the med bay. He turned to Finn and Ashley "I'm off to make sure I was assigned a top bunk. I'm in a room with three other guys."

"Good luck," Ashley said as he took a turn down a narrow corridor to the left.

"Headed to the bridge?" Finn asked.

"Yahuh," Ashley said. "I have to start the longest pre-flight check in history. How can a ship half the mass of the Triton have a list twice as long?"

"Everything important is new, and everything else is reconditioned," Finn said as he turned down a corridor to his right. He couldn't help but look at the welds in the ceiling and floor. The quality was incredible, there were no flaws anywhere he'd been in the ship since the Solar Forge and the bots it used had its way with the Revenge. It had gone in one end as the flawed, damaged Blessed Mission, and come out perfect on the other side. That was with the exception of the sections of the interior that had to be built while they were under way.

"Ah, I read that the checklist will get shorter as we go, that makes sense," Ashley said.

"You okay?" Finn asked. He'd never seen her have difficulty reasoning through the why and how of ship systems.

"Just a big morning. Your speech was wonderful, by the way," she told him. "After we finished there, I had to say goodbye to Zoe."

"How is she?" Finn asked.

"Growing by the minute. I think she really likes living in the same section of the Everin building as the rest of the nefalli. She's going to have a great time. She didn't want to let go though. When I left, I mean."

"She understood you'd be gone for a long time?" Finn said.

"Yes, when Panloo explained it to her. I've never seen Zoe cry like that before."

"All the more reason to get our mission done quickly," Finn said. They passed a bank of lockers and suspended their conversation as a crewman and woman argued over which locker they were assigned at full volume. He couldn't resist but to turn around, step over the threshold and force silence to fall as a crewman further down the locker compartment called; "Officer on deck!"

"At ease," Finn said. He looked at the locker they were arguing over and pushed the top door. It popped open. Then he pressed the bottom door, which opened as well. "There are two lockers here, not one. The top one is Row E, the other is Row D. Read your intro packets, pay attention, stow your gear, and get to your stations, we depart in two hours, twenty minutes."

"Sir, yes, Sir," said both of them without much enthusiasm.

"You will address the Chief properly!" shouted an enlisted man who was in the middle of sorting his possessions into a locker.

"Sir, yes, Sir!" the pair repeated, standing at attention.

"At ease," Finn said, leaving the locker compartment and continuing on. "I'll never get used to that."

"I think you will," Ashley said. "You've changed. You've grown up."

"Maybe," Finn replied. "I think I just understand how important discipline is now. There are thirteen grades of enlisted people below me. I didn't realize how powerful that was until I looked at the full command chain."

"I know, this is the military," Ashley said. "No more changing vacsuit textures on duty, I always have to set a good example, and we're in charge of so many people. More you, though."

"Yeah, Agameg and I seem to be in charge of forty percent of the crew in one way or another. Anyone wearing uniforms with blue, white or white and blue is one of ours. Thank God Ayan is going to help out for the first while."

"From the Triton?" Ashley asked. "She's a crazy multitasker."

"I've seen over the last few days," Finn said. "I don't know where she finds the time to sleep."

"Speaking of which, have you seen your room yet?" Ashley asked.

"I have a sink, a cupboard, two drawers, a single bed and a locker. Oh, and a door, which is more of a luxury than expected. Agameg's quarters are right against mine, exactly the same."

"Oh, you too, huh?" Ashley said. "Looks like Chiefs and Lieutenants get about the same digs. Well, except for the Lieutenants across the hall. I got a peek, they're two to a room, so they miss out on a row of cupboards and get a few more feet for an extra locker."

"What about Minh?" Finn asked. The noise of the forward berthing finally started to fade as they approached the main hallway. It was the widest place to walk on the ship other than the hangars or supply loading areas.

"His quarters have an extra closet for his flight gear and some weaponry, but somehow the ceiling is shorter. His head brushes the roof, and I have to duck a little."

"I always thought you were taller," Finn said with a smirk.

"A centimetre," Ashley replied.

"All stand at attention and check your nearest viewer, please," announced Lieutenant Commander Liara over the public address system.

"Oh, here we go," Ashley said.

Finn was already standing at attention, and elbowed Ashley, who snapped to as soon as she realized that she was surrounded by crewmembers that had dropped everything they were doing to do the same. A display appeared on the black and white walls every three metres.

On the display, Ayan was standing beside a simple control stick inside the Solar Forge with Jake beside her.

"I present Haven Shore Founder, Captain Ayan Anderson. She is doing us the honour of christening the ship," Liara continued.

"Oh, this means we're late," Ashley whispered through lips she kept mostly still.

"We're just de-tethering from the Solar Forge, they won't miss us for a few minutes," Finn replied in the same fashion.

A fellow in ancient butler's finery handed Ayan a bottle of Black Sail Rum, and she held it up so everyone could see for a moment. "Oh my God, that's Frost," Ashley said.

Finn took a closer look as the butler opened a small round cover, and she carefully dropped the bottle inside. "You're right!" It disappeared, and a few seconds later a green light turned on beside the joystick.

Half the images in the hallway showed a close up of the bow of the Revenge, so the name could be clearly seen. "The rig Captain Anderson is using to launch that bottle against the hull was developed by Chief Frost, and built by our crew."

"I name this ship the Revenge. May she conduct our sailors and soldiers safely to and from war. May she be a beacon of hope to our allies, and a dreaded nightmare to our enemies," Ayan said as she carefully aimed the launcher. She pushed the trigger and the bottle surged forward from the launcher.

"Is that even fast enough to break?" asked a crewman to Finn's left.

"Oh, God, she missed," breathed another.

Finn watched as the bottle moved through empty space. For a moment it looked as though it would miss its target entirely, striking on some random part of the ship or, even worse, flying past it entirely.

A new view angle revealed that it was indeed close to the target, and the bottle of old fashioned rum shattered right in the middle of the last E in Revenge. "A perfect shot! Now the last tethers will release, and we will be free of the station. We are officially ready for final prep," Liara announced. Finn could barely hear her over the cheers and applause of the crew.

Captain Valent and Captain Anderson kissed briefly, and then they walked away in a hurry. The displays along the corridor disappeared, with the show over, but people were still applauding. "Square away, and to your stations!" Finn shouted, even though he was smiling. He glanced at his command and control unit. "Yeah, we're running late now."

"Race you to the bridge?" Ashley asked, lurching into a run.

"Make a hole!" Finn shouted as he chased after her, and the crewmen and women moved aside to let them rush by.

CHAPTER 37
THE FIRST HOUR IN THE CHAIR

There was no extravagance aboard the Revenge. It was true that Jake had moments where he wished he still had the Warlord, but by the time they were under way, heading out of the solar system under power alongside the Triton, he started to fall in love with the simplicity of his new ship.

Knowing you'd done everything you could to improve the design of a ship in the schematic stage, and experiencing the ship first hand were two different things. The centre of the ship had the narrowest hallways and the most cramped spaces. The corridors were wider closer to the outer hull, where heavy equipment, supplies, munitions, and larger groups of crewmembers had to move on a regular basis. The ship was made to go into war, to take damage, and the triple hull design certainly made that clear. The original design of the ship by Regent Galactic was actually much better than Jake would have guessed. The touches and modifications that Ayan, Jake, and a few other crewmembers made to the blueprints were mostly to accommodate the ship's extended purpose. The Battlecruiser was converted into a carrier. Two hangars with short launch bays and extra armour plating made the ship look much more significant. More powerful weaponry that drew very little power but required more space for ammunition gave the ship better survivability in a multi-target fight. He felt confident that the ship would be able to protect the crew, but he was aware that there was much left to do.

The crew quarters had been cleaned up, the computers were replaced, they added the bridge in the middle of the ship, and there were some other minor changes, but, for the most part, the inside of the ship hadn't changed much.

There were a few problems that he had to work out with the Admiral before they made it past the furthest asteroid belt from the sun, however. The bridge of the Revenge was almost centremost inside the ship. Some of the design and layout reminded him of the First Light, with the least important components nearest to the outside of the vessel, most of the crew and critical components under multiple layers of armour.

The narrow bridge felt older than he expected, with dark floors, secure doors on the sides, and an escape hatch at the rear that led to five man pods. Some of them still had to be installed, one of the drawbacks of finishing things while they were under way. Navigation and scanning departments had their consoles at the front of the bridge, tactical to his left, engineering and damage control to his right. Right in front, but several steps down from the captain's seat were the communications consoles along with operations and three other stations. Each department was given two stations, and there were another four behind his captain's seat. It was only cramped if everyone stood up at the same time.

The Flight Operations Deck was still being configured, a task that Lieutenant Commander Stephanie Vega took upon herself. She wanted to know everything about the operation of the ship, and was studying at a break neck pace. As one of the people in charge of the Flight Operations Deck, where fighters and other ships from the Revenge would be directed, she would be one of the top experts on its operation when it was finished. The new opportunities and workload that came with being Jake's First Officer seemed to ignite something in her, and he couldn't wait until he could see what she could do as a commander on his ship.

He was sitting on the bridge, running through the status of their new thrusters when he got the call he was expecting. "Admiral McPatrick for you sir, on secure laser link," Liara announced.

"I'll take it in my quarters, you have command Minh-Chu," he said.

Minh-Chu got up from one of the consoles in front of him that he'd rigged for temporary flight operations and took the command seat. "Not much going on with everything strapped up in our bays anyway."

Jake passed from the bridge, across one of the main corridors where two heavily armoured guards saluted him, and into the Officer's quarters. A few more steps, and he was in his quarters. They were furnished with a half table against one wall with cupboards above, a bench that served as more storage space against one side, his double bed, which he'd already come to call his 'barely double' bed, double locker between the door and the table against the wall, and a soft easy chair. He pulled the easy chair a few centimetres closer to the table and gave up on trying to get it right in front of the middle, settling for slightly off-centre. "Display holographic data there," he pointed to the table.

He opened the cupboard door over his bed and retrieved a cup.

"Jake," Oz said. "Congratulations."

Captain Valent filled his cup with a thick brown nutrient drink. The mini-kitchen unit displayed it as a Chocolate Nutriment Beverage, and offered it in hot or cold temperatures. He tasted it and immediately wondered if it would be better hot. "Thank you," he said. "But I think there may be something wrong with my mini-kitchen. The drink mixer says this is supposed to taste like chocolate, but all I'm getting is chalk. Forma and chalk." He took another sip anyway. The last few days had run him ragged, he could use something fortifying.

"So, you know what this is about," Oz said. "You got Agameg, Finn, and Lieutenant Commander Erron. Not to mention, Governor Anderson hand picked your new medical staff."

"You mean those four bots and three medical technicians?" Jake said, sitting in the easy chair. It was just wide enough, if the arms were any closer together, they'd pinch his hips too much.

"Hey, picked by the Governor, they've gotta be something special," Oz replied. "But back to your two Chief Engineers and Lieutenant Commander Erron."

"You saw the enlistment files. One maintains the ship and keeps operations running smoothly, the other monitors and continues to develop the systems. Very different jobs."

"Yeah, but Agameg could continue developing your systems from the Triton."

"That doesn't make sense from where I'm sitting," Jake objected with a wince that was mostly from braving another gulp of his nutrient drink. "What if something goes wrong? Developing new tech can be dangerous. We both know the Triton is the ship we can't afford to lose."

"All right, but Lieutenant Commander Erron? Liara is probably the top communications and legal officer in the fleet," Oz said. "The Triton will be taking the lead in diplomacy, we need her here."

Jake smirked at the small hologram of Oz on the table. "Should I tell her your first tactic in negotiating to get her back was to understate her talents? We both know the only reason she's a Lieutenant Commander is because she's still under Order Agent watch. As soon as we're sure she's not spying for the other side, she gets Commander rank. She can run hacks and get through information faster than anyone I've seen, and she doesn't have problems running a brain-bud. Even with a direct connection to the ship, she doesn't show any signs of data addiction disorder, hell, she doesn't even seem mildly distracted."

"Kadri," Oz said. "You have your own genius in communications, she's just as amazing as Liara."

"She's wasted on communications. Kadri doesn't have the legal training, and she has a science background. On the Warlord she was playing double duty – communications and scanning officer – but on the Revenge, there's no way I could stretch her. I need her as our eyes, and I need Liara as our ears. Don't worry, I'll pair ensigns with them so new communication and scanning officers will be in training. Besides, you have three lawyers aboard the Triton, and I hear you've got five new scanning officers in training, all with experience. I read staff updates too."

"Where you find the time, I'll never know," Oz replied.

"What can I say? I don't miss my direct connection with the ship because I like reading," Jake replied. "One of the many things I'm discovering about myself on this journey of self-rediscovery. I'm afraid you'll have to do with the great big crew you've got over there."

"I could pull rank," Oz said.

"I'll make you look bad," Jake said nonchalantly. "Everyone will know Admiral McPatrick always has to have the bigger pile. Whether it's getting the nicer ship, or the bigger space superiority wing, or the most well known people, they'll know you just have to have the nicer toys and that's all there is to it."

"You wouldn't," Oz replied.

"You outrank me now, squarely, so the only thing I could do is get some scuttlebutt going about overcompensation."

"You're going to go on every acquisition run we have on this trip," Oz said, shaking his head. "There's no winning at the bargaining table with you."

"I've been doing it a long time," Jake said, happy that his friend was dropping it. "You let me pick my crew, so I did. Besides, you have people over there that were trained by Agameg and that shiny artificial intelligence you have running that ship. I still want a copy."

"We'll go into that later," Oz said. "For now, I'm wondering what we're going to do about the ships the British Alliance assigned to us. I've already sent a message telling them that they're no longer necessary. They said we should be grateful to have them along."

"I was wondering why you were calling on a secure connection," Jake said.

"No point in trusting them with anything when they're watching us like we're the lesser experienced, lesser armed on this excursion. They scan us every three minutes to the second, from bow to stern, and I received a brief introduction from each Captain, no more. When I requested a strategy meeting and orientation session for our command staff with them, they put me on the schedule for day after tomorrow. I wouldn't mind being put in my place if they could pull their weight."

Jake couldn't help but smile a little. The idea of the British Alliance captains putting the Triton and the Revenge commanders in their place was more than a little amusing. "They pack a third the firepower and a quarter of the shielding as the Revenge. They're going to have trouble keeping up with our thrust power outside of a wormhole," Jake said. "Those ships are old, even by our standards."

"I know we could learn a thing or two from the Captains aboard those ships," Oz said. "But technically, they're support at best."

"And the Captains think they're chaperones, and bad ones," Jake said. "I should have paid more attention, looked more closely at the ships the British were sending with us."

"Hey, as part of a defensive screen around Tamber, they're great, those commanders have service jackets that I could roll out the door, but those ships?"

"Hey," Jake said, putting the mug down. "They've got really thick armour."

"If that were enough," Oz replied. "Even if they had the power and speed, they don't have dimension drives, and I'm not comfortable showing them the technology. When we get that working, the game changes, but not if we have three millstones around our necks slowing us down."

"Agreed. It's too soon to share the technology," Jake said. "Everyone in the known galaxy is going to be after these if we can get them working."

"Mine's going to be ready to go in eight hours or less, I have an Ayan in engineering. She tells me the corrections from Lorander will be easy to implement using technology we already have."

"Show off," Jake said. "I'll be ready sometime after oh nine hundred tomorrow. I can't get it done any faster. Checks on the regular systems are going to run through the night."

"Considering the time we're going to save in transit, I don't think a few hours are going to make a difference. So, about these British ships," Oz said. "If I exercise my rights as Admiral of the Triton Fleet and order them back to assist with defence, you would support me?"

"Best choice you've made all day," Jake replied.

"So it's the Triton and the Revenge. Are we opening a wormhole, or are you doing the honours?"

"Our wormhole generator just got a full overhaul, and all our computers just got replaced, we've got to test those systems," he said with a shrug.

"Good idea. You start plotting, I'll tell the British to bugger off," Oz said.

"Oh, and tell Ayan I can't wait for her to be back aboard," Jake said

"Maybe I should have tried trading her."

"Tell her she's the horse in a horse trade," Jake said with a laugh. "I dare you."

"Excellent point," Oz replied.

"Besides, she transfers back as soon as she's finished there," Jake said. "I get the feeling she'll stick around for a while too."

"Until she gets tired of the food and the trademark hard rock Regent Galactic mattresses." The hologram blinked off and Jake picked up his mug. For a moment he thought he may have sloshed a bit over the side, but he discovered that it was too viscous to easily spill. "That can't be right." He muttered as he left his quarters, handed his mug to a Crewman's Mate in white and continued on to the bridge. Minh-Chu was out of his seat in time for him to sit down without breaking his stride. "Told you I'd be able to keep all three crewmembers," he told him.

"No," Minh-Chu said. "How?"

"I'll tell you later," Jake replied. "Helm, set best course wormhole for the Iron Head nebula, hard jump, quarter distance. Wide enough for the Triton to follow alongside."

"You mean, high compression?" Minh-Chu whispered, looking up front where Ashley was running the helm.

"She knows, watch," Jake said, confident in Ashley's knowledge and abilities.

"Yeah, but I don't know," Minh-Chu whispered. "What is a 'hard jump?'"

"It's a wormhole that crosses great distance in as short a space as our generator can manage without giving much care for how gradual the threshold changes space."

"Oh, so like taking a staircase five steps at a time on that first step," Liara said from communications.

"Good analogy," Jake replied.

"Okay, so I knew what that was," Minh-Chu said. "I just didn't know there was a term for it."

"It's in the new Fleet manual," Jake whispered. "We have a lot of reading to do over the next few days."

"You mean, you haven't finished reading it either?" Minh-Chu asked quietly.

"I think the only people who've finished reading it are our Communications Officer and my First Officer."

"You mean, Executive Officer," Minh-Chu said. "So many things are changing, glad I have my fighter squadrons. The squadron may be changing, but the rules are the same."

"Yes, that's because you were smart enough to start your fighter wing using real military regulations and organization," Jake said. "I should have taken your lead on that one with the Warlord."

"Do you want me to forward our helm data to the Triton and the British Alliance ships?" Liara asked.

"Just the Triton, the rest aren't coming," Jake replied.

"No?" asked Finn from his right.

"Why?" asked Agameg, standing beside him.

"When you look at their ship specifications, now that they've been released to us, you'll know why. Helm, how long until that wormhole opens?" Jake asked.

"Forty-nine seconds, Sir," replied Ensingn Clara Ramone, one of the few navigators who Ashley trained aboard the Triton and the Warlord.

"The Triton is signalling a go," Liara said. "And Triton Fleet Command reports that the British Alliance destroyers are slowing. They are off the mission, awaiting orders from British Alliance Fleet."

Minh-Chu looked up at him uneasily.

"Don't worry, it'll all make sense tomorrow on our jog," Jake whispered to him. He sat back and waited for the wormhole to appear in front of their ships.

The crewman he handed his mug to in the hall came through the bridge hatch and presented it to him. It had been washed, Jake's name and rank were freshly printed on one side with the ship insignia on the other. It was three quarters full with the cold nutriment drink. "Sir, I didn't know what you wanted me to do with it, so I put proper insignia on it, and refilled it from the galley, Sir."

Jake was as impressed as he was surprised. It looked like the young man had run extremely hard to have it all done in a handful of minutes. "Thank you so much, Crewman's Mate..." Jake trailed off.

"Viken, Sir. From maintenance, Sir," he said, gulping air.

"Well, thank you," Jake said taking a generous gulp. It was less chalky, but the pasty characteristic of a forma beverage was unmistakable. "Please, return to duty."

"Sir, yes, Sir," he said.

"Where did we find him?" Jake said when he was out of earshot.

"Haven Shore, Sir," Liara answered, to Jake's surprise. "He was an apprentice in the manufacturing shop."

"You don't have to answer every question, you know," Jake said as he pantomimed the act of looking for a place to put his mug. "Knew we missed something. Every command seat should come with a cup holder."

"Checking wormhole for viability and verifying trajectory," Ashley announced. "All checks passed, transitioning."

The ship rumbled slightly as it crossed the threshold into the wormhole's space. Jake checked his tactical screen and saw that the Triton was right behind them. Over the next few minutes they would carefully navigate so they were right alongside, making it difficult for a scanning officer on another ship to clearly see either of them.

Agameg stepped up to the Captain's seat, pressed a button on its arm and a cup holder popped out from the front. "We forgot nothing," he said.

"Thank you," Jake said, putting his mug down. He watched Agameg return to the engineering department where they were busy reviewing the ship's systems. He took a moment to look the bridge over and to enjoy the feeling of being on a military ship. The Revenge was the kind of ship he wanted to grow into. A little more leg room would have been nice, but it was the beast of burden they needed to win major engagements.

Every engagement while Captaining the Warlord was undertaken with a hull much thinner than a proper warship. The Revenge was what he needed, his crew would be properly protected, and properly equipped. Even still, he felt as though he had been killed as one man only weeks before, and woke up as another man. A man of military means and military methods who enjoyed life more than the previous one ever knew how to.

The view from the front of the ship appeared across the entire front wall of the bridge, and he couldn't help but smile. The space outside the wormhole appeared blurred, as usual, but somehow the reassurance that all the work they'd put in over the last few days was paying off made him feel extremely confident in his crew, even though there were over three hundred Crewman's Mates who were there for training.

He brought up a holographic schematic of the ship so he could take a closer look at it in the Captain's seat. The main body of the ship was at the rear, a thick V with the widest side facing front. A broad neck extended from the middle. The old bridge was at the head of the squared off forward section that connected to the rest of the ship in a neck of armour. To the port and starboard sides of the forward section were rectangular armoured rotary thrusters. They located just far enough forward along the neck of the ship's fore so they didn't scorch the hull, but they could turn two hundred and seventy degrees to fore and aft, and sixty three degrees to port or starboard. A railgun turret featuring three four hundred and twenty millimetre barrels sat directly behind the old bridge on top of the front of the ship's neck. On the bottom of the same section was one of the directed electromagnetic pulse beam weapons, capable of firing at anything beneath or in front of the ship through a low profile protective dome. The main launch bay door was located behind that, and the enclosed hangar ran the length of the ship along the bottom, connecting to the two additional hangars, which were sandwiched between heavy armour wings.

The extra armour plating that was added to the ship covered half the neck in a widening V shape, with the widest section at the rear. The whole of the neck section was only seven decks thick, with extra power and weapon systems adding to the thickness. The main section of the ship thickened to fourteen decks, not including armour. At each stage another main railgun turret with triple four hundred twenty millimetre guns were mounted, and two more were mounted at the broadest points of the port and starboard sides of the ship, making for a total of five deadly turrets.

Several other standard anti-fighter and countermeasure turrets were built into the hull, some were computer controlled, while others were manned, but none of them were railgun systems. The purely mechanical turrets used a variable shell system, where the guns could dumb-fire if the power in the ship went out, and the shells could still serve many different purposes.

The other directed electromagnetic pulse beam dome was on the bottom of the ship's main section, along with torpedo and missile systems that required crewmembers to man stations between the launch decks of the hangars and the outer hull. The rear thrusters were spread across the aft section of the hull, above the hangars, and the new rectangular rotary thrusters sat above and behind them. They were heavily armoured, but also had their own shield emitters that assisted the rest of the ship, and a pair of automated point defence guns. They also enjoyed a little coverage from the armoured communications section that was designed to look like another bridge built off the rearmost portion of the dorsal section of the hull. There was a secondary communications system inside the neck of the vessel as well.

Jake could see where crews were running basic tests on systems across the ship, and yellow dots marked where systems still had to be installed. There were dozens of dots throughout the main section of the vessel, and even more inside the new hangars under the left and right wings of the ship.

He was thankful that the ship didn't have rail guns when they faced it before, it could have changed the shape of their encounter entirely. Rail guns were bad enough, but the version he had installed used high explosive shells that spread the damage of the impact out significantly. Two hits from such a weapon would have slagged the Warlord.

He was just starting to bring up the status tracking displays in front of the captain's seat, a holographic scroll that he knew he'd be staring at for so long that he'd see it in his sleep, when Liara gently broke through his concentration. "Now that we're under way and nothing's fallen off, maybe you could do a ship wide?" she asked.

"That's a good idea, thank you," Jake replied. "Engineering, are we ship shape?" he asked.

"Aye, aye, Sir," Finn replied.

"Any problems coming up?" he asked the bridge in general, catching Frost's eye. The man looked a little out of place in a fitted tactical uniform, but happier than Jake had seen him in years. All the stations from his right hand around to his left and behind all checked in green on his display. They were safely under way.

"Well, then, ship wide announcement, please," Jake said.

"Your attention, please, for an announcement from the Captain of the Revenge," Liara said. She turned and nodded to him.

Jake didn't have anything pre-planned, so he started his statement the way he was trained to in the Freeground Fleet so long before. "We have begun our first mission. The Revenge is currently in wormhole transit to our first waypoint. All critical systems are green. I am proud of every single one of you for pulling together as a crew and getting us into space. I am confident that our first mission will be remembered as one of the greatest efforts in what will be the long service of this ship. We will see combat, but not for several days at least, so get squared away, get used to your duties, and stand ready. I encourage all of you to take a moment when your duty shift ends today to record a message for someone at Haven Shore or somewhere within the reach of their communications system. All operational data will be deleted, so don't talk about the state of the ship or our mission, or the message your loved one gets will be pretty short. It may be the last time you can send a message home for a long time. This is a great crew, look out for each other, follow the regulations, the directions of your superiors and you'll learn more than you can imagine. I am already proud to be serving with you."

CHAPTER 38
JACOB VALENT AND MINH-CHU BUU

There were few personnel lifts on the Revenge, and the computer aboard restricted most crewmembers from taking them unless it was an emergency or they were late for a duty shift.

This suited Jacob Valent fine. As the Captain, he could take the lifts whenever he liked, but he hadn't tried one yet. The ship also had a set of bulk movers that carried heavy cargo along the first, fifth, twenty eighth, twenty third and fourteenth decks horizontally, and up and down between all decks. They ran along the broad service hallways that were core to the ship's maintenance.

Jake decided to take his first jog on deck twenty-eight, where the Solar Forge had created quite a surprise for everyone aboard. The track for the bulk movers, square flat bed cars that were several metres across, was opaque, but the decks around them could be mostly transparent with the touch of a button.

The simple artificial intelligence saw fit to show him as soon as he arrived. His original reason for being there was that it was the only broad hallway that ran the full length of the ship, all three hundred thirty three metres, minus the hull thickness. It was perfect for he and Minh-Chu to have a jog on.

"Now that's something," Minh-Chu said as he looked through the smoky transparent metal floor running alongside the bulk mover track. "I can see my fighter from here." The whole main hangar bay was visible below. Jake and Minh-Chu could see that crews were already on shift, getting the ships into position so their only working fighter bay would be ready for use later that day.

"It'll take another week for the secondary bays to be ready, right now they're storage for the rest of the fighter wing," Jake said. "Ready to go, old man?"

"Look who's talking," Minh-Chu said, breaking into a brisk jog. "If experience were age, you'd be twice as old."

Jake had no problem keeping up with him once he got moving, it was starting the run that he was uneasy with. His balance was still not as keen as he would have liked. The extra muscle he'd been given during the six weeks he'd spent in stasis served him well, and he had good endurance, but he needed to keep walking and running as much as he could. They settled in at a good pace, running side by side, and Jake started to realize how long the main access hall was. It was twice as tall as any other floor, and had room on the sides for storage beside the walkways. That space was filled with components that had to be installed on the ship, and supplies that hadn't been moved to the right place due to time constraints. "So, did you check the report for the night shift?" Jake asked.

"Yes, Agameg ended up balancing the power distribution for the ship while he was in the Captain's chair. That one is a serious over achiever."

"Tell me about it, he got us down to using less than one percent of our output while we're under power in a wormhole. I knew the fusion generators on this ship were good, but I would have never imagined they were that good."

"Yeah, I meant to ask you about something," Minh-Chu said. "There's no antimatter aboard anywhere, did the Warlord spook you off the stuff?"

"That's part of it," Jake replied. "But antimatter also comes up on scans a lot faster than anything else, and we don't have any real cloaking systems right now."

"That makes sense," Minh-Chu said. "So the torpedoes you're going to be using, if they're not antimatter, what are they?"

"Guided drillers, with high explosives. Only useful once a ship's shields are down, and they take a little while to punch through the hull, but they make a big mess when they do."

"Nasty," Minh-Chu said. "So, do you think there's going to be a large need for fighters in the nebula?"

"Bigger than ever. Our sensors are going to have limited range in dense areas, so we're going to need to extend them using your fighters. That, and we're going to be up against the real Order of Eden Fleet in there. If they're after Freeground, there's going to be a lot of them. The new gunships can do a lot of damage if they take something by surprise, especially if they're each flanked by two Uriels. Mainly, though, we need your Fighter Wing because the Revenge is not a close combat carrier. She may have the armour, but her weapons are made for long range, so your fighter wing will be the first line of defence."

"We have a lot of green pilots. I don't know of I'd trust those nuggets to keep the enemy where you want them," Minh-Chu said. They passed a group of five Crewmen in white and blue vacsuits. Each of them were low ranking Enlisted, Grade three or below, the morning duty shift was just starting.

Jake replied once they were past them. "That's why we're going to have to rough it for the first while, take the Revenge closer than I'd like if your fighter screen doesn't work out."

"It'll work out," Minh-Chu said. "As long as I'm out there flying with the right wingmen. The gunships are going to make a real difference too, they've got good survivability, are about as heavily armed as the average corvette class warship. With the right loadouts, and good pilots, they will be kings of the strike and fade attack."

"Exactly. The Revenge will be a great big fat target though, so your fighter squadron won't get all the attention. The Clever Dream will play the role of scout, cloaked."

"What about the Triton?" Minh-Chu asked.

"They'll be thirty thousand klicks or more above or below," Jake replied.

"The Revenge will be the bait," Minh-Chu said.

"Our shields are good for it, and the Triton will hit them from out of nowhere," Jake replied. "The problem is, you have to find a place to fit in with your fighters."

"Nah, we'll run patrols, try to catch anything hiding on the outskirts of your sensor range. It'll work out, you'll see. Just get all my fighter bays working," Minh-Chu said.

"Yes, Sir, Wing Commander, Sir," Jake replied. He wasn't winded at all, so he followed the automated medical advisor's advice and turned the resistance of his suit up five percent. With all his muscles working against the suit, he immediately felt like he was starting to get real exercise.

"You know, the Rangers jog and do obstacles practically nude," Minh-Chu said.

"Yup, I've seen," Jake said. "I'm a space combatant, everyone on this ship is. We should be used to wearing vacsuits at all times."

"Old Freeground Fleet doctrine," Minh-Chu said. "I agree, but I have to admit, the Ranger outfits are something else. Have you seen the Ranger ladies jogging around Haven Shore?"

"My daughter's a Ranger," Jake replied, more to put Minh-Chu on the spot than to object to his statement.

"They look very athletic, warrior like, even," Minh-Chu said, backpedalling with a chuckle.

Jake nearly lost his balance for a moment, but recovered and kept running.

"You all right?" Minh-Chu asked.

"I turned the resistance of my suit up, just learning to fight through it," he replied. "So, how many people on your crew broke regulations last night?"

"Nine," Minh-Chu said. "Only two were pilots, and they were both fraternization rule violations. The rest were either out of bounds, or late for duty."

"Lucky," Jake said. "There were a hundred five violations made by the rest of the crew. Six were officers, one was a senior officer."

"What? That's a really high number, right?"

"For the first night in the military after taking people in only based on their records and their qualification testing? No, that's less than ten percent of the crew," Jake replied. "I was expecting about three hundred."

"Seriously?" Minh-Chu said. "So what are you going to do?"

"Well, I'm going to talk to Stephanie, but I bet we'll end up doing similar punishments across the board. Anyone who broke violence or substance abuse regulations will see me in Captain's Mast."

"How many will you be seeing?" Minh-Chu asked.

"Nineteen enlisted, two Officers. One is Frost, so that'll take ten seconds," Jake said.

"Whatever punishment you dole out for him will be nothing compared to what Stephanie does to him," Minh-Chu said. "I know it's confidential but-"

"Rum," Jake said. "Crewcast recorded him giving a cup of Black Sail rum out to his senior gunnery team. I doubt Stephanie will give him a hard time, she'll have some fun at his expense though."

Minh-Chu laughed, "But you've gotta set an example, right?"

"A light one for that, but he's getting restriction for a week, then it's his responsibility to punish his people."

"Oh, that's going to suck," Minh-Chu said. "I'll watch what you do to punish your people before I punish mine. There's a guide in the regulations, but I'm thinking I'll go light this time."

"Just a warning and a little restriction to duty?" Jake said.

"Exactly, except for the one who started a fight. Sticky got into it with an Engineer's Mate and broke his nose," Minh-Chu said. "You'll hear about it, the engineer is on your list."

"What Sticky getting?" Jake asked.

"No flight priviledges for three days, she gets to be my sensor intercept officer instead, and extra watch for five," Minh-Chu said. "Can't start fights across departments or across ranks."

"Or at all," Jake said.

"That too," Minh-Chu said. "Speaking of, have you thought of trying martial arts training? Great balance and discipline."

"I was programmed with some as a framework," Jake said, "And Doctor Messana made sure there was a good basis for martial arts in the muscle memory work she did on me. I should try. Are you offering?"

"I'm not your guy," Minh-Chu said. "All I have is the old Freeground training, and I'm rusty."

"That was good training," Jake said. "Served me well so far. Why don't we start something every third morning?"

"All right, but just you and I at first, we'll have to get a good grip on it before we start getting other people into it. We also need someone for more involved martial arts, you know, to keep things interesting."

"Stephanie," Jake said. "We need Stephanie in on this. She can throw people three times her size around, has a gymnastics background and they trained in cross discipline martial arts when she went through her military training."

"I am not surprised," Minh-Chu said. "Let's take a break. I'm in shape, but obviously not your kind of shape, we've been pinning it and you're barely winded."

Jake felt a little sweat on his brow, but had to admit that he was finding the morning jog fairly easy, even with his suit fighting his every movement. They sat down on a pair of crates along the side of the hall. There were over a hundred crewmembers within sight, starting their morning, loading equipment, parts and supplies onto carts. "Sorry, Minh," Jake said. "I'm only as good as they made me."

"You're going to have to start bench pressing railgun shells to stay in that kind of shape," Minh-Chu replied. "Or running with a gravity enhancement pack."

"Not a bad idea," Jake replied. "But I think this morning run is a good way to catch up before the day starts."

"Let's invite all the department heads," Minh-Chu said. "Better than sitting down for a morning briefing with bad coffee and a tray full of forma pastries."

"Good idea."

"For now, let's do one more lap, then I need coffee," Minh-Chu said.

They started running, Jake enjoyed a look through the last fifty metres of transparent hull as an army of skitters started moving boxes and major components for the aft launch bay under the direction of several crewmembers. Alone, a skitter was only a small shiny dome of metal, a smaller brain, and a bunch of tiny but strong arms that they used to walk, carry objects or interchange for tools. As a group, the skitters were strong, could pile up on top each other, and make repairs quickly. He made a mental note to order more from the Triton manufacturing bay.

"All brace for test firing," announced Frost over the public addressing system.

"Someone's pushing his crew this morning," Minh-Chu said, running to the wall and leaning. "Must be punishment for last night."

"I get the feeling it's going to be worse for them than it will be for him," Jake said. "At least we're out of wormhole transit on time."

The ship rumbled and shuddered as several thuds echoed from above. "I counted nine," Minh-Chu said.

"Same here," Jake added. "Where's the other-" he was cut off as three more of the main railgun turrets fired. "Are they not firing the last three?" The last three fired. Jake checked his command and control unit and found his fears justified. "That was supposed to be our first simultaneous load and fire."

"Those were all supposed to go off at the same time?" Minh-Chu asked. "Frost has some work to do."

"You know it, at least the ship is handling the stress well," Jake said.

"If that's what it felt like down here, then I'd hate to be one deck below," Minh-Chu said.

"All clear, all clear," said Chief Frost over the communications system. "Next test in ten minutes."

"Oh, that's going on all morning," Minh-Chu said.

"Fine by me," Jake replied. "I told him to get his gun crew in shape, that's what he's doing." He ran up a ramp then through a tall pair of secure doors. They opened for he and Minh-Chu as officers, and they came face to face with the dimension drive, sitting in the middle of a space surrounded by three levels of catwalks. Jake stopped and looked at the strange machine.

"So, first test on that today too?" Minh-Chu asked.

"Aye," Jake replied. "We're going to make it to the nebula by noon."

"Can I wait outside in a fighter, just in case?"

"If you wait outside, then I'll have to let everyone wait outside," Jake said.

"Going to be a busy day," Minh-Chu said.

"May as well get to it."

Chapter 39
New Ground

After dealing with crewmembers who broke regulations for over two hours, while Frost's gunnery team practiced firing their giant rail gun turrets all morning, Jake was ready for some quiet experimentation. He sat in the Captain's seat with a view of the bridge in front of him, and a view of the Flight Operations Centre above and in front. The floor was transparent, and they were connected through an independent communications system so he could speak to his Executive Officer whenever he needed to.

Stephanie sat in front of her pedestal style console in a high seat with the Flight Operations Team in front of her. The bridge and the Flight Operations Centre were reversed and miniature versions of the same thing on the Triton, made to direct everything that went on inside and outside the Revenge. Stephanie had her staff sorted out, and the consoles ready, they no longer needed help from the Triton to track and control launched fighters or other craft.

"We are ready, Sir," Stephanie said through their communications link. "Triton reports ready as well."

"All departments report ready?" Jake asked his bridge staff.

"All departments ready," Agameg replied. "I'm excited."

"Activate dimension drive," Jake ordered. He watched the status of the drive and the energy fields around his ship, ready to cancel the test at the first sign of trouble. A flash of light signalled the opening of a rift in space ahead of them.

"Reading normal radiation, there is an energy tunnel with directionality pulling at our ship, but we are holding," Kadri, the new Science and Sensor officer reported.

"Triton is launching their drone," announced Stephanie.

"Launch ours as soon as theirs is through," Jake ordered. He watched as the first drone disappeared into a rift in space that was invisible to the naked human eye.

"Our drone is away, approaching the rift at high speed," Stephanie said.

Their drone disappeared seconds later. Jake silently admitted that he was just happy to see one of their autonomous ship launchers work, none of them had seen practical testing.

"Rift is closed," Kadri reported. "Minimal residual radiation, most of what I'm seeing isn't exotic at all, anyone scanning would think it was energy and particles left over in the wake of a large ship. Almost exactly the same as our current hyperspace technology."

"Now we wait for a signal from our drone," Stephanie said. "We should see something in about thirty seconds."

"What about our drive?" Jake said. His console told him it was properly powered down to standby mode. "Anything in the details that could be trouble?"

"No power build ups, no anomalies at all," Finn said. "Everything is working as expected."

"Good."

"Our drone has made it across, and is signalling using a micro-wormhole through normal space," Stephanie said. "Data is coming in, the drone is undamaged. It had to make constant course corrections so it didn't collide with the Triton's drone."

"What about their drone?" Jake asked.

"The same, they report that their drone suffered no damage, even when it tried to break through the wall of the energy tunnel. The tunnel moved with the drone, but the containment did get weaker. The drones were being squeezed together though, and it took most of their thruster power to keep from colliding."

"Okay, so far we're learning a lot," Jake said. "Get ready for the next test."

"This is fast, Jake," Minh-Chu said. He looked excited. "That's a light year every twenty minutes. No deceleration or acceleration time, just really fast through dimensional space, then full stop."

Jake couldn't help but wonder what kind of foe the Edxi would be, if they had mastered dimension drive technology. It created many tactical problems, and he was already starting to rethink his decision to skip adding cloaking systems to the Revenge. "That is much faster than what anyone has right now," Jake replied. "Let's finish testing so we know we won't kill ourselves trying to use this thing."

Four hours and five tests later, the Revenge had expended a quarter of its drones, and all the results coming from the Triton and their own systems were telling them that it was safe technology. They'd tested both drives as well, and the results told them the same things. The only issue with the dimension drive was that bodies travelling together would be attracted to each other, making any kind of journey taken with multiple ships a dangerous proposition.

"It's our turn," Jake said. "All hands, we are going to attempt to use the dimension drive to travel with the Revenge. This will be a one-minute long trip."

"Dimension drive is charged," Finn said. "Ready."

"Helm is ready, Sir," Ashley said.

"Open the door, navigation," Jake said.

"Hey, that's not bad," Minh-Chu whispered.

"Dimension drive activated, rift open," Agameg announced.

"There is a viable corridor," Kadri said.

"We're going in," Ashley reported.

At first there was no difference in what they were seeing with the naked eye, the view was the same. Jake's console told them that they were entering a funnel like energy doorway that led to a slightly curved energy tunnel, or corridor as Kadri put it. A brief creaking sound filled the cabin and suddenly none of the readings he saw past ten metres away from the hull made sense. Inside the transit corridor, it looked like normal space with an energy much like gravity pulling them forward at great speed, but outside it was nonsense.

The view inside the bridge displayed on the walls was of a blue-white expanse of twisting energy. Glowing bodies of shadow drifted between eddies of light. "We've got to learn how to scan this space," Jake said.

"First we have to find out what we're seeing," Kadri replied.

They exited through another tear in space and Jake immediately saw their drones on his tactical display. "Predictable, stable, easy to manoeuvre,"

"And fast!" Minh-Chu said. "No difference in speed between us and the drones."

"How's our hull?" Jake asked.

"Sensors aren't picking up any cracks or other damage," Finn said. "Sending our army of skitters out to perform a close scan, it should take about half an hour."

"All right, move us out, we want to be well clear when the Triton arrives," Jake said.

"Getting out of the way," Ashley said, firing the main thrusters and accelerating away from their arrival point.

"The Triton is signalling that it is about to enter its own rift," Liara announced.

The Revenge moved well out of the way and decelerated, and the crew waited. Seconds later, the Triton arrived, as though coming out of nowhere and stopping instantly after moving at a great speed.

"Captain," Kadri said. "I'm scanning the Triton's hull and can't find any flaws. It matches our previous scans perfectly. Their scan data of us is the same. I'll admit I don't understand everything about this technology, but I'm going to clear it for longer distances."

"Captain Anderson is hailing us from the Triton, Sir," Liara announced.

"Put her through," Jake replied. The image of the Triton Command area of the Bridge, with Oz sitting in the middle seat and Ayan sitting beside him, appeared on the front wall of the Revenge's bridge. "This technology works," Ayan said. "The information and schematics that Lorander provided got us over the hump, and it's working reliably. Not only that, I understand why it works. We've always had theories that there are infinite dimensions, but this proves it and takes advantage of our most advanced science in that field."

"So you think it's safe to use it for travel?" Jake replied.

"Considering what these drives do for us, yes," Ayan replied. "The energy corridor does not appear as a natural phenomenon, it's completely the result of a subsystem inside the drive, I can pinpoint all the subsystems and tell you what they do, I'm sending the document to your engineering team now so they can start performing component by component checks."

"Congratulations," Jake said. "You may be one of the first humans to understand this technology."

"Thank you," Ayan said, distracted by the work she was doing on her console. "I think it's time for us to go to the Iron Head Nebula," Ayan said. "The technology is ready, and once your people look at this information, they'll be ready to use it safely."

"We weren't ready to use it safely before we went through the dimensional tunnel?" Minh-Chu muttered under his breath. "I really am going to go outside in a shuttle next time you test new toys."

"All right, so we recall our drones, finish our integrity scans and the rest of our good scientific practices, then we get moving?" Jake asked.

"Sounds like a plan to me," Oz replied. "Don't forget to send your crew's email packet through a wormhole pointed at Haven Shore before we go, it might be the last mail call we get for a while."

Chapter 40
Balance and Truth

Captain Valent was actually glad to be summoned to the infirmary by their new lead medical technician, Ensign Levine. The distraction was welcome. Even though he was about the business of running a ship, which was a sixteen hour a day job where he was always on call, he still found himself thinking about the strange space they were moving through. If one thing went wrong, they could be flung into an unpredictable maelstrom of strange energies and objects. When he managed to bury those anxieties, and he happened upon a quiet moment, he remembered the people who he missed most.

He already wished he could have brought Alice along, and wished he could check on her, even using Crewcast. What made matters much worse was that he knew that Governor Anderson, the last research doctor he knew and the only one he trusted, had inherited everything from the Fallen Star and was busy relocating it. He was also doing an intense study of Doctor Messana's research into curing Alice, and was optimistic. Whether he could use the ill-gotten methods if they were effective was another question, one which Jake trusted Governor Anderson with.

He wished he could speak to someone about his daughter back home, and the developments there, but Ayan didn't transfer from the Triton before they entered the dimensional rift. She had too much research to finish there, and it was the best thing for the fleet. Jake understood, and felt childish for missing her already, but there it was. So, he endlessly read reports – no matter how boring or trivial – checked systems, and ran efficiency simulations while sitting in the Captain's chair. That was, until the Ensign called him down to the infirmary.

Jake had to admit that he found Ensign Zachary Levine, their new doctor, amusing. Ensign Levine was born on Kambis and raised on Tamber in a small mining and manufacturing town. He was trained as a medical technician by the local military and had a decades experience in the field and in space. Everything about the man's service record made him the perfect candidate to lead the Revenge's medical team. Another thing Jake liked about him was that he was in no way interested in experiments or long-term research.

The infirmary was neat, clean and surprisingly busy. There were still people who needed their obligatory stop shots. They were lined up outside and there was an injured crewman he didn't see straight away. Jake sat on one of the treatment beds like any other patient, a narrow bot with a smiley face painted on its flat, featureless face. "The medical technician will be with you shortly," it said.

Jake could hear the groans of a patient behind a curtain. "You're not a medical bot, are you?" Jake said to the slender droid that greeted him, looking for the bots that he'd managed to get his hands on for the Revenge. He could only see one of the four-armed, circular machines.

"I am not. I'm a receptionist and host bot that has been serving Medical Technician Levine for four years. He found me in a junk heap while he was serving on the Plains of Gusette and decided that I could be useful at holding non-critical objects, cleaning and speaking to patients while they wait. It was a glorious day when he turned me on and put me to a finer purpose, serving ailing humans."

"Who painted that on you?" Jake asked.

"What? Is there something on my face?" the droid asked, mildly alarmed.

"Never mind," Jake said.

"Someone forgot to activate the medical features on their vac-suit," Jake heard Ensign Levine say to the patient behind the curtain. "No wonder you broke your leg. Let me show you how to activate all the features of your suit so it protects you next time."

"Wait, aren't you going to treat my leg first?" asked the patient behind the curtain.

Jake had an idea that he knew what was about to happen, but listened quietly. "Do you need anything, Captain?" the hospitality bot asked.

"No, just be quiet, I want to hear this," Jake said.

"As you wish, Sir," replied the hospitality bot.

He listened to what was happening on the other side of the curtain closely. "Well, since the technology in your suit would fix your leg the same way I would, I'll activate it so you never forget to enable it before your shift again," Ensign Levine said. "Let me show you, the activation is right here under the critical systems control menu on your command unit."

A yelp of surprise and pain signalled to Jake that the suit, and the emergency medical systems had been activated. He knew that nanobots had been injected, the suit gripped, stretched and flexed to set the bone properly, and in a moment the bone would be mended. "Son of a Bitch!" the patient shouted. Ensign Levine most likely neglected to activate anaesthetic on the man's suit.

"You can swear all you want in my med bay, but don't insult my mother," Ensign Levine said as he emerged from the curtained area of the infirmary, his attitude perfectly pleasant. "Now, your leg is fine, but you can take a minute to relax, and man up before you get back to work. I need that bed." He turned to Jake, who was thoroughly amused. "Captain! I didn't expect you to report in so quickly."

"Good to meet you," Jake said, shaking Ensign Zac Levine's hand. "Welcome to the Revenge."

"Good to be here, thank you for my infirmary," he replied. "I was surprised when the Governor tapped me for this job, I couldn't wait to get back to space."

"I'm sorry about Kambis," Jake said.

"Not your doing," Ensign Levine said. "So, what brings you in, balance issues?"

"Yes," Jake said. "I think its just part of my recovery. I wasn't able to walk at all a few weeks ago, but thanks to physical therapy, I'm on my feet, but I'm not steady yet."

"Log says you went for a jog this morning," Ensign Levine said, bringing up a holographic display of Jake's records using his hospitably droid. "Have you ever gotten dizzy while sitting?"

"A few days ago, yeah," Jake said.

"Okay, let me do a quick scan here." Ensign Levine pointed a small box at Jake's head and clicked it. He looked at the scan results using the holographic display and nodded. "Your brain is getting conflicting information from your eyes and your inner ear. Your suit's diagnostic missed it because it calibrated with the problem in place. It got tricked into thinking that it was a normal defect for you."

"So, the balance issue isn't a normal thing for my kind or recovery," Jake said.

"Not at this stage," Ensign Levine said as he accepted a small pointed tool from a round medical bot. "Look over there, Captain," he told him.

Jake did as he was told and Ensign Levine put the device he was holding into his ear slightly. He felt a cool pinch. "Lay down for a moment, you're going to get real dizzy in a sec."

Jake barely made it to a flat position before the world seemed to spin. "That's normal?"

"The nanites I just sent into your head are correcting the inner ear problem, so you're going to be very dizzy for a minute or two. You can expect severe dizzy spells for a few hours following.

"What was it, exactly?" Jake asked.

"A tiny abnormal growth on the vestibular nerve connecting the inner ear to your brain. After we're done here, the chances of it recurring will be very low, but your command and control unit will know how to take care of it."

"Captain Valent, please report to the bridge," announced Lieutenant Commander Liara over the intercom.

"And we're done here," Ensign Levine said. "Just take it slow for the next few hours, and your equilibrium should restore itself. Trust your suit, it'll help you walk upright while you're trying to find your balance. Oh, and you're confined to the completed areas of the ship for the next two days."

"Is my balance going to be that screwed up?" Jake asked, sitting up. A wave of dizziness overcame him and he slipped off the treatment bed. The world seemed to wobble around him as he fell on his side.

"Wow, you went down pretty fast there," Ensign Levine said with a chuckle. "Sorry I didn't catch you, Sir, I didn't have a chance."

One of the medical bots pulled Jake up onto his feet, and he had to admit, he was anything but steady. "I have to get to the bridge," Jake said.

"Okay," Ensign Levine said, taking Jake's command and control unit into his hand and programming his vacsuit's artificial muscle layer to do all the balance and walking work for him. "Marionette time," Ensign Levine said. "Now, when the bot lets go, just go limp."

The medical droid backed away, and Jake had a moment where he couldn't catch his balance, then it partially subsided. "Can't really catch my balance here," Jake said.

"I'll have Marion here follow you to the bridge," Ensign Levine said, gesturing to his hospitality bot. "She's good and sturdy, just put your hand on her head and let your suit do the work. Oh, and you may feel some nausea, your suit will treat that as it comes up, pun intended. That'll get you to the bridge, but you're staying in your chair for the rest of your duty shift, then straight to your room. A bunch of balancing exercises will come up when you get there. Do them for an hour at least before you go to bed."

"How long will the recovery be?" Jake asked, feeling his suit adjusting for his unsteady stance.

"You'll improve over the next three days or so. No jogging for at least five, Captain," Ensign Levine said. "I'm clearing you for some fitness meds so you can keep your physique up."

An alert came up on Jake's command and control unit. They had just arrived in normal space. "Thanks, Ensign," he said, putting his hand on the slender hospitality bot.

"No problem, just do those balancing exercises whenever you can. I'll watch your progress. The nanites I put in your head should start helping you gradually balance out. You'll see a real difference sometime tomorrow."

"No way to speed this up?" Jake said as he fought the sensation that he was about to fall down again. His suit forced him to stand straight.

"Sure, there's a cybernetic assembly I could have built in your head. An army of nanobots would go in there and replace all the pertinent bits with cybernetic versions that we could calibrate in about an hour. I'd rather not, though," Ensign Levine said. "And if I'd rather not, you'd better not."

"I'll take your word for it and stick with what I've got," Jake replied.

"Now, off to the bridge with you. I have every confidence that you'll make it. Just don't fight your suit, it knows which way is up."

He found walking out of the infirmary, down the hall and into a lift was almost as bad as his first attempts at walking. His legs were cooperating, it just seemed that nothing else – the deck, the walls, the other crewmembers in the hallway – were. It seemed as though the deck was moving under foot, and he grasped the thin hospitality droid's head for dear life as the muscles in his suit did their best to keep him upright.

Frost met him in the hall and put himself under one of his arms. "Are you all right, Captain?" he asked quietly.

"Just had a tiny tumour removed and it's going to take me a bit to find my balance, a few days, maybe," Jake said. "Have to get to the bridge."

"Into the lift," Frost said as they made the transition from corridor to small box fit for five people.

Jake got a notification that he had just gotten a shot of anti-nausea medication, and was thankful he didn't have to deal with the embarrassing alternative. "Wow, if I knew this was what I had to look forward to as a cure, I think I would have waited."

"Our new medical master doesn't do much waiting around," Frost said in agreement. "He sees there's a cure, gets you fixed and moves you on. Normally, my kind of medic."

"Same here, but," Jake jerked and fought for balance as he suddenly felt as though the floor of the lift tilted violently. With the help of his suit, Frost and the bot under his other hand, he recovered.

"Floor's perfectly stable," Frost said. "Was this what it was like when you were in recovery?"

"It was a lot worse," Jake said. "And Levine said this would only last a few days if I do the exercises." The trio left the lift, and everyone who saw them in the corridor stopped and stood against the wall until they passed. "What do you think of the ship, Chief?" Jake asked.

"Loving it so far, Captain. My gunnery team hates me just enough. I got those bastards out of bed an hour early this morning for extra cleaning duty. There's something satisfying about seeing racks of thirty-two soldiers jump out of their bunks and stand to when you hit the action alarm."

"You're an evil man," Jake said. "I didn't hear guns firing at oh six-thirty this morning though."

"Ah, we practiced loading, clearing, aiming, but not firing," Frost said. "I don't need to torture the rest of the ship to get my gunnery boys and girls into shape."

"Glad to hear it, how are they doing?" Jake said, jerking again as he felt the floor tilt forward and back.

"Getting into shape," Frost replied. "They're not as quick or clean as I like, but they'll get the guns firing on time. They'll be fit by the time we get automation installed, and ready to take over if that automation fails."

They reached the bridge and Jake saw that there were only seven paces at most between the hatch and his chair. "Going to take this on my own," he said to Frost quietly.

"Aye, easy lad," he said as he let Jake go.

Jake tried to relax and let his suit do all the work, then let go of the hospitality droid. "Go on back to medical," he told it.

"Yes, Sir," Marion the hospitality droid replied.

Jake caught himself jerking to compensate for a deck that seemed to be tilting, and tried to relax. The door and deck straightened for a moment and he forced himself to walk forward. The suit kept him upright for the most part, and he sat in his chair hard.

"Are you all right?" Stephanie asked from above him in the Flight Operations Centre.

"Now that I'm sitting?" Jake asked with a snicker. "Much better."

CHAPTER 41
SAMURAI SQUADRON

"it is good to have women in the Wing," Hottie said as he leaned against the back wall of the Samurai Squadron Briefing Room, eying Sticky appreciatively from behind. She was leaning over the mission table, a gridded white surface with holographic projectors built in, trying to fix it. "I just love the way a vacsuit stretches and clings when it's worn by the right curves, and she has the nicest aft section in the fleet."

"You're grounded for three days," Minh-Chu said, putting his hand on Hottie's shoulder as he came through the door.

"Seriously? For admiring the view?" he replied.

"There are places where you can talk like that if you want, but it's not on this ship," Minh-Chu said.

"What? We're just waiting on you, and only these guys heard me."

"You remember how you got that call sign, Hottie?" Minh-Chu said, taking no care to keep his voice down. The entire Samurai Squadron, all twenty one were there, and they knew something was going on at the rear of the briefing room. "Let's take a look at that footage."

"What? No!" Hottie said.

It took Minh-Chu only seconds to recall the footage in question, then send it to the working holographic table in the middle of the Briefing room. An image of Hottie with his vacsuit re-shaped so he had fake exaggerated womanly curves appeared. He was in the Pilot's Den aboard the Triton, sitting down seductively and pretending the table in front of him was a control panel. "Oh, Captain, would you like me to change course?" he said in a breathy, overly sexed manner. "You know, training is so easy, they all pay so much attention to me."

The spectacle was made worse for Hottie, who was cringing at the sight of himself pantomiming Ashley in an oversexed way, the gathered pilots of Samurai Squadron weren't whistling and catcalling at the hologram, they were doing it in his direction. Minh-Chu shut the playback down and turned to Hottie. "Quiet," Minh-Chu said. He didn't have to say it loudly or forcefully for his pilots to calm down. "So, that's how you got your call sign, and I get that you had twelve shots of Hakri Slider in you when you put on your show, but now I've got you leering and commenting at one of our own, while you're sober. There are three big reasons why we don't do that here. First, you make people feel like objects, like they're only a stack of parts. Second, you risk making a whole part of this fighter wing uncomfortable. Third, there's a no fraternization rule for each department, do you know why that is? It's because we're all brothers and sisters in here. You may not like some of these pilots, they may not like you, but because we're brothers and sisters, we get each others backs, we are a family. I just caught you staring at one of your sisters, and what you said would definitely get spread around. If I get the feeling that someone in this squadron will have a second thought about saving your ass out there because of something you said in here, I will have to remove you. If Slick doesn't want you on the Triton, then you'll have to pull duty somewhere where it doesn't matter what anyone thinks of you until we get back to Tamber and we can dump you off. That's where you're headed if you ruin the confidence this squadron has in you."

"You should have heard what he said before you came in," said Fury, an older female pilot who Minh-Chu just drew into the Squadron from the Triton. "It's on Crewcast, I'm sure."

"Do you have time to come to Captain's Mast tomorrow, Fury?" Minh-Chu asked. "So we can address this pilot's problem the right way?"

"I have watch, then mandatory rest for the rest of the day," Fury replied. "Just tell me when to be there."

"C'mon," Hottie said. "For looking and a bit of appreciation?"

"If you make her uncomfortable, you make us all uncomfortable. Besides, that's no way to treat your sister," Minh-Chu said mildly. "Communications is giving a course on fraternization and appropriate dating aboard, you're going to be there."

"Grounded and a class? That's overkill," Hottie said.

"Those aren't even your punishments. I'm just grounding you because it'll make everyone feel better, the class is so you can learn a thing or two. Your punishment will be decided in front of the Captain, our Communications Officer of rank and me at Captain's Mast."

"So, I can't even compliment someone?" Hottie said.

Minh-Chu sighed. "Quick demonstration before we get to the briefing," he announced. "Sticky, can you pay a respectful compliment to Fury?"

Sticky, a petite young woman with large dark hair, turned to Fury and smiled. "You look great today, I wish I could do that with my hair," Sticky said.

"See, that's not as colourful as what you were saying," Minh-Chu said. "But you can pay someone that compliment anywhere, and no one will feel uncomfortable about it. Now, grab a seat and be quiet while everyone who will be launching when we reach normal space discusses our mission."

The whole room shifted focus as they took their seats. A third of the room was occupied by comfortable seats made for long mission analysis and briefing sessions, the middle had the two holographic tables, and the rest of the room was still unused.

It was refreshing to see a full sized squadron, with twenty-one pilots including himself, in a proper squad room. He hadn't had as much time to know them as he would have liked, but he could tell most of them either had a good professional attitude, or looked up to him. He hoped he'd get as lucky with the other squadron, the Marauders. "We will return to normal space tomorrow at sixteen hundred hours. At that time Samurai Squadron will launch."

Minh-Chu brought up a tactical display showing the mess they were going to head into. Hundreds of thousands of massive shards of ice were strewn between patches of gaseous clouds and other particles. "The mystery in this section of the Iron Head nebula, called the Death Cap, is where this ice rich asteroid field came from. The shape of the ice suggests that it comes from something shattering, but no one on record has proven what that was. The best guess is that the original object that this ice belt originates from was approximately two hundred times the size of earth, and it suffered a collision with another body travelling at incredible speeds, a body that was mostly ice as well. The belt is relatively calm, drifting through nebular matter in the same direction we'll be travelling."

"Relative to what?" asked Flex, a pilot transferred from Haven Shore who earned her name because of her bodybuilder's physique. "Sorry sir, but are you saying it's calm relative to a blender, or to a lake on a calm day?"

"Ah, this will help," Minh-Chu said as he brought up another projection. A close-up hologram of slowly churning ice shards and debris appeared, the components of which were lazily travelling against a backdrop of white and brown nebular matter. "The light is from a cluster of stars half a light year away, but as you can see from this recording taken four years ago, the ice belt is calm. This image is time lapsed, we're looking at it sped up forty-times, so most of it should look stationary when you're out there.

There are billions of objects though, so none of you will be riding alone. Gunships will have a scanning officer, and a systems officer as well as a pilot. Uriels will have a pilot and a sensor intercept officer. I'm not going to have any of us smashed on our first time out. Questions?"

"I'm seeing iron and some other minerals as minor components in the chemical analysis," Jinx said. "Can we expect sensor issues?"

"Only at long range," Minh-Chu said. "That brings me to the mission objectives. Our first objective will be to safely extend the range of the Revenge's sensors. If we encounter any resistance from Order of Eden or their allies, and we can take them out without causing great risk to each other or the Revenge, we are to do so. If you encounter something you can't slag in five seconds or less, then we are to attempt to take it on as a squadron. We are not to let any target we can take care of near the Revenge. Heavily armoured ships out of our class are the exception, and we'll be told when to regroup. The good news is that most of the asteroids are so big that our weapons won't stir things up."

"So the Revenge is going through this?" Carnie, a pilot with intentionally knotted, long blonde hair asked. He was one of Minh-Chu's favourite new pilots, and was named Carnie because he was found at a carnival when he was a baby and raised by the travellers who found him.

"That's right, and we don't get to know where the Triton is. They will be cloaked. We move through this field, and save a couple days travel going around it," Minh-Chu answered.

"Sorry, Sir," Sticky said. "But I have to ask; Why don't we use our new dimension drive and skip right through this?"

"We've recently learned that the dimension drive doesn't completely remove us from our home dimension. We're in a shadow of our dimension, where solid objects with sufficient mass could still get in our way. At least, that's how it was explained to me.

That is why we always emerge in our home dimension, because we never stray too far from it, we just skim along the top for a while, then nature gets its way and forces us back out, closing the door behind."

Minh-Chu looked at the twenty pilots in front of him. He had their complete attention. "Now, we have old intelligence that tells us that there are patrols in the Death Cap section of the Iron Head Nebula, real Order of Eden patrols with support. Our intelligence shows that they pass in these three areas, and we have to go here."

Minh-Chu said, pointing to a space in the middle of the opposite end of the ice field, an area two million kilometres to the left, and another four million kilometres above. The last point he indicated, their destination, was between the middle patrol and the one to the left of it. "Those patrols passed through those areas every seven and a half hours, give or take a few minutes. As far as we know, they use fast corvette class Regent Galactic built ships that report to a larger central battle group somewhere behind them."

"Oh, good," Hot Chow said. "So if Regent Galactic built them, then they're low on sleep and all beat up because of their mattresses. Man, I could feel the springs on those things." Minh-Chu didn't know exactly why the pilot was called Hot Chow, but he guessed it may be because of his thick middle.

"Right," Minh-Chu said. "If we run into any patrol craft, we have to make sure they go missing, and don't have a chance to report. Be ready to go after propulsion and main power systems, wipe out emitters if you can't get a good shot at those. If we meet anything worse, we are to wait for orders. If we are being jammed, and cannot get orders from the Revenge, then one of you will be sent to laser link range in order to update them on our situation while the rest of us leads the enemy away from the Revenge."

"So, this is real war action," said Jinx. "We're in it for real."

"Absolutely," Minh-Chu said. "And I expect you to be the best you can be, because you're my wingman for this trip," he said, pointing to Jinx. "The rest of this run is pretty simple if there are no surprises. The objective is to get a good scan of the area, finish escorting the Revenge through this mess. We join the Revenge and Triton in wormhole transit to the next point."

"Why not use the D-Drive again?" asked Hot Chow.

"It saved us five days time travelling here, but since there is no way to curve a course with a dimension drive, a wormhole makes more sense for these complicated, short term jumps. If we don't meet any resistance after that first jump, then we're in for a shift. Six short jumps in one eight hour period and two passages through light particulate clouds. That is, if plans don't change." There were a few groans and rolled eyes. "Hey, it's time we work for a living, so let's start prepping," Minh-Chu said. "We start sims in ten minutes."

CHAPTER 42
DEATH CAP

The first full day of dimension drive travel came to a close, and Jake could feel the entire ship breathe a sigh of relief as they emerged into normal space. Captain Valent was sitting much more firmly in his seat, recovering from having the tumour removed was on track with Ensign Levine's predictions. There had been less than twenty breaks in regulations while they were in transit, and all of them minor. The most common complaint about the new rules was how long it took to read them, but almost everyone was reading the summarized version, so the rules were getting around.

"Position?" Jake asked.

"Confirming," replied Ensign Ramone replied from where she sat beside Ashley at the navigation station. "We are nine thousand kilometres from the Triton, on their port side. We've arrived in the section of the Iron Head Nebula that is called the Death Cap, exactly where we predicted we'd emerge. The asteroid field is dead ahead."

"I have several emergency transponder signals and distress calls coming through," Liara said. "It'll take us a moment to find out how old they are."

"Kadri, start scanning," Jake said.

"The Triton has signalled that all systems are nominal," Agameg said. "They are cloaking and beginning to move on. Their course is logged into our tactical system."

"Helm, follow our pre-determined path through the asteroids, make as few adjustments as possible," Jake ordered.

"Sticking to the plan, moving ahead."

"Launching fighters," Stephanie announced from above. "Ordering Samurai Wing to begin their patrol."

The main hangar began launching four fighters and two gunships at a time from the front and rear of the ship. They stayed together in groups of three, with a gunship in the middle and two uriel fighters flanking it. The three groups spread out, increasing the Revenge's scanning range.

The Clever Dream was the last out, and after it moved three hundred metres away from the Revenge, it cloaked. The hangar doors closed, and the Revenge's combat shielding began to fortify its charge. "All right, let's get the best sensor readings we can," Jake said. "Kadri, set to maximum power active scanning, three hundred cycles per second."

"Aye," Kadri replied. "Maximum power to all sensors, three hundred cycles per second."

Jake's tactical screen began populating quickly, and with extremely high detail. He sent what he was seeing to the larger holographic projector that filled the middle of the bridge with an expanding image of the white and brown asteroid belt. Light from the massive distant star cluster reflected and refracted through the ice, painting the area in hues of white and gold. The sensors picked up more detail further out as their signals travelled.

"We have energy readings," Kadri said. "There are fighters in the asteroid belt."

"Tactical, ready point defence and make sure our fighter screen is aware," Jake ordered.

"Aye," Frost replied. "Safeties off, point defence ready."

"Samurai Squadron are aware of the fighters. Scanning confirms, twenty five fighter class ships, Tyri Raider Class, definitely

Order of Eden, three generations behind their top fighters. Ronin is looking for a go on pursuit," Stephanie reported.

Jake looked at the large tactical map in front of him, the fighters were in groups of five, scattered throughout the field ahead. "Denied," Jake said. "Fire only if they have a clear line of sight." He looked at the private tactical screen on his command seat and verified where the Triton was supposed to be. "All right, these groups," he said, marking four of the locations of the enemy fighter groups ahead. "We're going to hit them with shard missiles while they're a good distance out. Launch five at each group as soon as you have a firing solution."

Frost's mate at tactical, Ensign Surelle, activated the missile turrets on the belly of the Revenge and began marking the targets. "Confirming, targets marked according to tactical display." Jake watched as the marks he put on the tactical map turned red with the number of missiles and the type of projectiles linked beside it. "Launching, missiles are away." The rapidfire rocket launchers on the bottom of the Revenge sent eight high speed projectiles weaving between the slowly moving asteroids. "Retracting rocket pods."

Instead of striking any of the fighters, the rockets exploded into thousands of white-hot flak shards in front of the fighter groups. Their countermeasures were ineffective from where they were hiding behind icy asteroids.

"Updating the number of active fighters based on power readings and scanned integrity," Kadri said as nine of the enemy fighters turned grey on the tactical display. It was an indication that the fighters or their pilots had taken critical damage according to their scans.

"New contact at the edge of our range," Kadri announced.

"Ronin here," Minh-Chu said through their communications link with him aboard his gunship. "Sixteen fighters are moving to intercept us. Tell me we can break and take these guys out."

Jake checked the nearest group of five fighters and saw that most of them were damaged. "You are free to engage the enemy fighters. Make it quick. We're getting a large energy reading ahead."

* * *

"It's about time," Jinx said through the communicator.

Minh-Chu set his course for the nearest enemy group. He had Sticky and Maid with him. Sticky he could trust with every system in the craft, so she monitored their systems, their sensors, helped with navigation and operated their rear turret and heavy munitions. Maid was brand new to the Squadron, and a heavy set fellow, so he had the pleasure of manning the top turret.

Both of them sat in the cramped space behind him, Sticky facing port side, and Maid facing starboard. "All right, we're going to wolf pack these bastards. All fighters, all gunships, attack the nearest fighter group. We need to wipe them out before the rest move in."

Minh-Chu led his pair of Uriel Fighters, both fully loaded out for heavy combat, between massive ice asteroids, through white shafts of light, and under a large, rocky formation. He saw that the other two groups, each led by a gunship and flanked by two uriels, were approaching from the sides, so he passed under the enemy fighters, putting the large stony asteroid between them.

"I can't get a shot," Maid said. He was a complainer, Minh-Chu had discovered in the minutes he'd spent with him in the small cabin.

"Wait for it," Minh-Chu said.

They came up behind the enemy fighters before they could turn and compensate for their approach. "Now, shoot," Minh-Chu said as he lined up one of the lead fighters and opened up with his pulse cannons. The shard turrets on his gunship, fired by Sticky and Maid, sent a hail of solid projectiles into the group of five fighters as they scattered.

The uriels flanking Minh-Chu ripped into them as well, splitting to pursue the enemies closest to the edge of the asteroid as their foes accelerated towards cover. Minh-Chu took the middle enemies, flying near the two fighters that decided to try him head on, and opened up with his rotary micromissile launcher for a burst of three shots in one second. The nearest fighter exploded, sending shrapnel into the path of the second, which was getting pecked apart by Maid, who quietly giggled to himself, a disquieting sound for such a large man.

"Five more coming in," Jinx announced from his Uriel. "I just finished mine off, and Carnie is playing with the last fighter from group alpha."

"Got him," Carnie said. "He has ejected."

"Leave him," Minh-Chu said, looking at his tactical display. "Regroup, protect the gunships and don't let anything past us to the Revenge. Use your heat seeking micro rounds."

"This early on?" Carnie asked. "The Uriels are twice the fighter those guys are flying, so their ten against our nine is a bad bet, especially with the gunships."

"Orders are to clean this up fast," Minh-Chu said. "That's what we do."

"Aye," Carnie replied.

The six Uriel fighters and three gunships formed a line for several long seconds as they marked targets and traversed an open area of space in the icy asteroid field. Minh-Chu marked three targets, fighters to the right of the centre, and saw that he shared them with the Uriels flanking him. "Time for you to earn your way out of that new handle, Jinx," he said to his wingman.

"Done, breaking right and high," replied Jinx.

They entered a vast cluster of ice asteroids. The enemy was ready, they were waiting on the edge of that complicated space.

As soon as he passed across the top of one large asteroids, all ten of the enemy fighters launched missiles and broke in different directions. There was a wall of medium sized, high speed projectiles coming their way, and Minh-Chu evaded.

"Activating high-temp flak," announced Sticky. Minh-Chu cringed as he saw Hot Chow's Uriel fighter weave through the tail end of their countermeasures, doing minor damage to his shields, but providing a target for a pair of missiles that were meant for his gunship.

The missiles struck Hot Chow full on. His fighter spun away from Minh-Chu's gunship into a broad opening, where several fighters opened fire on him. Minh-Chu pointed his nose into the group of three enemy fighters and opened fire with his guns, striking two of them several times. It took several seconds for Maid to start firing in the same direction.

To Minh-Chu's surprise, Hot Chow got control of his ship and retaliated, raking the enemy with explosive shells mercilessly as he tried to evade. A pair of needle-like enemy fighters rushed to the aid of their comrades, falling into Jinx's trap. They were greeted with a volley of gunfire and small missiles. Minh-Chu's pair of targets burst, venting their atmosphere and coming apart in pieces. The third was completely Hot Chow's kill, and the pair coming in to finish him off were split by Jinx, who killed one and thrust off in pursuit of the other.

"Major strike on my ship, lost shields, down to two thrusters, I'm down to one gun," Hot Chow said.

"Retreat to the Revenge immediately and await orders from Flight Operations," Minh-Chu said. "Good recovery there, Hot Chow."

"This is Carnie, I've been hit, had to eject my port missile pod, but I still have one gun and my other missiles."

"Crane here, my Sensor Intercept Officer is dead. Nemo is dead. Ejecting," he announced. Minh-Chu glanced at Crane's signal on the tactical display in time to see two enemy fighters finish him and his Uriel off before he managed to get clear.

A pair of enemy fighters broke off in pursuit of Hot Chow's Uriel as it accelerated towards the opening they'd left behind. Minh-Chu marked them as his new targets and started turning around, making his way through the asteroid field as safely as he could so he could get a shot at Hot Chow's pursuers. "I've got Hot Chow's back, everyone else, clean this up."

Minh-Chu saw a missile launch from nineteen hundred meters above him and forced his gunship into a spiralling dive. His upper turret had a clear line of sight to fire on the fighters going after Hot Chow, who was flying backwards, firing at his pursuers.

Maid was slow on the gun again, firing rounds at a fighter that had been marked by Carnie. "Get on targets beta two and three," Minh-Chu ordered. "Maid! Targets beta two and three, now!"

"What? Where?" Maid said as he struggled to turn his turret in the direction of the fighters firing on Hot Chow.

Minh-Chu swung the nose of his gunship in the direction of Hot Chow's pursuers and opened fire as soon as he had a good shot that wouldn't stand a chance at striking his comrade if he missed. "These two," he said as he raked the fighters with pulse fire and waited for a missile lock. The enemy fighters wove effectively, keeping Minh-Chu from locking on, and, in that moment he wished he was in the cockpit of a more manoeuvrable Uriel fighter.

"We've got you, lad," Frost said over the communicator. The forward countermeasure guns, turrets that fired three thousand rounds per minute dotting all sides of the Revenge, opened fire and the pair of fighters who followed Hot Chow into their range disintegrated.

Minh-Chu spun his gunship back towards the active engagement and started to accelerate. There were three enemy fighters left, and Jinx was tearing into the closest. Carnie was closing in on another with the help of two other Uriels, and the last was being hunted by the rest as it took desperate measures to evade in a cluttered portion of the asteroid field. "Stay back," Minh-Chu instructed, marking that fighter, theta three. "Let him kill himself, or catch him on the other side. Don't follow him in."

"Twenty five more contacts," Sticky said. "At extreme scanning range, fifty one thousand kilometres out."

"Why doesn't the Triton come in on this?" asked Uppity from the back seat of her Uriel.

"Because we are the fighter screen, the first line of defence," Sticky replied. "And before you ask why the Revenge doesn't just rush through here and tear it up with their point defence guns, I'll explain it again. A fighter can carry a weapon that does a lot of damage to a big ship, but can be avoided by another fighter, so we take care of this kind of mess for them."

"Thank you," Minh-Chu said. He managed to conceal his concern. The last three fighters from the defence the Order of Eden had in the asteroid field were destroyed, and his fighter squadron started to form up again. They moved carefully forward, ever closer to those five groups of fighters, which each had five fighters. "Resetting targeting labels, starting at alpha one and counting up," he said.

Sticky carried out the target marking for him. "Revenge Flight Operations, we're about to be outnumbered here."

"This is Flight Operations. Stand by."

* * *

Jake eyed the tactical display. There was a difficult to read energy reading in the distance and twenty-five fighters between them. The Samurai Squadron, which has been reduced to seven ships from nine, were between the Revenge and the enemy.

"Jake, if there's a larger ship here, they're not going for us," Stephanie said from above.

He looked at the distant energy reading. It was large enough to be a destroyer or bigger, but the reading kept changing. "Signal the Clever Dream to get a scan on that," he said. "They have two minutes. Tell Ronin and his squadron to fall back. I have a feeling about what we're seeing."

"A base," Frost said.

"If it is, we're in for more resistance than some fighters can help with," Jake said.

"This is the Clever Dream," Lieutenant Garrison said. "We got close enough for a scan, were detected, on our way back. Those fighters are in our way. Forwarding data."

A shielded asteroid appeared on the tactical display, so high in iron content that it was black. "That's a base, looks like a small repair and supply station," Jake said as two Order of Eden battleships appeared well above the base, in a large clearing inside the asteroid field.

"The Triton acknowledges the scan," Liara said. "Putting their low powered laser-link through."

"Jake, I don't want to see the Clever Dream go down, I'm launching fighters," Oz said through the audio system.

"Re-cloak as soon as you can, we're going to have to make a run for it," Jake said. "But towards them."

"Can you do that? The Revenge is agile for her class, but-"

"I can," Ashley called back over her shoulder from where she cracked her knuckles at the helm.

"Be sure," Oz replied.

"If she says she can do it," Jake replied, looking at Ashley. "She can do it."

"All right, we're launching all three of our fighter squadrons. They are under your command. Where will you need me?"

"High and ahead. Try to stay out of that base's line of sight, I think that's how they caught the Clever Dream. They must have higher resolution scanners there." Jake watched as fighters appeared on the tactical display, in the space of a minute there would be sixty three more ships on their side. "All fighters, you are to wipe out the nearest wave of bogeys, follow Ronin's lead, then return to the Revenge, where you will follow us."

"Slick here," replied the leader of the Triton's Space Superiority Wing. "We are on our way, Clever Dream, hold tight."

"Helm," Jake said. "Take us in, as fast as you can." He reconsidered for a second and added; "But don't try to impress anyone."

"Impressing people is just a by-product of my excellence," Ashley said, her lisp very intentionally absent.

The Revenge fired all its thrusters and rotated a few degrees as it began to weave between asteroids many times its size. Jake caught Frost making the sign of the cross out of the corner of his eye.

* * *

Slick had set his squadron up almost the same way Minh-Chu had, only he had one gunship to every six fighters, and one Uriel to every light Ramiel fighter. Sticky made a mad scramble to make sure that they were all locked into the tactical systems they were all looking at, and she had it finished in under a minute.

"Welcome to the real show, ladies and gentlemen," Slick said as another twenty-five fighters appeared between the initial wave and the base, trapping the Clever Dream in the midst of fifty enemy fighters.

"Did the Clever Dream take fire from those fighters, or the base?" Minh-Chu asked Sticky.

"That damage is recorded as being from the base, the Clever Dream is about to come up on the wave of fighters nearest us."

"Garrison here," the long-suffering pilot and Captain of the Clever Dream announced over communications. "We're going to evade, put as many asteroids between the fighters and us as we can while we head your way."

"Good idea," Minh-Chu said. "All fighters, we are going to form a moving wall, be careful not to fly too close to each other so we have plenty of room to manoeuvre between the asteroids." He brought up the formation on his screen and made his adjustments by glancing at the different icons to control the size and shape of the formation he was ordering. When it was just the way he wanted, he sent the order.

"Good flying with you again, Ronin," Slick said. "Let's make this look easy."

The enemy fighters decelerated and began to turn, most likely to join the wave well behind them before engaging the Triton and Revenge based fighter Wings. "Oh, no you don't," Minh-Chu said. "Scan for traps, mines, everything."

"On it," Slick replied.

Minh-Chu took a moment to focus on the view outside his ship using the direction connection to his ship. Their small warships wove around and between a field of slow moving giant ice asteroids, catching up to the enemy. White light flashed against the hulls of the Uriels and the icy surfaces around them, making the scene seem almost ghostly. Small jewels of ice deflected off their shields as they passed through a dense patch of particles, and the first fighter in their long wall of ships fired for a second then stopped as they saw an enemy appear in the open for a moment.

The enemy was staying ahead, but according to Minh-Chu's tactical display, they were about to hit an opening, and on the other side of that nine thousand kilometre opening, foes would meet reinforcements. The Clever Dream was staying well above, weaving between icy bodies, forcing the ten fighters after it to risk life and limb to get a shot off before they were outnumbered.

"Something just launched from the base," Stick said. "I can't get a good scan at it from here, it's not a fighter though."

"Keep your eye on it," Minh-Chu said. "The Clever Dream is about to reach the clearing, it's going up and over through denser areas. They're going to need someone to break off and give them cover, Slick."

"Hatter Squadron, go help them out," Slick ordered. Twenty-one fighters broke off, turning upwards to cut the fighters chasing the Clever Dream off. "When you're done with that, return to assist us."

"Do not engage these bastards in the middle," Minh-Chu said as he started to guide his fighter towards the outer edge of the clearing. "Stay near the edges and fire from cover. We do not know how desperate they are to win this engagement."

"Good thought, Ronin," Slick said. "Repeating: All fighters, stay to the edges of the clearing. Cover is your friend."

Minh-Chu's gunship and his wingmen's Uriels all got their first clear shot at the enemy as they reached the edge of the clearing and started flying from one asteroid to another. Sticky and Maid started firing their turrets, Carnie and Jinx fired their guns and seeker missiles.

A flash of light rendered Minh-Chu's sensors useless for three seconds, and he looked through the transparent metal canopy of his cockpit, flying by sight. "EMP, I repeat, they dropped an EMP," Sticky said into the communicator.

"Antimatter alarm," crackled Jinx in return. The same reading came up on Minh-Chu's computer. It was launched from the other side of the clearing. "Break, get behind the biggest rock you can find!" he ordered as he twitched his controls down, pointing his nose at the missile.

He manually slapped the power controls to his left to shunt all available energy to his forward shields and opened fire with all the weapons on the nose of his fighter. Pulses of light crossed the extreme distance between his fighter and the opposite end of the clearing at the missile that was just breaking through the asteroid cluster there. He started launching micromissiles before he managed to obtain a lock, and continued after.

All the while he rotated his thrusters so his gunship was pointed backwards, between two massive asteroids that read high in iron and other metals. His heart seemed to jump as he scored two hits on the missile with his guns, but it didn't detonate. It was twelve hundred kilometres into the clearing on the opposite side when his first micromissile struck it, and the enemy missile twisted in space before the second struck and Minh-Chu wholly concentrated on getting his fighter behind the asteroid he was manoeuvring around, praying it had the mass to protect him and his co-pilots.

They were bathed in light, but his gunship's sensors only flickered for a moment. He made it behind the asteroid in time, and the metal content saved them. "Get ready to engage," he said to his gunners, knowing no one else would be able to hear him through communications yet. He fired his thrusters on maximum towards a space between asteroids that would lead his vessel to the clearing. As soon as they came out from his shelter, he saw the havoc the enemy caused with his own eyes. The other side of the asteroid field was in motion. The massive asteroids that had hung almost still in the white silence were turning and drifting into each other slowly.

His tactical display showed that all but three of their fighters had checked in as soon as communications began to function. "All fighters, cross the opening at full thrust and engage those fighters at close range. We turned their dirty trick against them," he said.

"Good shooting, Ronin," Slick said.

"I aim to please," Ronin replied.

The Uriel and Ramiels well above the clearing amongst the asteroids engaged the enemy fighters, taking the first three out in seconds with gunfire. It was twenty-one Triton fighters against ten up there, and Ronin was sure they'd be finished wiping out the enemy soon. Minh-Chu was at the lead of the fighters crossing through the clearing, with the remaining seven ships in his squadron, and forty-two from the Triton behind him. The open distance was crossed quickly, and they were within ten thousand kilometres of the enemy fighters where their Order ships gathered together as a group of thirty-five. "Order of Eden fighters, you have one chance to stand down and allow us passage. Otherwise you will be fired upon."

The entire group of fighters began accelerating to meet Minh-Chu and his allies. He didn't expect a response, but he got one. "Raider fighter group," replied a fighter pilot from the other side. "We will hunt you down and kill every last one of you. This is the sacred space of the Order of Eden, and you are trespassing."

"You know, your religion is a lie, and your Queen is just some cyborg bitch who's really high on herself. Oh yeah, and there's every chance that your families, who you think are safe under the protection of the Order are actually being fed to a race called the Edxi. That's who you're really protecting, a bunch of insect people who feed humans to their children."

"You are a lying worm, and a terrorist," the enemy pilot replied. "I am The Revenant, and I will kill you."

"I'm Ronin," Minh-Chu replied. "Are you sure you don't want to be friends? I make a mean lo-mein stir fry."

"Terrorist," repeated the Revenant.

Minh-Chu closed the channel, then marked the fighter who was broadcasting and the four surrounding him. "Those are ours," he told his crew and wingmen, Jinx and Carnie.

"Looks like we're in for a good one," Slick said. "Good hunting everyone, watch your spacing."

Minh-Chu started guiding his gunship around a massive asteroid. "Get ready to fire as soon as we clear this."

"Gotcha," Sticky said.

"Yup," replied Maid.

Minh-Chu flipped his fighter so the dorsal side faced the asteroid, released the safeties on all four of his micro-missile racks and tipped his nose at the spot where he knew the nearest enemy fighter would come up on the asteroid's horizon. It was the one who issued threats. As soon as the enemy fighter was in sight, he fired his thrusters and began the fight to get behind his target while he gestured for his missile system to lock on to the four wingmen with him. His four missile pods each focused on one fighter as they broke formation, and Minh-Chu had only two seconds to rapid fire his missiles, sending two dozen seeking projectiles after them. He wanted this Order of Eden Wing Commander, and he wanted him to die alone. "Take his wingmen out," Minh-Chu told his gunners as well as Jinx and Carnie.

"I've got Delta three," Carnie replied.

"I'm getting the best of Delta four, looks like Delta two is using our targets as lures while he tries to get behind us," added Jinx. "Have to keep those asteroids as close cover."

Minh-Chu set his shields to adjust automatically and spun his fighter so he was flying backwards. His nose was pointed directly at the Revenant, who was ducking between two asteroids and fighting to get behind him. Minh-Chu fired his thrusters on full, turned to skim the surface of a massive asteroid and hit his afterburners. He let the Revenant come at him, and when the needle-nosed fighter crested the horizon, Minh-Chu opened fire with his guns, sending ice up between them and striking the enemy ship's shields head on. A missile lock warning sounded, and he stopped accelerating, spun his thrusters so they pointed straight

up, then fired them as soon as he reached the edge of the asteroid. It took the full thrust of his ship to slow down, turn to avoid
a small cluster of ice and stone, then spin so he could get another
shot on the Revenant as he went by. The missile lock on him was
broken, and he almost got a lock on the enemy Wing Commander before he ducked behind another asteroid.

"He's too manoeuvrable," Sticky said. "We're not going to get
him. Get Carnie to take him out while Revenant's chasing us."

Minh-Chu ignored her, noticing that delta two was trying to
close with him from the other side of the asteroid he was approaching. He maintained his course at a drift, rotated his ship
towards delta two then waited. "We'll piss him off, then."

Delta two, one of Revenant's wingmen, came into open view,
Minh-Chu obtained a missile lock, and he opened fire with two
of his pods for a second, launching six guided mini-missiles at
the enemy fighter. Delta two was too close, moving too quickly
towards Minh-Chu's gunship to avoid any of the missiles, and
the fighter exploded as they struck, ripping the cockpit to shreds.
Minh-Chu casually thrusted to the side to let the wreckage pass.

Revenant was coming around, and Minh-Chu wanted
Revenant to follow his lead, so he blasted towards the area where
most of his allies were successfully cleaning up the enemy fighters. His tactical display flashed red, and he saw that there were
fifty more fighters coming. "They're just too eager to die," he
whispered to himself.

"My bogey is down," announced Jinx.

"Just a second before mine," said Carnie. "And I'm on another."

"I'm coming up on you, Jinx," Minh-Chu said as his missile
lock warning notified him that Revenant was behind him, trying
to lock on. "Their Wing Commander is right behind, take him
out."

Sticky fired at Revenant with the rear turret, sending the enemy under cover over and over again as he moved from asteroid to asteroid, trying to get a quick lock on Minh-Chu's gunship with missiles.

"I see you, coming in from your eleven o'clock, right behind him. Easy with that gun, Sticky," Jinx said.

"I'll stop when you're tearing him up," Sticky said.

Minh-Chu passed under a stony asteroid and watched as Jinx began to move in. He was almost in position when Revenant reversed, ducked behind a narrow asteroid, and spun his fighter around so he would be ready for Jinx when he came into sight. Minh-Chu tried to decelerate and turn so he could cover his wingman. He saw what was happening. Jinx was moving past the asteroid too quickly to adjust his course and avoid getting into Revenant's crosshairs.

A hail of close-range missile and gunfire tore through Jinx's shields. Revenant began accelerating after him, locking missiles and firing. Minh-Chu was able to catch sight of Revenant just long enough to lock missiles as he tried to give chase, and he tapped the trigger in time to strike.

As Jinx's fighter was torn apart by a stream of missiles and a hail of bullets, three of Minh-Chu's missiles struck Revenant from behind, damaging his port thruster pods. Revenant's ship spun into one asteroid, chipping off a spray of ice, then collided with another, his fighter lost power.

"Jinx and Rigger are gone," Sticky said. "Revenant is dead. No power, no life signs."

Minh-Chu fired a burst of parting shots at Revenant's fighter, and was satisfied as a compartment burst open, releasing air from the rear section of the ship. It didn't make any difference to his mood. "Triton to all craft," announced Chief Mendle. "Recovery, recovery. Time to return to the nest."

374 · RANDOLPH LALONDE

The Triton appeared amongst the icy asteroids above and well ahead. "We're being directed to the Triton," Sticky said. "The Revenge is going to be too busy to take us in, I guess."

"Then that's it," Minh-Chu said. "We're packing it in."

CHAPTER 43
THE CHARGE

"Jake, we're going to take care of this fighter problem," Oz said as he stood in front of his command seat on the Triton. "We've got antimatter alarms going off, they're bringing in heavier munitions to take you out."

"Understood, where do you want us?" Jake replied, the image of him in his captain's seat appearing in the middle of the Triton Bridge.

"One of those Battle Ships is already taking a position in front of the base, so take it out. They are covering the side of the base with the least shielding and weaponry coverage."

"Changing course now," Captain Valent replied.

Ayan sat down in the seat to the right of Oz. "Jake," she said to the hologram in front of her. "You're running your scanners so high, you should be able to find the number of times their shields pulse per nanosecond. If you sync your DEMP beams up with the exact time that their shields are weakest, right before they are reinforced during that charge cycle, you might be able to break through a little more and knock out their shield emitters. Those DEMP beams are perfect for overloading sensors and emitter systems."

"Then I'll crack their hull open with my guns," Jake said. "Thank you, Ayan."

"Good hunting, luv," she replied with a wink.

The holographic image of Jake faded off as he flashed a roguish grin.

"Tactical, order all gun turrets to fire on those fighters," Oz said. "Flak and high explosive rounds." He looked at the holographic tactical display and saw that the Triton's dorsal side was alread facing towards the enemy fighters. They were on course to pass by.

"Aye, Sir," replied Lieutenant Gwen Yore.

The gunnery deck began to fire, sending tens of thousands of rounds towards the fifty enemy fighters that were trying to close with the Revenge so they could fire antimatter missiles. At first, much of the anti-fighter fire struck the asteroids that were still between most gun emplacements, then they passed into a clear firing area. The fighters scrambled for cover, but in seconds their number were reduced by half.

The rounds his gunners were using barely scratched the asteroids, keeping the field of combat calm, but the fighters didn't stand a chance. A group of nine broke through and headed for the Revenge, using cover.

The Revenge was moving between asteroids so quickly, weaving as though it were a fish in water. It was about to pass well beneath the Triton's gunnery deck. They started decelerating to match speed. As the nine fighters emerged from cover to fire their payloads, the Revenge's anti-fighter guns tore the first three to shreds.

Something in the corner of the tactical display caught his eye then. Minh-Chu and four of his Samurai Wing fighters were moving in on the Revenge from above instead of going to the Triton to land. "Ronin, you are off mission," Oz said. "The Revenge can take a couple small antimatter hits if it has to, get into the landing bay, we are trying to make a fast getaway."

"The Revenge doesn't have to take antimatter strikes with us here," Minh-Chu said as his fighters moved in behind the enemy, holding nothing back as they raked them with gunfire. He had trained the pilots he had with him well. They used guns to kill the pilots or disable their engines instead of missiles, so they reduced the chance of setting off the enemy's antimatter ammunition by mistake.

They killed all but one of the fighters. The last enemy ship attempted to retreat by pulling up and using asteroids for cover, but it made itself vulnerable to the Triton's turret fire. "Hold fire!" Oz ordered. It was too late.

"Roll out!" Ronin ordered to one of his pilots who were following the enemy too closely.

The gunnery deck made quick work of the fighter, but set off the antimatter missiles inside at the same time. The fighter exploded, taking one of Samurai Squadron's Uriels with it.

"Ronin here, requesting emergency recovery in Revenge's rear hangar. I have injured, and that blast took out my shield's capacitor array."

"You are cleared, we are opening the door," replied Lieutenant Commander Stephanie Vega.

Minh-Chu's gunship and his remaining Uriel wingmen looped back towards the rear of the Revenge and slowed to approach.

The only enemy fighters left were returning to the base. It was a low structure built onto one of the largest asteroids with two towers above it. They both had numerous large antennae and emitters. "Okay, let's take those shields out," Oz said, selecting the base as their target. "Hold on torpedoes, but all other weapon emplacements are clear to fire as soon as you have a shot." He looked at the systems summary and saw that the Triton's shields were fully charged with a reserve that could regenerate them five times, all torpedo tubes were loaded, and the rest of their primary systems were in the green. The Triton had never been in better shape. *'This is not what we are here for,'* Hausgiest said in his mind.

'My intention is to make it look like this is why we're here.' Oz replied.

'Then why have you not signalled the Revenge that you intend to fire on the station until you are clear of the asteroid field? Jacob Valent is readying his most significant weapons, and will be firing soon, as though you are here to destroy the Order of Eden installation,' Hausgiest replied.

Oz entered a suggested course for the Revenge that would take them up, towards the base, then to a stretch of space clear enough to enter a wormhole.

'Did you forget?' Hausgiest asked mentally, slightly amused.

'No,' Oz replied in his thoughts. *'I wanted to do as much damage on our way through as possible, but you're right. Taking out one battleship and damaging a base won't make a difference in the course of the war, but keeping the Triton and the Revenge in the best shape possible could.'*

"Sir," Ensign Shane Gallow, one of the junior communications officers said. "The Revenge acknowledges your new orders and is changing course so they can move under cover while we clear the area. They will fire when possible, but are making your order top priority."

"Answering through communications," Ayan said. "Sounds like Jake is disappointed that he won't get a chance to take that battleship out."

Their torpedo guidance system continued to track the base and the Order of Eden Battleship, but there were still thousands of large asteroids between them and the Triton. The Revenge began to change course, weaving through the mess of giant ice shards, then rotating so their main guns were facing the base and the battleship blocking it.

The directed electromagnetic pulse beams fired as soon as they passed between asteroids. Oz could see that the weapon system was pouring energy into its beam, taking the enemy shields down a two to three percent at a time whenever it pulsed. The Revenge was struck by nine enemy shells as it passed into the open for several seconds, but their shields held. While they were in that opening, they fired their DEMP beam weapon constantly, draining all the power they held in reserve. The enemy battlecruiser's port side shields were down to twelve percent power as the Revenge passed back behind several asteroids.

When Jake's ship emerged, they were caught in the middle by a barrage of explosive shells. Their shields were down to half power. The Revenge fired their large railguns at the same time. Several shots struck the edges of asteroids, but the rest struck the battleship square on, bashing through their shields and ripping several holes in their outer hull.

A second later, the Revenge fired its lower beam weapon, a white shaft of light with power readings higher than he'd ever seen ran across the fore section of the battleship then onto the base's shields before deactivating. The enemy battleship sustained electromagnetic pulse damage along the fore half of its port side, and Oz could see systems on that ship going dark, including its sensors, antennae and many computer systems.

"Sir, we are now close enough to the base for our torpedo guidance systems to make it through the asteroids," Lieutenant Yore.

"Fire all torpedo launchers and reload with conventional warheads," Oz said. Thirty-six antimatter torpedoes fired from the Triton's launchers and began to zig-zag between the asteroids towards the station.

The base fired their main cannon at the Revenge and the Triton, attempting to roll asteroids in their direction, but the icy masses were too dense to move any significant amount. Their secondary weapons – particle beams and flak cannons – began to fill the space around them with light and hostile shrapnel. The Revenge and the Triton were too far away, with too many asteroids between them to take any damage, but Oz watched the line his torpedoes must cross so the antimatter explosions wouldn't damage either ship if they went off closely.

Some of the flak the base was firing was beginning to get close to that line, moving in between narrow spaces between asteroids. He was relieved to see the first fourteen torpedoes push through or avoid the flak. The ten behind, the ones that took wider routes around the asteroids were still too close.

A beam weapon swept across the front of one, and it tumbled, the guidance system fried as it passed behind a large asteroid between it and the base. "Shut down main sensor systems," he ordered.

The Revenge was safe, but the Triton was still too close. The torpedo caught the outer edge of the asteroid and spun into open space. The base's beam weapon missed, sweeping wide.

"Sensors are off and our antennae are disconnected," replied Ensign Kessen from communications.

A relatively small chunk of ice, no more than twelve metres in length collided with the antimatter torpedo, cracking it open and exposing the antimatter to space. The explosion that followed went off against a cluster of ice asteroids.

"Reactivate sensors, now," Oz said, imagining the worst. "Reconnect antennae."

When they came back online he saw the mess the detonation made, a wave of lighter asteroids were spinning towards the Revenge. A shard fifty metres long glanced off its shields, but he could see the thrusters rotating, fighting to stay on course. "C'mon, Ash, you can make it through this," he whispered under his breath.

A larger boulder of ice rolled towards them, barely slowing as it nicked a heavy asteroid. The Revenge's main guns rotated towards it and fired simultaneously, cracking a small chunk that was sent spinning away off. "They're going to collide," Ayan said.

To Oz's amazement, the aft-starboard compartments as well as the starboard launch bay of the ship depressurized as all their thrusters pointed towards the rear and they powered ahead. The ship turned slightly as it pressed forward into a narrow opening between heavy stone asteroids. The Revenge rotated to fit between them and then turned their main engine pods again, pointing upwards this time. then stopped thrusting as the massive ice boulder barely caught on their aft most armour plating. The Revenge began to rotate, nose down, back up, and then they fired their rear thrusters at maximum, stabilizing the ship. "God, I want that woman back at my helm," Oz said as the Revenge managed to fit between two gargantuan asteroids, getting clear of danger.

"You'd have to fight Jake for her," Ayan said. "Ash is his first adopted daughter, so I think you'd lose."

The first of their torpedoes went off several hundred kilometres away from the base, not doing any significant damage. There were nine left, all approaching from the sides of the station, and four of them made it through their defences and detonated. Globes of white light enveloped the base.

"Now!" Oz said. "Fire another volley and make best speed to our escape point."

They were much closer than the last time they launched torpedoes, but the high explosives they were firing were not nearly as risky. With less manoeuvring to do, they moved around the asteroids at a much greater speed. "Keep firing as we reload," He ordered.

The Revenge was almost at the same height as the Triton, firing all fifteen of their main railguns, torpedo launchers, missile emplacements and beam weapons in the direction of the station.

"Sir, the other battleship just came up on scanners, they were hiding behind the station. They are making maximum thrust towards our exit point," Lieutenant Yore reported.

A new marker appeared on the tactical display named the *Order Hand*. "What kind of capabilities does that base have?"

"Their stationary guns could do some real damage if we lose our cover for long," she replied.

"Helm, keep us moving between asteroids, but get us to our exit point. We'll deal with that battleship when we get there."

"We're going to try another high burst on that thing as soon as we're clear to fire," Jake said, his hologram reappearing on the bridge of the Triton. "It's a bigger ship, but their hull is thinner than ours for fairly large sections."

"We'll try to keep that base blind so they have trouble getting shots off," Oz said. "Intensify fire on the base, try to aim for their main batteries," he said, marking three large gun turrets, each with five barrels, that would be able to fire on them on their way through the asteroids.

The Revenge moved around a large cluster of asteroids, curving through the space so it faced the battleship nearly a hundred thousand kilometres distant and fired its beam weapons at the same time as letting lose with a railgun volley. The battleship let loose with sixteen torpedoes and its three main guns. The torpedoes were rendered useless or smashed by the railgun rounds in the narrow corridor between asteroids. The heavy shells from the battleship exploded against the Revenge's shields. Another round of fire followed right behind the first, costing the Revenge her forward shields.

"C'mon, Jake, move," Oz said, hoping to see the Revenge move back under cover.

The Revenge let loose with another volley of railgun fire, launched torpedoes and missiles then thrust upwards. The instant before they reached the safety of cover, a trio of large shells struck the front of the Revenge, cracking their nose section open and destroying the old location of the ship's bridge.

The Order Hand had done little better. The Revenge was able to render a narrow section of its shielding on the port side useless, and they were venting atmosphere from as deep as five compartments in from their primary hull. Chief Frost was directing the gun team on that ship, and they weren't loading as quickly as Oz would like, but their accuracy was deadly.

There was an arrogance to the way the Revenge moved, accelerating around several gargantuan asteroids as it stalked towards the battleship from behind cover. "Let's keep up with them, Helm," Oz said.

"Sir, the base is recovering, we have detected motion from the main gun batteries. They are tracking us," reported Lieutenant Yore.

"How long before they have a firing solution?" Oz asked, looking at the tactical map, trying to find a way to direct the helm better so they could keep more asteroids between them and the base.

"Forty seconds or less," the Lieutenant replied. "We will still be moving from one asteroid to the next, there are no easy lines of fire."

"Let's keep it that way," he said. Another volley of torpedoes issued from the Triton's launchers, most of them had no difficulty pushing through flak and impacting on the base's shields. "How much damage have we really done here?"

"Their shield energy is down to seventeen percent," reported Lieutenant Yore's assistant Tactical Officer.

'Suggestions?' Oz asked mentally. *'The Revenge is about to try to take on a battleship with equivalent armament, and we're trying to distract a base that would have had us slagged by now if it weren't for all this cover.'*

'Disappear,' Hausgiest replied in his mind, sending him a mental image that served as a tactical diagram.

"Comms, signal the Revenge that we're cloaking," Oz ordered. "Cease fire, cloak the ship."

"All attention will be on the Revenge, it won't last more than two or three minutes when they break cover to escape," Ayan said.

"I know what I'm doing," Oz said as he turned towards the helm at the front of the bridge. "Helm, adjust heading to three, eighty nine, two eight seven and follow that chain of asteroids to the Revenge. We're going to pass behind them and fire a full salvo of antimatter torpedoes at the base as soon as we have a clear shot."

The base fired their main guns at asteroids nearby, sending showers of shards towards the Triton. "They're trying to get our location by seeing what bounces off our shields," Ayan said. "I can only compensate so much with our projection system."

Chunks of less dense asteroids exploded in bursts of white, filling the space around them with debris. Three rounds struck their shields, one breaking through to the hull.

"Hangar three has taken damage, but it is still intact," reported tactical. "Aft shields are charging back up from thirteen percent."

"Is our cloak intact?" Oz asked.

"Yes," Ayan replied. "Cloaking shields are compensating for the damage to the outer layer of our hull."

The next shells missed narrowly, and they moved back behind cover. The station's attempts to strike at them became less and less accurate over the next few seconds as the Triton moved towards the Revenge.

"Sir, you're not going to believe this," Communications said. "We're getting a direct connection to the base computers. Someone on the Revenge hacked in."

"Can you deactivate the station's guns?" Oz asked.

"Not yet. I haven't found that system, it might not be net-worked."

"All right, then, download everything, starting with naviga-tional and patrol information," Oz said.

"I'm going to see if we can increase bandwidth," Ayan said as she brought up a data control hologram in front of her seat. "And I'll try to prioritize our downloads so we don't get a bunch of copies of letters home and speeches from Eve."

"God, I've been trying all this time, and they get it first," mut-tered Ensign Gallow.

CHAPTER 44
RUN AT THEM

The Revenge was expertly guided around one of the largest ice asteroids that they'd seen by Ashley. "I have confirmation, there was no one in the forward observation section when it was hit," Finn reported. "Nothing important was damaged."

"All right, line up your shot, Frost, and wait until we've discharged are DEMP arrays before you fire," Jake said.

"Aye, gunners ready," he replied.

"I'll take control of the torpedo and missile launchers," Jake said, bringing up an old-fashioned key style control. "We're going straight at them one more time." He sighted the port side of the enemy battleship, where their sensors said the armour was thinnest. "So far, so good, Ashley. Bring us out of cover right where you promised."

"Ready with beam weapons," Agameg said. "We may fuse the controller system in beam number one if we fire at this intensity."

"Take it down ten percent, Chief," Jake replied. "We may still overheat, but the damage shouldn't be as bad."

"Sir, I have hacked their entertainment systems and non-essential mechanical assemblies aboard the Order Hand," reported Liara from communications.

"All right, start playing their entertainment library in thirteen seconds, and what mechanical assemblies?"

"Well I don't have control of hatches, or machines in main systems, but things like food processors, lifts, the bed adjustments in the bunks," she replied. "That kind of stuff."

"The Captain's chair?" Finn asked. "You would have control of its rotation and adjustments."

Liara looked through her display and nodded. "Oh my God, I do!"

"Do whatever you can to make the Captain's seat act like a rodeo bull," Jake ordered.

"What's a rodeo bull?" Liara asked.

"Something Oz showed me a long time ago," Jake replied. "It spins and bucks back and forth really fast, trying to knock you off."

"Aye," Frost said. "I'll have to make one sometime."

"Sounds like fun," Liara said. "But it won't be for this captain. Sending you the controls to the enemy Captain's seat, Finn."

"Adding a random testing cycle to his seat's pre-sets," Finn said.

"Send him on a ride," Jake said, wishing he could see it. "Are you playing their library back as loud and as bright as you can?" he asked.

"What part of their library?" Liara asked.

"All of it at the same time," Jake replied.

"Done!" Liara said with a grin.

Frost snickered to himself, visibly forcing himself to focus on the task at hand.

The Revenge moved to the last large asteroid it was going to use as cover. "Forwarding all the commands, the chair should be bucking, and the entertainment system should be blaring," Liara said.

They broke cover and Agameg fired every beam weapon on the ship, draining the battleship's shields down to critical levels as three rays of white light swept across their vessel. "Firing all guns," Frost said as the roar of fifteen heavy railguns shook the ship. Jake followed up with twenty-eight heavy missiles and the eight torpedoes they could launch. "Begin opening that wormhole," Jake ordered. "Reload, fast as you can."

A hail of antimatter torpedoes fired past them towards the base, and the Triton de-cloaked. "We are ready to go," Oz reported.

"Jake, stop generating a wormhole," Ayan said from the engineering section aboard the Triton. "We'll have one open in three seconds."

Five solid thuds sounded against the Revenge's port side hull, and Jake's missile launchers reported that they were disconnected. "Stop generating a wormhole," Jake ordered. "Damage?"

"Our shields are down to twenty three percent on aft port sections," Finn reported. "Minor hull damage, our missile emplacements are gone. Shells struck one of our missiles as it left, setting off all twenty eight and destroying our main turret."

"No ammunition explosion in the magazine?" Jake asked.

"None, which is a miracle. I need to get some bots down there to make sure we don't have munitions jammed somewhere."

Another pair of shells struck their fore portside as Frost announced; "Firing all railguns."

All but four of their shots missed. The ones that struck tore holes through the middle of the hangar bay on the enemy battleship.

"The Triton has opened their wormhole, and I have a course set to enter," Ashley announced.

"Execute," Jake said. A massive explosion surrounded the base in the distance, indicating that most of the Triton's antimatter torpedoes made it through. They were into the wormhole behind the Triton before they got a scan of the damage.

"Permission to join the damage control teams, Captain?" Finn asked.

"Aye, granted. Make sure we don't have any munitions ready to blow near that gaping hole where our missile launchers used to be, please." Jake said.

"We will be in transit for twenty three minutes," Ashley said.

"Thank you, great job everyone," Jake said. "Liara, did we download any updated information that we can use to find Free-ground Alpha?"

"I'm starting my search now, Sir," she replied.

CHAPTER 45
HIDDEN IN HAVEN SHORE

Carl Anderson missed research. His medical career was often interrupted by it, and his research career was, in turn, interrupted by his work in the clandestine service. As Governor of Haven Shore and master of the Rangers, he was able to balance all sides, and ignore politics when it was convenient. Ayan's old aide, Lacey Rosedale was perfect to take his place as Governor, and was happy to fill in when he was busy. He would serve as long as he could, and make sure she got the seat when he had to leave it.

The mess left behind by Doctor Messana was something he could not ignore. When he directed Triton Fleet soldiers to deliver the contents of the lab to a new section of Haven Shore medical along with most of the other experiments, there was no resistance. He didn't want the dimension drive, and there was only one issyrian who had a tenuous claim to the Fallen Star and whatever was aboard.

The Fallen Star was originally a Freeground Fleet ship, making it more his property than anyone else's. His final order for the vessel was for it to be recycled by the Solar Forge, the records of whatever was removed from the vessel deleted.

Everything from the research sections of the Fallen Star was transferred to a lab that he and four Ando Model androids knew about. He hoped that the Haven Shore Medical Centre would match the Triton's medbay in technology and capability soon, but there was so much work left to do, so many devices to have manufactured, it would have been months if he didn't steal everything from the Fallen Star. With the technology from that ship, he'd cut the time down to days. He only had to make sure that the medical equipment that he'd taken was fit for use on normal patients. Extra features or programming could do more harm than good.

He looked at one of the results of Doctor Massena's experiments as it lay on the table. It was the result of the perfect conversion of the Alice copy from framework to pure human. The last three days had been tiring, but he'd gone through all the research, checked all the simulation data and made sure all the relevant equipment was set up exactly the same way as it was aboard the Fallen Star. His testing began where hers ended using all the things Doctor Messana created, and he could not believe the results, so he spent an extra day performing the simulations over again. "She found it," he said to the red-haired corpse on his table.

A male Ando android stood at his side, ensuring that everything he said and did was clearly recorded. "Doctor Messana was trying to solve the problem of removing framework from a living body, and she succeeded, but she also gave us a way to reprogram the software any way we want. This is the secret to destroying the indestructible army. The thing that brings them into being is their greatest weakness. We can infect them with a virus that tells their framework systems to destroy their organic material, and, if we have a gifted programmer, maybe even take control of the soldiers themselves."

He touched the cold cheek of the converted Alice copy briefly. Unlike so many autopsies and inspections he'd done before, this one was difficult to take. There was something about the way she looked, with features that were unmistakably the result of Ayan and Jake; that made him want to avoid looking at her. "Again, I do not condone Doctor Messana's methods. Her logs indicate that she became obsessed with getting Jacob Valent back into shape, to the point of replacing fractured segments of memory with grafts from the original Jonas data found in the Fallen Star's computer. The work she did repairing the emotional centre of his brain has had obvious results, he is more the man I met almost a decade ago aboard the Sunspire than the hard edged warrior I have come to know. Jonas and Jacob are both killers, there is no doubt there, only the first had a better moral compass, and I think that has been given to Jake, and now I have no misgivings about him and my daughter. I don't know if Doctor Messana would ever tell him that she made those grafts, or that she adjusted his pheromones to be highly compatible with Ayan's. It is as if she was so driven to help Jake that she had to ensure his future happiness at the same time. The muscle enhancement and enrichment packages that she installed perfectly were all intended to make his transition from a framework super-man to a mostly normal human as seamless as possible. Scar removal was another art she had mastered, I can't help but admire the range of skills she had. It is a shame she lost her way, and a tragedy that she was murdered."

Doctor Anderson realized he was rambling, avoiding the most difficult topics of the day. "Details on all that are on record. Doctor Messana's work on Jake led her to begin thinking that she could find a way remove framework systems from the hosts they create, starting with Alice. That was the top of her slippery slope into ethically questionable research."

He sighed and forced himself to look at the young red-headed corpse on the table. "This body is a testament to rushed research and an ethical code that was largely ignored. I would not have gone this far. That is coming from a man who made a daughter for himself without her mother's permission. That is, while removing the mother's DNA from the daughter I created and replacing it with programmed material instead. I will not apologize for how my daughter came to be, I broke no actual laws, but I did irreparable emotional harm to the first Ayan's mother. If we're comparing sins, and it is only human nature to do so, I admit Messana makes my transgression seem small. I admit, I have gone far and a little wide of my own ethics more than once, but never have I stretched that code to the point of breaking. This is a child, and the records show that she was not only alive, but was awake and aware."

"Are you sure you'd like your last statement, comparing your transgressions to Doctor Messana's, on the record, Doctor?" the Ando asked him.

"Absolutely. Anyone who dares to judge someone should be examined for hypocrisy. I'd hope that whoever gets access to this takes a minute to examine my records, and they'll find my worst crime is a brutal one, emotionally speaking. I regret cutting the blood ties between Ayan and her mother, it hurt Jessica Rice deeply, and I loved her with all my heart for a long time. Part of me still does. So, no more asking if I'm sure about what's going on the record, all right?"

"I understand. Thank you for explaining, Doctor."

"You're welcome, let's continue. The research I've examined here can save Alice, and then save millions more by defeating the soldiers of our enemy bloodlessly. That raises the question: do the ends justify the means? Would I be proclaiming that they do by using the methods she discovered if I used her research? This is a question I've asked myself more than once in my career, and I have almost always answered no. I have seen medical technology that could have accomplished miracles, but had a hand in judging them based on how they were discovered. Locked away are the secrets to automatic limb regeneration, instantaneous memory transfer from any range, and not to mention the crush gate technology that Lorander has kept from the rest of the galaxy for over a century. My former association with the British put me on a council that judged the researchers of these and other technologies based on ethics before the first Ayan was even born, and I have to wonder if putting those secrets away was truly good for mankind. No one had to know how the technologies were discovered and the researchers could have been kept from reaping the rewards for their work. In this particular case, Doctor Messana is dead, along with all but a few members of her team. One is being delivered to a place where he will most likely not survive long, while the others are hiding somewhere on Tamber, a place that will soon be more dangerous than ever thanks to a food shortage. If riots or random crime don't kill them, my Rangers will find them and I'll have them imprisoned. No researchers will be rewarded for what they've done yet ethically using the technology to cure Alice is wrong. It validates their actions.

At the same time, her future is in question because she is not suited to do the one thing she wants to most: become a soldier. I have been watching her progress for long enough to confirm that her ability to process traumatic events will not improve over time regardless of any therapy. Whereas the Framework technology stifled Jake's ability to properly process positive emotions under most circumstances, something I admit I'm surprised my daughter was able to break through, Alice's framework does something different. As Alice participates in, and witnesses more real or simulated violent acts, her mental trauma will steadily increase. A memory lock will prevent therapy from working. Reprogramming the framework technology so she is more receptive to therapy is not an option. Doctor Messana tried, and something inside the framework detects intrusions and reacts, sometimes destroying the framework host permanently. No, the only way is to trick the framework into thinking it is critically damaged, then to alter the software during repairs so the framework removes itself. It took seven tries to find the right method. Six copies of Alice were mutilated and destroyed before she got it right with the seventh. The solution is here, and I'm not supposed to use it to cure this bright girl of a system that will eventually take everything but life from her?"

Doctor Anderson ran his hand down his face.

"Am I supposed to answer that question?" asked the android recording him.

"No, Ando Three," he replied. He looked a little like Minh-Chu Buu, so Doctor Anderson left him that way instead of customizing his appearance. Doctor Anderson stared into the face of the Alice copy that had been cured for a long moment. "Wait, why not? Go ahead and answer."

"Putting emotions aside," the Ando Three said. "You are questioning the ethics of using Doctor Messana's research thoroughly and well. You're also putting your thoughts on record, which offers people who question your decision later an insight into the process that will lead to whatever action you take."

"All right, so my butt is at least partially covered," Doctor Anderson said. "What conclusion is your android brain coming to?"

"It tells me to refer to the law. A machine that is proven to be fully aware may be copied legally if there is no other solution to continuing its existence, and only if that machine agrees to be duplicated," Ando Three answered. "That is the law where I was manufactured on Albin Five. The law is a result of several judgements spanning the past seventy years. Those judgements answer the questions you've asked in a particularly clear way. Was it right for her to attempt to cure Alice? Yes. Was it right for Doctor Messana to conduct her research using sentient copies of Alice? No. Now that the crimes have been committed, does it matter if anyone makes gains from it? Yes. Are those gains satisfactorily prevented according to the Albin Courts? Yes, but only if the last two researchers who could have reported and prevented the crimes are apprehended and kept from making future gains. Will further harm come to the people who the research methods damaged? No. The subjects are all dead. Should you use Doctor Messana's research to prevent further harm? Yes, but only if those benefiting from that research are made aware of how the treatment was discovered and refined."

"So, according to the laws governing sentient life on Albin Five, I should show Alice the records then ask her if she wants this cure," Doctor Anderson said.

"Yes," Ando Three answered. "A difficult situation, especially since Alice is not known for being perfectly logical."

"Good point. What would you want, if you were Alice?" he asked.

"She is a teenager. According to the Marson Guide To Raising Adolescents, all teenagers want to be treated as an adult sentient. They want to feel that they control their own destinies. If I were acting on the advice of that guide, the most popular guide on adolescents in the galaxy, I would show her the materials surrounding the issue and assist her in making an informed decision. I caution you that most teenagers want more responsibility than they know how to handle, sometimes leading to failure. It is one of the ways in which they grow."

"But Alice will never grow," Doctor Anderson said.

"Then I don't envy the decision you have to make. It makes her problem unique, all living things change, but she does not, even though she qualifies as a living thing in every other way."

"I think I agree with you, Ando Three, thank you. One more question: What do you think of using this technology as a weapon to shorten a war that could kill billions?"

"Two wrongs do not make a right. This research resulted in the destruction of sentient life. Using it to kill more sentients will only continue that legacy, especially when there is another way. Use the weapon the Order of Eden already made to kill unregistered frameworks instead. Even considering that framework tech-

nology may eventually be made immune to that option, the result will still be similar."

"I should just leave and let you make all the decisions," Doctor Anderson said.

"I don't think that would help, since I wouldn't get myself into
your kind of trouble," he replied.

"Fair enough," Doctor Anderson said. "All right, preserve this
body for now. How is our VIP doing?"

"She is stable, and ready to wake," said Ando Two from the
next room.

"All right, wake her up," he said as he left the main room of
the lab, leaving Ando Three behind to carefully re-insert the
body back into a stasis tube.

An open, heavy reinforced doorway led to the next room
where a woman was propped up on a table set to a sixty degree
angle. Her chest and arms were visible but the rest of her was
covered by a long tube. The room was simple, with life support
machinery that was sealed and silent. The woman strapped into
the table began to groggily open her eyes.

"Welcome to our facility. You are the prisoner of a clandestine
organization with no name, have no rights, and will not escape
unless we decide it is good for us if you do so. Answer my questions, and we may consider making your stay more comfortable,"
Doctor Anderson said as though reciting something he'd said a
hundred times.

She stared at him, and Doctor Anderson simply looked back
at her, keeping his attitude and demeanor light. "You were put
into full stasis after technically dying aboard the Fallen Star. They
brought you to me on my request, and the records say that we
were not able to save you, and that your remains were inciner-
ated then put into this storage box." He took a long silver box
from the android standing next to him and shook the contents.
It sounded like ash and bone fragments. "This is what we'll be

cataloging. About half of it is actually you, since I didn't bother saving your legs or lower torso." He handed the box back to Ando Two. "Catalog that in the official record please, we need to finish reporting her dead."

"Yes, Doctor," Ando Two replied. "I'll send Ando One in with some water for our patient."

"Thank you," Doctor Anderson said. He looked at her and could see that she was trying as hard as she could not to react to her situation. Her arms did not move within their restraints and her breathing was steady. He brought up a medical hologram that verified that she was stable, and perfectly connected to the life support systems that did everything her missing organs were supposed to. "I'm not a ghoul, or a torturer, and I'd like to give you your independent health and mobility back some day. Until then, I'm not going to harm you, I'm going to maintain your life, and keep you as healthy as you are right now. You will be comfortable, but alone except for me and the three androids who maintain this space. That is, unless you give me information. I think we should start with your name. I don't care if it's your real name, though that would be preferable, but I don't want the Andos to keep calling you 'patient' for the rest of your life, so anything will do for now."

Just for a moment there seemed to be a little fear in her expression. He was sure he caught it around the time he told her she would be alone. He waited. He did not move, but stared at her calmly and watched every motion on her face. Every few seconds she looked her up and down, calling her attention to what wasn't there: nearly everything from the rib cage down. For several minutes she stared back at him, but then her gaze began to wander. His unmarked vacsuit didn't warrant much attention. The open door kept her staring for close to a minute, where she could see the copy of Alice being put into a stasis tube by an android. She managed to look the rest of the room over in a few seconds. Then her eyes fixed on the hologram that displayed what was left of her body, everything from the mid-torso up, and her life data.

Ando One arrived with a water bottle and offered it to their captive. She drew on the straw, drinking long gulps of the cool water calmly. Then Doctor Anderson saw the first crack in her armour, and it was a large one. She closed her eyes after the first few sips and continued drinking. A tear rolled down her cheek. She breathed raggedly and when she opened her eyes she was more a young woman in distress than she was a Citadel Special Forces member. "My name is Paka."

Ando One, who looked like a pretty young woman with almost overlarge cheeks and eyes, mopped up Paka's tear with a soft cloth. "Are you finished drinking?"

"Yes, thank you," Paka said. "This was my first mission as an agent, I was a soldier with medical training before I was noticed, then retrained as an agent. I was told that you would torture and kill me if I was caught."

"Well, you're safe here. I'm not interested in torturing you. I'm wondering what you were after in the Fallen Star? Why did you kill everyone aboard?"

"They were playing with technology they did not understand, a trans-dimensional drive that could tear the galaxy apart," Paka replied. "I was to kill the researchers and destroy the drive's core."

"From what I understand, you had gained access to the main controls for that system. Otherwise, you wouldn't have been able to overload it. It would have been easier for you to destroy the drive then."

"It was my first mission," Paka offered. "I thought it would destroy the drive, but it just killed most of the crew instead."

"And you finished the rest off yourself," Doctor Anderson said. "I've been involved with the military, I understand. You had your orders."

"Yes, I had my orders."

"Well, thank you," Doctor Anderson said. "It'll take me some time to confirm your story. For now, you're going to be kept still from the neck down so you don't disconnect from any of the equipment keeping you alive. If you feel any pain or discomfort, the androids here will take good care of you. They will do their best to keep you entertained using the holographic system in the room, but you won't be able to access anything yourself, the androids will process any of your requests and enter them into the system. I'll see you soon," Doctor Anderson said, leaving the room. The armoured door closed behind him.

"She lied," Ando Two whispered. "I could hear it in her voice, everything she said was a lie."

"I know," Doctor Anderson said. "Keep her comfortable. Record everything, and start installing what we were talking about yesterday."

"The direct access device? Are you sure?"

"It won't do any permanent harm to her, and we can keep her partially sedated to eliminate most of the discomfort. I'm willing to walk this line if you're willing to delete the records."

"You are sounding like the scientists you seem to have a general distaste for," Ando Two said.

"You're right, and I'll have to live with it unless she starts telling the truth. The answers in her mind, the insight she can give us into Citadel are more important than preventing a mild period of discomfort."

"I understand," Ando Two said. "I was only mentioning it because you told me to question acts that you may regret later."

"I know," Doctor Anderson said. "Hold the door closed and keep things running until I get back. I have to go talk to Alice."

CHAPTER 46
OVERLORD PATTERSON, THE BEAST OF
THE ORDER

The bridge of the Dominant was made of dark blue near seamless plating trimmed with silver. Three-metre thick transparent metal fronted the grand space, providing an expansive view of the brown, white and gold section of the Iron Head Nebula. To the sides were two railing ringed levels of control stations. Over sixty officers worked there. Beneath was a pit of less important stations, where technicians and lower ranking officers performed more pedestrian tasks at their stations. The broad, circular pit was split down the middle by a wide walkway leading to a platform in front of the tall transparent section of forward facing hull. Clark Patterson stood in the middle of a raised island at the centre of the bridge, he could see every officer at every station, and the only way to join him on the circular observation platform was a stair at its rear.

The Dominant was the creation of Fleet Admiral Dron, a servant to the order unlike any other in the fleet. It took three hard years to build five of the Regal Class ships, an incredible feat of resource procurement, worker handling, engineering, and sheer ruthlessness. Building one of the base ships should have taken eight years, by the Beast's estimation, but Dron had forced the building of five in three years. He took one for himself the moment he saw it.

The gargantuan killing machine was made for intimidation and sector superiority. Broad, pointed twin forks with thick layers of armour and covered weapon emplacements graced the front. Beneath were heavy grade mooring systems that enabled the ship to transport six full sized destroyers.

The main body of the ship was a hulking mass of armour plating arranged in a broad semicircle with thick shards jutting out from its sides. Many of those extensions were launch bays for middle and small class ships. There were mooring points for five more destroyers across the bottom of the vessel.

No weapon emplacements, exterior sensors or antennae were left without a layer of armour ready to cover them. Unlike ships built by Regent Galactic, there was enough space for most of the crew to make the ship feel like a home, a necessity when the vessel required a minimum of nine thousand crewmembers. Optimally, the vessel was crewed by twenty eight thousand. It was a supreme show of force, with enough firepower on its own to suppress a planet populated by millions. With the addition of the destroyers and corvettes that made up its accompaniment along with thousands of small ships, they were a highly mobile fleet.

The Regal Class vessels were the key to controlling the Iron Head Nebula, and the vessel wasn't just presented to Clark Patterson in a complete state, it was presented to him with plans. The man who was responsible for their construction built them with a set of strategies in mind, and it was thrilling to see a commander who spent so much time meticulously testing his creation in tactical simulations before it was finished.

Fleet Admiral Dron wasn't a member of the Order because he believed in the religion, or because he strove to become immortal and indestructible. He joined so he could exercise his military mind, and to find a place of power in the galaxy. His determination and ferocity was attractive to followers, and he had brought millions into the fold while recruiting workers for his little known shipyard. None of them were paid, but they were all taken care of in return for their service. This was the man who could stand up to Eve, his charisma and drive was exactly what Clark needed. The success he had in building the monstrous ships was a testament to how Dron could lead the population of one single planet in quietly but quickly undertaking a massive project. The control it must have taken to keep it secret from the galaxy and even most of the Order was impressive.

The Beast didn't know the man existed until two months before. Dron toiled as an Admiral in a region of space still controlled by Vindyne, a company that Regent Galactic acquired some time before. He did have control of a shipyard, power over a solar system, and he made good use of them while he spent only as much of his attention as he had to on holding the territory.

When Freeground was almost destroyed, Admiral Dron couldn't escape notice. Freeground Fleet discovered Dron's massive shipyard. How exactly it happened, no one could say, but the Admiral made sure Freeground would be too busy to tell anyone else what was happening in the Aurora Bella system.

Admrial Dron took it upon himself to set Freeground's destruction into motion. Without expending a single ship, he created an alliance with an unheard of group of militant humanoids, the Isek, who hailed from a nearby galaxy. They already had a foothold in the Milky Way, and were warring amongst themselves for control over the Thun Solar System, well outside of Order of Eden territory. Dron convinced the two largest clans that their philosophies and objectives in the Milky Way were similar enough to the Order's to be joined, and that the Order of Eden would be critical to their goals in the galaxy. They only had to take care of one problem to prove themselves, and that was Freeground.

The report that his plan worked was startling, and seeing Freeground reduced to its Alpha segment then forced to run gave Clark a very human feeling of gratification. He showed his

404 · RANDOLPH LALONDE

thanks by making Dron a Fleet Admiral, a position that he earned with cunning.

The Beast watched the eleven new destroyers that accompanied his new flagship, the Dominant, as they crossed his view through the transparent section of the upper hull. The bridge was busy, the main fleet of the Order of Eden was preparing to enter the nebula. Most of them would traverse the space, but nearly a third of the massive fleet of thousands of ships would remain there, taming and taking worlds, rooting out undesirables.

Just on the left side of his railing were translucent holograms that displayed news from the fleet, the overall status of the main departments on his ship, and the status of each of his destroyers. The holograms to his right highlighted news from the rest of the fleet, their overall position, their destinations and orders. The middle section of the railing was mostly clear of information, reserved for information he needed to focus on and the announcement of emergencies.

The sectors of conquered space behind his fleet were well in hand. Strongholds surrounded by shipyards and billions of followers that unwittingly protected a secret that their enemies should have already known. It had taken too long to begin manufacturing on that side of the Iron Head Nebula, but it was well under way, so they wouldn't need as much finished equipment from Regent Galactic. The Order of Eden could grow on both sides of the nebula at a much greater speed.

He was also confident that the crisis of information was over for the time being. The risk that Order followers would try to abandon their posts at hearing that the Edxi were taking control of a few of their worlds did not manifest in any meaningful way. Jacob Valent and his followers on Haven Shore had failed to frighten Order followers by spreading the truth, that the Edxi were using some of the Order of Eden worlds as hosts to their broods. Broods that fed on humans.

The galaxy did not believe. The ones that the Order had not yet converted or conquered thought the allegation was too horrific and outlandish. The members of the Order who heard the rumour saw it as propaganda, lies meant to pull them from the path to elevation in the Order. It was a situation Clark could not have expected. The efforts of one of his most dangerous enemies was hampered by simple scepticism.

Fleet Admiral Dron approached the Beast's perch. The man did not flinch as Overlord Patterson turned towards him, the partially transparent red plates covering his body grinding against each other slightly. The sound was like small, wet, sand covered stones being rubbed together, and Clark had learned to love it. If it made him the Beast to everyone else, so be it.

"My Overlord," addressed the Fleet Admiral. "One of our stations has reported that they have seen the Triton. They attempted to stop their progress through the Iron Head nebula, but failed. Most of their ships were ordered to spread out and search the region for Freeground Alpha, so they had a minimal defence. There was another ship with the Triton as well." Dron made a gesture towards Clark's left hand side, bringing up a full report in holograms spread out across the railing.

"Thank you, Fleet Admiral," Clark said. "You may come up."

The Fleet Admiral calmly climbed the steps, his long legs taking them two at a time. "Thank you, my Overlord, it is an honour."

"My assumption is that the Triton is looking for Freeground Alpha," Clark said. "What do you think?"

"My first thought was that Valent and McPatrick were leading a strike to raid the facility. There are stores of high-density materials there, as well as a warehouse of fabrication systems that just arrived three weeks ago. That's not to mention the food production systems that base maintains in order to supply ships in the area. My first assumption was based on both of their ships being fully functional, however. They are not." Dron focused in on a hologram of a ship named the Revenge. "This is one of our ships, captured by Valent, I have no doubt. They made some significant modifications, but the scan the base was able to take indicates that two of the ship's main launch bays are incomplete. Supplies for construction clog their cargo holds. That only indicates one thing."

"They launched early," Clark said. "Earlier than was convenient. They know where Freeground Alpha is, and want to join them."

"I agree," the Fleet Admiral said. "I have run the scenarios and can see no other reason why they would rush launching such a ship. Significant damage was done, so the final construction of their vessel will take even longer. The Triton will be forced to protect the Revenge, which does not seem to have a cloaking system."

"They can be tracked," the Beast said. "They could lead us to Freeground Alpha."

"My Overlord, I know you have been waiting for the right time to move the Dominant into the nebula so we can join the forward elements of the main fleet. I submit that you may have found the perfect time. We can reach Station Five-Oh-Three in four days from our current position."

"Prepare the prototype jump drive, order all ships to mooring positions," Clark said. "If they had no choice but to pass through this ice field, and get past that station, then there can be only a few courses they would take. Project them. Send twice the combined power of the Triton and the Revenge to search along each course. We will position the Dominant so we can respond as quickly as possible when Freeground Alpha is found."

"Yes, my Overlord," Fleet Admiral Dron said.

"I will brief my knights," the Beast said. He descended from his perch on the bridge and strode through the thick double doors at the rear. He mentally ordered the computer to pass a message to all of his personal army of Order Knights to assemble. This is what he brought them together for. He would take Freeground Alpha and use it as a new base of operations on the other side of the nebula. He would stand on the Command Deck of that base as its new master.

CHAPTER 47
STARK TRUTH AND AMBITION

It was times like these that Carl Anderson was glad that the position of Governor came with a private office. He only had to begin telling Alice that Doctor Messana was doing serious research into her condition to get an immediate and clear response. She leaned forward in her seat with a deadly serious expression on her young face. "If she found a way to get rid of it, the framework, I mean, I want you to do it."

"I need you to know how the cure was found if we're going to go forward," He replied. "I have all the information here, and I've made a guide so you can get through it in a few hours."

"Show me, then," Alice said. "She did something wrong, otherwise the method wouldn't be important. Just show me so I can decide and get on with things."

"She did cross some ethical lines, and you're going to find parts hard to watch," Carl warned her.

"I see worse when I try to get some sleep," Alice said. "Trust me."

So, he left her alone in his office with the report, including the recordings and the forensic analysis. He couldn't help but be a little proud of how quickly and thoroughly she looked through the information. The training she'd had in the Rangers about processing information had taken root.

He gave her three hours to look through everything on her own, and she was finished in two. When he returned to his office, she found that she'd had time to walk all around the government and operations centre in the upper half of the Everin Building. Carl Anderson met her at the doorway to his office and he had difficulty judging her mood as they sat down. Alice was quiet, but not pensive or morose. She seemed on edge instead.

The light from the transparent section of the wall above and behind Carl's desk bathed her in hues of gold. She was still in a Civic Watcher's uniform, black with a wide white stripe down the sides. Her two weeks off before the Fleet Academy opened would not be wasted. Alice was just starting her first patrol shift with The Watch when he called her in.

It was remarkable that someone with Alice's mental maturity could train to have new instincts with the Rangers, that she could sustain and persist despite her mental problems, and then refuse to remain idle when she was given the opportunity, taking a temporary full time position instead. It was remarkable, and Carl Anderson admired her drive and potential, even though he couldn't help noticing how small she looked in the chair in front of his desk. There was a frailty to her that he'd never noticed before.

"Do you need more time to think?" Carl asked. "There is no time limit on this cure." he said, knowing that she had visited her therapist in the middle of the previous night. The note in her file said that she woke up sweating, screaming, and panicking.

"I don't think so," Alice said hesitantly. "You left the whole ethics debate you had with your Ando at the end of the file. I listened to it while I watched the other me wake up. She must have been terrified." She exhaled slowly and leaned forward, much of her nervous energy disappearing. "No one else will be hurt if I tell you to do it, if I die and get rebuilt as this next version of myself without the framework."

"That's true," Carl replied. "It won't be true death either. Your brain will only be modified to the point of removing any memory blocks and framework devices."

"I know," Alice said. She took a moment to think. "If I decide that using the cure is wrong because of how it was made, the suffering that it already caused will be for nothing," Alice said. "And we can never know if Messana would have given the girl she made a life of her own once she was finished. She was killed by that energy wave on the Fallen Star."

"That's true, Doctor Messana never had a chance to record her intentions."

"I can't believe that she went too far over the line," Alice said. "Or that she wouldn't do everything she could to make things right if she did. Not everyone liked her, but she only ever helped us, especially my father. I have to do it. I am the girl that Messana copied, so I know all of those copies would have the same answer, they wouldn't want their suffering to be for nothing. I can't believe that Messana's end game was evil, and she seems to be one of the only people who could see what my framework could do to me, that it would only get worse as time goes on. I have to grow, but I'm regressing while I'm carrying baggage I can't handle. I can't carry a weapon anymore, because I'm not even sure what I'm seeing from one moment to the next is actually what's going on, and I get these paranoia attacks. I'm falling apart."

"Mentally, yes," Carl said, amazed at how well Alice understood her situation.

"What about physically? My health tracker says I've rolled back younger than ever, it doesn't make sense," Alice said.

"I can check that, but I suspect your tracker is right."

"Doctor Anderson," Alice said. "Show me to the operating table."

"You're sure?"

"Yes, I need this, I need to have control of my life. The last time I felt free, I was running across a battlefield. That can't be it, I need to feel like my body, like my life is my own again. I want to be a real girl, with all that comes with it, and I think I'm pretty sure I could do worse than be genetically tied to your daughter and my dad. I guess that's the problem, I'm going to have to wait for him to come back. I'm technically not an adult."

She was desperate, excited, and then morose. Watching the sway of her emotions, then the final downturn made him want to help her. "I've seen framework technology send scientists into a frenzy," he said. "There is something about the combination of technologies that made then carry the research forward, try it under the most inappropriate circumstances. The Order has turned framework systems into a method of building a soldier wrapped in flesh, and there are strings attached. I have a theory I was afraid to share before. Your framework is the latest generation the Order has, and I believe a part of what you're experiencing was made to act as a kind of corrosion, just in case a soldier becomes fully self-aware and decides to escape. I also believe that there is something undiscovered in your system that can be activated by an Order of Eden device that could erase everything in your system and reboot you as a blank soldier. That is one of the reasons why I suggested that you stay here, though I am pretty sure your father already wanted the same thing."

"Okay, now I'm not just sad, but bloody terrified," Alice said with a nervous laugh.

"You won't have to be for long. You are such a brilliant girl, you remind me of both my daughters, the one I could not admit fatherhood to, then the one I made. I need you to be well."

"Thank you, but, we'll still have to wait," Alice said, surprised.

"No," Carl said. "Technically, no. Your father left your care in my hands. While he is out of the solar system, you are my responsibility. I can't watch you suffer, and I can't have you at this level of risk."

"So, how soon can I do this?" Alice asked.

Carl Anderson thought for a moment, considering what could go wrong one last time. There were so few risks, and no matter what, he knew he could keep her alive. "You sat through all that footage, and the reports," he said. "So, any time you're ready. Understand, you will feel different when it's finished. You won't be left on your own either, not for weeks."

"Yes, just, yes!" she exclaimed.

"That sounds certain to me," Carl said.

Chapter 48
Ronin or Samurai?

There was a scratch on Minh-Chu Buu's helmet that would never come out. It was a near miss. Shrapnel from the inside of his gunship would have done him critical harm if it struck just twenty centimetres lower. He was more fortunate than his crew. He watched Sticky and Maid get pulled out of his gunship and dragged off to medical. When the medical technician gave him the thumbs up for both his crewmembers, indicating that they'd be all right after some attention in the infirmary, Minh-Chu just leaned against the damaged port side of his ship.

He could not stop himself from reviewing the events of the last hour in his head. He was in a gunship, armed with heavy fighter turrets, missile pods, and heavy munitions. He was one of the most protected members of his squadron, and it was his responsibility to not only use his tools effectively, but to make sure his squadron was where they had to be, when they had to be there. He couldn't get past the fact that it was his responsibility to make sure that his wingmen weren't ordered into unnecessarily unsafe situations. No matter how he considered the very real scenario in his head, he couldn't come to any conclusion other than that he'd underestimated their enemy then led Jinx and his co-pilot to their deaths.

Minh-Chu took several steps away from his gunship and looked at it. There were holes straight through the ship's armour surrounded by dents and scorch marks. They didn't have to use the main hatch to pull his two crewmembers out of the shuttle, the break in the starboard armour was larger. He stared at it until his vision blurred and he was seeing nothing but blurred colour. Jinx followed his orders without question straight into a trap. Revenant was a good pilot, no, he was a great fighter pilot. Minh-Chu should have treated that differently, he should have called half the wing down on him, given him nowhere to run, no place to hide.

Instead he took the job of killing the loudest mouth the enemy had himself for no logical reason. He was running a gunship, and should have assisted the more agile Uriels, not pretended he was still flying a starfighter. Every gunship in the field had more assists than he did.

"Sir?" asked an Ensign in a heavy yellow vacsuit. The extra layers of armour and synthetic muscle didn't match the face behind the visor. It was like seeing a bodybuilder with the head of slim fifteen-year old girl. "Are you all right? You've been standing here awhile," she said quietly.

"I'm fine, sorry," Minh-Chu looked back at his fighter for a moment. "Guess you have to drag this wreck off for repairs."

"Yes, Sir," the Ensign said. "And we're coming out of wormhole transit in a few minutes. Your squadron will be returning to the Revenge, escorting three personnel shuttles."

Minh-Chu glanced at his command and control unit, finding that there was an update from the Flight Operations Centre telling him the same thing. It was several minutes old. "Heading back into another wormhole after that. Thank you, Ensign, carry on," Minh-Chu said softly. Everyone who could contest his next decision would be busy on the bridge. He waited until he was inside the lift and behind closed doors before he accessed the Officer's controls on his arm unit. "Am I sure?" he asked himself. The lift moved up one level and stopped.

Carnie loped into the elevator car. The man was a full head taller than Minh-Chu, and the knotted strands of blonde hair made him recognizable from almost any distance. At least, that's what everyone assumed.

Carnie looked at the command and rank display screen on Minh-Chu's control unit and shook his head. "Yeah, you're not gonna do that," he said. "I need you, man. My mates in this wing, the ones on duty and the ones who are coming on line when the other hangars are done need you to get us through this shit storm."

"I've been here before," Minh-Chu said, not thinking about the words coming out of his mouth, not filtering for once. "I've never been trained to handle this rank, Wing Commander. I didn't go through Officer training like our Captain, like the Admiral. I got a month of Officer Prep, nothing compared to their year, and some of them got even more," he said sourly. "I can barely make the right decisions for myself, what business do I have taking your life in my hands. I can come up with a strategy in a briefing room, but I lose focus out there."

"Man, you look at my training logs," Carnie said. "Sixty three hours of watching your combat playbacks and counting. Not including the ones I watched over, and over. I watch your dashboard too, what you're doing, what you're telling everyone else to do and when. That's me watching your greatest hits, in simulation and in real combat. I've been flying since I was nine, but I've never learned as much about tactics, running a ship, systems management, or shooting as I have in the last few weeks. Yeah, maybe you made your duel with Revenant personal, a mistake you warned us about in those training recordings, but it happens once in every pilot's career if they see enough action. Until I joined your outfit every fight was personal. Defending our convoy wasn't my job, it was my duty, like some kinda higher purpose. I was fighting assholes off so they wouldn't steal our kids, kill our families, take our shit and leave the survivors stranded.

416 · RANDOLPH LALONDE

That's personal, and we lost focus all the time. We were a bunch of idiot hotheads. I didn't know it then, but I do now. If we had just one guy that was half the leader you are up there with us, we wouldn't lose people in almost every fight. Our convoy would have been untouchable, no one would even bother messing with us carnies after a while."

"Some of us have grown as much as we can as leaders," Minh-Chu said. "I'll stick with the wing, but I won't lead."

Carnie mashed the STOP button on the elevator. "Hell, no. You're not putting this burden down. I might not know you as well as the Officers on this ship, but I see a leader when you're in that briefing room, a role model. I didn't have a dad growing up, the repair droids on my ship took care of me as much as anyone did. The guy I dreamt about, the one who would swoop in and adopt me, the one I made up in my head sounded a lot like you do. He wouldn't leave his wing to deal with these Order pricks on their own. He wouldn't walk away from his kids."

Minh-Chu looked at Carnie and realized how very young he really was. His height, his scraggly hair and sure step were deceiving. In truth, the man was only eighteen, too young for a stop shot. "I don't know what to say, I led someone into a trap today and didn't see it coming. I wasn't in the right place for most of that fight."

"Not from where I was sitting," Carnie said. "You did lead us through that, and you took the most dangerous targets on, like that antimatter missile. I don't think there's one of us who would have thought of detonating it on purpose so it caught the tails of those Order fighters, and if anyone did think of it, I don't think they'd have the guts. Except for maybe Hot Chow, but he was out of the fight. Oh, and you saved his ass too. What's this, man, why am I not getting through to you here? This is just a gut check. What would you tell one of us if we had a bad mission?"

Minh-Chu couldn't help but admit that the young pilot was right, and deactivated the interface that would allow him to demote himself. "Thank you, Carnie. You've saved Slick from doing double duty, commanding the Triton's and the Revenge's fighter wings."

"Buy me a drink sometime, Angry Grape if you can find it," Carnie said. "Besides, did you think about who Slick would eventually put in charge of this outfit?"

"You'd be close to the lead, your stats are better than almost everyone here." Minh-Chu suddenly realized that he was standing next to a solution to another problem. "I'm putting you in for Squadron Leader along with Sticky. I have to take another look into the third spot, but you two are going to start taking command level qualifiers tomorrow if we stay in transit."

"I don't know if I'm ready," Carnie said.

Minh-Chu pressed the STOP button on the elevator so it would continue moving to the command deck. "That's what the qualifiers are for. Oh, and start memorizing regulations, they'll be part of the command qualifier."

"Yes, Sir," Carnie said with a little smirk. "Holy shit," he muttered to himself.

"Oh, and stow the language," Minh-Chu said. "That's not how Officers sound."

"Yeah, I'll work on it."

The lift doors opened and Minh-Chu turned towards Carnie, shaking his hand. "Thank you, and good luck. Remember, this isn't a reward, this is an opportunity to do more for everyone in your wing and on your ship."

"Thank you, Ronin," he replied.

"You'd better pass those quals," Minh-Chu said as he walked out of the elevator car into the relatively narrow concourse. "I'm not going to run this wing alone, you know what they say."

"Misery loves company?" Carnie replied as the doors started to close.

"True, but I was thinking; 'when this job drives me crazy, I'm going to take you with me.'"

"No one says that!" Carnie shouted after him.

CHAPTER 49
CREATURE COMFORTS

Minh-Chu joined Stephanie on the Flight Operations Deck above the main bridge to help as the Samurai Squadron and a few personnel shuttles made their way to them from the Triton. Jake enjoyed seeing him on the bridge, upper or lower half, it didn't matter. As commander of their fighter wing, he would be spending more and more time there.

It was a strange experience seeing Minh-Chu and Stephanie work together though. Minh-Chu had only been there a moment before Jake realized how all the people who survived his previous lives were coming together in his new one.

Jake hadn't seen Stephanie laugh since he woke up, not even during the welcoming party on the Solar Forge, but Minh-Chu had the magic combination to crack her stern expression. Her mood was so improved that she was leisurely rocking from toe to heel as she oversaw landing operations from the command podium above the bridge. "All craft are aboard and secure, Sir," she said to him through the intercom.

"Thank you, Stephanie, good work," Jake replied. The counter said it took them only nine minutes to recover Samurai Squadron and three personnel shuttles, two of which weren't planned.

"The Triton is forming the wormhole that will take us to way-point three," Kadri announced.

"Helm," Jake addressed. "Careful entry, please. Don't get too close to the Triton."

"Aye, Captain," Ashley replied.

The bridge was half empty of familiar faces. Finn, Agameg, and Frost had left their subordinate officers at their posts while they made inspections, supervised damage control and made plans to rebuild based on the supplies they had on hand. The Revenge was crossing the threshold into the wormhole behind the Triton when Jake received a surprising report.

Agameg and Finn had found a way for a component inside the dimension drive to safely project shield barriers without requiring an emitter directly behind the protected area. It was so simple, and they were able to use a small piece of software written aboard the Triton to enable it immediately. Jake looked the procedure over and checked for risks.

The part of the dimension drive that created the funnel through outer-dimension space was the key, and in normal space it could create powerful barriers that stopped objects and high energy from getting in, while letting anything they liked leave from the inside of the field. The system that opened dimensional rifts would not be used at all, so Jake opened a channel to Finn. "You can implement this right now?" he asked.

"Absolutely. It'll give us time to repair and replace the forward emitters and increase the rest of our shield defensive capability by…" Finn replied trailing off.

"Approximately three hundred percent," Agameg finished for him.

"I know, I was just double checking that number," Finn said. "It seems high, even though we're going to have to feed those systems about thirty seven percent of our generated power to do it."

"How long will it take to calibrate the system?" Jake asked.

"First, Agameg is right, we get a minimum of two hundred and fifty percent boost in our shield intensity, and a maximum of three hundred thirty five percent. I know, that sounds huge, and it is, but we can't open a dimensional rift while we're doing this.

So, if we want to jump we have to shut down our enhanced shields, then wait a little over a minute for the capacitors to recharge before we open a rift."

"I think we can live with that, considering we can barely shield the nose of the ship without it," Jake said. "Now, calibration?"

"I'm almost finished," Agameg said. "I only had to feed the shape of the ship into the computer, add a few metres in all directions, allow for a pocket of space around our launch bays, and now it is complete."

"Good work, you two work three times as fast together," Jake said.

"The new program came from the Triton, actually," Finn said. "Ayan and the artificial intelligence there finished putting it together while she was on her way here. We'd never have been able to do it without her code."

"It was easier than it looks," Ayan said as she stepped onto the bridge. She had a hard, meter long case slung over her shoulder in addition to her personal carry bag. An Ensign at the rear of the bridge took them from her. "You can put that in the Captain's quarters," she said. "Thank you."

"Welcome aboard," Jake said.

"Thank you," Ayan said, walking to him. She stopped beside his command chair, resting her hand on the back of his neck and leaning against it. "The information you got from Lorander is going to make using the technology in the dimension drive a lot more possible. I've been reading through it non-stop since I boarded the Triton, and there are absolutely no mysteries about the systems in the dimension drive. Lorander started studying the prototype aboard the Fallen Star as soon as Shozo approached them. Now we have all their work on the technology."

"So, you're happy with what I was able to get out of them?" Jake asked.

"Jealous, to be honest," Ayan said. "All I ever got were kind words and philosophy lessons, which were invaluable, if I'm being honest. They made seeing you in a stasis tube much easier during those six weeks. I don't know what they saw in you that convinced them that we should have an instruction manual to improve every technology we already have the keys to."

"Pardon, Captain," Liara said; addressing Ayan. "Did you say every kind of technology?"

Jake couldn't help but recognize that, not only was the entire bridge listening to his and Ayan's conversation, but they were glancing at her and smiling a little as well. Were they just happy to see her? Was it the spectacle of seeing him and Ayan together that keep them glancing?

"There are interactive documents dedicated to teaching us to move forward with everything from agriculture to weaponry. The weaponry portion of the database is thinnest, but I don't think they saw a need to tell us how to weaponize technology, it's something we're already a little too good at. Have you had much time to look through the information package?" she asked Jake.

"Honestly? Not really," he replied. "Running the ship and trying to keep my balance has kept me busy."

Ayan cocked her head, concerned and curious.

"It seems all that extra muscle growth in the tank had a side effect. At least, that's my theory. Our medical technician found a small tumour, it was causing problems with my inner ear. It's gone now, but it's going to take a little time for me to find my equilibrium again."

"So, that's what's wrong!" Ashley exclaimed from the helm. "Sorry, eavesdropping. It's just, I didn't know why you needed help walking around awhile ago, a few of us were worried."

"It's all right, Ash," Jake said. "I'll be steady on my feet again in a couple days."

"Okay, whew," Ashley said. "Nothing serious."

"Do you have time for a break?" Ayan asked in whisper.

Jake checked their disposition in the wormhole and the ship status then nodded. "We don't come out of this wormhole for about forty minutes."

Stephanie surrendered control of the Flight Operations Deck to Minh-Chu, and descended the short staircase at the rear of the bridge by picking her feet up and sliding down the railings on her hands. "Good time for a break, Captain," she said.

"I'll take half an hour," Jake replied, carefully standing up. The deck didn't seem to tilt nearly as much as it did the last time he attempted to rise.

Ayan tucked herself under one arm and walked off the bridge with him. She chuckled a little when they finished the short journey. "I remember seeing how close your quarters were to the bridge on the schematics, but actually making the trip in ten steps, seven for you, is another thing entirely. If you're not careful, you'll serve your whole command in a ten by fifteen metre area."

"Not if I can help it," Jake replied. "I've never wanted to explore the ship more than I have today. Getting knocked off my feet, not being able to help with repairs or check damage myself has been a pain in the ass."

"No one expects you to do any of that," Ayan said. "Your place is the command centre."

"I'm a mission driven Captain. I'm too good on the ground, or in a boarding team to get stuck on the bridge full time," Jake said. "At least, I used to be." A wobble in his balance made him overcompensate, fighting the support of his suit, and he leaned against the lockers beside his door, pulling Ayan into his arms. It wasn't intentional, but he was glad to have her to himself in a private space, even if it was for a short time. "Lapse in balance there."

"Sure, sure," she said, looking up at him.

"While we're here," he said before kissing her. She wrapped her arms around his shoulders and reciprocated warmly. The world spun a little, but he did his best to ignore it, and held her, one hand around her waist, the other across her back. Ayan leaned against him fully, and even through his light armour the feeling of her in his arms, the long, open kiss, the light rose and lilac scent of her was nearly overwhelming. Nothing he could re-member from his life could compare. He did not press the situa-tion, but kept trading intimacy, enjoying the moment with her without showing intentions for more.

He didn't have expectations or designs for the half hour they were stealing, but having time to be with her was something he needed, though he didn't know it until she was there. The sound of her breathing, of her body against his, her parted lips and the play they enjoyed between was more than enough. Jake would not have been able to guess how long they spent together against his storage locker, but when it ended he knew it was longer than he would have guessed, and not long enough.

He drew back a little, offering an opportunity for the long moment to end, but she followed him, and they continued. A short time later she began to withdraw, and he squeezed her to him a little, she squealed and giggled lightly against his lips. A parting kiss later, and they were extracting themselves from each other. She brushed her red curls out of her blushing face and straightened her vacsuit, even though it had already adjusted it-self. "I swear that's not why I wanted to drag you off to your quarters," she said through a smile. "Not this time, anyhow."

"Sure, sure," he said.

"No regrets, though," she said. "I brought you something." Ayan picked up the hard case that was delivered to his quarters and opened it to reveal a collapsed adaptable bed frame. "I plun-dered the Triton's storage for all the spare beds they had. There are two crates with seventy-five of these in each one of them. I didn't mark them, so no one knows what's inside. I put a low-priority order in for more too."

"A hundred fifty of these?" Jake asked, taking the slender frame, collapsed to no more than a thin pair of poles a meter long, in his hands. "We'll start giving these to senior officers and work our way down."

"I thought you'd say that," Ayan replied.

"And the Chiefs, I have to make sure they get them."

"I was wondering, since this is one that can expand into a queen size, if you wanted to pull this wall out?" Ayan asked sheepishly, pointing to the wall with his small table against it.

He stared at the wall blankly for a moment. That would get rid of his tiny hygiene alcove along with its vibro-shower, a slender cupboard beside it, and it would open his quarters up to the next, a space that was identical to his. The conversion would take only a few hours, but he would be occupying two of the best rooms in the ship beside the bridge.

"If you think it's too soon, you can just use the bed here as a wide single," Ayan said. "I just thought we could share resources this way, but if you need your privacy, I'll understand."

He looked to Ayan, who was staring at him expectantly and realized that she had been assigned the quarters next door. "Yes, I mean, we'd both feel like we had more space, and the fixtures that they take out with the wall could be used somewhere else," he said, sticking to the practical side of things. "We're not breaking the fraternization regulation either, we're from different departments."

"How romantic," Ayan said, her enthusiasm wilting.

"I'm just thinking about how the rest of the crew would take it, I have to follow the same regulations." He took her hands, she turned her head away from him. "I just didn't expect us to share quarters so soon," he said. Jake could see her fighting a grin and losing. "I'm excited to see that we are though," he said, lowering his voice. She was drawing the awkward moment out to watch him squirm, so he set himself to turn that around. "We're going to have to have to improve the sound proofing and anchor the bed frame to the deck really well though. Oh, and we'll need to install localized gravity controls, maybe a few reinforced strap loops in the ceiling-"

Ayan laughed and blushed, boggling at him. "What were you watching while you were stuck in recovery?"

"I'm kidding," Jake said, "serves you right for putting me on the spot. Of course I'll share quarters. You just surprised me."

She breathed a sigh of relief, blushing nonetheless. "I don't want to rush things either, but I feel like we lost time, and it was my fault."

"Don't think about that," Jake said. "You're here, we can take time together when we can, and on the other side of that door there are much bigger problems. A ship like this, a cause like ours will eat every scrap of energy we have and stay hungry for more. Sharing quarters might be the only way we can steal time, even if it's only a few minutes before we pass out."

"I'll take that," Ayan said. "And we'll still take it slow, get to know each other again."

"That's what I want," Jake said. "But it's going to be a couple days at least before maintenance can put our rooms together. I'll put everything on this wall on the list of available components for the build they're working on near the hangars, but those alert quarters for our other fighter squadrons won't get worked on for a bit."

"That's all right, we'll set up your bed for now, I'll do mine later," Ayan said, picking up the slender bed frame and pulling the rods apart. Jake took one end and held it out over the cheap mattress that was there. The thin, membrane mattress expanded as Ayan drew her rod to the head of the bed and anchored it against the bulkhead. Jake anchored his end inside the sleeping alcove and let Ayan stretch the rod width-wise, to match the modest sized mattress beneath. "I'll signal maintenance to remove this mattress," Jake said, poking the old one that seemed to fight him the night before. "I'm going to sleep so much better tonight, thank you."

"You're welcome," Ayan said. "Pass me the blanket."

Jake pulled a dense sheet from inside the case. He thought the soft crimson material was the lining of the container, forgetting that the Triton's quarters also made use of variable material bed covers. His memories aboard that ship were surprisingly faint, but his recollections of the amenities aboard that ship were just sharp enough to remind him of what he could expect. Fully adjustable beds, blankets, pillows that could be pulled apart to make several cushions or one big one of any shape were faint, but still fond. Having that technology aboard his ship would help morale immensely, not to mention that it was all self-cleaning, heating, and the blanket doubled as a survival bubble in emergencies. "I'm going to forget where I am when I lay down tonight."

"I think that's the point," Ayan said. "Wait until you see my adult-sized swaddle blanket, a going away present from Lacey."

"I don't think that would suit my image as the tough and combat ready Captain," Jake said. "Maybe if I get quarters at Haven Shore some day-" A beep on the intercom in his quarters interrupted Jake. "Go ahead," he answered.

"We have picked up a distress call through the wormhole," Liara said. "It is from a Freeground Fleet ship, within actionable range."

"To combat stations, red alert," Jake said, passing through the hatch and walking straight to his command seat. Minh-Chu was already on his way out. "Good hunting," Jake said.

"Thank you, this looks good, Jake," Minh-Chu said on his way off the bridge.

Ayan took a place at the engineering station. "I'll make sure our new shields are ready to go and run them from here."

"What does the Admiral want to do?" Jake asked.

"Our orders are to begin charging our emitters so we can open the next wormhole," Liara said. "I have the Admiral on now."

"Put him through."

A hologram of Oz sitting on the edge of his command seat appeared in front of Jake. He'd never seen so much suppressed excitement. "Jake, it's the Huntress, one of the new Sunspire class ships. It's Captain Lawson, I know her from the last time I served with Freeground, and she was a Lieutenant then. We can be there in nine minutes if you can create a wormhole to their coordinates as soon as we emerge from this one. Do you think you can get the new shields running in time?"

"Yes," Ayan said. "I'd test them now, but that would destabilize the wormhole. They'll work though."

"What are we up against, Admiral?" Jake asked.

"Four destroyers and a battleship with advanced interdiction technology. The Huntress has managed to take out two of the destroyers so far, but won't be able to hold out without support. We're forwarding all the information we have to your tactical system."

"Will we get there in time?"

"We're going to try."

"We'll be ready," Jake said.

CHAPTER 50
A NEW FACE

"How do you feel, Alice?" asked a friendly voice she didn't recognize. "I'm Ando Five, Doctor Anderson thought it would be more appropriate if I were here when you woke up, since I am a female model with medical training."

Alice opened her eyes and sat up. She was in the bedroom of her own appartment in Haven Shore. She was still in her dark vacsuit, but that was where the similarities ended. "I was afraid I'd get these from Ayan, they are going to be inconvenient," she said, looking at her chest. "Wow, my voice is so different."

"You have physically progressed through the most difficult parts of puberty thanks to the transformation. To quote Doctor Anderson, 'you dodged a bullet.' By my estimation, you've flowered into a lovely young woman, if you don't mind me using the expression, and are fairly well proportioned. You could have alterations done like any human, but they're not recommended."

Alice took a better look at herself and couldn't help but feel gleeful. The boyish body was gone, and she could remember what her first body was like clearly, a memory she had difficulty recalling before. What she had become was better than the grown woman she remembered the first time she transferred her consciousness into a human body. She felt like she was made of rounded corners and circles instead of lines and boxes, but in no way weaker than that first form. "This is so weird," she said, closing her eyes for a moment. Her memories were much clearer, her mind felt free again, able to recall the people she'd known since she became a human being.

"Are you all right?" the Ando asked.

"Just doing a head check, things seem great," she replied. Her mood darkened slightly at the memory of people she'd lost and left behind. It wasn't a small number, and she'd have to find out if some of them made it through the trials of the past two years.

"That brings me to the next point of your current status. Your brain is in the optimum state to develop new skills and adopt good habits that could last the rest of your life. The framework left it in excellent condition, and at an optimal stage."

"But, is the framework gone?" Alice asked, finding the sound of her own voice strange, still youthful, but the tone had a much more musical quality to it.

"All but this tiny, inactive sliver of the framework was eliminated. I extracted it when the procedure was finished, then healed the wound with regeneration gel," she said, holding up a small jar with a silver sliver inside. "Would you like it as a souvenir?"

"The Governor can have that," she said. "So, who am I related to now? Did it turn out the way he expected?"

"Yes and no," Ando Five said. "You are the daughter of Jacob Valent, and Ayan Anderson, but with a distinct leaning towards Ayan. Genetic traits from a normal combination of the two – as if they had you like any child – are all present, and there is no presence of influences from other lineages. A full body scan reveals that there are no defects, which is slightly unnatural, but in a good way. Your ideal image of yourself did change between the time your framework data was copied by Doctor Messana and when your transformation was initiated today. I'm afraid the difference in body shape and facial structures could be more surprising than he anticipated. Take a look." The android projected a mirror image of Alice that was so different that it startled her.

She had a mane of ringlets that ranged from deep red to bright, flaming hues. Her face was heart shaped, with big blue-green eyes, full cheeks and lips.

"Red hair! So red! I look a lot like Ayan too, but younger. I definitely don't look like her daughter, more like her kid sister, but not a kid, definitely not a kid." She turned the hologram so she could look at herself side-on. "Okay, I'm not as big as I thought on top, I can deal with this. Everything matches, but I've never been cute like this," she smiled and blushed at herself. "I'm cute and curvy, like really old poster girls before people got into the skeletal thin craze. It's so weird. I don't know if I like it."

"Judging by your reaction – smiling, blushing, and other signs of excitement - I think it's likely you do like what you see," the Ando said.

"Okay," Alice looked the image of herself up and down again, looking the image of the young woman there in the eye. The full smile on that person's face was a mirror image of the one on her face, but it still seemed to beckon her on into a new phase of her life. A life led by an adult woman who had an infectious grin, and a face so much like Ayan's, a woman she had come to admire. To look like her, but still unique, an adult, it was more than she could have asked for. "I'm a grown woman again," she said aloud, keeping the rest of her thought to herself. *And I'm pretty,* she thought to herself. *How could I think I deserved to be so pretty, even subconsciously?*

"By my estimation, which is medically sound, you are equivalently between seventeen and eighteen years of age. A scan of your body reveals that you are in perfect shape for a young woman your age, and at your stage of puberty."

"Would you stop saying the p-word?" Alice said, watching herself blush a deeper shade of red. She couldn't help but giggle. The sound was so foreign, almost child like. "Why do I sound like this?"

"Your vocal chords are on the small side for a female with your physical maturity thanks to a trick of genetics. You will probably always sound youthful unless you make an effort to lower your intonation, which is a skill they can teach you at the Fleet Academy."

"Wow, it's strange, but I feel lighter somehow, like a weight has been taken off," Alice said. "A really heavy one."

"That does not make sense, you are actually a few grams heavier, despite the difference in height. I suspect you gained some mass thanks to moving things along towards becoming a woman."

"Nice, found your way around saying the p-word," Alice said.

"Do you feel ready to stand?" Ando Five asked.

Alice swung her legs down over the edge of her bed and got to her feet. She held Ando Five's hand for stability, but once she took a few steps, she felt fine. "I'm shorter? Tell me I'm not shorter."

"You are three centimetres shorter, but I predict you will slowly gain seven more centimetres over the next three years."

"I grew sideways instead," she said, patting her hip. She hopped and landed on her heels hard. "Okay, ow," Alice said, crossing her arms over her chest. "Going to make sure my vac-suits keep those strapped in properly."

"Can I come in?" Doctor Anderson said from the opening door.

"Oh yeah, you have explaining to do," Alice said.

He came through the door, and she gave him a running hug. "Just kidding, but seriously, this isn't what was advertised."

"I was a little concerned that there would be differences," he said, practically beaming at her. "I did a last minute scan of what your ideal mental image of yourself was, according to the framework, and this was close enough to what you saw in that copy to go ahead. I pressed on because your subconscious mental image was constantly changing. For all I knew, you could have ended up with the DNA of your best friend, combined with that of a teacher. I didn't think you'd mind."

"No, I'm a little disappointed to be shorter though," Alice said, letting the Doctor go and sitting down. "I really thought I'd get at least ten more centimetres. Maybe a few years too, skip the whole teenage chapter completely."

Doctor Anderson sat down across from her and took her hand. "We can use gene therapy to cause a long growth period to supplement what's going on, but I don't suggest that until you're about twenty four. Your age is a gift though," he said. "If I could go back and be a teenager again, with the advantages and opportunities you have, I would do it in a heartbeat. The experiences I had when I was your age weren't just formative, they were incredibly intense. Teenagers your age feel everything more keenly, learn faster, take in experiences differently, and even feel the effects of excitement more powerfully. Fill these years with as many meaningful memories and learning experiences as you can. Something in your subconscious mind wanted to be on this cusp between adolescent and adulthood, so I hope you run with it, because you're not going to be this young and fresh to the universe forever."

"Okay, I'll give that a try, but only if I can call you Gramps," Alice said.

"I'll take that trade," Doctor Anderson said. "Now, all the testing is finished, and you're completely healthy. What do you want to do?"

CHAPTER 51
A CAUSE LIKE OURS

The Triton and Revenge emerged from their wormhole with a dust cloud between them and the Huntress. The Triton led the way through, ploughing a path into the iron rich matter for the Revenge using antigravity shielding.

"We have been detected, and are being ordered to surrender," Liara announced. "We are to finish moving through the dust cloud, power down all but essential systems and prepare for boarding."

"What's the Admiral doing?" Jake asked with a smirk.

"He's agreeing to their terms," Liara replied. "Our official encoded orders from him still tell us to do the opposite."

"All right, signal the Order command ship that we intend to surrender as well, try to get as much information about their communications systems as you can while you're at it, though," Jake ordered.

"Time to hack the battleship," Liara said.

Jake examined the main tactical display and shook his head. The Huntress was venting atmosphere from a large opening in her aft section. Two of their five main thrusters had been destroyed, and their launch was open to space from the aft section. Several small tug ships and boarding shuttles were moving in to dock with the kilometre long war ship. The Triton's gunnery deck were marking them as their primary targets.

"We are being ordered to take out Destroyer Alpha and De-stroyer Beta. The Triton are taking on the battleship," Frost said from his left at the tactical station.

"Beam weapons first, we'll discharge one DEMP beam on each of the destroyers. They are turning to come straight at us, so focus on their bridges. I'll fire driller torpedoes at the one on the left while our beams discharge, you take care of Beta with the guns," Jake said. "How are those new shields coming?"

"I'm having trouble with power switching," Ayan said. "I can only get twenty eight percent of what I need, something's not connecting."

"It's power junction four," Finn replied. "It's failing under full load."

"All right, I'll reset and try starting the new shields up with less power."

"Hurry please," Jake said, looking at the minimal shielding on the nose of their ship. "Helm, fit us in behind the Triton, flying sideways. Our shielding is still strong on the sides." He looked at Ayan out of the corner of his eye, hoping she wouldn't take the change in tactic personally. She seemed completely unphased by his decision.

They were seconds away from clearing the dust cloud, and their scanners began to reveal damaged sections of the destroyers that they were ordered to defeat. Alpha already had significant damage to their fighter launch bay, and Beta had an opening in their port side hull that yawned open for nineteen meters. Both of them were still regenerating their shields.

"Fighters detected," Kadri announced. "Five squads on scan-ners, they are flying an escort formation around the boarding shuttles."

"Can the Triton's gunnery deck take care of them all?" Jake asked, watching as fifty-six new enemy contacts appeared on the tactical display.

"At that range, there is little chance," Frost said. "They'll make a dent, but the delay between firing and striking is too long to guarantee hits."

Jake checked the status of their fighter wings to find that Samurai Squadron, and three Squadrons from the Triton were reporting ready. "Oz," Jake asked through an encrypted channel. "Are we launching fighters once we clear this dust?"

"Yes, we need the cover," the Admiral replied. "So does the Huntress."

"Then we launch," Jake said, nodding at Stephanie, who was watching him.

"Launch all fighters?" she asked.

"Samurai Squadron," Jake said. "And whoever Minh-Chu wants to take with him. Launch at maximum speed as soon as we clear the dust, they have to cover a lot of distance." The Triton and Revenge were approaching the edge of the dust field, it was seconds away. "How are our new shields?"

"Activating, I can give you a one hundred and forty percent improvement overall, and repelling coverage across the nose of the ship. Warn the fighters. As they cross the field, they will get bounced forward, about twelve G's."

"Helm, take us down under the Triton, facing the enemy destroyers," Jake said.

"We need to be at least four hundred meters away from the Triton so our shield doesn't interfere with their antigravity field," Ayan said. "Nine hundred would be better."

"You heard her," Jake said to Ashley.

"Nine hundred metre distance under the Triton," Ashley repeated back from the helm. "No problem."

Jake watched his status displays, glancing up at the tactical hologram as fighters rushed forth from the Triton and Revenge's fighter bays. Their shields were reporting a ninety percent boost in strength. "Everything all right with the shields?" The first of the torpedoes from the enemy ships were twenty nine seconds away.

"I'm holding at minimum power while the fighters launch," Ayan explained. "If I turn them up all the way too soon, they'll get thrown out of our shield barrier at about forty nine gravitational units."

"New technology, new rules," Jake said. "Looks like I have some learning to do."

"Don't we all?" Ayan said. "I have to manually balance the power here, so I'm going to be busy."

The last of Samurai Squadron passed through their forward shielding, catching a boost of speed as they did so. The entire squadron split and continued their indirect course towards the cluster of enemy fighters around the Huntress. The Triton's gunnery deck and the high rate of fire pulse turrets aboard the Revenge opened fire on the first salvo of enemy torpedoes.

"Raising shield intensity," Ayan reported.

All but three of the enemy torpedoes were torn to shreds by thousands of energy and solid shots. One of the remaining torpedoes was deflected by the gravity field emitted off the nose of the Revenge, detonating hundreds of metres away. The other two struck the gravity field and exploded, barely making any difference to the high-energy barrier beneath. Jake checked and saw that Ayan had managed to rebalance the power distribution so they were well protected. She was keeping up with the task of drawing power equally from different parts of the ship, and maintaining the intensity of the field across their entire exterior. It all had to be done manually, and Jake didn't think he could do the job nearly as well, if at all. He didn't complain that it wasn't as powerful as originally promised, it should be enough to get them through the situation they faced and more.

"Fire DEMP beams," Jake ordered.

"They will be three percent effective at this range," Frost said.

"Drain our capacitor bank, then we recharge and fire again."

"Aye, firing."

The white beams fired, one striking each destroyer. Their shields registered an eleven percent dip in power. The Revenge would not be able to fire again for forty-nine seconds. The enemy destroyers kept firing torpedoes. Another twenty-four were on their way into range, and Jake looked up in time to see that their point defence weapons reduced that number to only two with no help from the Triton.

The last two torpedoes hit them head on, covering them with a nuclear flash, and their sensors went dark for two seconds. "Our shields registered a nine point eight percent loss in power," Kadri reported. "Scanners and antennae are back online. We can keep this one, right Captain?" she said, turning and nodding towards Ayan.

"All right," Jake said, watching the Triton alter course to pursue the main battleship. "Helm, full thrust ahead, we want to pull right up alongside these destroyers. If they're going to start firing nukes and antimatter torpedoes, we're going to have to make sure they take just as much damage from them as we do." He glanced at their power generation and shield integrity. Only twelve percent of their main power was being used for their new shields, and they were already fully regenerated.

"Closing into close range with Destroyers Alpha and Beta," Ashley said. The Revenge's large rotary thrusters burned white, accelerating the vessel towards the enemy. Their point defence turrets burned like flickering fires along the surface of the hull, tearing through another salvo of twenty four torpedoes that never made it to their mark.

The waiting while they closed in was what tested Jake. He knew well enough that the time could not be spent idly, and he checked on the status of his ship, then on Samurai Squadron. Minh-Chu was directing his squad to come at the Huntress wide, and Slick – the commander of Triton's fighter wing – was following his lead. There were hundreds of small bursts of light against the enemy battleship's shields as the fighters tried to blind their sensors by unloading the smaller nuclear munitions on it. They would be useless when they closed in on the tugs and fighters around the Huntress, so it made sense that they'd assist the Triton while they could.

The anti-fighter guns on the Order battleship were slow and inaccurate thanks to the frequent bursts of nuclear fire that scrambled their sensors and made communication impossible. The Triton was closing in as the fighters moved on, things were about to get difficult for the enemy battleship.

The main thrusters on the Revenge reversed so they wouldn't rush by the enemy destroyers. They were still moving quickly, but they would almost match the enemy's speed by the time they finished closing in. These kills had to happen quickly, Jake knew. There were definitely Order of Eden reinforcements on the way.

The Revenge rumbled as all fifteen of their main rail cannons fired. The capacitor banks for their directed magnetic pulse beams were fully charged. "How effective are our beam weapons at this range?" Jake asked.

"Thirty nine percent," Frost replied.

"Wait until fifty, then drain all our beam weapons on Destroyer Alpha. Aim all weapon emplacements at that ship, I want it gone before the Triton has fully engaged that battleship."

"Aye, Captain," Frost said.

"Helm, keep our nose pointed right at Destroyer Alpha until we're under it," Jake ordered.

"This is Ronin," Minh-Chu said over his communicator. "All squadrons have engaged the enemy fighters. It looks like there are still some gun crews working on the Huntress, too. Five turrets just started firing."

"Incoming torpedo salvo," Frost warned. "They're spacing them out this time."

Jake looked up in time to see a series of torpedoes spaced several kilometres apart, and knew what was coming before the first one detonated. A nuclear flash erupted out of range, an attempt to blind their sensors. The next one in line was destroyed by point defence weapons fire, hundreds of high-energy bursts ripping the casing apart. An antimatter warning appeared above that torpedo a moment before it exploded. That was the first of seven explosions that followed, each one getting closer to the Revenge until the last four exploded against their shields only three seconds apart.

Jake watched their shield energy level drop to three percent before the barrage was over. Their sensors took four seconds to reset, and their communications were out, but, to his surprise, their shields recovered to twenty eight percent in five seconds, and their power level increased steadily. Jake glanced over to Ayan's engineering station in time to see her fingers moving across the controls at a frenzied pace. Finn entered the bridge in a rush, "I'm sorry, I got here as fast as I could." He said to her.

"Don't worry, it's my fault," Ayan explained. "I thought I could do this and manage engineering for you from here at the same time so you could help with things down there. But, no."

"I don't think Agameg could do both if he grew a third arm," Finn said, glancing at Ayan's station. A complex, ship-wide power diagram was in front of her along with the active equations that represented the energies that made their shield, she was interacting with both at the same time. "I wish there was someone who was already an expert at this so they could teach me how to do it," she said.

"You're doing great," Jake said. His tactical display showed that they were at fifty one percent effective range for beam weapons. "Fire DEMPs," he told Frost.

"Aye," Frost said. The main guns thundered, and a straight line of white light connected the Revenge with Destroyer Alpha for five seconds while the energy drained from all three of their directed electromagnetic pulse beams. For the first time in his life, Jake saw the beams break through their enemy's forward shields and penetrate their bridge.

"Enemy shields are down to zero on their forward quarter," Kadri announced. "I am getting no power readings from their bridge or any exterior systems on their forward hull."

Jake was about to order Frost to turn their main guns on Destroyer Beta when they went off, firing fifteen four hundred twenty millimetre railgun shots packed with high explosives directly at the nose of Destroyer Alpha. He watched the rounds close the distance and barely had time to feel sorry for the enemy before they struck. Destroyer Alpha's bridge was gone, and the high speed explosive rounds broke through over a hundred metres of the ship's interior, creating a gaping exit wound in the dorsal side. "Oh, that's rude," Frost chuckled to himself quietly.

"Focus all firepower on Destroyer Beta. I need that ship gone."

Every particle beam weapon, slug turret, pulse weapon and missile launcher aboard Destroyer Beta opened fire on the Revenge. Jake was almost stunned at the sight of every last bit of their firepower either getting stopped by their shields, or glancing off because of their repellent gravity field.

"We can take this for another ninety," Ayan said, "Maybe. I can't get power to the shields fast enough to maintain them while taking constant damage like this."

"Frost, main guns, now," Jake ordered.

"They're loading," Frost said. "Slow buggers." Their main guns howled, battering their enemy, and Jake took direct control of their beam weapons, burst firing them across their lower shielding. Ashley guided the Revenge so it passed beneath them and slightly to port. The guns had a perfectly clear close range shot.

When the enemy's shields failed, all fifteen of their main rail guns fired at a range of eleven hundred metres, and milliseconds later, a section of their hull thirty nine metres wide was gone. Jake drained their beam weapons, sending their harsh light directly into the heart of their ship. "How is our fighter wing doing?"

"Two Uriels have taken minor damage," Stephanie reported from above. "We have three new aces in Samurai Squadron, the Mad Hatters have two new aces, and Skykeeper Squadron has three. I would say the Order of Eden are having a very bad day."

Jake couldn't help but smile as he looked at the status of the Triton on his tactical display. To become an ace by the rules their squadron followed, they had to make five confirmed kills. By the numbers he was hearing alone, they were well on their way to freeing the Huntress.

The Triton was firing a final salvo of torpedoes at the enemy battleship, which had several large hull breaches and all but their aft shields were failing. Jake checked on the type of torpedoes the Triton was firing to discover that only two were high explosives, the rest were targeting a gap in the battleship's dorsal section, and were loaded with small bots that would invade their power systems.

Their main rail guns fired another salvo of fifteen shots through Destroyer Beta, leaving the fore and aft sections of the ship attached by a thin strand of hull.

"Aim at Destroyer Alpha, fire one more full volley, then we move into range with those fighters," Jake said. "Let's give our secondary gunners some close range anti-fighter practice."

"Aye," Frost said. "Reloading and putting Destroyer Alpha out of business."

"Aim at only unshielded sections," Jake said, marking the forward section of the ship.

"You really mean to make a mark here, Captain," Frost said.

"I am disarming our enemy. We will not leave them with ships worth repairing."

The main guns fired, sending high speed explosive rounds through the front of Destroyer Alpha, reducing the forward quarter to shreds of red-hot metal. The shielding across the rest of the ship lost power, and it began to list to her port side.

The Revenge turned and thrust in a graceful arc. "We are on our way," Ensign Clara Ramone reported from navigation, looking a little surprised at Ashley's work.

"Enemy fighters are opening wormholes," Stephanie reported. "Anyone who can is bugging out."

"Sir," Liara addressed. "We are being directed to waypoint theta to recover fighters and prepare to enter the wormhole. The surviving crew of the Huntress has enough control to follow us through."

"Switch to standard shielding," Jake said. "You can take a break, Ayan, great work."

"You are amazing," Finn told her. "I didn't understand half of what you were doing."

"To be honest, I spent a quarter of the time compensating for my own mistakes," Ayan replied as she slowly powered their new shielding down. "At least I know what the software we need for this has to do now. Training someone else to do this just in case the software fails is going to be a task."

"I'm volunteering to be your first student," Finn said.

"Audio message from the Huntress, its Captain Lawson," Liara said.

"Put it through the bridge intercom," Jake said.

"Thank you for coming to our aid, we were sure we were about to be captured. We have basic navigational control back, and are sending one of our probes to you with the coordinates of Freeground Alpha. I'd send it to you over an encrypted channel, but we don't have a common key, so the probe will have to do."

"Good to run into you again, Captain Lawson," they over-heard Oz reply. "We will begin generating a wormhole as soon as we read the data in your probe."

"I look forward to buying you and Captain Valent a drink, see you at Freeground Alpha," Captain Lawson replied.

"Channel closed," Liara said.

"It looks like we've found what we were looking for," Jake said, settling back in his seat. "A good, long day."

EPILOGUE
HOPE

The Command Centre of Freeground Alpha was silent. Every crewmember across all forty-nine stations knew what was about to happen, they had been tracking three special ships through a wormhole exit point for the better part of half an hour.

The Huntress was returning, and they had found the Triton and a new ship called the Revenge. Fleet Admiral Rice could scarcely believe it. After everything they had gone through since arriving in the Iron Head Nebula, the incredible losses, and the awful trials, there was finally a ray of sunshine.

For her tastes, the good news was coming in a package that couldn't be more perfect: two significant fighting ships. According to the preliminary report sent ahead by Captain Lawson, they made quick work of three Order of Eden vessels, had their own fighter wing, and were fully crewed.

The Sun Spire moved into position at the lead of a wedge of Freeground carriers, destroyers, cruisers and other medium vessels that were set up to welcome them. The Huntress emerged from the wormhole first, showing significant damage. There were repair and recovery crews standing by in service vessels for them.

The Triton and the Revenge came through next, flying in close formation with each other. They signalled friendly intentions the moment they were in regular space. The staff gathered on the Command deck to witness their arrival applauded. They truly were fighting ships. Fleet Admiral Rice admired the smooth curves of the Triton, shaped like a Sting Ray with extra broad wings, showing no serious damage and high power levels. She couldn't help but notice all the torpedo ports, the railguns across the dorsal side, and the three hangars under her wings.

The Revenge was more function than form. The nose of the ship had been smashed, but there were still high energy readings, and a fantastic amount of firepower. They also sported three smaller hangars.

"Open a channel, please," she said. A channel opened to the Triton and she cleared her throat. "This is Fleet Admiral Rice. Welcome to Freeground Alpha."

Admiral Terry Ozark McPatrick appeared on screen. He was all smiles. "Thank you, are you ready to follow us back to Haven Shore?"

"More than you know," Fleet Admiral Rice answered. She knew that the arrival of these two ships didn't mean that they would make it all the way to Haven Shore for a certainty, but it was a slim hope where there was none before. "Just show us the way."

"Admiral," her personal artificial intelligence said through her sub-dermal communicator. "You're shaking. Are you all right?"

Fleet Admiral Rice simply nodded.

Please Visit www.SpinwardFringe.com
for a preview of Spinward Fringe Broadcast 10.
Thank you for reading.